# TIME STEP

A Novel by
## Brent Monahan

## ALSO BY BRENT MONAHAN

*DeathBite* (with Michael Maryk)
*Satan's Serenade*
*The Uprising*
*The Book of Common Dread*
*The Blood of the Covenant*
*The Bell Witch/An American Haunting*
*The Jekyl IslandClub*
*The Sceptred Isle Club*
*The Manhattan Island Clubs*
*To Move the World*

## WTF BOOKS RELEASES

*Nevermore: A Novel of Edgar Allan Poe and Allan Pinkerton*

Copyright © 2012 WTF Books

ISBN-13: 978-0615705729
ISBN-10: 0615705723

Printed in the United States of America

www.wtfbooks.net

# CHAPTER ONE

Nathaniel Allen looked up from an episode of The History Channel *Dogfights* playing on his ultra-thin laptop screen. He studied the two Ministry of Public Welfare guards standing at the waiting room's outer doorway. The AK47s hanging by straps from their shoulders did not frighten him. Rather, they spoke with silent eloquence of Zimbabwe's instabilities. The volatile and immoral political climate was precisely what provided opportunity for Nate and his partner.

Ceiling fans installed in the colonial era stirred the heavy waiting room air but did little to relieve the heat. Nate knew the early September weather was typical for 17° south of the Equator. He had dressed his slim body in a tropical-weight, pale linen suit, an orange-and-black striped silk tie, a crisp, oxford cloth white shirt and oxblood Gucci tassel loafers. He consulted his watch and scowled with mild annoyance, even though he had fully expected the scheduled meeting to begin at least half an hour late.

Daniel O'Shea sat across from his partner. His very muscular frame wore a well-tailored, lightweight cotton suit in olive drab, a maroon, matte-cotton tie and brown Florsheim lace-up shoes. A portable computer lay open and hummed softly on his lap as well. A wire ran from its side to headphones on his ears. He swiped his hand across his forehead and held it out for inspection.

"I'm sweating like a pig."

Nate glanced up from his documentary film. "I can see. What are you watching?"

"*Lawrence of Arabia.*"

"No wonder. All that sand is making you hot. Watch *The Thing* or *Alien versus Predator* instead. Something that takes place in the Antarctic." He returned his attention to his computer. A sly smirk stole across his face. "Don't you have *March of the Penguins?*"

"*March of the Penguins?* Up yours." Danny reached down for his shoulder bag.

The antiquated Bakelite phone on the secretary's desk jangled.

The antiquated Bakelite telephone on the secretary's desk jangled harshly.

"Mr. Allen, Mr. O'Shea," the secretary said after replacing the handset, "Vice Minister Dube will see you now." She stood and opened the double door. A powerful voice spoke from the other side.

"Gentlemen!"

Nate noted as he entered the room that Simbe Dube did not rise, much less venture from behind his oversized mahogany desk. Nate added this to the list of clues he had gathered to choreograph how the meeting should be conducted. Dube was insecure enough to feel he needed the fortress of a desk to maintain control.

"Sit, sit please!" Dube pushed to the side a vase filled with fragrant flowers, so he could take in both men. "I trust the Sheraton is up to your American standards." English was the official language of Zimbabwe, a legacy from the colonial era. Dube's words were accented but perfectly intelligible.

"Indeed it is," Nate lied. "Mr. O'Shea and I are simple men, doing God's work. We don't need much to make us happy." Danny took the chair on his right, automatically ceding the power seat to Nate. Just before parking their posteriors, the pair drew their chairs in tandem closer to the desk. As was their custom, they immediately became motionless, fixing their stares exactly on the bridge of their quarry's nose to subconsciously unnerve him.

Dube blinked. "Yes. Well. The Ministry of Public Welfare is delighted to welcome representatives from the World Assembly of Churches."

"I assume you are delighted to welcome any organization that delivers a half million dollars in food relief," Nate replied, punctuating his remark with an affable smile.

"We are."

Dube reminded Nate of a Mississippi River catfish. He shook off the image and said, "We bring other good news. The WAC has instituted a program to collect unexpired drugs from American AIDS patients who have died or whose prescriptions have changed."

In a country with 2.3 million infected by HIV and AIDS out of a total population just under 13 million, Nate knew this program could keep the gangplank between the World Assembly of Churches and the Zimbabwe Ministry of Public Welfare in place for many years to come. Dube's eyebrows elevated with patent interest. Nate adjusted downward the bribe he would offer.

"How much of these medicines can you deliver?" the vice minister inquired.

Nate knew the man meant value and not quantity. "On our next visit to Zimbabwe, probably two hundred thousand dollars' worth." He watched the dark eyes on the opposite side of the desk drift as their venal owner calculated the black market prices in his country for such expensive and hard-to-get drugs. Nate glanced theatrically over his shoulder at the closed door and lowered his voice. "This is our first meeting with you, sir, and only our second visit to Zimbabwe. The last thing I want to do is to insult a high official of your country. Please correct my ignorance as soon as I speak an offensive word."

Dube nodded. He glanced for a second at Danny, as if wondering when the bigger, more older-looking of the young men would speak. Nate cleared his throat. "I assume that your undersecretary has kept you informed about our preliminary conversations. He led me to believe it is customary to offer directly to your office a portion of the incoming shipment. We understand this is so that your ministry can oversee special distribution without the complaints and interferences of other bureaus within the state."

The vice minister seemed pleased to be supplied with such a well formed rationale for thievery. "Continue."

Nate dipped his head apologetically. "Unfortunately, since we work for very heaven-focused people, they don't want to understand how this world works. If they learned of such an accommodation, they would shift future deliveries of food and drugs to other worthwhile countries."

"That would be most unfortunate," Dube echoed, "since we have only begun our relationship." His hands had rested quietly, palms down, on his desk until that moment. He had been sitting bolt upright in his high-backed, stuffed chair, with his shoulders squared. Suddenly, the shoulders relaxed. He leaned ever so slightly forward. His hands rotated toward each other, and his fingers interlaced. "There must be some way around this problem."

"Although we work for many churches, we are men of the world," Danny announced in his resonant bass, startling the vice minister.

Nate pivoted toward his partner and nodded. "Exactly. We...Mr. O'Shea and I...are willing to overlook a percentage of our shipment leaving the warehouse before your charitable organizations arrive for the distribution. All that is ultimately important to the World Assembly of Churches is that the three men in this room sign their good names to the distribution document."

Nate noted that Dube's fingers began wiggling impatiently after the word 'warehouse', but he resolutely finished laying out the realities.

"What percentage?" Dube asked.

"Five."

Dube snorted. "It is customary for this office to 'oversee' twenty per cent."

Nate looked at Danny. Danny delivered his rehearsed part by shaking his head as if with grave misgiving. Nate nodded somberly at him and puffed out his cheeks. Even though they were in unfamiliar territory, the dance was proceeding as he had anticipated, movement for movement. Nate regarded the vice minister in silence for several seconds, rubbing his forefinger back and forth across his lips.

"I'm very sorry, sir. If we allowed that to much not to reach the designated organizations, my partner and I would risk losing our jobs. Twenty per cent is far too much."

"Unless you have an incentive to equal the risk," Dube returned. "You mentioned to my undersecretary your interest in our native gems." He pushed his chair back several inches and reached into his top, center drawer. He removed an Altoids peppermints tin from the drawer, set it on the desktop and opened it so that its contents faced his guests.

Danny and Nate leaned forward. Inside the tin rested eleven uncut emeralds.

"May I?" Nate asked.

"Certainly."

Nate studied the collection and figured they would yield cut stones between one-and-a-half and two-and-a-half carats. With hardly any embarrassment, he reached into his inside jacket pocket and pulled out a jeweler's loupe. He selected three of the stones and held one after the next up to the light for inspection. Judging from the color, clarity and slight imperfections, Nate estimated that these most valuable among gemstones would produce finished product selling from between four and seven thousand dollars each in legitimate stores. He rubbed the third stone between his thumb and forefinger. Somewhere along the route from the emerald fields to the minister's office an ill-informed character had given the gems a bath of fine machine oil.

Nate knew well that crystal growth during the formation of emeralds creates inevitable inclusion flaws. In order to disguise the streaks of imperfections, dealers cooked stones in oil to fill in the spaces and give a more lustrous, uniform look. The practice was so common and so successful that many emerald owners arranged to have their stones professionally bathed every few years, because the oil eventually evaporates. The ignorance of what Nate looked at was that oil baths only helped increase the value of emeralds once they were cut, polished and had smooth surfaces. The discovery of the Zimbabwe emerald fields was recent. The oil suggested to him that he was dealing with novice criminals, at least regarding the business of negotiating gem values.

The backfire of a large truck reverberated from the street below. Nate tensed. The explosion was quick-followed by a woman's annoyed outcry and then the confused chatter of the street crowd. Dube, who had thrust his hand into the center drawer an instant after the noise, withdrew it slowly and shrugged, as if in apology.

"Are these from the Marange district?" Nate asked of the emeralds.

"No. They are from newly opened fields in Buhera and Chishanyi."

"A little more yellow than buyers are used to," Nate observed, to depress his adversary on the other side of the desk. "Especially compared with the standard greens and blues of Columbian emeralds."

"Which makes them unusual. Certainly no less valuable," Dube insisted.

"Perhaps. What interests me is that they are less dangerous to come by." Nate replaced the stones in the tin box and slowly shoved the container back toward the minister, indicating the deal was far from concluded. "Between the guerrillas and the drug cartels, dealing in South America is worth one's life. Do you know what dealers have begun calling Columbia, Vice Minister?"

"Tell me."

"Locumbia."

Dube laughed. "'Crazy country,' eh? I speak a little Spanish."

Nate knew the fact already, as well as fifty other pertinent pieces of personal information about the man. While the vice minister depended on weapons of steel and lead for his power, Nate's power derived from knowledge. In three years of such global dealings, he had never entered into a negotiating dance poorly informed. He was not the sort to assume he would be partnering in a dignified waltz only to find himself instead trying to survive a leg-kicking, cross-armed kazatsky.

The minister's room was even hotter than the waiting room had been. A trickle of perspiration escaped Nate's hairline and weaved down his temple. He refused to acknowledge it and rather concentrated on the Altoids tin. "We would like to accept your offer. But I heard you say twenty percent."

"That is what I said."

"The average lifespan of a Zimbabwe citizen is thirty-eight years. Our future food and drug shipments might increase that statistic to forty within five years. What a coup that would be for the Ministry of Public Welfare! Let us agree on ten per cent."

"The prosperity of our people is what I live for," Dube asserted. "Fifteen." One eyebrow cocked. "Please be sure your next word is not that offensive one you feared to speak."

Nate nodded toward the desktop. "My sincere apologies, but both sides must not be offended in order to move forward. Let me make no mistake: You wish us to accept this private gift of uncut stones in exchange for diverting fifteen per cent of the materials in our care."

The vice minister's eyebrows knit. "Not all the stones. Not for fifteen per cent. Choose six."

Nate picked out the three largest emeralds and set them on the desktop. He snapped the tin lid closed and slid it two inches toward his chest. "We'll take the eight smallest. We are, after all, simple men of God."

Dube laughed. "I am happy we have agreed. Let us sign the necessary documents and then bid each other good day, gentlemen."

Nate picked up the Altoids tin from the huge desk. "Curiously strong," he said to his partner.

Nathaniel Allen had just turned twenty-five. He had the physique of a welterweight boxer, even though, at five-foot-eleven, he could easily have bulked up to a middleweight. Between the ages of ten and fourteen, he had attended a karate school, gaining confidence and balance along with the ability to defend himself. He had also learned graceful movement from his mother, who had personally taught him ballroom dancing. His dirty-blond hair was like a bristle brush, so thick it would not lie flat. His eyes were the color of the sea before a squall.

Nate exited the Ministry of Public Welfare onto the dusty sidewalk and shielded his eyes from the low, merciless sun.

At six-foot-two, Danny O'Shea was built more like a wrestler. His two-hundred-and-twenty pounds of muscle and sinew came from an obsessive regimen of weightlifting and running, and from a prodigious appetite. He possessed deep-set, chocolate-brown eyes, set in a square face. Although he moussed and used a blow dryer on his dark-brown hair, his crown betrayed signs of male pattern baldness. He was 28.

"They really mean it when they say 'vice minister' here," Danny quipped as he came up beside his partner. "Nice touch with the excuse for not taking the three stones too big to smuggle. He didn't flinch at giving us two more smaller ones."

Nate made no reply, too busy studying their surroundings.

A vacant taxi waited in front of the building.

"How convenient," Danny remarked.

Nate grabbed his elbow and steered him down the crowded sidewalk. "Maybe too convenient. I'd hate to lose the stones so soon after getting them."

"Dube isn't gonna screw with us," Danny said. "He's got a signacure now."

"He can deny he had anything to do with a robbery. And the word is pronounced *sinecure*, Big Dog."

Danny winced imperceptibly, then swiveled his head and offered Nate a toothy smile. "I know, I know. I don't forget what you teach me, Big Fox. I just thought I'd make a joke:  Our signatures give him a sinecure."

Nate led the way across the street. "What's really funny is that the original meaning of 'sinecure' is a payoff from the Church without the recipient having to care for any souls."

Danny transferred his bag from his left shoulder to his right. "And Dube's payoff is from hundreds of churches." He patted his jacket at chest level. "I feel naked without a gun in this town."

"More trouble than protection." Nate took a hitch in his step and pointed toward an oncoming, unengaged cab

"Fifteen per cent siphoned off. Exactly what you predicted he would agree to," Danny said with admiration.

Nate's face remained like stone as he hailed the cab. "It will still feed people. They'll just have to pay for it in favors, prostitution or whatever. One way or another, we're keeping people from starvation. And next time from dying of AIDS. It's not like we're merchants of death, selling land mines, submachine-guns and RPGs."

Danny stared at his partner with incredulity. "Exactly! What's this about? After three years of world-class conning, smuggling and black marketing, are you developing a conscience?"

"Actually, I always had one. It just took a microscope to find it."

"Maybe not anymore. This is the third time you've brought up the subject in the past month. And that worries me, because you are the icy brains of our little operation, Nathaniel."

The cab pulled to the curb. Nate opened the door. "Harare Sheraton."

Nate and Danny sat side by side in the taxi, which smelled like sweat and decaying flesh. Nate consulted his right wrist. It held a solar-powered Casio Pathfinder watch that reset daily via satellites linked to seven atomic clocks distributed around the globe. Among its many features were a digital compass, barometer, altimeter, and thermometer.

"You gonna get another rubdown from that awesome, tawny masseuse?" Danny asked.

"I think not."

"Or are you skipping directly to the main course?"

"You can try for her if you want," Nate said.

Danny made a couple tsking sounds as he opened his shoulder bag, lifted out his Sony Vaio laptop, and removed *Lawrence of Arabia* from the DVD drive. He pushed aside the Nikon 16 megapixel SLR digital camera, his wireless cell phone with Mobile Web 4.0, removable memory, V-Cast music, built-in camera and video messaging, his iPod 24GB Nano, and his Sony stereo FM/AM/LW/MW/SW world band receiver radio with 100 station memory presets. "How are you gonna reach that magic number of three hundred by your thirtieth birthday? When were you laid last?"

"We have the day off tomorrow," Nate said, ignoring the question. "Your turn to pick the entertainment."

Danny reached the case for his DVDs and tucked the movie away. "Victoria Falls."

Nate sighed peevishly. "What is it with you and waterfalls?"

Danny shrugged. "With some men it's climbing the tallest mountains. Me, I like running water."

"Then take a bath. I should think dragging me to Multnomah, Yosemite, Angel and King George would be enough."

"You forgot Gavarnie and Trümmelbach."

"I'm trying to forget them all. Victoria isn't even that high, Danny."

"But it's wide and it's carved out this fantastic gorge. It's the best one on this continent, and we were in a hurry on our first visit. We're not in a hurry this time."

"It's a 500-mile round trip from here," Nate complained weakly.

"Fair is fair. Like you said, it is my turn. I'll do the driving," Danny negotiated. "We'll rent something fast."

"Five hundred hard miles," Nate restated. "Nothing a sports car could handle."

"Have you been to Victoria Falls?"

"No."

"If you don't want to drive, I'll hire a plane or a helicopter."

"You know how much that will cost?"

Danny made a choked noise deep in his throat. "Excuse me. Flying by helicopter over Zimbabwe is my definition of exciting hours. We just scored another connection, so we have plenty of—"

Nate lifted his hand, and put his forefinger close to Danny's lips.

Danny looked at the taxi driver's rearview mirror. The man refocused on the street. Danny dropped his deep voice to a near-whisper. "I figure this deal is like a franchise. Bring in about thirty thousand tax-free dollars a year. Why worry about rental costs? At the rate we're raking it in, we'll never spend it all by the dreaded Four Oh."

"My tastes keep getting more and more expensive." Nate opened his wallet and fished for money to pay the driver. Before he pocketed the wallet, he took several moments to stare at his mother's photo.

"C'mon, Nate! I'm bored."

Nate gestured beyond the taxi windows. "How can you say you're bored? We're in the capital city of a great African nation."

"'Great' my hairy ass. Let me rephrase that: I feel like I'm wasting my time, which, according to you, is Big Sin Numero Uno." Danny pushed up on his legs, to free the bottoms of his trousers from the damp and sticky taxi backseat. "I tell you what: When we get to London, I promise to go with you to any event, any tour, any stupid history museum if you go with me to Victoria Falls tomorrow."

Nate studied the sad storefronts of downtown Harare. "I *guarantee* you'll regret your promise."

# CHAPTER TWO

Aside from the protracted length of the lines at Heathrow's customs and the fact that a child in front of Danny and Nate smelled of vomit, nothing seemed out of the ordinary.

"Several big planes must have landed around the same time," Danny speculated as they inched down the ramp toward the solid line painted on the floor.

Nate did not respond. He consulted his watch, fixing on the sweep hand as it ticked off the seconds. His mind totaled the number of air miles he and his partner had amassed over the past eight months. It was truly staggering. The World Assembly of Churches' directorship was generous. Officially, the team received one paid vacation day for every seven workdays accumulated on the road or twelve spent at the New York home office. The understanding was that if schedules required them to travel on multiple back-to-back missions for many weeks they would suck it up and take vacations during lulls. Further, they were paid the usual, reasonable per diem even though they merely waited at liberty in a foreign country for a shipment to arrive, to be unloaded and to be distributed.

In truth, the job required fewer than a hundred diligent days' work per annum. This year, he and Danny had already had forty-nine "working" weekdays completely to themselves, and he anticipated that they would have eighteen more by New Year's. Even their time in the air was usually bearable, since they traded their tickets up to first class. Nate told himself that he should not feel as weary as he did.

"Doesn't it get rainier in England in September?" Danny asked.

"Absolutely, Cholmondeley," Nate returned with a crisp, upperclass British accent. "That's why the Glorious Twelfth signaled the end of The Season."

I have no idea what you're talking about, and don't bother explaining it." Danny lowered his voice as he nodded toward a pretty woman of graduate-school age who stood in the other line on the ramp and was absorbed in reading a hardback book. "Here's your kind of femme." Nate glanced at the book's title. It was *An Inquiry into Meaning and Truth.*

"Bertrand Russell," Danny read the author's name. "He's a philosopher, right?"

"Right."

"I'm interested in life's meaning. Do you think I could understand it?"

Nate transferred his attaché case to his right hand. "I read it. It's not that kind of meaning."

"What other kind is there?"

"Epistemological. He says that humans formulate meaning based on the kind of knowledge that comes through our limited senses. Russell is concerned with both the knowledge gained through science and also the problems of establishing the nature and validity of all knowledge."

"Forget it. Too deep for me," Danny decided.

Nate pinched the bridge of his nose, trying to relieve the weary pain around his eyes. "I'll tell you without a book what you're looking for. There's no guiding force beyond what we can sense. Life has no great, hidden meaning. You're born; you claw whatever joy you can out of it; you die. End of story." He noted from the changed position of the young woman that the other line was moving slightly faster. He watched her reach into her raincoat pocket, to drag out a yellow and black, thin paperback that Nate recognized as a study guide. Her action freed her passport from the same pocket and Nate watched as it fell onto the rubberized surface of the ramp, barely making noise. The next second, the man standing in line just behind her stepped onto the passport, covering it from view. Under normal circumstances, the booklet was thick enough that the man should have sensed its presence. However, he not only failed to register the passport but also moved his other shoe closer, completely concealing the document. Nate maintained his watch as the woman took another two steps forward. The man set his carry-on bag down, directly over where the passport lay. He bent and reached blindly for the passport with his left hand. As he was straightening up, Nate pushed forward and tapped the woman on the arm.

"Pardon me, Miss," he said. She turned with at surprised look. "You've dropped your passport, and this gentleman has picked it up for you."

The would-be thief blinked at the unexpected turn of events, regained his composure with the speed of a practiced felon, flashed a smile at Nate and then beamed it at the woman.

"Indeed I have," the man said, handing the British passport over. Nate noticed then that at least half a dozen Euro bills were tucked into the passport. He rolled his gaze back up and fixed his unblinking gaze on the man, even as he addressed the woman. "A passport is not a good thing be without. You should keep it in a safer place."

"You're right, of course," she agreed. "Well, thank you both!"

"Glad to have been of service," the man standing behind her said. Nate smirked.

When the two in the other line had advanced even farther down the ramp, Danny asked Nate, "Didn't like her looks?"

"No. She's pretty."

"I don't get it. That was a perfect opportunity. Why didn't you make use of it?"

"I'm calling Catherine tonight," Nate replied, reaching for a plausible if untruthful excuse.

"Okay, that's one night of revelry. But two in the hand guarantees one in the bush," Danny quipped. When Nate failed to respond, he lapsed into silence.

A customs agent crooked her fingers to draw Nate to her desk.

"Good afternoon, Mr…Allen," she said in a bureaucratic monotone, as she opened his passport. She turned to her computer screen and tapped out several strings of keystrokes. Even though she had his paperwork in front of her, she said, "Anything to declare?"

"It's a beautiful day?" he ventured.

She glanced up with a blank stare. He offered her his best Steve McQueen smile.

"No, nothing to declare," Nate retrenched.

"What is the nature of your visit to the British Isles?"

"Strictly pleasure."

"You departed from Zimbabwe last night."

"Yes. Late last night. Arriving London via Rome."

"And previous to Zimbabwe, you were in Columbia."

"That's correct."

The agent raised her hand and waved it, to catch the attention of another agent who stood near a door.

"Would you be so kind as to take your carry-on and follow that officer?" She held up Nate's passport and declaration form.

"Certainly."

"This way, sir," the male agent said, gesturing toward the door.

Nate glanced back briefly at Danny, who was having trouble concealing his discomfort.

The room beyond the door was fitted in Government Modern. The parts of the walls not covered in plastic or official signs were painted a bland blue. A gray, metal table dominated its center. On it sat a detector wand. At the far end of the room stood a man in a white smock. An X-ray machine loomed in the far corner.

The man in the smock wore an unctuous smile and had his hands folded in the attitude of a Dickens antagonist. "Please step into the room beyond that door and remove all your clothing. Put on one of the paper gowns you'll find on the shelf."

"I assume this has something to do with my having just come from Zimbabwe and Columbia," Nate returned.

"A routine check, sir."

Nate locked the official's eyes with his. "I travel as a representative of the World Assembly of Churches."

"Very interesting. Please allow me to do my job."

Nate entered the bathroom. He hung his raincoat over a hook and removed his jacket. For the rest of the disrobing, he sat on the padded steel chair. Above him was affixed the unwinking eye of a television camera, turning the privacy of the changing room into a farce. First, he removed his watch. Then he placed his socks inside his shoes, folded his trousers and underpants over them, and followed with his shirt and undershirt, creating a neat bundle.

In the outer room, Nate's ears, nose, mouth and thick brush of hair were minutely inspected. Finding nothing, the agent asked him to step onto the base of the X-ray machine. While he waited for it to make its automated journey from head down to feet, he watched the agent who had ushered him into the room complete his inspection of the attaché case. Finally, Nate and the emptied case traded places.

"What are you looking for…drugs, diamonds, or state secrets?" Nate asked in a mildly curious tone.

"These days, we're looking for many things, sir," the second agent replied. He shut off the X-ray machine and returned the attaché case to the table.

The first agent turned over each of Nate's shoes in turn, felt around the insides, measured the thickness of the soles, and tugged and twisted the heels. Without expression, he handed the shoes and Nate's underwear back to him.

Nate kept his hands at his side. "I'll wait for my shirt and jacket if you don't mind. Actually, it's a blazer. It was named for His Majesty's Ship *The Blazer*, you know."

"I did not know that, sir," the agent admitted, while patting down the double-breasted, heavyweight, navy jacket with its large brass buttons.

"As I understand it, the ship's captain designed it. He had buttons sewn onto the outer edge of the sleeves because he was tired of watching his men wipe their runny noses on them and leaving behind trails like slugs."

Finally, the agent's impassive mask slipped. For a moment he looked surprised. Then he laughed.

"Imagine a Yank teaching us our own history, Harry," the agent said to his partner.

"Live and learn, I say," the second agent remarked, as he carefully replaced the contents of the attaché case.

The first agent handed over Nate's shirt and blazer. "Don't wait at the…you Americans call it a carousel…for your bags, sir. You'll be picking them up at the Luggage Claim office in the same lobby."

"May I dress now?" Nate asked.

"Certainly."

Nate dug into one of the blazer pockets and pulled out something the agent had already scrutinized. He opened the Altoids tin and offered the "curiously strong" peppermints.

"Can't accept gifts, sir," the agent declined. "Apologies for the delay. Have a lovely time in England."

The Berkeley double-bedroom suite at the Ritz London was everything a five-star accommodation should be, including authentic oil landscapes from the nineteenth century in gaudy gilt frames. Danny had immediately headed to his bathroom to shower off the grime of nineteen hours' travel. Nate had elected to delay unpacking and instead stretched out with *The Times* along the sumptuous teal-color sofa.

About two minutes after the shower water stopped hissing, Danny opened his bathroom door. Steam cascaded around his legs. The hotel's plush bathrobe was too small for him.

"Do you think we're on some international list?" he asked the figure hidden behind the newsprint.

"The Notorious Gem Smuggler List?" Nate replied.

Danny began massaging his scalp with eight fingers. "It's not funny if we are."

"Why do you keep saying 'we'? You weren't dragged into an examining room."

"I guess they figured if they found nothing on you they wouldn't on me." Danny let out an exasperated sigh. "I don't know. I didn't see them haul in anyone else from the flight."

"Did you see anyone else from Zimbabwe who caught our connection in Rome?"

"That woman and her child."

"Who else?"

"Nobody."

Nate lifted his blazer from the glass-topped coffee table and pulled a Cross ballpoint pen from his inside pocket. He wrote across the top margin of the newspaper. "Well, a woman in her early thirties with a ten-year-old is less likely to be transporting illegal Zimbabwe emeralds than a guy in his twenties. It could have been completely random."

Danny wandered toward the nearer window. He gazed down on Green Park. "But you're with the World Assembly of Churches."

"Oh, right! I forgot: Religious people never commit crimes."

"We're not Catholic or Muslim priests."

"Muslims have imams, mullahs, or ayatollahs." Nate held up the newspaper. "Just have faith in our innocence and in the protection of God." Across the empty upper margin he had written, "IF I'M ON A LIST, THIS ROOM MAY BE BUGGED."

A baleful expression swept onto Danny's face. "Okay, fine; it was random. So…are you gonna ring up Catherine?"

"I did. I left her a voice message. She texted back that she's getting married."

"Married? Hah! She'll be cheating on him by the end of next year. Just as well. Time for you to find a new London 'bird,'" Danny decided. "What about entertainment? See anything interesting in the paper?"

"As a matter of fact, I do. A ride in the London Underground."

"What's special about that?"

"This ride uses a powered coach restored from the 1930s. It runs into sidings at various places around the city. We get out and learn about the history of building the subway, about the sewer and water systems, about the cemeteries, and how the Underground is an integral part of London history."

Danny looked manifestly disinterested. "I'm in the mood to wet my whistle and my willie. If you want an exciting ride, I'll rent a Lotus

Exige tomorrow and blast us around the countryside. Tonight, why don't we check out Fox and Hounds, Wibbly Wobbly, or the Cartoonist?" he suggested, speaking of notable London pubs.

"You'll be wetting your train whistle," Nate replied, undaunted. "They provide wine and champagne on the tour." A wicked smile came onto his face. "And I haven't mentioned the best part yet: They put you in period costumes."

"Over my dead body," Danny vowed.

"Relax. Ten to one they won't have anything in your size anyway. It's very exclusive. A hundred pounds each. We might meet some rich chicks also looking for exotic excitement."

"A strip club is exotic excitement. I guarantee no chick, hot or rich, would be caught dead on your tour. What a waste of money *and* time!"

Nate waggled his forefinger. "Remember your word when I flew with you over Victoria Falls."

"You only picked this because you guaranteed I'd regret it."

"Not true. You know me and history."

Danny cinched in his bathrobe belt. "Christ on the Cross! When? "Tonight."

"But we won't have time—"

Prepared for his partner's reply, Nate swiftly lifted the newspaper and pointed to his printed message. "We'll both have time for the hotel's exercise room. The tour starts at midnight. We have an hour for supper as well. Get changed. I'm calling for reservations."

"Why not tomorrow night?"

"It happens just once a month, and we're gone in five days."

"An entire evening down the Tube, literally. We were just in two tubes the better part of a day," Danny complained, referring to their flights.

"Sorry, partner. It's my choice. Besides, it's supposed to rain tonight. I want to do something where I won't get wet…at least not on the outside."

"London in September," Danny groused. "Fine. Saves me from torturing my hair."

Nate lifted the newspaper so that Danny couldn't see his emerging grin. "From what I see, it looks like all that torturing has killed a lot of it."

The throw pillow ripped *The Times* in two parts.

The roof deck of the parking garage on Cockspur Street had two staircases, as well as the lanes for vehicular traffic. With the workday ended, only twelve cars remained. Along the building edges, three were isolated and four more stood paired up. In the center, three were side by side. At one edge of this group stood a late-model, light-gray Range Rover. Nate stood next to the passenger side, huddling under a doorman-sized umbrella. The rain had been pelting down. On the stroke of ten o'clock, it relented to a shower. The clouds hovering low over London masked the starlight above and devoured most of the city lights below.

At three minutes past ten, a lone figure emerged from the north side staircase. As it approached Nate, it stayed out of the overhead stanchion lights, but the fedora on the man's head and the cigar glowing in his mouth were plain enough. Nate stood his ground within the umbrella's shadow.

The figure kept his head tucked into the collar of his coat until he was within five paces of Nate. Then he looked up suddenly and stopped. Nate took a step backward.

"I recognize the hat and the brand of cigar, but you're not Arthur," Nate challenged. He noted well that the man had both hands stuck into the side pockets of his Burberry raincoat.

The man took another two steps closer. He was about three inches shorter than Nate and twenty years older and did not look dangerous. Water dripped off the fedora. "True enough. Arthur gave me his hat and treated me to this excellent Cuban so's you would know I'm here on his behalf."

"What did he tell you?" Nate asked.

"That you would be bringing in emeralds, and that I was to pay you for 'em."

"Let's see the money."

The stranger took his time turning a full circle, assuring himself that they were alone on the rooftop, dropping his cigar and letting it hiss to death in a puddle. When he stood once more facing Nate, he said, "Let me see the stones first."

"It doesn't work that way," Nate told him.

The man withdrew his hand from his right pocket. In it, he held a small automatic. He pointed it at Nate's heart. "This says it does."

"It's not much good with the safety on," Nate said.

The man glanced involuntarily down at the weapon. His focus on the gun rapidly shifted to his feet, where a hand closed around his right ankle.

Nate took the two moments of distraction to drive the ferrule of his umbrella into the gunman's face and then to rush forward into his right side, beyond the muzzle of the automatic, advancing his left foot foremost and grasping the man's elbow on the top with his right hand. In a swift, fluid series of motions, Nate let the umbrella fall, jerked the captured appendage forward and slipped his left arm through the loop of the man's arm, placing his left hand on the gunman's shoulder. He gracefully pivoted around on his left foot and circled his right leg to face the same way.

"You can let go," Nate told Danny as he pressed down on the captured elbow and levered up the forearm.

The man grunted in pain.

Nate put his left foot in front of the man's right one, to prevent him from twisting away. He yanked the gun out of the man's helpless grasp.

"Who the hell are you?" Nate demanded.

"I'm a friend of Arthur's."

"Arthur doesn't do business with a gun."

Danny rose up from the opposite side of the Range Rover and jogged around it. "The tires must be under-inflated. It was a tight fit," he complained.

"Or you've gained weight."

"The water was beginning to soak my goddamned trousers," Danny continued, ignoring his partner's verbal jab. He reclaimed the umbrella and took the gun from Nate. "Not much of a piece."

"But it fits well in pockets."

"A Webley .32," Danny recognized.

"Ease up on me arm, mate!" the man pleaded.

"Shut up, asshole!" Danny commanded, as he kicked the fallen fedora away.

Nate nodded at the little weapon. "It's one of the only handguns common in England. Used for decades by the Metropolitan Police."

"Please!" the man groaned.

In reply, Danny delivered a short jab into the man's solar plexus. The air whooshed from his lungs. Nate let him collapse to his hands and knees on the rain-slick asphalt.

"More facts from The History Channel?" Danny asked.

"Yeah. A fascinating hour."

While the man attempted to hold himself up and resume breathing normally, Danny thrust his hand into the stranger's left coat pocket.

"Nothing," informed Nate. He bent over the moaning figure and patted down his jacket and trousers. He found a wallet, which he opened and inspected.

"Jack Eastwood," Danny announced. "Doesn't Arthur live up in Hampstead?"

"He does," Nate confirmed.

"This one's a neighbor."

"Maybe they *are* friends."

Danny planted his right foot on Jack's posterior and gave a strong shove. The man went off his hands flat onto his chest and planed a couple feet through the water.

"What's the story, Jack?" Nate asked.

Eastwood took in several shallow breaths. "We're friends. Art's in prison. Got nicked for receiving stolen goods. I supply him swag from time to time. He asked me to look after his flat while he's away. I came across a note he had made about this meeting."

"Swell!" Danny said to Nate. "No wonder Arthur got caught. The guy makes notes!"

"But not stupid ones," Jack insisted. "He always forward-dates his meetings by a day. For example, he had this one down for tomorrow." Nate exchanged a grim glance with Danny. To the prone man he asked, "What exactly did he write on the note?"

"It wasn't a note exactly. It was in his appointment book. It said 'Nathaniel Allen, green'…which is his code for emeralds…'Cockspur car park, ten o'clock.'"

"Green. Real sneaky. Jesus!" Danny railed into the drenched night.

"How long has Arthur been in prison?" Nate asked.

"Only ten days."

"Have you tried any other of his pick-ups?"

"You were the first one wrote down since I began taking care of the flat."

Danny gave the Range Rover's fender a frustrated kick and squinted at his partner. "That's why you were searched at the airport. They're on to us."

Nate lowered his head in thought. "The police wouldn't have left his appointment book in the flat unless they thought they could catch more flies with it. They want to see if they can nab you, too, Jack."

"We're probably on some Interpol list by now," Danny added.

Jack Eastwood dared to roll over. He had a gash on his left temple, where the tip of the umbrella had dug into his skin. He lifted up his hand to shelter his eyes from the rain. "But they won't come here looking for you until tomorrow."

"Wonderful," Danny said. "And you thought you could just show up tonight with a gun and rob Nate."

Jack shrugged. "After paying for his defence, Art didn't even have enough left in his bank account to take care of his flat for more than three months. I would have paid you just like he did if I had the money. If you want to give me the emeralds on consignment, I have another acquaintance I can dump 'em off on for a fair price."

"In your dreams," Danny said, fishing under the Range Rover for his leather shoulder bag. "You'll be lucky if we don't plug you with your own gun." He looked at his partner. "Now what?"

"We revert to just plain tourists," said Nate. "We eat, drink and make Merry and her sister for four days and nights, and then we blow this town."

"Can I have my gun back?" Jack dared. "You can keep the bullets."

Nate grabbed the man by his raincoat lapels and hauled him roughly to his feet. "You cheeky bastard. I'm sure felons aren't allowed to have guns in England. I'm doing you a favor. Besides, it's the VAT on your stupidity. If I were you, I'd think about going straight for awhile, Jack. Pick up Arthur's hat and take better care of it!" He took the man's wallet from his partner and thumbed it open. He removed all the pound notes except for two bills. "Just so you don't think we're bad guys, I'm leaving you enough to get back to Hampstead. It's a lousy night to walk."

# CHAPTER THREE

The tour began a few minutes after midnight from London's Transport Museum. It was located in the center of the city, in a large building that formerly housed part of the world-famous Covent Garden Flower Market. Danny had begun grousing ten minutes earlier. According to him, the period costumes looked like they had been recycled from "some musical comedy where the dancers sweated a lot." He allowed a Victorian dockworker's porkpie cap and white neckerchief to be placed on him and no more. He pronounced the wine second-rate, which it was. Further, as he had predicted, there was not one good-looking woman on the tour.

Nate studied the ten other tourists from under his borrowed derby hat. One was a couple in their early forties. The only other person under fifty was a teenage boy in the company of what appeared to be his grandmother. The tour guide was an upbeat gentleman who had attained at least seventy years of age.

"Sorry the shop is closed," he told the group, as he handed out a current 'Tube & Bus/Map out your day' tri-fold to each member of the party. "Come back tomorrow, why don't you, for your 'Mind the Gap' paraphernalia. I'm Reggie. Although I may look it, I was not around when the London subway system, or Underground as we natives call it, was started. After tonight, you will be able to tell your friends and relatives that you touched one of the first walls of the very first stretch of underground in the world."

"Whoop-dee-oo," Danny exhaled, loudly enough that the couple in front of him heard.

"It was opened in between Paddington Station and Farringdon Street. And that is only our initial treat. The tour lasts three hours. On the way we will discuss the building of the system, we'll see part of a cemetery from below, learn the use of the Tube during the London Blitz of World War II, and visit the site of bomb attacks and other disasters from 1883 right up to the terrorist suicide bombers of July, 2005. This way to the bus that will carry us to Charring Cross Station."

At the halfway point of the tour, the refurbished 1930s railway car returned to Charring Cross. Sparkling wine masquerading as champagne was foisted on the patrons. While the prompt tourists waited for the stragglers to return from the restrooms, Reggie kept them entertained with lurid descriptions of the earliest Underground bombings, products of the Irish struggle for Home Rule.

"That very first bomb was exploded on 30 October, 1883, between Charring Cross and Westminster Stations. Down that way," Reggie supplied. He pointed from the side spur where their train waited into the darkness beyond the station lighting. "Charring Cross has had its share of sorrows. During the morning rush hour on 17 May, 1938, a Circle Line train ran headlong into the back of a District Line train waiting at a stop signal between Charring Cross and Temple. Like this car, both trains were made mostly of wood. The damage was considerable, as they compacted into each other like a concertina being squeezed. Six unfortunate travelers died. The cause of the accident was later discovered to be an electric signal repaired with the wires crossed. The Circle Line train had received a green light that allowed it to proceed."

Reggie crooked his fingers several times, encouraging the dawdling old couple to hurry down the platform. He signaled to the train engineer, who he called 'Bertie the Driver.' "Right then. If everyone will kindly climb onboard again, and..." He gestured down to the opening formed between the platform edge and the lip of the railway car. "...mind the gap!"

"Why in hell can't they say 'Watch your step' like we do?" Danny complained to Nate.

"Why do you have windshields instead of windscreens and elevators instead of lifts?" asked Reggie, dropping the perpetual good-humored up-glide of his speech as he came parallel with Danny. As he passed, he added, "Shaw said, 'Britain and America are two nations separated by a common language.' If you will all take your seats, I believe we can get back on schedule."

His last word was spoken with the preferred English pronunciation and with particular emphasis.

"I'll bet he learned that word in elementary shool," Nate quipped to Danny in a half-whisper, causing his friend to burst into laughter.

Reggie eyed the pair coolly. He, however, had no visual clue that Nate was making the same kind of frigid judgment of him and the tour. The refurbished coach, the dress up and liquor were obvious compensations for a lack of truly impressive sites. Reggie's lurid and adjective-filled recreations were barely supplying sizzle to cover up for the lack of steak. Unless the tour concluded with something spectacular, the American connoisseur of historical presentations would give it only two stars out of a possible five.

The single coach car started back onto the main line with creaking of wood and squeaking of undercarriage. Hats and heads bobbed from the constant jostling.

"We shall conclude the tour in the East End of the city, by walking through an authentic public air raid shelter from the Second World War," Reggie announced. He began telling the tour group that the British government had been unwilling to allow the public to shelter from the earliest air raids on the platforms and in the tunnels of the Underground, the fear being that crowds would congest the platforms so badly that use of the city's vital transportation system would be prevented.

"We're gonna be exhausted tomorrow…I mean today," Danny carped. "We both got little sleep on the plane yesterday, and we won't be back to the hotel from this expensive subway ride until at least four."

"So? You and I aren't prisoners of time," Nate riposted. "We have no plans, nobody we have to report to. We'll crash till noon. You would have had us up until at least this time carousing at pubs anyway. True?"

Instead of answering, Danny said, "I've been thinking about what Jack said on the roof." He spoke in what he intended to be a soft voice. The sounds of his resonant bass words, however, were audible over the noise of the moving car and the guide's speech. "I'll bet Scotland Yard or whoever hasn't informed Interpol about Nathaniel Allen yet. Hell, there must be thirty Nathaniel Allens on this island alone."

Reggie allowed Danny to finish his third sentence, then trained his stare on him and cleared his throat. Danny looked at the guide and stopped speaking. Reggie continued uninterrupted for another twenty seconds.

"Maybe you're right," Nate rejoined in a subdued tone, picking up the thread of the subject. "As long as they never find out we met with Jack, all we have to do is to behave ourselves for the next four days and fly home."

"We can sell the stones to Jerry in the Diamond District," Danny suggested.

Reggie shot another annoyed look at the two men.

Nate nudged Danny into silence.

Reggie persevered.

"But the Underground did not assure safety. Twenty Londoners were killed when a Luftwaffe bomb hit Marble Arch Station on 17 September, 1940. Seven more were killed at Trafalgar Square on 12 October when an aerial bomb penetrated the ground and exploded at the top of the escalators. This, in combination with ruptured water pipes, caused a mudslide, which smothered the platforms. Similarly, Balham tube station on the Northern Line, was struck on 14 October of 1940 by a large bomb that penetrated nine meters into the road above. The water mains and sewer pipes were broken, drowning sixty-five persons."

"So we just do our normal thing," Danny decided with enthusiasm. "Survive this tour and move on to pubs."

The dawdling couple turned in unison and glowered at Danny.

"Excuse me, gentlemen," said Reggie. "If you're finding my talk of insufficient interest, would you do the rest of the group the favor of moving to the back of the car?"

"With pleasure," Nate obliged, before Danny could unload both barrels of his verbal shotgun. Not simply from being American-born Irish had O'Shea inherited an antipathy toward Brits who acted in any way supercilious, condescending, or short-tempered. "Let's go, Lord Waterford," Nate said, pulling Danny by the lapel of his raincoat. Danny resisted for a moment. With a little ceremony, he set his porkpie cap and scarf on the seat and snatched up his shoulder bag.

"To misuse your favorite quote," he said to Nate, "I'm glad I'll never pass this way again."

The special train hurtled down the track with more speed than the normal Tube traffic. Lights, signals, stations and walls of tile flashed by in a seamless blur. The sight sparked in Nate a sudden revelation about the members of his family. Their attitudes toward New York City's subway system neatly epitomized them. His father would not be caught dead in the common man's transport system. Simply "getting there" was not sufficient for Simon Allen; the style of transport mattered immensely. Any time one of the pharmaceutical companies sent him a limousine or helicopter, his mood was jovial for the rest of the day. Nate's mother, a lifelong denizen of the City, only took the Lexington Avenue and Broadway Lines, through the "better parts of town." Stepbrother Simon, Jr. prided himself on never having been in the subway. He caught taxis everywhere, even for a three-block ride crosstown in Midtown rush-hour traffic, never thinking it ironic that he swore at the delays.

Stepbrother Hammond feared all manner of transport. He refused to enter any large city and, in spite of his Princeton degree, lived like a hermit in a Princeton Junction apartment, using the mails to deal in coins and rare metals. Stepsister Whitney occasionally "braved the system." When she did, she referred to herself as "a poor, white mouse among a swarm of black rats." Pseudo-liberal Allysia, the youngest of the "steps," publicly applauded the concept of egalitarian transit but privately begged off by using its dangers as an excuse, even after Nate proved its low crime rate compared to that on the street. In spite of his obsession to live the good life, Nate made use of all world subway systems. They were fast, dependable and saved him money for his many excesses. Extravagances and indulgences, he reflected as the stations flew by beyond the windows, which increasingly cost more and satisfied less.

Nate shook himself from his reverie. Ironically, once seated at the far back end, Danny remained totally quiet. He had turned his head as if no longer even pretending to listen, staring at the passing scenes without blinking. Nate concentrated again on the lecture.

"We are now on our way to Bethnal Green station," Reggie reported. "The most horrific incident in the Underground during World War II took place there in March of 1943. During an air raid, a woman with a child tripped at the base of a spiral staircase leading to the Central Line platforms there. A new class of anti-aircraft rockets fired off from nearby Victoria Park panicked the citizens. The river of descending souls could not be stopped. Many fell and were crushed to death by the mass of those trying to push their way down to safety. After the staircase was completely cleared, it was found that 173 people had died from trampling and suffocation."

"I'll bet this guy digs up graves on his day off," Nate murmured.

Danny did not acknowledge the quip but rather kept his attention fixed on the exterior images flashing by.

The hand of the teenage boy shot up. Reggie nodded at him.

"Was that the worst accident ever in the Tube?" the young man asked, in a proper Kensington accent.

"In a station, yes. However, on trains it would be the Moorgate crash," Reggie was happy to supply. "A little before 9:00 P.M. on 28 February, 1975, a Northern City Line train failed to stop. Old Street is a terminus, which means the end of the line. The train continued on through the station and into the closed-ended tunnel south of the platforms. It ploughed through the sand drag barricade piled there against such an eventuality. An autopsy on the driver found no illness such as a failed heart. For whatever reason, he never tried to slow down. It was estimated that the train hit the end of the tunnel at 30 miles per hour. It crushed the first three coaches into a space that would normally fit just one. The driver and more than 40 passengers were killed." Reggie smiled broadly. "I see several looks of apprehension, but have no fear. Following that disaster, signaling systems were changed to ensure all trains stopped or slowed down in plenty of time. Also, a ten mile-per-hour speed limit was added on the approaches to termini. Any time now, we should—"

Nate, who had his shoulder pressed against Danny's, felt his friend tense.

The car suddenly rocked to the left and bounced lightly.

The car's brakes came on hard with an ear-splitting squeal. Nate could feel the car wheels leaving the rails and the right side clattering over the ties.

Danny grabbed Nate in a bear hug and rolled him flat onto the aisle flooring, covering him with his larger frame.

Several people screamed.

With sharp snaps of disintegrating wood and shrieks of sheering metal, the coach struck the right tunnel wall. Half the top and much of the right side of the car peeled off. Glass shattered and exploded in all directions. The surviving frame of the car rebounded wildly to the left. For a moment, it threatened to overturn. It hit the left wall, crushing the front in an ear-punishing boom. The momentum of the rear end swung it around so that it faced nearly backward. Once more it teetered. Then, with a groan like the final breath of a giant, it shuddered one last time and came to a stop.

"Jesus!" Nate exhaled, as Danny rolled off him. "Are you all right?"

"I'll live," Danny replied.

Both men coughed from the volumes of dust swirling through the near-total darkness. Nate pulled at his friend and coaxed him toward a faint light beyond the back of the coach. He realized with relief as he crawled that only his knees ached, from his fall to the floor.

"I'll see to the others. You get help," Nate ordered.

"Okay."

As Danny staggered away from the accident, calling out again and again, Nate cautiously moved forward through the wreckage. He found one after the next of the other ten tourists, Reggie and the engineer.

Everyone was dead.

The word "carnage" came unbidden into his mind. Two victims had been beheaded. A foot in its shoe was separated from its leg. Nate slipped slightly on a pool of blood. He felt his stomach roil. For the first time, he was glad he had seen so many movies and television shows that graphically depicted human gore. Only that rich catalogue of inurning images kept him from fainting. He swallowed several slow, calming breaths and continued his exploration. He found Danny's shoulder bag wedged under a wrecked bench and carefully worked it free.

"It's nothing but tunnel for at least half a mile back," Danny called out as he returned. "It's worth your life to walk that way. Anybody alive?"

"Not one."

"Jeez. Then we are really lucky."

Nate set down the shoulder bag. "Yeah. Thank God your talking made us move to the back end of the car. We have to leave them and find help."

"Right. Be careful, man."

Nate worked his way carefully through the shadows, the twisted metal and splintered wood and thence slowly down to the track. Danny stood erect, waiting for him.

"You seem okay," Nate appraised.

Danny held up his left hand. "All except for this." He rotated it so that it caught the light coming from a distance down the track. He had a deep cut in the flesh of his palm. Blood trickled down his wrist. "I held on tight to one of the bench legs, to keep us from sliding forward during the crash. It had a sharp edge on it. A couple things landed on my back, too. I'm gonna be damned sore tomorrow."

Nate nodded as he extracted his pocket handkerchief and tied it carefully around Danny's wound. Then he encouraged his partner forward by tugging on his raincoat.

"Help! Someone help us!" Nate's pleas, directed toward the line of feeble light bulbs, echoed off the tunnel walls. He paused for a moment and heard no response.

"I knew we were going to crash," Danny said with conviction.

"When?"

"When I saw the guy with the switch changer."

"What?"

"I was looking out the window."

"And?"

"And I saw a guy in a railway workman's outfit standing on the other track. As we came up on him, I saw the tool in his hand. Then as we passed I caught a glimpse of his face and his hair. Bright-red hair. And he had a bandanna tied around his neck. Just like the one they gave me for the tour, except red."

"How do you know the tool was for changing a switch?" Nate asked.

"Because my uncle works for MBTA…the Boston subway system. He's what they call an MOW – maintenance of way – worker. He's responsible for the track and the switches. When I was a kid, I asked him so many questions about what he did that he arranged for me to come with him on a day off. Not underground. Part of the system above ground. He had one of those tools."

"That's crazy," Nate judged.

"Or another godless terrorist attacking a subway."

"Help!" Nate yelled again. He received no answer.

The pair walked in the direction the train had been moving when it crashed, heading doggedly toward the intensifying line of lights. Nate noticed that the tunnel seemed new. Its walls had no covering of dirt or soot. Likewise, the rails shone as if recently laid down.

"Hug the wall," Danny cautioned. "I'll be damned if we survived that crash to be hit by another train coming down this track."
From far off came dull but profound noises.

"Stop!" Nate commanded. "You hear that?"

"Yeah, so? The rain must have changed to a thunderstorm."

"I don't think so. Thunderstorms can't shake the ground this far down. Put your foot on the rail, and you can feel it better."

The muffled concussions continued.

Danny said, "Maybe they're blasting a new tunnel."

"At night?"

"Why not?"

"Other than a thousand locals calling in complaints?"

Nate thought about his partner's first supposition. "You're convinced that guy purposely messed with the track?"

"With a switch," Danny corrected. "There's plenty of radical Muslims living in London."

"Redheaded radical Muslims?" Nate doubted. "Maybe it was one of your relatives in the IRA."

"If it was, I'll personally kneecap the bastard."

The unusual verb made Nate think of his own knees. He felt them swelling, but the emergency was too great to baby himself. They continued on for about a hundred and fifty feet.

"These crossties are murder on the feet," Nate complained.

"They're called 'sleepers' in England," Danny corrected.

"'Two nations separated by a common language,'" Nate muttered.

The noises grew louder and more distinct. Also, a cool breeze blew down from above. When it was at its strongest, Nate looked up and saw that the highest reaches of the left tunnel wall were exposed. Rock and dirt alternated in a cliff that angled up and away, as if the initial excavation for creating the tunnel had started here and still had not been closed. Secured into the rough, natural wall was a wooden ladder, fashioned from lengths of two by fours. At its apex was a narrow wooden platform, and then another, similar ladder climbed the wall into a gloom too dark to see its top. Far above was what Nate took to be sky. It was a darkness suffused with a lambent, orange glow. From the area appeared periodic bursts of light, followed a few seconds later by deep rumblings. The brighter, louder examples were accompanied by more shaking of the ground.

"It sounds like cannons," Danny judged.

"Cannons? In the middle of London?"

"The East End, actually. Or maybe bombs."

Nate had to acknowledge that the noises did resemble elements of warfare. "That sounded like the whistle of a falling bomb."
An instant later the sky flashed orange-yellow, and then a concussive force shook the earth so hard that both men took an involuntary step backward to brace themselves. A great "boom" rang down through the tunnel opening.

"Jesus Christ!" Danny cried out.

"It's an effect," Nate decided. "It must be coming from a theater above the old air raid shelter. They…they recreated the noises, light and shaking of the bombs and the anti-aircraft guns from World War II for the tour."

"After the shit-poor first three-quarters, they owed us going out with a bang," Danny said.

"Not funny, O'Shea. Let's get to that platform."

The string of lighting illuminated the beginning of a station platform to their left. A set of steps rose to a pair of posts that Nate assumed would later hold a gate to prevent travelers from descending to the tracks. Everything about the area seemed roughed out and only partially finished. Electrical cables were exposed. The unpainted ventilation ducts did not have covers. No tiles covered the concrete walls, which exuded the chalky odor of newness. Stripped wires and insulation lay strewn on the platform. Nate studied one of the light bulbs. It looked to him like a good copy of an outdated type, with clear glass and large tungsten filament. He wondered why anyone would go through that much trouble for authenticity before they were finished retrofitting the rest of the station. He pulled back his right sleeve and checked to see that his watch was still ticking. It had sustained no visible damage.

"Was this the first time the tour was offered?" Danny asked.

"It didn't say so in the article." Nate felt a tingle of warning at the base of his brain. He let Danny lead the way down the platform until it opened into a small foyer.

"'Shelter'!" Danny exclaimed. He pointed to a sign and arrow on the foyer wall.

Nate gestured for him to continue. Not much farther along, they came to the back of the foyer. They were confronted by doors on either side of a large, vertical, metal tube painted red. It had an opening for a door but no door. To its right, concrete steps ascended. Nate understood that the red tube was intended to hold a small elevator. He and Danny had once experienced a general escalator failure in a central London Tube station. All detraining passengers had been directed to a similar, tiny elevator and spiral stairs. Being young and impatient, they had elected to climb. They were both amazed at the depth of the station and the rigors of the on-foot ascent.

"What now?" Danny asked.

"You walk up and see if there's a theater." Nate bent and massaged his knees, as a visual demonstration of his next words. "My legs got banged up pretty bad in the accident. I don't want to climb that far unless I have to. I'll explore down here."

Danny looked up to where the tenth step disappeared around the dimly lit curve of the elevator shaft. He did not look happy. "Yeah. All right. Don't go too far." He began climbing.

Nate pushed open the first door to the left of the elevator. Across the red door was stenciled the words "Danger! Keep Out!" It was clearly the lift plant room, but there was no machinery other than a non-operating ventilation fan in front of a black shaft. The fan was covered by a thick wire mesh to prevent accidents. Nate backed out and explored the other door to the left. On its white face in black lettering had been stenciled "Medical." No tables, cots, cabinets, or counters had been installed. It was simply a large, white room. In between the two doors, a much larger ventilation fan protruded from the wall about five feet. Behind its wire mesh covering was an unmoving fan that looked like the engine propeller of a World War II vintage bomber. A large panel door had been inset immediately to the left of the fan system. It had two flanges that allowed a padlock to secure it, but there was no lock to be found. Nate swung the door back. He saw that the area was a crawl space fashioned to house several banks of electrical service panels. Only one had been installed.

Nate crossed to the door opposite "Medical." It was larger than the other two. It opened to a short, semi-circular corridor. This, in turn, led through another metal door into a passageway that had two large, tiled rooms to the left. From the unfinished piping and fixtures, it was clear that these were lavatories for large masses of people. Inexplicably, everything in the lavatories looked shiny new. So had the ventilator fans. A shiver shot down Nate's spine. He lifted a trap door in the floor and looked down. A series of pumps had been installed. This was the high-pressure system needed to move human waste up to the normal sewer system. From their pristine look, they had never pumped filth. He let the door drop. It made a loud, hollow clang. No guard, no custodian, no attraction employee hurried in to ascertain who had made the noise.

Beyond the lavatories was room after room that would have housed air raid refugees. Nate calculated that, together, the chambers might have sheltered six hundred. He pictured in his mind stacks of metal bed frames three high. No frames had been moved in. More strangely, the walls bore no marks of bolts or stanchions.

At the far end of the hive of chambers was another spiral staircase but without the elevator at its center. The staircase was dark, dissuading him from venturing up. He could hear his heartbeat in his ears, pulsing out the passing moments.

From a schematic Nate had once seen in a World War II history book, he knew absolutely that he was wandering around a deep level air raid shelter. He also understood that it was months, if not years, from being finished. Yet it did not look like a relic, a curiosity piece to end a twenty-first century subway tour. It rather looked like it was an antiquated design in the process of active completion. Shaking his head, he started back toward the station foyer.

"Nate!" Danny's strident voice echoed through the empty corridor.

"Here!" Nate called back. "I'm coming." When he emerged into the foyer he found Danny shambling back and forth from one foot to the other, looking like a circus bear extremely annoyed at being made to dance.

"This is a damned maze!" he complained. "I went all the way up to the top. Let me tell you, if you're claustrophobic don't make the trip. The stairs opened up into a little station room. I tried both doors, but they were locked. No windows either. No way out at all. So I walked back down and came out on what I thought was this floor. It wasn't. It had no lights. I came pretty close to panicking. There are two levels, Nate."

Nate nodded. "That's right. Some of them had two levels. Up on the street, there's an entrance at opposite ends of the block. It was in case one of the entrances was bombed."

Danny's eyes widened with amazement. "You knew that and didn't tell me."

"I wouldn't have remembered it unless you reminded me."

"Great. Thanks. Listen, there was no theater up there, but the noise was really loud, the shaking was lots stronger than down here. It was like World War II was actually happening on the other side of those locked doors."

Nate rubbed his chin nervously. "I explored this shelter, and it sure isn't ready for prime time. Something is really wrong here, Dan."

"So what do we do?"

"We have to go back as quickly as we can and see if we can straighten that switch. If it hasn't happened already, another train is going to derail."

"Christ, you're right!"

They quit the station and hastened along the track toward the destroyed railway coach. Nate encouraged Danny to run ahead. He watched his partner reach the V point where the left wall opened up into another tunnel. The lights spaced along the walls flickered and then returned to full power.

"No trains," Danny yelled. "That's lucky."

"No. It should be impossible," Nate countered. "We were gone for at least half an hour. A dozen trains should have come down this track."

"Why didn't they?" Danny asked.

Nate made no reply but added the observation to his rapidly growing list of the eerily unexplained.

"Look at this," Danny directed as soon as Nate stood at his side. "Do you understand how a track switch works?"

"Only that it moves."

"When two lines of track come together, eventually the wheels of the engine and cars have to cross over one pair of rails. The whole thing where it happens is called a turnout. This V where they come together is called the frog; don't ask me why. You see these extra pieces of rail on the inside? They help keep the car wheels on the main rail or guide it back. They're called guardrails."

Nate nodded in mild astonishment. He had rarely heard Danny so well versed on any subject much less one as arcane as railroad switch configuration.

After a quick pause to draw in a big breath, Dan plunged on. "Railroad wheels have circles of extra metal on the outer edge. They're called flanges, and they hug the inside of the rails so the train won't slide off. The flanges have to pass through a space between the rails. Right here. That creates two gaps. These are the real gaps you have to mind on a railway system. And here are the movable rails. You see how they get thinner at the end? They're called the points. These points were not completely closed. It's lucky the coach we were on didn't jump the rails immediately, or we'd have plowed into that sharp-angled dividing wall back there."

Nate looked up and down the track. "The points aren't closed because somebody moved them mechanically?"

"Yes, to the middle. The fucking redheaded maniac!"

"I don't see him," Nate said, craning his neck to one side and then the other. "I don't see anyone."

"Why would you? We're nowhere near a working station."

"Where did he go?"

Danny lifted both arms and pointed up and down the main line. "Take your pick. How the hell can I move these points so there isn't another wreck?" He walked down the track a little way, gave a little shout of triumph, bent and picked up a long-shank metal tool with sturdy, right-angled handles.

"See? I wasn't crazy! This is what the guy was holding. I'm gonna switch the rails back to the main line."

While Danny labored on the box beside the rails, twisting the tool slowly around, Nate took the "Tube & Bus" tri-fold map from his back pocket and walked under the nearest tunnel light. The print was small, so he held the map up high. He found the red-colored Central Line and traced it from Liverpool Street station east to Mile End. In between the two stops was Bethnal Green. A tiny dash of red extended north at right angles, suggesting the spur behind him. Nate had never before ridden a Tube line into the East End. He had no expectation of what to look for, but he felt something was very wrong. He suddenly remembered the words of Reggie the tour guide. Bethnal Green had been the site of the worst Underground disaster in history, when panic during an air raid on a spiral staircase had resulted in the death of 173 persons. One of the two staircases Nate had just looked upon had been that very site. His body shook with the realization.

"Crazy bastard! He smashed open the lock is what he did," Danny growled as he worked.

"That noise is still shaking the earth," Nate observed. "I'm going back to what's left of the car and collect your bag."

"Right."

Nate hobbled toward the destroyed carriage, feeling not only the pain in both knees but now also the friction burns on his legs where he had slid partway down the coach floor. When he reached the ruined car, it took him some time to boost himself up without injury. He crossed carefully to where he had left Danny's shoulder bag and grabbed it. Nate turned to leave and then stopped. Screwing up his face with revulsion, he pivoted. If indeed a redheaded maniac had sabotaged the train, Nate did not want him plundering the bodies as well. Feeling like a ghoul himself, Nate moved carefully among the corpses. He collected purses and removed all items of identification or value to hand over to the police. He fished into jacket and trouser pockets for wallets and billfolds. Then he removed watches, earrings, rings and other pieces of jewelry. He stuffed everything into Danny's bag. Before he abandoned the wreckage, he picked up the porkpie cap and the derby. He met Danny walking toward him.

"Why are you wearing that stupid hat?"

Nate handed over the shoulder bag and then pushed the porkpie cap into Danny's free hand. "To keep my head dry. The umbrella was destroyed."

"There's no rain down here," Danny argued.

"For when we get out onto the streets. You must have been right; those noises are a thunderstorm." Nate began walking toward the intersection of the main line and the spur.

"Yeah. With wicked lightning. Where are you going?"

"I'm walking out of here, if my knees will hold up."

"You'll get hit by a train!"

"Have any trains come by in the last half hour?"

"No."

"According to my ever-reliable Casio Pathfinder, it's three-thirty in the morning. The only thing I can think of is they must stop running for a couple hours in the East End."

"Subways never stop," Danny asserted.

"Then where are the trains?"

"Ah, shit! Fine. Whatever will get me into that big bed at the Ritz." Danny clapped the cap onto his head. As he started after his partner, he reached into his shoulder bag and took out the flashlight he never traveled without. Although neither man had ever mentioned the subject, it was clear that big, powerful Daniel O'Shea feared total darkness. In one of his suitcases at the Ritz London was also a nightlight with every outlet adapter known to mankind. The flashlight was of the survival variety, made of shatterproof plastic, with a built-in replacement bulb housed in the back and consisting of a magnet and moving coil. Shaking the flashlight for long enough produced a blue-white beam that was never strong but which could be infinitely renewed. Danny shook it for all he was worth.

When they were still almost a hundred feet from the junction of tracks, the noise of an approaching train came to their ears. Danny looked over his shoulder with an expression of triumph. Rarely in differences of opinion was he right, and he wanted Nate to acknowledge it.

"So, they just started up again," Nate replied.

"Up yours! I'm gonna try to make it stop." Danny loped toward the main line.

The train noise came from the direction of central London. Wincing from the pain of swollen knees, Nate struggled to keep up with his more long-legged partner.

"Stop!" Danny yelled at the growing noise, waving his flashlight beam down the tunnel at the far-more-powerful approaching headlight. In answer, the engineer sounded his horn, filling the tunnel with an eardrum-splitting racket. No sound of brakes, however, augmented the ruckus.

The din of metal rolling on metal became painful to Nate. The train's lamplight swept across his face, making him wince. He forced his lids to stay open, so that he could study the train and its passengers as it passed. It was not moving particularly quickly, but neither did it slow down.

"Stop, damn it!" Danny screamed at the three passing cars, immediately after retreating.

The train rumbled on into the darkness.

Nate's eyes following the disappearing train. A moment later, his legs failed him, and he sat down hard on the track bed.

"What happened? Did your knees give out?" Danny asked.

Nate lowered his head toward the ground, desperately needing the blood to return to his shocked brain.

Danny squatted next to his partner, his face filled with concern. "What's the matter, Nate?"

"I'm pretty sure we can't go back to the Ritz. At least not the Ritz we left this evening. Did you see the men and women inside those cars?"

"No."

"Almost every one of them was wearing a hat. Derbies, poor boys, fedoras. And the cars all looked like the one in pieces behind us."

"It's another one of these stupid tours," Danny asserted, reaching up to touch the pork pie cap on his own head.

"There is no other tour. That train is in another time. Just like we are."

Danny's eyes narrowed as he studied Nate's face, looking for signs of the head injury that he was certain had happened during the crash. "What are you talking about?"

"The impossible. 'Boom. Crump, crump, crump.'"

"And what does that mean?"

"It was how Ernie Pyle described bombs landing in London. He was a famous American war correspondent. World War II."

"You're scaring me, man."

"Good. Because I want somebody scared with me."

"You musta hit your head in the crash."

"My head is fine. Help me up."

Danny pulled Nate to his feet. "What do we do?"

"We can't walk down the tracks. The shelter's locked. The only sure way up is those ladders just beyond the train wreck."

"You didn't want to climb them."

"I do now. Stop staring at me like that!"

Danny averted his eyes.

"And you can let go of me while you're at it. I'm not the problem."

Nate pulled away and started once again toward Bethnal Green station.

"You had to have imagined that old train," Danny insisted.

"Did you see a new one?"

"I was just trying to get it to…. I saw a train. That's all."

"Then let's see what's topside."

The system of ladders was not quite as dangerous as it looked. The ascent was several degrees from vertical, and two intervening platforms broke up the climb. By resting every dozen or so rungs, Nate was able to work his way toward the orange-glowing sky. He had insisted that Danny go first, so that if his knees buckled and he fell he would not kill both of them.

With virtually every new rung climbed, the volume of the strange collection of noises increased. The ground, however, had stopped shaking and the rain had ceased. Danny reached the top while Nate was still more than a dozen rungs down.

"Holy God Almighty!" Danny's words were not spoken with his usual booming delivery but rather seeped out in a prolonged gasp.

"What?"

Danny did not respond.

Nate recruited the last of his strength to haul himself up and over the top of the ladder. He stood.

Nate followed Danny's frozen focus. He faced the southeast, where the entire horizon pulsed in orange, yellow and red. Miles of the landscape were not just dotted with fires; an entire quadrant of the city was engulfed in flames. The air above for at least two thousand feet was a living black entity, like a giant and still-growing fungus. The black mass was not storm clouds, like the ones Nate and Danny had left behind when they exited the bus from the Transport Museum and descended into Charring Cross Station. These were billowing clouds of smoke, the product of terrifying, out-of-control burning consumption. London was an open-hearth furnace.

The writhing flanks of the clouds were caught in moving shafts of light. Nate looked around and saw that no fewer than fifty powerful search beacons cut through the concealing night. And then one of the things they sought burst out of the black, amorphous monster, its engines making the sound of a million angry hornets as it skimmed over the city. Nate watched in horror as six small bombs dropped from its belly, flashing silver in a spotlight cone for the briefest moment and then plunging earthward.

Like a steady death march drumbeat, the six high-explosive bombs unleashed their destructive force as they met with ground, structure and street.

Grimly congratulating himself, Nate was still weathering shock but not surprised. Too many gathered clues under the earth had prepared him for the hellish scene.

"You've gotta be fucking kidding me," Danny exclaimed. "That plane had a swastika on the wing!"

Nate glanced to the south. Something resembling a silver whale, with a smooth body and short tail fins, floated in the sky. Nate recognized it as a barrage balloon.

"I'm glad I'm young," Danny managed, "because otherwise I'd be having a heart attack right now. My ticker is trying to jump out of my freaking chest."

"Stayed zoned in, Big Dog," Nate said, keeping his voice calm and even.

Close by, a group of cannons blasted ordnance into the sky, bracketing with a diamond pattern of shell bursts the bomber that had just released its load. None hit the enemy aircraft, which dipped its left wing and started a turn over what Nate figured must be the Thames River.

More bombs landed. More cannons erupted.

"Maybe the crash killed me. You and all of this is a creation of my mind set free from my body," Nate speculated aloud, as if guessing the truth would set him free from the flaming world.

Danny slapped Nate hard on the shoulder. "Did you dream me hitting you? I have the opinion I'm pretty damned real, pal. What is this?"

"The Blitz," Nate answered. "The German air attack on London that started a year after England declared war on them."

# CHAPTER FOUR

Danny tugged on the sleeve of Nate's raincoat. "We have to go back the way we came. Right now! We don't belong here."

"We don't belong then," Nate replied. "The train that went by us down there was from another time."

"That's impossible!"

Nate swept his left hand across the fiercely flickering panorama, through the breeze that blew toward the fires. "Then what is this?" Before Danny could reply, he added, "More than sixty years ago."

"This is your fault," Danny accused. "You were the one who insisted on the trip back in time on that railroad car. You were the one who used the phrase 'we're not prisoners of time.'"

"I also said we could crash until noon. So, even if I am guilty, what do you want me to do about it?"

"Talk us out. Walk us out. Anything but this!"

"Yelling will only make you hoarse. Let's relax and explore a little," Nate said, to keep his partner from melting down. He executed a slow circle.

The Americans stood in the middle of a fenced-in field. It was heavily rutted from the movement of many construction machines. To their right and left, at either end of the long block, stood white buildings. Nate moved toward the one on the right, finding himself suddenly in waist-high weeds. Some of them had nettles that pricked his hands and stuck to his raincoat. He ignored them and brought himself close enough to be able to study the building. From where he stood it looked like a one-story rectangle backed by another rectangle twice as high. He figured the taller section housed hoisting and ventilation shafts. The shelter entrance structure had no windows. It looked extremely solid, like the German "pill box" bunkers the Allies faced when they assaulted the Normandy beaches on D-Day. When Nate turned and estimated the distance between the identical structures, he calculated that they lay at either end of the shelter far below.

To Nate's back extended more field, including the gaping excavation hole from which they had just climbed. At the opposite limit, a high wooden fence ran the length of the block between the shelter entrances. Nate moved toward it, with Danny tailing noisily behind. He found the entrance, but it was a gate formed by two metal doors and secured with a sturdy chain and padlock.

"It's like a damned video game," Danny lamented. "We're trapped again!"

Nate took the flashlight from him, shook it for several seconds, and trained it on the ground. "Not this time. The fence is only made of wood."

"Listen!" Danny said as Nate swung the beam back and forth along the ground.

Nate paused. The sounds of warfare had almost died away. No more airplane engines, no more bombs or anti-aircraft fire disturbed the night. However, horns and sirens of emergency vehicles echoed from every direction.

"Strange," Nate mused to himself, regarding the burning cityscape.

Danny came up close beside him. "You mean something specifically strange or the whole impossible thing?"

"There were no 'all clear' sirens."

"Maybe more planes are on the way."

"I don't think so." At last, in spite of the eastward direction of the breeze, Nate smelled the stink of soot and ash.

"Why not?" Danny demanded, venting annoyance at Nate's sudden calm.

"They flew in tight waves during this war. They stuck together as much as they could, to protect their squadrons from fighter planes and to keep from flying into each other. Also to give the enemy too many targets to fire on all at once."

"More History Channel?"

"No, reading. When I was around thirteen I became fascinated by war. Especially our Civil War and World War II."

"I read too," Danny said defensively. "Just not dry stuff. Have you read anything about going back in time?"

"Nothing that wasn't pure speculation."

A lone concussion off in the distance cut through the vehicle noise.

"Another bomb," Danny decided. "I thought you said the attack was over."

"Probably a time-delay. Nasty tricks. People come out of their shelters, and then the things go off."

Danny turned his back on the cyclorama of fires and smoke. "Jesus, London is black. No lights at all. Unbelievable. One of the biggest cities in the world, and it looks like we're in the middle of some country village."

"It was the biggest city in the world back then. Back now." Nate angled the failing flashlight beam toward the watch on his right wrist. He pointed. "That way is west."

"We can't move away from the tunnel!" Danny said in a strident voice. "It's our only way home. We just have to figure it out."

"You stay here if you like. I need to learn more." Nate's foot chanced on a length of iron pipe. He brought it to the fence and used it as a battering ram. The targeted board groaned with the abuse. He grabbed it and twisted left and right until it came off in his hands. He went to work on the board next to it. The second one gave him more resistance but finally started to move.

"Who goes there?"

A male voice came from the dark street beyond the fence. A faint beam of light swept along the ground, found Nate's feet, his legs and then his face.

"It's all right. We're lost," Nate called, swinging the loose board out of the way. Then, in a near-whisper, he told Danny, "Let me do the talking."

"Don't I always?" Danny rejoined.

The second board suddenly dropped to the ground of its own weight.

A moment later, the owner of the challenging voice came close enough to the new opening in the fence that the fire glow from more than a mile away lit his form. He wore farm boots and a rather formless unitard with a black belt around the middle. An armband identified him as a member of the ARP. From his belt hung a gas mask. A tin whistle hung around his neck from a lanyard. On his head sat a shallow metal helmet with a wide rim, like an inverted formal soup bowl, secured by a chinstrap. In his left hand he carried a galvanized bucket with a hand pump extending from it.

"You're destroying city property," he declared in a matter-of-fact tone.

"Only because we couldn't get out."

"Blimey! Are you Americans?" the man inquired, keeping his light on the pair.

Nate noted that the flashlight had a half-circle cover so that the light it cast would be hard to see from the air. "We are."

"Bad time to be visiting London," the Englishman observed, looking Nate and Danny up and down. "Come out of there."

Nate said, "We're here on business from our government. For the war effort. Our train stopped running."

"I'm not surprised, this being the first big raid," the Englishman replied. "But I'm sure it won't be the last. I'm Worden Miles." He held out his hand first to Danny, who stood closer to him. While Nate waited his turn, he registered that Mr. Miles's speech carried a hint of cockney. It suggested that they were indeed on the western verge of the East End.

"You're an air raid warden," Nate said, offering his hand.

The man smiled. "True enough. And my first name is Worden." He spelled his given name. "Perhaps my father was prophetic."

"Nathaniel Allen. New York City."

"Danny O'Shea. Brooklyn, by way of Boston."

Worden said, "Pleased indeed. My official title is Air Raid Precaution Warden. Where in London are you staying?"

"In a residence off Green Park," Nate dissembled.

Warden Miles's thick eyebrows elevated. "Must be important government business indeed."

"But it's very inconvenient," Danny chimed in, fixing his gaze on Nate to let him know he had elected to speak for a very good reason, "because our business is out this way. We need someplace to stay that's closer."

Worden nodded. "Well, you won't be getting back to Green Park tonight. Not after all this Bosch mayhem. Come with me."

For two minutes, they walked down the middle of dark roads without trading comments. The near-total darkness begged for silence. Then Worden said, "They knew exactly where to bomb. I'd say they went after Woolrich Arsenal and all of the docks. Many big factories are down there."

"We know," Nate lied. "One of them is why we're here."

"It also looks as if our anti-aircraft and barrage balloons did next to nothing," Worden observed. "We'll see what the newspapers tell us tomorrow and the next day."

Then he lapsed into another silence. They crossed a main road, which was disturbingly devoid of traffic. Nate and Danny found themselves ascending slightly as the air raid ward negotiated the street of tightly huddled houses. They turned yet another corner and, in a few steps, came to a collective halt. Worden held open a wooden picket fence gate. The wall on either side was formed of stone and mortar, but a white canopy trellis festooned with white Tudor roses softened the line.

"Welcome to my humble home," Worden said. Three steps up, they entered a back yard. Off to the right side, a large semicircle of metal with a door in it shined dully in the homeowner's flashlight beam. Just behind lay a mound covered with vegetation.

"Is that you, Worden?" a woman's tense voice inquired from inside the structure.

"Yes, Mother. Safe and sound." Worden moved to the bottom end of the structure, where its stubby door was located. As the sound of unblocking came from inside, he told his guests through a sly smile, "We're very lucky, don't you know. We have a summer home, as well as our ordinary one. But, then again, so do a million and half other Brits. Welcome to Casa Miles."

The door opened. After the unremitting darkness of the neighborhood, the glow from inside was welcome.

"Duck your heads, gents," Worden advised. "Especially you, Mr. O'Shea. This is my better half, Millicent Miles."

Mrs. Miles merely nodded her welcome, not offering her hand. She was as tall as her husband, who stood at five-foot eight. She, like he, was attractive and in her forties, with no middle-age weight on her frame. In fact, under her flower print dress and apron, she seemed underweight. Both husband and wife had gray-blue eyes, and when Mr. Miles removed his helmet, it was revealed that both had brown, slightly wavy hair. Nate noted that they might be mistaken for brother and sister.

"Have you been inside an Anderson shelter before?" Worden asked.

"Can't say we've had the pleasure," Nate replied, looking around. He saw that the shelter was formed from six large, corrugated steel semi-circles bolted together. The bottoms of the walls had been sunk into the ground. The Miles family had set their interior up to sleep four. Roughly built bunk beds occupied either side toward the far end, with a tiny aisle in between. The front end had just enough room for a small, folding card table and two folding chairs. On the table sat a large book, its double columns betraying its nature. Nate saw that the Bible lay open to Psalm 46. The shelter's equipment stood on duckboards.

Under the bottom beds were stored several round troughs of galvanized tin. These were crammed with bedding and cooking materials, as well as tins and cardboard packages of foodstuffs. From the apex of the shelter hung a Coleman kerosene lantern.

Worden said, "Cramped and damp, but they tell us, between the metal and the foot of dirt covering, it can withstand all but a direct hit." He ran his forefinger along the curve of the wall and withdrew a bead of water, leaving a dark line behind. "They weep terribly from the night air and our exhalation. We're lucky, because we're up on a hillock. I was able to dig a trench down to a sump hole. Many others find themselves standing in inches of water. But we're safe."

"Don't the houses just above you drain onto your yard?" Nate noticed.

"They do. In fact, Archie Wilcox next door fed a hose out of his shelter right to the edge of his property line. I said to him, 'Archie, where in blazes do you think your water will go?'"

"I'd have sued him," Danny said.

Mr. Miles looked at him like Danny had suddenly grown a second head. "Sue him? He's been my neighbor for more than fifteen years. No, we put our backs together and dug an underground line from his place into my sump. It works fine. Can I bother you for the time?" Without thinking, Nate held up his watch.

"Glory be!" Worden exclaimed, staring at the digital wizardry. "What's this?"

Nate cleared his voice to give himself a moment for thought. "It's part of the reason we're here in London. This watch tells the time in numbers, but it also gives the compass direction, our altitude, the temperature and the barometric reading."

"I see. For airplane crews, no doubt," Worden said, studying the watch with great interest. "Where's the winding stem?"

"It doesn't need one. It runs on solar power."

"On sunlight? Astonishing! And there's the correct date in your system. Oh-nine, oh-eight. September eighth, four-nineteen in the morning. How wonderful!"

"What's wonderful?" a female voice inquired from outside the shelter.

"Come in and see, Penny!" Worden called. To his guests, he said, "This will be my daughter, Penelope."

"Hello."

The first impression Nate received came from Penny's eyes. There was no mistaking the intelligence radiating from within them. Unlike those of her parents, hers were a brilliant green. They reminded Nate of the color of the stones he had so recently smuggled out of Zimbabwe. He lowered his gaze to her smile, which was broad. He marveled that, in this time before braces or operations to remove wisdom teeth, her teeth should be so even and white. He noticed as well her "English rosebud complexion," the brown, shoulder-length hair that framed her oval face, and the single strand that had just fallen over her left eye. Her hair was wavier than that of her parents. When he realized his silence was becoming rude, he searched for something cleverer than a return hello.

"Ulysses' faithful wife," he managed.

"I'm nobody's wife, thank you" she replied. In her hand she held a gas mask.

"These gentlemen are Nathaniel Allen and Daniel O'Shea. From America," Father Miles introduced.

Penelope also wore a uniform. Hers, however, was well tailored, dark gray and paramilitary in look, with a white blouse under a waist-length jacket and a matching skirt running about two inches below her knees. Her lace-up shoes were flat, almost male in character, and dark brown.

"Pleasure," Penelope returned. She looked past the two to her mother. "How are you holding up, Mum?"

"Better than Mrs. Wilcox." She dipped her head to the left. "I thought she'd run out of screams yesterday afternoon, but she had plenty left for tonight. I hope you're home for good."

"I am," confirmed her daughter. She collapsed onto one of the folding chairs, set her elbows on the table, let out a large puff of air, and dropped her head onto her hands. "My shift was officially over three hours ago. Whole rows of houses flattened, not much more than a mile from here at the bottom of Stepney. I don't know why we put up all these home shelters if people don't go into them. They went out into the street to watch the bombers, and the next thing you know a bomb lands beside them. And then there were all those trapped inside their homes."

Nate tucked away the fact that Penelope spoke in a neutral British, with almost no trace of the quasi-Cockney accent of her parents.

In Poplar, the houses have no back yards," Worden Miles reminded his daughter. "They've been reinforcing their homes with timber." He patted Penelope on the shoulder. "We'll get better protecting ourselves now that the Phoney War is over."

"They dropped tonnes of incendiary sticks. The fires are far worse than the bombs," Penelope shared. "I counted more than one hundred pumps on the streets we covered, and they were barely doing anything. The water pressure was so low that their streams hardly reached the rooftops. You couldn't go within fifty feet of the raging fires, the heat was so bad. We made nine trips."

"So, *Ordeal* has finally arrived, my love," Worden told his daughter. To Nate and Danny he said, "Penelope drives an ambulance for the ARP. Out of the garage they built in the park."

"What park is that?" Danny asked.

"Oh, sorry," Worden said. "Victoria. You're in Bethnal Green. Where's your cap, Penny?"

"What? Oh, I must have left it in the ambulance."

Worden looked at his wife. "I told these gentlemen we could accommodate them for the night."

Millicent's eyes grew wide with surprise.

"In the house," Worden assured. "I'm sure the Luftwaffe is done for this round. They did a set of afternoon and then a set of night runs each day when they destroyed Rotterdam and Warsaw. No reason to think they'd mess with success."

"I concur," Nate said. He noticed that Worden's eyebrows were slightly elevated when speaking his last words. Whatever he was feeling on the inside, his façade was one of pluck, colored by his dry, English sense of humor.

Penelope covered a yawn with the back of her hand and then immediately excused herself. She rose slowly and moved toward the bunk beds. "I'm all in. If I'm like this after one night, what will I be like if they bomb like they did Warsaw?"

"You'll do fine, because you *must* do fine," her father told her.

"Gentlemen, shall we make the arduous trek to the other Miles abode?"

Nate stole a last glance at Penelope, wondering if he would see her again.

The Miles' home was bigger than thousands in the East End of London, but still it seemed claustrophobically small to Nate. They entered through an open back door that Worden explained had been left that way "to minimise the overpressure from the bombs and hopefully keep our windows intact."

They immediately entered the kitchen, which adjoined the dining area. At the opposite end was the hallway and, a few steps later, the front entrance, which had also been left open. To their left lay a small living room. To the right, a narrow set of stairs led up to three bedrooms and a bathroom. Nate and Danny were not shown the parents' bedroom but were first led to the one across from the stairs, which was ten feet by eight. The back bedroom, which shared the rear wall with the bath, was not much larger. Nate saw from the furnishings and decoration that it belonged to Penelope. Worden had tried the stair light, to see if the electricity was still functioning, and had left it on only until his guests had climbed to the top. He showed the bedrooms and bathroom by "torchlight."

"Why don't you take this, Mr. Allen? It's Penny's room," Worden invited. "My son's bed is longer, made for a man of Mr. O'Shea's proportions." The sweep of his light showed a glossy promotional still of Fred Astaire and Ginger Rogers tacked to the wall.

"Where is your son?" Nate inquired.

"Ralph was killed holding the eastern front during the evacuation of Dunkirk. We just removed our armbands after three months of mourning."

Nate was glad he could not see Worden's face.

"We're very sorry, sir," he offered.

"Thanks." He turned to Danny. "I would ask you to disturb the room as little as possible. His mother has everything just as he left it. A shrine of sorts, I suppose. I don't agree with her, but there you are. We must each mourn in our own peculiar manner, mustn't we? I'll leave you then."

Only after the reverberations of Mr. Miles's boots retreat from the house did Danny dare to speak.

"My walk-in closet is bigger than this guy's bedroom."

"What do they say about beggars?" Nate replied, little surprised but more than a little appalled by Danny's lack of reaction to Mr. Miles's parting speech.

"Just making an observation. I wonder if this house is still standing in our time?"

Nate shrugged out of his raincoat, registering as he did that Danny was making at least a token effort to adjust to the bizarre situation. "There's a good chance it isn't. You heard what Mr. Miles said. Today is the eighth of September. I can't remember exactly when the bombing of London began, but I'm pretty sure it was early September 1940. He said this was the first time."

Danny scratched his neck. "And how long did it go on?"

"For the rest of the war."

"Refresh my memory: How long was that?"

"Until May of 1945."

"Fuck!"

"The Blitz will be brutal but, in fact, a blessing," Nate informed. "Until Churchill sent bombers to Berlin a few times, the German Luftwaffe was concentrating on England's airfields and their support installations. They had almost wiped out the Royal Air Force. Shifting their attention to London will allow the RAF to survive."

"Wonderful," Danny replied, his voice thick with irony. "Except we're in London, not at some airfield."

"The heavy bombing will stop after a time," Nate offered.

"That's good. How long?"

"I think it was almost every night for about four months."

Danny shoved Nate hard. "Why don't you set me up and knock me down one more time?"

"And then Hitler got distracted by the partisans who overthrew Yugoslavia. That was around April of '41. He didn't fixate on England again until the invention of the V1 and V2 rockets. I think those started hitting London in early '44."

"Was Bethnal Green ever hit?" Danny asked.

"I'm sure it was. Everything in this city was eventually hit."

Danny collapsed on the dead soldier's bed. "Great. Just great. We gotta escape this nightmare quick."

# CHAPTER FIVE

Nate woke to the furtive sounds of wooden hangers clicking against each other. The room was dark from the black paint spread across the windowpanes, except for several streaks where the brush had missed or someone had felt a need to let in at least a little light. He recognized Penelope's shape, however, from her nipped-in waist. She wore the same outfit she had on when he met her, but she had removed her jacket.

"Oh! Sorry to wake you," she said in a hushed voice. "I was so tired last night I wasn't thinking straight. I should have taken my clothes down to the shelter then." She pulled a dress and hat from inside her armoire.

"What day is it?"

He could see her form tensing, signaling her confusion at how he could not know the day. "Sunday."

"Right. Sorry. Danny and I don't work normal hours or days, so we lose track."

Penelope stood stock still for a moment. "I see."

"Where are you going?"

"To church. If ever there was a day to pray, it's this one."

"True. I'm glad you're here," Nate said. "It drove me crazy wondering until I fell asleep. What's 'ordeal'?"

Penelope turned and looked down at Nate. "Beg pardon?"

"Your father said something to you like 'Ordeal has arrived at last.'"

A decidedly feminine laugh escaped the bedroom's owner. "Ah. *Ordeal* is a novel that came out last year, by a writer named Nevil Shute. He predicted what last night would be like, and that there would be many more days and nights of air bombing. He wrote about lack of food and a tainted water supply, a collapsed sewer system and all of us huddled in inadequate shelters."

"A prophet of doom, eh?" Nate responded.

Penelope's silhouette stopped moving. "I like to believe his intent was to frighten us into preparing ourselves. We've done well, but what can prepare any people for such warfare?"

The negative topic and her rhetorical question fostered a sudden and overwhelming desire for Nate to gift the young woman more than some fiction author's precautionary warnings. He came up on one elbow and searched through the gloom for her bright eyes. "Britain will triumph. It will take some time, but she will prevail."

"You're certain of that?"

"Absolutely. I'm also certain that you don't need to carry your gas mask everywhere."

"Well, pardon me if I doubt you on that matter."

"I mean it," Nate said.

"Nice to know. I'll tell you what Mr. Shute did not predict: The amounts of soot and grime thrown into the air from aerial bombing. Rationing strictly limits the use of water, you know, and I'm absolutely covered in dust. Every time I licked my lips or brought my teeth together yesterday, I tasted and felt it." Penelope shuddered slightly in remembrance. "I shall have to be satisfied with a sponge bath, I suppose."

An image of alabaster skin in a porcelain bathtub, a luffa dripping water as it traced along perfectly smooth curves came into Nate's mental eye. He pushed it aside with effort.

"Stiff upper lip and all that rot," he offered, imitating an upper-class accent.

Penelope giggled. "I really must go. Hide your eyes while I fetch my knickers."

Nate lowered his lids but could not resist leaving them open a slit, to watch the tightening of her skirt against the taut muscles of her buttocks as she bent to a bottom drawer.

Penny turned. Nate squeezed his eyelids shut. The armoire doors closed. He listened to her moving down the noisy steps. He replayed her voice in his head and remembered how big a sucker he was for a English accents in the alto range. Eyes now adjusted to the dimness, he looked around the cozy room. The wallpaper was patterned with nosegays of posies. He discerned the outlines of stuffed animals and throw pillows. It was definitely a female's bedroom. He closed his eyes again and inhaled the lingering scent of something subtle and deliciously pleasant, completely the opposite of the burnt world outside.

Nate had been in many women's bedrooms. A number of them

had been the impersonal, rented furnishing of hotels. Many had been spare and smart, to suit the look of the up-and-coming businesswoman. Some had been professionally decorated, revealing nothing of their occupant but a large purse and a desire to appear chic. This room was unique to his experience. He realized he had never slept in a bedroom so redolent of true femininity. It felt wonderfully comfortable.

In the middle of his thought, Nate fell back asleep.

"Hey, man! We're still in this time warp, damn it." Danny stood in the doorway to Penelope's bedroom.

"What time is it?" Nate asked.

"Eleven fifteen."

"I'm surprised there haven't been more raids," Nate said, swinging out from under the bedclothes.

"Lucky us. Get your clothes on, Nate. We've gotta get back to that tunnel and figure out how to get home."

Danny disappeared from view. Nate crossed to the primitive light switch on the wall near the doorway and flipped it up. He saw from the external wiring stapled to the wall that the house's construction had predated use of electricity in this sector of London. The switch powered a lamp sitting on Penelope's desk.

Nate studied up close the photograph of Fred and Ginger gliding into a dance step. He noticed that the room's owner had tacked another photograph to the wall opposite. The glamour pose had been taken from a distance on a set or sound stage, and the woman's face was too small to make out clearly. She wore a man's formal outfit, including top hat, but her trim figure in the well-cut costume and her heeled shoes betrayed her gender. She had brown hair. What he could make out of her features seemed to match those of Penny Miles.

"Hurry up!" Danny yelled from the first floor.

Nate pulled on his shirt, yanked his trousers up beyond his aching knees and stabbed his feet into his shoes. The day seemed warm. After tucking in his shirt and securing his belt, he grabbed his blazer and raincoat and hobbled down the stairs after Danny.

Danny stood in the kitchen, holding his shoulder bag. He stared at a large, off-white appliance.

"Is this an ice box?" he asked Nate.

"No. Look at the circular thing on the top, inside the wire cage. That's a motor. This is an early refrigerator."

Danny looked around. "Nobody's home."

"They're at church."

"I'm starving. I wonder if I could take something."

"If you're thinking of catching lunch outside, forget it," Nate told him. "We don't have any money from this time."

The refrigerator motor came to life, as if awakening to defend itself. Danny reflexively retreated a step. "Then I have no choice," he decided. He unlatched the door and bent slightly. "Not much here."

"Then leave it," Nate said. He looked at the crate of bottles sitting on the floor in a corner. "Have some liquid calories instead."

While Nate opened a wall cabinet, Danny picked up two full bottles. He tried in vain to twist the cap off one. "Man, this is ridiculous. I need a church key." He opened and closed drawers until he found a bottle opener.

In the meantime, Nate had found a tin filled with shortbread cookies. He brought it to the kitchen table and opened it. "There you go. Lager and cookies. Breakfast of champions."

"Just enough to tide us over until we cross back," Danny said.

Nate opened his bottle. "You're sure about that?"

"Not the food; the crossing back. You bet. Grab a couple more, and let's find that tunnel."

They wandered for almost half an hour through the twisting streets of the Bethnal Green neighborhood. All the street signs had mysteriously been removed. In desperation Nate asked a woman pushing a baby carriage for directions to the shelter.

"It ain't finished yet," she said, eying him suspiciously.

"I know. We're American architectural consultants," he assured her.

The woman recited a series of lefts and rights and patiently repeated herself. They thanked her and moved off for the first time with confidence. At last they sighted one of the pair of white, bunker-like shelter entrances. From the street, Nate saw that the building had one more element. Its curving front side undoubtedly held a double helix of spiral staircase.

The partners squeezed through the damaged wooden fence and located the ladder system. Danny went down first. Nate's knees compelled him to descend much more slowly. By the time Nate reached the track, Danny was striding back toward him, lit by the reflected sunlight pouring through the hole in the earth. He had his bag over his left shoulder and held the Webley pistol in his right hand. His face was anguished.

"Gone! The car is gone!"

Nate stopped walking. "I guess the damage crews thought it was just one more casualty of the bombing and cleaned up the mess."

"Every fucking splinter?" Danny countered. "It's like it never existed." He squatted in his disappointment. "Or it vanished. Sucked backed into our time. Without us."

Nate bent and squeezed Danny's shoulder. "Don't give up."

"We never should have left the tunnel."

"How could we have known that, even if it's true? Let's keep exploring."

Danny reached into his bag for his light. "You're damned right we'll explore."

They returned to the main line. The tracks were empty. The walls echoed with their exchanges of words. Danny stopped abruptly. He shone his light groundward.

"It's gone, too."

"What?"

"The switch changer. I dropped it right about here."

Nate turned a slow circle. "They must have picked it up when they removed the wrecked coach."

Danny shook his head gravely. He swept his flashlight methodically back and forth.

A crunching noise sounded from somewhere down the tracks.

Danny raised the flashlight.

From the opposite distance came the sounds of an approaching train.

Danny played the beam up one end of the main tunnel.

The train came closer, throwing sparks, pushing air ahead of it in waves.

Over the noise of the train, from behind Danny, came a series of quick crunching sounds.

Danny swept the beam around. It caught the image of a man in a railway worker's uniform jogging away. Around his neck was a thin line of red cloth.

"Hey!" Danny yelled.

The figure stopped and turned.

"It's him!" Danny told Nate.

The train was almost upon the junction point.

Danny started running toward the worker. "I have a gun! Stop!"

The worker ignored the command and resumed his retreat.

"Danny! Watch out!" Nate screamed.

The headlight of the swift-approaching train caught Danny. A deafening air horn blast escaped from the top of the lead car.

Danny hopped off the track bed and pressed himself against the tunnel wall. The train rushed by.

Nate was so intent on his partner's safety that he could not tear his eyes away from the tunnel wall long enough to study the train. Only after the last car had passed O'Shea did Nate change his focus. He saw enough to assure himself that the train was a product of the early twentieth century.

The moment the trailing coach passed, Danny leapt back onto the track. He played his flashlight frantically up and down the length of the tunnel.

"God damn it! He was here. He was just here." He looked back at Nate. "It was the redheaded worker." When Nate failed to speak, he said, "And don't ask me if I'm sure it was him. It was the goddamned bastard who sabotaged our train!"

"I believe you," Nate said, coming closer. "But maybe it wasn't the smartest idea screaming at him that you had a gun. Guilty or innocent, if I were he I'd have hotfooted it out of this tunnel as well." He looked at the opposite wall near where the mysterious man had stood. "What's that?"

"Rungs."

"Into an escape tube. He must have gone up the ladder."

Danny rushed across the tracks and started up the soot-encrusted metal rungs into blackness. Nate waited on the opposite side of the tunnel and listened to a series of grunts and oaths. Eventually, Danny climbed down.

"There's a hatch about twenty feet up. He locked it from the other side."

"Now what?" Nate asked.

"He must have come back for a reason."

Nate had never seen his friend so jangled. Dan's shoulders jerked up and down as he swallowed air in short gulps. Nate asked, "What reason?"

"He's the key to getting home," Danny asserted with conviction.

"Why?"

"He can obviously get from one time to another."

"Dan, this is stranger than Alice falling down the rabbit hole. Do you think he's like a leprechaun you can catch, and then he'll grant your wish and let us go home?"

"That's better than clicking ruby slippers," he shot back.

In spite of Danny's extreme agitation, Nate could not help laughing.

Danny's arms relaxed to his sides. He shook his head. "This is in no way funny, man. I am not leaving this tunnel again."

"Yes, you are."

"I'm gonna sit right over there in the dark and wait for him to come back. And when he does, I'll turn on my light real fast and kneecap him. Then I'll wring his scrawny neck until he tells me how to get home."

"You've frightened him away…at least for the moment," Nate argued. "Come back to the Miles house with me. I'm starving. Let's charm them into a good meal. We clean up and then come back around ten o'clock. He must have opened those points a little before two o'clock this morning," he reasoned. "Otherwise, an earlier train than ours would have crashed. If he returns, it will be just before two a.m."

Danny nodded. "Maybe. But let's stay one hour now as well. He may figure we gave up. If that doesn't work, we'll return at ten tonight. You have to come with me. We can't risk you missing the train home."

Nate remembered a short story by Ambrose Bierce that he had read as a teenager. It was called "An Occurrence at Owl Creek Bridge" and told of the detailed story that flashed through the mind of a man between the moment the scaffold swung out from under him and the noose snapped his neck. Nate wondered if he was right then a millisecond from his head slamming into the back wall of the destroyed coach. He decided that even if it was the truth, there was nothing he could do about it.

Nate put on the same convincing smile he used when closing a smuggling deal. "Of course I'll come with you, Dan."

Supper at the Miles home was navy beans and fried potatoes with canned string beans and fresh beets. Nate had developed a habit of eating small portions, which he augmented between meals with power bars. The lack of a sugar rush for more than twenty-four hours made him feel tired and headachy. When Millicent Miles forced another helping of the beans and potatoes on him, he did not refuse.

Worden and Penelope excused themselves for their volunteer

services, even though there had been no direct attack on London during the morning or afternoon. Nate and Danny excused themselves "to do some work we've fallen behind on." In reality, they retired to the bedrooms they had been made guests in and lay down to fortify themselves for a long vigil in a dark tunnel. In spite of deep misgiving about the possibility of success, Nate said nothing.

# CHAPTER SIX

At three-twenty in the morning, Penny trudged up the stairs of her completely dark house and into her bedroom. She sighed with exhaustion. Although the night attack on East London had been light and brief, many ambulances had been called to service, to move the wounded to hospital all the more quickly and save more lives with speed. Penny started to shrug out of her service waistcoat when a noise from inside the bedroom caused her to gasp.

"Sorry," Nate's voice came out of the blackness. "I didn't want you to go any farther without warning."

"My God! I had no idea you would still be here."

"Your mother made the invitation after you and your father had left. They elected to sleep in the shelter again. Just give me two moments to get my clothes on, and–"

"No, I'll sleep in their bedroom," Penny said. "Stay under the covers. I can fetch what I need blind."

"You're very kind to do this," Nate told her.

"It's my duty. 'These are the times that try men's souls,'" she replied, as she stepped into the room.

Nate's head reared back in surprise. "You know the words of Thomas Paine?"

"I know a quite a bit about American history," Penny answered evenly. "Just because we lost that war, should we pretend it never existed?"

"No, I…" For one of the few times in his life, Nate found himself at a loss for a reply. Penny came to his rescue.

"There are thousands of homeless wandering around looking for a roof. Many more than just our family will have to extend hospitality in the coming weeks."

Nate found himself wanting the conversation to go on and on. "You're right. Are you tired?"

A drawer opened and closed. "Completely fagged. I'm fetching my work clothes, as well. I must rise early. I'm sure it will take much longer to get to work this morning."

"You mentioned a ministry. Is it in the center of the city?"

"Yes."

"You go by the Underground?"

"That's right."

"Danny and I have to get to Piccadilly early as well. If we promise to stay out of your way and be ready quickly, would you mind leading us to the station?"

"Not at all. By the by, Monday is washday. My mother would be pleased to add your shirt and Mr. O'Shea's."

"What would we wear?"

"My brother left behind two white shirts. One will be a little big on you and the other a little small on your friend, but it's better than going the week in your own."

"That's very kind as well."

"Duty. Good night, then."

Only the creaking of a few steps betrayed Penny's departure. The house grew quiet once more, allowing Nate to replay the comforting sound of her voice over and over inside his head.

The sounds of the house in use woke Nate in a hurry. Danny had to be aroused from his usual sound sleep. Nate returned to Penny's room and surveyed his clothing. While the hem of his raincoat had been badly scraped and discolored from the coach accident, his blue blazer and charcoal slacks had survived relatively unscathed. His black loafers were smeared with mud but nothing that a rag and some water could not fix. For the first time in his life, Nate had no choice of wardrobe.

In the kitchen, Millicent Miles had listened to the many footfalls from the floor above her and had trebled the recipe for porridge. She offered it along with warm milk flavored with Ovaltine. Mr. Miles, they learned, was "lying in an extra half-hour." The food was eaten quickly, with a minimum of talk. The three early morning travelers were each sent off with an apple as well. For her part, Mrs. Miles moved around the kitchen like a well-oiled automaton, with her jaw so firmly set that no one expected comment from her. The acrid, stinging smell of smoke and soot pervaded the air, but talk of the devastating attacks was avoided.

The train that arrived at the Mile End station platform had been constructed more than forty years before the American's births. In spite of the stop lying so far from the center of London, the cars were nearly filled. Many of the commuters carried lunch pails, and almost all, including Penelope, carried gas masks as well. Nate and Danny stood like buttresses on either side of the young woman, their legs spread to absorb the rocking and lurching of the train.

"May I see this fabulous watch that my father talked of?" Penelope asked with no preamble.

Nate pulled back his raincoat and blazer sleeves and held up his hand.

"Unbelievable!" Penelope marveled. "Technology from America."

"At its finest," Nate replied, even as he pictured the watch being assembled somewhere in Southeast Asia.

"Then perhaps you can say with assurance that we shall win, if your country offers such modern help. You'd best not show that around to too many people."

"I don't. I only pulled up my sleeve because a beautiful woman asked," Nate answered. He was rewarded with the sight of a quick blush suffusing Penelope's cheeks.

"I deal with secrets as well, but I never reveal them," she said, leaning close to Nate's ear and whispering above the noise of the train. "Secrets that can't be seen."

Nate lifted his hand and guided her head gently around so that her ear was now directly in front of his mouth. He, in turn, leaned close and whispered, "It wouldn't be...radar, would it?"

Penelope gasped. Her head jerked around so that her enormously wide eyes locked with his.

Nate was equally surprised by the verbal bullseye he had scored. He brought the tip of his nose to hers and said, "We're more than we appear, Miss Miles, but we're not spies. Believe me. Your father chanced on us; we didn't seek out him or you."

"I...I can't say more," she told him.

"I don't want you to say more," he assured. Nate looked around the immediate space. Several travelers studied them with curious expressions.

Nate thought about a ride he had taken in the New York City subway the day after 9/11. The faces then and there had been remarkably similar to these in the Underground, sober and resolute. The difference, he thought, was that that attack had been isolated, with no further assaults to endure. These people would have to withstand month after month of aerial bombings, citywide explosions and fires inexorably reducing London to rubble. Ignorant of the eventual future triumph, they would daily contemplate complete annihilation of their capital, their government, their freedom and way of life. There was also the major psychological difference between enduring a limited number of terrorists who hijacked four airplanes to create havoc and standing against entire enemy armies that had swept across Europe in a matter of months, occupying virtually every country but yours with not one defeat. Both were horrific times, but this was far worse. It made Nate's chest ache.

Nate tapped Danny on the shoulder and swept his forefinger down the length of the coach. "You see how calm these fine people are, in spite of the last two nights?" He spoke with theatrical projection that guaranteed more than half the car would hear him. "You know why Hitler's army will never cross the Channel? The little corporal's in awe of the British. These people were building a world empire while Germany was still a pack of duchies. England brought civilization, not brutality. Britannia has ruled the waves for centuries and still does. Besides, he can't attack a ruling family that comes from Hannover."

Several commuters laughed; three applauded; and one offered Nate a rousing "Well said!"

When Nate turned again to Penelope, he found her studying him with what he hoped was admiration.

"That's a lovely expression you're wearing," he told her. "Does your boyfriend see that face often?"

"My boyfriend is an aircraft maintenance engineer in the RAF," Penelope replied.

Nate felt another tug inside his chest. For a moment he thought it might be jealousy, but then he told himself he was immune to the emotion. Jealousy meant a desire to possess. When one's life was dedicated to the constant pursuit of excitement, a succession of smart, beautiful women was obliged. Jealousy over one woman from another time would be insane. One way or another, he would be out of her world as quickly as possible. Nate was certain the pain he felt was physical rather than mental, a fleeting remnant of being slammed around in the coach crash.

"He has informed me that he is my boyfriend at any rate," Penelope went on. "I dare not disappoint a young man serving my country in uniform."

"You can't be seeing him very often," Nate guessed.

"No. Not with 'so few doing so much for so many'. He's only returned to London twice since June, and both times for just a night."

Nate thought of the photos on her bedroom walls. "And he takes you dancing."

"Not Brendon. He has two left feet. He would if I asked, but my toes can't stand the abuse. Do you dance, Mr. Allen?"

"Please call me Nate. I dance a little."

"He's being modest," Danny said, looking past Penelope to shoot Nate his mocking look. "I can tell you personally that he's the best dancer I've ever worked with."

Nate understood that Danny used a double entendre, speaking Nate's favorite analogy for carefully arranging illegal introductions and negotiations. He offered a cloying smile in return. "My partner is jealous because I always insist on leading." When Penelope looked more confused than amused, he quickly added, "As we were leaving this morning, I saw your next-door neighbors pushing a pile of belongings up the street inside a tall wagon."

"That was a dust cart and they're Mr. and Mrs. Wilcox."

"Ah. She of the leather lungs and the pusillanimous disposition."

Penelope burst into laughter. "Right on both counts. I've never heard anyone actually use that word in a sentence before."

"Oh, he's stuffed with fifty cent words, Miss Miles," Danny interjected. "He was prep school educated."

The train came to a stop at Bank station.

"I see," said Miss Miles "I wish you would both call me Penny. I believe the Wilcoxes were in the process of vacating the city. Mrs. W threatened to run to her aunt's farm the minute a German bomber flew over her roof. The farm is in a little village in Somerset called Uphill. We're now obliged to look after their house for them. I don't blame them for fleeing if they have a place to run to. However I think it a rather cheeky request, seeing as how we may be required to climb upon their roof as well as ours to pull out incendiary spikes."

"I agree," Nate told her. "Certainly your father is too busy. What does he do in the daytime, before marching around the streets in the dark?"

"He's an editor at a private printing company. It's very busy now, doing government contract work. You know, the leaflets our planes dump over occupied lands. And instruction manuals. Also many of the posters you see around London: 'Save Fuel,' 'Make Do and Mend,' 'Careless Talk Costs Lives.'" Her eyes darted with embarrassment as she pronounced her last words, as if thinking of her imprudent mention of her work.

"All true," Nate replied. "Our posters say 'Loose lips sink ships.'"

"I've never heard that. It's very clever, isn't it?"

"Yes. It's wonderful that your father also spends his spare time as a warden."

"Especially in light of the fact that some have been paid for more than a year to do the same work. People would walk by them in the street and call them freeloaders right to their faces. Well, they'll be earning their keep from now on. Of course, if my Dad wasn't a warden, he'd be required to join the Home Guard."

Nate shook his head to indicate he was ignorant of the term.

"All able-bodied men between the ages of 45 and 51 are required to drill and be prepared to defend our shores at a moment's notice."

"Were you required to serve in the ambulance corps?"

"No. But England expects every woman to do her duty as well," Penny replied, misquoting the great British admiral's famous phrase. "I'll feel a good deal better when the statue of Lord Nelson is back on his pedestal in Trafalgar. He was left-handed as well, you know."

"Are you left-handed?"

She smiled. "No. You are. You wear your fancy watch on your right wrist."

The train slowed. Penny looked at the station wall and its Holborn sign.

"This is your transfer to Piccadilly." She held out her hand. "If you're gone by the time I return home, it was lovely meeting you. And you as well, Mr. O'Shea."

"I assure you, the pleasure was ours," Danny said as he turned to the opening coach door.

Nate backed away, wanting a good look at the warm, unpretentious woman. He bumped into a rider just entering the train.

"Try walking forwards, mate!" the man scolded in an Australian accent.

The train pulled away, and Nate stayed rooted to the platform watching it go.

"Nice to see your appetite's returned, lover boy," Danny said, grabbing him roughly by the elbow, "but forget that one. The sooner we're done here, the sooner we can get back to the tunnel."

"We need money and we need food," Nate reminded him.

Danny got behind Nate and guided him against the flow of

humanity heading toward the platform. "Not very much of it if we figure out how to get back to our own time today. This way to the Northern Line."

When they emerged from the bowels of the earth into Piccadilly Circus, the first thing that Nate observed was the lack of damage to the area. The fountain with its statue of Eros had been covered by an eight-sided structure made of wood and which faintly resembled a pyramid. Its pinnacle was capped by a superstructure that looked like the tip of a stubby pencil. A huge poster encouraging Londoners to "Keep on Saving" had been neatly affixed to each wall face. The Criterion Theatre, the London Pavilion, the many retail stores were all intact, as were the billboards and neon signs for Bovril, Wrigley's, Gordon's Gin, Schweppes Tonic and the like. Not far above the tallest building one of the silver barrage balloons was moored, ready to float up to the limit of its steel guy wires when next the Germans attacked. Double-decker busses whizzed around the circle, as did a number of taxis, but private automobiles were conspicuous by their absence. A majority of the travelers were pedestrians or bicyclists.

Nate noted that the citizens of London did not saunter or window-shop but moved with purpose. He thought again of New York the day after 9/11 and how alike the citizens of both great cities appeared. Nate assumed that, long before the start of the Blitz, Londoners of 1940 daily faced the added stress of big-city life, with its crowding, its hectic pace, bad air, transportation delays and harassment by the homeless and crazies that all large cities attract. Even worse, they had faced the Depression for more than a decade. The screw had simply turned a few more twists, but it was clearly nothing unendurable.

Nate crossed to a news butcher stand next to the station entrance and assured himself from one of the newspapers that the date was indeed September 8, 1940. When he straightened up, he realized that Danny was not tugging at him. He turned to find his partner holding his cell phone up to his ear. Several persons stared at him in bewilderment as they walked by.

Nate yanked Danny into a nearby alley. "Are you out of your mind showing that?"

"I don't give a damn if they think it's Dick Tracy's two-way wrist radio," Danny returned. "I'm trying to see if we can at least talk to our time." He looked at the screen. "No signal. It wants to roam. Fine." He punched a button. "Do your best."

Nate looked over his shoulder. "I think you need microwave towers around a city for that to work. Yep, I'm right. Nothing. The distance is too long, pal. So stow it in your bag and let's go. We need money. I was so desperate for subway fare that I opened Penny's piggy bank and stole everything in it...which was not much."

Nate walked out onto the sidewalk. He waited until a shabbily dressed man approached and stepped in the fellow's way. "Excuse me, sir, could you tell me where to find pawn shops?"

The man's head rocked back. His eyebrows shot up.

Nate at first thought the man had been insulted because a stranger assumed his clothing meant he would know about pawning. Then he remembered the unwritten English rule of "poor form" to speak to anyone who had not been introduced by a mutual acquaintance. "I'm very sorry to bother you, but we're from America."

"I can hear that," the man replied. He looked toward the north. "I know there are several in Camden Town. Take the Northern Line. Excuse me."

"Back into the subway," Danny said.

"No. Let's save money and walk it. Catherine lives up there...or will one day. It's only about two miles from here."

"Time," Danny said with irritation. "We're losing time."

Nate headed onto Shaftesbury Avenue. "I hope not. We already lost one time."

The brokers that the pair found, Thomsons/Chalk Farm Road and Camden Town Pawn Shoppe, were located in the district's marketplace. On the way, Nate had determined how they would transact. He would walk into the first shop carrying one of the woman's watches and a pair of gold earrings taken from the train wreck. Danny would enter the store half a minute later and hang back, listening to the dialogue and watching the body language of the shop person. Then they would trade roles at the second establishment. If necessary, when the money they had collected began to run out, they could trade places in the shops or hunt for other places to unload the valuables.

A thin man in a well-worn but stylish three-piece suit was dusting the cases when Nate walked in.

"Good day, sir," Nate greeted.

"And to you. May I be of service?"

"I hope so. As you can hear, I'm over from the United States closing an estate. It belonged to my mother's sister. I don't care to bring these items home and wonder what they would fetch." He laid down the watch, whose face glass was surrounded by diamond chips, and the pair of fourteen-carat gold earrings in the shapes of oak leaves.

The man took his time examining the pieces.

Danny walked through the door and pretended to study the musical instruments on one wall.

"You realise, of course," the man began, "that between the Depression and the war, many more people are in the market to sell jewellery than to buy."

"I do," Nate returned. "I also realize that these are items of value in any economy."

"Nevertheless. For the watch, four pounds sixpence. For the earrings, three pounds. The watch is, naturally, functional as well as decorative."

"I couldn't let them go for less than eight pounds together," Nate bargained.

"I can stretch as far as an extra half a crown, being as how you've come all the way across the pond," the man said affably.

"Not quite enough stretch, I'm afraid. Thank you." Nate picked up the three pieces and turned toward the door. As he walked with a steady pace, he looked to Danny's face. His partner gave the smallest shake of his head, indicating that the businessman was about to let him walk.

Nate pivoted. The Thomsons employee had indeed returned to his dusting. "Perhaps you've made a better offer than I thought. Your currency is confusing to me. Our dollar is on a decimal system."

The man dipped his head in a genteel manner. "We English march to our own drummers. We shall hold to the foot and the inch and drive on the left until the devil himself compels us otherwise."

"I wonder if you would provide me a primer on the values beneath the pound," Nate invited.

"Delighted." He explained the system from the pound down to the farthing, and then said, "You'll find us as generous as any other shop in London." He erected the faintest semblance of a smile. "After such a long and dangerous trip to the Isles, you shouldn't need to traipse farther."

When they both stood outside the shop, Danny asked, "Did you know they had a different money system during the war?"

Nate stuffed the transaction coins into his pocket and started walking. "I think the system went back at least as far as Shakespeare's time. They changed over to decimal values around 1970. Will change, I should say."

"Excuse me if I couldn't care less. I hope you understood what he said."

"What I understand is that we got about twenty per cent of what it would cost to buy the things new."

"So we were robbed."

Nate rolled his eyes. "A rather ironic statement, considering we didn't own what we just sold. No, I'm sure we won't do well anywhere selling the stuff in your bag. On top of it, we'll either need to eat every meal at a restaurant or else buy food on the black market. This country is on rationing."

"Then we really need to get back to the twenty-first century, Nate."

"I agree. Take out one wedding and one engagement ring and that gold necklace. It's your turn to play the nephew from America."

They ate an early lunch at a place designated as a British restaurant, where prices were reasonable and ration cards were not used. They had seen another similarly labeled establishment on their walk up Tottenham Court Road. For desert they munched on the apples Mrs. Miles had given them.

"The Brits don't cook any better back in 1940 than they do in our time," Danny complained as they walked. "I'm gonna starve if I have to live here."

"You could stand to lose a few pounds," Nate answered.

"Said Jack Skellington. I'll do it at home, thank you."

Nate looked at the blue September sky, unusually cloudless for England and perfect weather for more bombing. His gaze lowered a bit, and he found himself looking at a brown-skinned man wearing a white turban. "Have you noticed on our walks how cosmopolitan the city is? Pardon the pun, but the complexion looks the same as modern-day London. The product of a world empire and of sheltering refugees from France, Germany and Eastern Europe."

"Don't do so much gawking," Danny ordered. "It slows your stride. Let's get into the Underground and back to the tunnel quick-time, okay?"

"One last stop: That market we passed on the way up. It's only another two blocks or so."

At the market, they were confronted with a queue in front of every food shop. It was clear that serial standing in line for the butcher, the baker, the green grocer and the dairyman would use up the better part of a day. After buying a "torch" and batteries from an enterprising salesman who roamed from line to line, Nate led Danny around to the backs of the shops. Using the excuse of being Americans and not having ration cards, along with the phrase "What do you have under the counter?," they were able to secure eleven potatoes, two onions, a bunch of carrots and half a wheel of cheese for cold coinage.

When a quart glass bottle of milk with a cardboard stopper was offered for two sixpence, Danny inspected it with suspicion. "For that much, we should be getting cream, not skim milk."

"All the milk is stretched," the dairyman replied, looking offended.

"Watered you mean," Danny argued.

"Exactly."

Nate thanked the dairyman and paid the price. They slipped their purchases into an old net bag picked up for a penny or into a small wooden crate that had held onions.

At the far end of the market stood a stall that advertised "Slightly Used Suits." The only suit that fit Nate was black with narrow, white pin stripes. It was double-breasted with trouser cuffs too high but with extra material underneath. When Danny started to protest the expense, Nate quashed him in mid-sentence with a look.

"Do you want me wearing my blazer everywhere?"

Danny eyed the blazer underneath the half-opened raincoat. "Fine. Buy it. Steal the food from this poor lad's mouth."

"'Please, sir, may I have more?'" Nate quoted *Oliver Twist* in a boy's voice. Then he made the sounds of a pig nosing for truffles.

"Just pay and let's go." Danny punctuated his reply with a pointed consultation of his watch.

The nearest subway station, Great Portland, was mobbed with people pressing urgently toward the entrance. Every one of them was weighted down with pillows, blankets, clothing and foodstuffs. Policemen struggled to keep the entrance to the station open to commuters. Nate and Danny elected to walk east to Euston Square but found precisely the same situation.

"You chaps lookin' for a ride east?" a driver called from a truck that had stopped for the traffic light.

"We are," Nate returned before Danny could speak. "Much obliged."

"I'm going as far as Whitechapel. Hop on the back."

The delivery van was tall and open-backed, with a pair of stirrups to help climb inside. The side of the vehicle identified it as "Genuine Danish Bacon," which Nate seriously doubted was still the case. The two men pushed carefully past the three, dressed pig carcasses swinging on hooks and grabbed onto empty hooks closer to the truck cab. The vehicle lurched forward.

"What a muck-up!" the driver called back through an open port. "Everyone's heard of all the deaths the last two days and they're tryin' to hide in the stations. But the government doesn't want 'em down there. Afraid it will cripple the system."

"That will change," Nate said, sure of his words. He heard in his head the faint echo of Reggie the Underground tour guide telling his charges about this exact situation.

"I suppose, if they don't want a revolution. Are you from Canada?"

"No, the States."

"Rotten time to be visitin'. Where's your next stop:  Hell?"

"Amen," Danny said.

"I hope not," said Nate at the same moment.

"I see you've been shoppin'. You care to buy a pound or two of bacon?"

"If the price is reasonable," Danny called out above the traffic noise.

"Very. These are from pig clubs, freshly butchered."

"What's a pig club?"

"Various groups, choral societies, cricket and football clubs, even gent clubs, get together and care for one, two, or three pigs in a back yard. Fatten 'em up on leftovers and garbage. Then they have them butchered and either use the meat themselves or else sell it off. I was deliverin' the Three Little Pigs to the Big Bad Wolf, but I'm not sure he can pay for all of it. Make me an offer."

Nate's offer was immediately accepted, which educated him to quote less the next time such an opportunity arose. Once they were inside the Whitechapel district, the driver pulled the van to the curb and came around brandishing a butcher's knife. He wore a bloody apron and reminded Nate that Jack the Ripper had murdered at least six times within blocks of where they stood. As the long strips of bacon were deposited in Danny's crate, an Air Precaution Warden came running down the street, blowing his whistle.

"Everyone to shelter! Bombers will be overhead in five minutes!" the warden shouted.

"Ta-ta, gents," the driver said in haste. He popped back into his cab, mashed his foot on the clutch and grinded the gears into first.

The pedestrians walked double-time or ran, but they hurried in every direction, indicating to Nate how new the experience of air raids was to them.

"Where are the sirens?" Danny asked no one in particular.

"They must not have them yet," answered Nate.

"But they've officially been at war for a year. Not real smart. Where do we hide?"

"Not here. This district is too close to the Thames." Nate consulted his watch compass. "That way."

He and Danny sprinted north until Nate's swollen knees threatened to lock up. They maintained a quick march until the first ack-ack antiaircraft guns opened up with their hollow, booming noises, followed by the Bofors guns making a rapid, staccato rattle.

"Under here!" Nate decided, darting beneath the tall, granite archway of a business establishment that faced west. It was the first building Nate knew for a certainty still stood in his time. A minute later, as both men recovered their breaths, the far-off sounds of ground explosions began. Sheltered by the massive building from view of the bombing run inception points, all they could do was strain their ears to pick up clues as to enemy size and targets. The shrill whistle of falling bombs and their duller explosions came nearer and nearer, and still the slice of God's heaven above them remained blue and unblemished.

Shortly after realizing how few among the buildings on their path to and from Camden Town jibed with his twenty-first-century memory, he began silently comparing them. He knew that even without total warfare, the face of the dynamic capital city would surely have changed in sixty-some years, but the disparity between what should and would come to pass appalled him. It was one thing to have read that twenty percent of the city's structures were flattened in five years of aerial bombing; it was another to see, block by block, just what that actually meant. It was like owning a genuine crystal ball; he could say with assurance and more than a little awe, "This will stand. But this will disappear. And this. And this."

"It's just beginning," Nate muttered.

"What's that?" Dan asked.

"It's just beginning."

Dan faced the building's doors, as if he could peer eastward through the mammoth structure. "Not back there it isn't. Maybe the Miles's house is burning right now."

Nate thought of Penny's bedroom. When he put his back against the edge of the archway, he could just make out one of the barrage balloons drifting into view. The hum of powerful aircraft engines grew steadily into a grinding roar, and then, for the briefest instant, two German bombers dashed into view and out again, about three thousand feet up. He waited for the building to disintegrate over him, but there were no nearby explosions except for an intensification of anti-aircraft fire. Danny took a step toward the street, and Nate yanked him back.

"It sounds like it's over," Danny said.

"Wait!"

A few seconds later, silver objects of various sizes appeared in the air, some drifting down, others plummeting. Several hit the pavement in front of the archway with sharp, metallic noises.

"Shrapnel from the cannons," Nate explained. "It injured…will injure a good number of those who come out too soon."

"Jesus! If this isn't Hell, it's the waiting room!" Danny railed.

"That couldn't have been more than a dozen–" Nate paused as a pair of RAF Hurricanes buzzed by in pursuit of the bombers. "Not more than a dozen bombers. I'm sure they were assessing the damage of yesterday's attacks and coordinating targets for this evening."

"Can we please go to the tunnel?" Danny implored.

Nate peeked out from the alcove. "Yes. If you don't walk too fast, we will go to the tunnel."

The subway tunnel was dark, dank and, except for the periodic passing of train passengers and the vigil of Danny and Nate, devoid of two-legged life.

Every five or six blocks in their day's journey, Danny and Nate had encountered build-ups of sandbags against a sturdy building, piled to protect the occupant at least from three sides and partially from above. A telephone line led down into each shelter. It was from these Air Raid Precaution shelters that wardens forwarded reports to fire companies, bomb disposal units, ambulance squads and rescue units or else received reports on where survivors were to be evacuated, which roads to close and so forth.

On their way back from the latest frustrating watch inside the Bethnal Green tunnel, they passed such a shelter three blocks from the

Miles's home and half expected to see Worden seated there. The inhabitant was instead a wizened man with a long white beard, nodded off in sleep on his wooden folding chair.

They entered the Miles property as they first had, through the backyard garden gate. They found Millicent Miles with her hair under a kerchief that was knotted on the forehead, with the bottom folded forward over her crown and the corners tucked in. Nate had seen the unusual style depicted in war posters of the period. She had fed non-insulated wires from an upstairs window down through a hole she had managed to punch through the side of the Anderson shelter by first exposing the covering earth with a spade and then employing a claw hammer and concrete spike.

"If I'm to spend my middle age in this half-buried coffin," she explained, "I at least want a decent wireless signal."

Danny helped plug the hole while Nate secured the reception wires to the radio.

"I've been listening to the BBC," Mrs. Miles divulged. "They're saying four hundred killed in the two attacks Saturday evening and night. Four hundred dead and nine hundred wounded. From all that noise and fire, I should have thought more. Oh, you've got food and new togs."

"Part of this food is for your family," Nate said. "For your many kindnesses."

Millicent waved away the thanks. "Lovely but not necessary."

"Actually, it is," Nate went on. "Penelope told us that the Wilcoxes have fled the city, leaving you to look after their house. That is quite unfair." Since Mrs. Miles did not contradict him, he plowed on. "What is also unfair is that very little damage was done on the West End, but wouldn't you know the house that Mr. O'Shea and I paid a month's salary in advance to let had a bomb go right through the roof and blow out the central staircase!"

Without missing a beat, Danny nodded at the bald-faced lie like a bishop granting absolution.

"How terrible!" Millicent lamented.

"We thought so. Started a fire as well that consumed our belongings. Every suit, all our ties, our spare shoes. We're left with the clothing on our backs and what Mr. O'Shea has in his shoulder bag."

Mrs. Miles' eyes turned heavenward. "But you were not there! I prayed so hard the last two nights for lives to be spared. Not only did the Lord see fit to take you from that house, but to deliver you here."

"Quite possibly," Nate agreed. "I believe the Lord also prepared us an alternate dwelling place in the vacant home of Mr. and Mrs. Wilcox."

"Oh." Mrs. Miles sat and thought about the notion for a moment. "I think you may be right."

"We'll earn our keep," Danny interjected. "We can't be there tonight, but as long as we stay here we can watch for incendiary spikes, shrapnel and other falling objects. And we could sweep away the dust and water the garden."

"They took everything of value," Millicent rationalized. "Yes, I think it's a capital idea, as W. S. Gilbert would say. Besides, your mothers must be worried sick about you. I might serve in their place." She studied the two Americans with a practiced eye. "How do those shirts fit?"

"Well!" Nate chirped, before Danny could damn the gifts with faint praise or less.

"I've washed and hung up your shirts. They came out amazingly well. I've never seen two shirts wash with fewer wrinkles! More improvements from America, no doubt." She assessed the suit Nate had laid over the other chair back. "There's a great deal of wear left in this. Does it fit you perfectly?"

"It's short in the legs," Nate replied.

"Go into the house and change; I have a few pins and my darning kit here. I'll fix it right as rain." The woman's dour demeanor was brightening by the minute. She looked up at Danny. "And, you know, Ralph was only an inch shorter than you. Not as broad across the shoulders, but I believe his brown suit would fit you with alterations, Mr. O'Shea. Now I know why I couldn't bear to give it away, in spite of the clothing drives; it wasn't the right time. You'll find it in his wardrobe."

The first thing Nate did after he entered Penelope's room was to replace the money he had taken from her piggy bank. He had found two keys inside the bank when he first opened the bottom. They remained inside the porcelain container, still joined by a large safety pin. He studied them for a few moments, wondering what they opened and why they were hidden. Baffled, he pushed them back into the darkness and replaced the circular wedge of cork.

After he allowed Mrs. Miles to measure his trouser lengths and then delivered them to her, Nate returned to her daughter's room for a rest. His knees were no longer visibly swollen, but they ached from the miles of walking and the squatting in the railway tunnel. He longed for ibuprofen or acetaminophen but took two aspirins from a brown bottle Penelope had on a shelf. He found a throw pillow and raised his feet above the level of his chest. He reveled in the delicate smell of the bed but could not place it. Enough sunlight penetrated the painted windows to allow him to continue his study of Penelope's room. He tucked away the fact that she was a fan of American entertainment. While Fred and Ginger decorated one wall, a little statuette of Disney's Pinocchio sat on her desk and a souvenir booklet for *Gone With the Wind* stuck out of the line of books on her second shelf. She had also clipped a picture of the New York City skyline from a magazine and displayed it under her reading lamp. She owned no fewer than fifty books. Several were textbooks. What impressed Nate most was that the subject of the thickest one was United States history. She, like he, was clearly attracted to the subject. Nate paged through the textbook, making sure the past into which he and Danny had been thrown was the same one he had been taught in school. He counted seventeen novels, five of which were American authors. In the middle of studying the room for more clues, he fell fast asleep.

"Who's been sleeping in my bed?" the pseudo-deep voice demanded to know from the hallway.

"It's not Goldilocks," Nate replied, laboring to unstick the pollution and mucus that had cemented his eyelids closed.

"My minister would be scandalised," Penny declared without appearing. "A man in my bed three evenings in a row." Nate sat up. "At least it's not three different men. How was your day?"

"Not as bad as I hear yours was. Get decent and come down for supper. Father Miles is here, and he's likely to play Home Guard with you if you're not out of my room double time."

Supper was served at the dining table. Worden Miles was more than ready for an audience as a rasher of black market bacon was served up with non-ration mashed potatoes and onions.

"It's good to have a job close to the insiders," he shared with those gathered, adding a wink to make his meaning completely unambiguous. "The unadulterated truth is worth more than the *Home Intelligence Report*, *The Times*, *Evening Standard* and the *Daily Express* rolled into one. Saturday, German and Italian fighters and bombers attacked from along the Thames estuary at 5:00 P.M. Their objective was the East End, the Beckton Gas Works, Woolwich Arsenal and the docks – the Albert, Victoria, Surrey Commercial, West India and Millwall. The estimate is that they dropped 600 tonnes of high explosives and 17,000 incendiaries. Naturally, Silvertown, Woolwich, Millwall and East Ham all suffered as well. The first strike ended at 6:10. Unlike the reports going out on the BBC, closer to 1,000 were killed and another 1,600 wounded. The worst catastrophe to my thinking is that many who were evacuated from houses following the first attack were transported to Keeton's Road School. On the second run, the Hun scored a direct hit on the school. A score were killed by one bomb." Mr. Miles dug into his potatoes but stopped the fork before it entered his mouth. "They are so desperate to stop our sea shipping that they've actually dropped sea mines into the Thames!"

Throughout the meal, Worden Miles recited at a rapid pace the many lurid particulars of the combined first eight hours of horror. He spoke of a crippled tar plant spreading pitch everywhere, of the Russia, Greenland and Canada Yards stacked to their limits with lumber, melting everything in the vicinity with their tremendous heat as the wood was reduced to ash. He related that several barges filled with burning lumber were untied from the docks and allowed to move seaward with the ebb tide, only to have them reverse their direction a few hours later and cause more havoc. He also spoke of looters who had invaded food stores, warehouses and shops. But when he changed his focus to the many acts of heroism and utter selflessness, his pace slowed and his voice grew richer with nationalistic pride.

Off and on during the day and even as Mr. Miles spoke, Nate had scoured the far recesses of his memory for facts on the London Blitz and the defense of England. He realized he remembered a great deal more about World War II than he would have supposed. However, if everything together could be compared with a work the size of the Bible, information pertinent to his present situation would comprise only a book the size of Job. His knowledge of London's Underground shelters, for example was limited to a few photographs and several paragraphs.

"Tell us about the local deep level shelter," Nate invited. "Why isn't it finished?"

"I believe they diverted a large part of the money to move children to the countryside. They stopped work about two months ago, and there's no word of starting up again in the near future."

"So they're just gonna let people die up here," Danny criticized.

Mr. Miles shrugged. "I believe, after ten months of the Jerries doing nothing, they hoped such an expensive project wasn't necessary."

What little of use he did know about the war Nate wanted to pass along privately to Penny. When she rose from the table and said she needed to hurry to cover another driver's shift for ambulance duty, Nate announced he would walk her there.

"After you mentioned looters, sir," Nate said to her father, "I worry that some desperate people may use the coming nightfall in Bethnal Green to prey upon those they feel were more lucky. Public parks are not known to be the safest of places."

"Thank you," Worden responded. "I can't chaperone her myself, as I have ARP duty."

Victoria Park, where the ambulance depot had been hastily erected, lay four streets distant from the Miles residence. As soon as they were out the front door, Nate said, "I've noticed that most of the major road signs have been removed. Is that in case of invasion?"

"Precisely," Penny answered.

"It's a real nuisance, especially for out-of-towners. Thank goodness I've been to London several times before."

Penny gave him a sidelong glance. "Several times?"

Caught in an unguarded truth, Nate had no recourse but to nod and push beyond. "The Germans will never set foot on your beaches, much less London streets."

"You sound so certain."

"I am. Listen, Penny, I don't want you to say another word to me about what you do during the day. But I do want you to listen. I happen to know that the Germans are far behind the British in the development of radar. You have something like twelve or fifteen large listening posts dispersed on the cliffs above your southeastern and southern beaches. They'll bomb them if your radio directions to RAF pilots aren't better disguised. You must make a suggestion to your superiors to have attack formation reports to the pilots seem to come via fishing boats and submarines in the Channel."

"You're frightening me," Penny confessed.

"Don't be. When you have time to think about what I've said, you'll feel elated instead. I happen to have overheard this special knowledge in Washington; but it's not my official reason for being here. I'd get someone in my government in trouble if I brought what

I just told you directly to your superiors. We have informants monitoring your war efforts, but for the best of purposes."

"All…right."

Nate jerked his head up and down, a punctuation to show that he considered the subject closed. "Enough about the war. Tell me about the textbooks in your room."

"I finished University a bit more than a year ago. I received my degree in primary education. I know your system and ours have different names for levels. Last year I taught those who were seven and eight. It was not the best year to begin. When war was declared, almost the first thing the authorities did was to ship a million children away from London. Then, about a month after the great evacuation, when nothing had happened, families wanted their children back. So the tide reversed. It made a shambles of the teaching plans."

"You liked it anyway?"

"I did."

Nate looked at Penny in profile. "And you like dancing."

A smile spread like sunlight at dawn across Penny's face. "Dancing? I live to dance. Especially tap and ballroom."

"Like Fred Astaire and Ginger Rogers."

"Spot on."

"Was the woman in the other photograph you?"

Penny laughed. "Don't I wish! That's Eleanor Powell. She's my idol. She can tap as fast as machinegun fire. I'm amazed you didn't recognize her. Don't you attend the cinema frequently?"

Nate's internal warning system sounded an alarm. So many of his friends, Danny in particular, were prejudiced against all black-and-white motion pictures. Nate, however, enjoyed much of the industry's work from the era between silent films and the end of World War II. He had seen *Casablanca* three times. Cary Grant, Errol Flynn, Humphrey Bogart, Jimmy Stewart, Loretta Young and Bette Davis were some of his all-time favorite stars. But he was hardly an expert on the era. And when it came to the many dance films, he barely recalled anything.

"Actually, not much," he replied. "The government keeps me very busy, moving around the world."

"Evidently."

Nate remembered a bit of their morning subway conversation. "If your would-be boyfriend, Brendon, has two left feet, then you'd better find a partner you can dance through life with. You don't want to become an old maid school teacher in sensible shoes."

Penny stopped walking and faced her chaperone with a cold stare. "I happen to know that you're a criminal, Mr. Allen, so you might as well confess it."

The truth of the accusation made Nate blink with astonishment. Then he thought of the impossibility of the young Englishwoman being able to learn anything about his 21st-century life, and he regained a bit of equilibrium. "What makes you think I'm a criminal?"

"You're American and from New York. Aren't all persons from New York City gangsters?"

"I get it. You're having back at me for using the old maid schoolteacher cliché. The truth is, I don't know why there isn't a line of suitors at your front door, air raids or not. I don't think Loretta Young or Donna Reed ever played old maid school teachers."

Penny's scowl softened. "'Ever played? Their careers are just starting. Give them time. If comparing me to those starlets was supposed to be a lame apology, I accept it."

"Thank you."

"Speaking of lame, I'd show you a step or two if you weren't walking so gingerly. Is it a permanent injury?" She looked down in the direction of Nate's knees.

"No. Only temporary. I took a fall on Sunday during the first bombing."

"So Danny wasn't joking. You can dance then."

He knew she did not mean silly steps like the Hokey Pokey, the Electric Slide, the Chicken Dance, or the Conga line that all bachelors were required to master in order to pick up ceremony-and-liquor-softened young women at weddings. Dancing to Nathaniel Allen was something far beyond moving smoothly in time to music.

"I dance a little," Nate confessed. "My mother taught me."

"You're built for it," Penny judged. "Tall and wiry. Perhaps we should step out on a night when I'm not on duty."

Nate wondered if the sting of the still-sooty air was all that made her eyes shine, or if it had anything to do with his company. "I would like that very much."

The park came into view. After an awkward silence, Penny said, "At least the perpetual blackout order is at last for a worthy reason. I read a report that, in the last year, 4,500 persons were killed in accidents because of the lack of light. Mostly pedestrians. At least they now allow us a slit through the headlamp glass."

"What's with the moat?" Nate asked, looking at the long stretch of water fronting the park.

"Actually, that's Regent's Canal. There's another one, Hertford Union Canal, on the south side. They serve to set the park apart from the houses, which is a good thing. We're about to walk through the main entrance." They crossed a bridge over the canal and strolled along a broad thoroughfare. Penny pointed to statues on either side of the entrance. "Our dogs of Alcibiades."

"The Athenian statesman, orator and general," Nate supplied.

Penny applauded. "High marks for you! You must have read Plutarch."

"I love history."

"And I admire men who love history," she said in a voice that sounded mock serious. Before he could explore her meaning, she said, "Unfortunately, most of the park is blocked off for anti-aircraft. It's really a lovely place, with some special features. What time is it?" Nate lifted his Casio watch and held it up to Penny's face.

"I have a few minutes." She pointed. "Over that way is the Bathing Pond."

"Is it actually used for bathing?"

"Not anymore. Many older homes still don't have a bathtub or shower. It was useful. However, it was closed to bathing about four years ago. This way." Penny grabbed Nate's hand and pulled him onto a path that led off to the left. It went through trees to the edge of the park, where a walled enclosure hid perhaps a quarter acre within.

"An elegiac churchyard?" Nate guessed.

"No, but a place to inspire poetry nonetheless. A rose garden."

"Why hide it?"

"Ah! At last something the privately educated Nathaniel Allen does not know. The English feel roses don't bloom enough of the year to display in our normal gardens. So we hide them behind walls and open them up only during the growing season."

They came to an iron gate that bisected the crumbly, damp brick wall that ran at right angles to the main park wall. The garden wall stood a little less than six feet high, and the gate about six inches shorter. Nate reluctantly let go of Penny's hand when she reached for the gate.

"Oh, bother! It's locked."

"The season for roses isn't over," Nate said. "The roses in your parents' garden are still in bloom."

"I suppose they want to discourage use of the park while the guns are here," Penny sighed. "Pity. I should have liked to have shown you."

Nate glanced at the lock. It was a thick but simple affair, one that he knew he could open with the help of the Swiss knife on his key ring.

"Turn around," he ordered.

"What?"

"Turn around, hide your eyes and count to twenty out loud. Not too fast."

Penny obliged.

"Now face the garden and open your eyes."

As she turned, Nate swung the gate back.

"How did you do that?"

"Magic." Nate swept his arm inward, inviting Penny to enter.

It was indeed a rose garden. Except for two trees, several dozen clumps of ferns and a number of luxuriantly thick beds of moss, nothing else grew in the garden. A brick path laid out in herringbone pattern ran straight from the gate to the park's outer wall. On either side near the path were planted banks of hybrid tea roses, with their bright, platooned colors. Wherever Nate bent, the air was filled with delicate fragrances. Behind them grew profusions of rose bushes. Toward the rear were rose trees. Halfway down the path had been placed an arbor, through which tendrils of wild white roses ran.

"Shall I lead you down the garden path?" Penny asked in a coquettish voice.

"It would be my pleasure," Nate replied.

"The bushes are mostly Tudor roses. You can recognize the petals from ancient crests."

They came to the curved trellis and stopped. "Another traditional reason roses were segregated," Penny said, "was because their colors were not vibrant enough. Until recent crossbreeding, they were only white, pink, crimson, purple and a washed-out yellow. Now we have scarlets, tangerines, peaches and indigos." Penny cast a critical eye around the place. "Except they seem to be failing early this year."

"It's undoubtedly the soot and ash," Nate told her.

"I suppose."

Nate looked at the masterly landscape design, with not only the green hues of the moss and ferns setting off the roses, but also employing the patterns and textures of stones and statuary. He envisioned it as an exquisite hidden treasure in high summer.

"I must be getting to my station," Penny said. "Coming?"

Nate followed behind, admiring the young woman's feminine gait and her figure. He locked the garden behind them and followed Penny toward the center of the park in the gathering dusk.

They approached a shelter opened on three sides, under a corrugated iron roof. Two "ambulances" were parked in the space. They were large saloon cars modified by cutting off the back end of the bodywork, substituting the rear seating with planks and adding a canvas cover with a back which could be rolled up.

"Ah! If it isn't our own William Grover-Williams!" one of the two men servicing the cars exclaimed as Penny entered the shelter. They were both in their sixties, long of what teeth they still possessed but both giving the impression of good physical strength.

"Mr. Donald Davies, Mr. Osgood Brown," Penny presented, "this is Mr. Nathaniel Allen from the States."

Hands were shaken. "You don't mind a woman driver?" Nate joked, shying Penny a sly smile.

Mr. Davies said, "Surely you're having us on! Neither one of us manages the crash gearbox in this thing. Penny double-clutches with the best of them."

Penelope knelt beside the front right wheel well. "This tyre looks suspect. Can we get another before dark, Ozzy?"

"I fear not."

Feeling like a deflated fifth wheel, Nate took several steps backward. "Nice to meet you both. I have to get to my own business." Penny shifted her focus to Nate, causing him to halt. She came up close, regarding him with a cocked head and a narrowed eyes, and spoke in an intimate tone. "Your own business indeed. I'm glad you shall be spending more time in our neighborhood. You are a puzzle, and I am determined to piece together at least a part of it. Thank you for the escort, Mr. Allen."

Penny turned without waiting for reply and strode toward the vehicles. Nate felt again the fleeting pain in his chest. The sound of her saying "spending more time" played in his head. He realized that he would not be completely disappointed if that became the truth. He executed a graceful about-face and moved in the direction of the supernatural railway tunnel, thinking about Nathaniel Allen the puzzle.

Nathaniel was the only child of a soap opera starlet with a brief career and the considerably older head of a law firm that specialized in representing pharmaceutical companies. He grew up in exclusive Basking Ridge, New Jersey, squarely in the center of "the world's medicine cabinet." His father earned obscene amounts of money, running a firm that made sure generic labs were bought off from producing drugs that had lapsed into public domain, senators and representatives were greased in exchange for favorable legislation and putting pressure on the Food and Drug Administration, and other lawyers and their class action lawsuits were squashed.

Simon Allen did not have to work as hard to spend what rolled in. There had been two spouses before Nate's trophy-wife mother, and there were four other children. She had died of pancreatic cancer at fifty, when her only child was seventeen. On the day of her funeral, Simon Allen announced to his youngest son that he finally needed to concentrate on saving for retirement. Therefore, Nate would not get what his stepbrothers and sisters had received. Although Nate had been accepted at Princeton and Yale, Simon had no intention of footing either university's hefty bills. Nate was not particularly disappointed. He loathed his father and wanted to owe the man as little as possible. Instead, he went to Rutgers University, the New Jersey public Ivy.

After eighteen years in the Allen household, four years at college and a year on Wall Street, Nate thought he had the world pretty well figured out. He had formulated his thoughts into a philosophy by the time he met his partner-to-be. Daniel O'Shea possessed an average intellect. He was a grandchild of the last great Irish influx into Boston. His grandfather had gotten his first job digging ditches for sewers. His father had lived better, moving his family to the suburb of Beverly and tarring and shingling roofs.

Never a scholar, Danny had attempted community college but dropped out to become the dapper greeter and, when necessary, the bouncer at increasingly fancier bars. He interrupted his career path with a tour of duty in the Marines. Unsolvable military situations in the Middle East convinced him to decline reenlistment. At age twenty-four, he landed in New York City and became the general factotum at the Bowery Ballroom. The upscale establishment on Delancey St. offered a swank, well-stocked bar and a superior selection of music. It was the class of watering hole favored by Nathaniel Allen. It was Nate's pronounced opinion that fate had brought the two men together.

One night, just before closing time at the Bowery Ballroom, when Nate was seated at the bar, an over-the-hill British movie star with a "tough guy" persona sat down two stools away. The actor was a nasty drunk. He had a reputation in major cities and their jails for picking fights. If it looked like he could not finish what his tongue started, his ex-commando bodyguard came to his rescue. On this night, he met an equally belligerent American drunk who thought he could make a local name for himself by decking a pretend action hero. Several punches were traded. The star received a bloody nose. His protector stepped forward with fists cocked, but Danny was already there. He matched the street-fighting tactics of the ultra-tough commando blow for blow and soon had him in a sleeper hold. The star, reliving a scene from one of his lesser-known motion pictures, broke a beer bottle against the bar so that the jagged bottom became lethal. He advanced on the distracted Danny. A moment later, Nate's instep swept across the drunk's trailing ankle and sent him flying to the floor, where he stabbed himself in the forehead with the makeshift weapon.

After the dust had settled and the police hauled the three troublemakers away, Nate hung around while the bartender and Danny closed the upscale pub. He had engaged Daniel O'Shea in revelatory conversations several times prior to the momentous evening. Now he had seen enough to know that this handsome-but-dangerous-looking, deadly-with-his hands character was the perfect partner to help him turn his evolved theories into practice. When the large man offered his hand and his thanks, Nate asked him to sit at the deserted bar and listen to his credo.

"A day has twenty-four hours. A week has one hundred and sixty-eight hours. A year has eight thousand seven-hundred and sixty-six hours," Nate revealed. "How many of those are exciting?"

"I never thought about it," Danny answered.

"Most people don't. But let's think for a moment about your past year," Nate invited.

"Okay," Danny agreed.

"Good. The hours you come up with must be exciting and not just mildly entertaining."

"That woman Elaine I told you about was exciting."

"For how long?"

"Maybe a month."

"Not every hour in that month. Do you mean about thirty hours in the sack?"

"Maybe more. We'd do it several times on the weekends," Danny said with pride.

"Let's be generous. Say fifty total hours. How many hours outside the sack was she exciting?"

Danny shrugged. "The ten until I nailed her. But then Caroline came along. She was more exciting."

"How many hours in total?"

Danny calculated. "A hundred?"

"According to what you've told me, that takes care of your recent love life."

Danny nodded toward the bar office. "Except for the quickies Jennifer throws me."

"Ah, Jennifer. The proverbial good time had by all. I'll add ten. You get high on exercising. The Saturday morning basketball league, the runs, the workouts all year. Tote up the good hours, not the routine ones."

"Eighty."

"Watching television. Your *24* and *LOST*, your sports events that are really fun and not just a pacifier to fill in time."

"A hundred-fifty?"

"Your vacation to Bermuda was three nights. You go to a movie about twice a month, you go out to a good restaurant once a month."

Danny raised his forefinger. "Those are limited because of my job."

"You mean because of the hours. But I know it's also because of what you earn. Anything else?"

When Danny took too long thinking, Nate said, "Take my word. Everything together does not total more than ten hours a week. Five hundred and twenty hours in a year. That leaves more than eight thousand two hundred hours, Dan. No matter what you told me, I already knew the real answer to 'How many hours in your life are exciting?' The answer is: Too few." Nate held up his half-finished blue martini.

Danny's back arched. "Hey, don't make it sound like you have two thousand to my five hundred. Just plain staying alive takes up lots of time. Everybody's gotta sleep. Everybody's gotta travel from place to place. You gotta shop for food, cook it, eat it and wash the dishes. You gotta work."

Nate smiled. "But where will you sleep, and with whom? You can walk to Gristede's for your Chef Boyardee Spaghetti-O's, microwave it, eat it in a ratty, little apartment and wash the plates and spoons when you run out of clean ones, or you can leave your suite at the Grand Hotel Plaza in Rome and take a chauffeured limousine to enjoy a salad

Niçoise, breast of turkey and fettuccini Alfredo at Alfredo á la Scrofa. And how you work…."

Danny shrugged again. "You're talking about the lucky few who inherit a bundle. Or those who step into a top job at dad's company or marry the boss's daughter. Otherwise, you have to bust your ass earning the credentials to be a doctor or a lawyer or a banker or whatever. Then you pay your dues moving up the ladder. And that uses up tens of thousands of hours of your best years."

"What about the guy who invented the pop top on aluminum cans?" Nate countered. "One great idea, and he had earned free hours for life."

"You telling me you've got one great idea?" Danny asked. "And don't say drugs."

Nate's eyes narrowed. "Not street drugs. Now, the kind that buys my father his new Jaguar is another thing."

"You're gonna work for a drug company?"

"No. We…are going to work for a charitable organization. A Christian charitable organization. Tens of thousands of Christians are either just plain generous folk or think they can buy their way into heaven by throwing money at charities. But they won't get out of their pews to do it. They need healthy, daring young men to gallop around the globe on their behalf. Young men not afraid to travel to dangerous, exotic places. Like Columbia, Ecuador, Brazil, Zambia, Myanmar, Afghanistan, Vietnam. Interestingly, all of these countries have something else in common: Precious gems. Diamonds, emeralds, rubies."

Danny's sleep-heavy eyes grew wider and wider as Nate laid out his schemes for using a Christian charity and its funds to front their travels and to help pay for illegal, uncut black market stones that could be sold in great cities like New York, London, Paris, Rome, Al Kuwait, Al Riyad, Dehli, Singapore, Hong Kong and Tokyo.

Having laid out his scheme, Nate relaxed against the high-backed stool. "'I shall pass this way but once.' Losing the hours of your youth is the great human tragedy. You're twenty-five, right?"

"Right."

"Life can only be fully enjoyed up to forty, my friend," Nate stated with assurance. "After that, you're a dirty old man to the women. Your muscles and bones hurt if you explore too hard or play too long. Your stomach starts rejecting rich food and wines," he said, tapping Danny's knee. "And all of that assumes that you get to live to forty. Do you ever read the obituary columns?"

"No."

"You should. About every tenth dead person is under forty. None of us knows how much future we have. I say there is only today, and it must be seized. *Carpe diem.* If you live for the future, the todays all slip away. Why tread water when I can show you how to sail around this magnificent world? I have a solid plan, but I need a partner. I need a guy who's not afraid to use his fists, who knows how to handle a gun, who will watch my back while I make the partnership tons of money. While I secure the two most precious commodities on the planet: Time and money. Whaddaya say, Mr. O'Shea?"

Mr. O'Shea said yes.

Danny flicked on his flashlight for a moment, to check his watch. In spite of his having hunted up a plank of dry wood to sit on, he found the tunnel damp and cool and uncomfortable under him.

"He'll return," Danny recited, speaking of the redheaded railway worker who was still myth to Nate. The words had become Daniel's mantra.

Nate did not bother to aggravate Danny with his own belief. His opinion was that so many fiction stories and magazine articles over the years had dealt with travel back in time that it had to be part of the collective unconscious. And, if so common a belief, then possible. Writers since Einstein's theory of relativity had defined an unbroken path called a time-space continuum that could be traveled back upon, given the right set of circumstances. The reason it had not been proven, Nate assumed, was because it was a one-way street. The future was the future because it had not happened. Therefore there was no path to travel on. As far as he knew, no one had ever been able to retrace travel to verify a backward trip. The sooner he and Daniel resigned themselves to the fact that they had been permanently dislocated in time, the better off they would be.

Recent memories of his mother teaching him to dance had dredged up other thoughts in Nate's consciousness. He recalled the day he discovered the engraved invitation to his parents' wedding. The date had been only been six months before Nate had arrived. His mother said that he was premature; but, given his birth weight of eight pounds, six ounces, thirteen weeks more than strained credulity. Furthermore, he looked like his mother but nothing like Simon Allen or his stepsiblings.

His legal father had never bothered to get emotionally close to him.

It was little wonder to him that Simon had footed the Ivy League educations of all the previous Allen children, but Nate, who was smarter than any of them, he would not support once his mother died. Nate was happy to believe that he shared none of Simon's genes. He did not like his lawyer father's value systems or his ethics. Sitting in the prolonged, reflective silence within the sensory-deprived dark, quiet tunnel, he realized with a start that, in spite of hating the man as much as he did, he had become merely a different version of the selfish, morally bankrupt individual.

At quarter past ten the next wave of bombing began. It seemed closer than the previous night. The tunnel shook more; the whistling of the bombs could be distinguished hundreds of feet inside. The attack went on for almost an hour. Nate worried about Worden Miles on his patrol, Millicent in her Anderson shelter, and Penny driving the ambulance.

The hours dragged on. Trains swept by in both directions with regularity, even during the raid, but no one else appeared in the tunnels.

"It's almost three," Nate pointed out when he could stand the boredom, the lack of answers and the self-recrimination no more. "He's not coming tonight. Maybe he'll never come again, Dan."

Danny whipped the earphones attached to his iPod from his head. "Bullshit! He'll come. He has to come."

"Why?"

"Because otherwise I'm stuck here. Haven't you been missing the Jacuzzi, the internet, your wide-screen television?"

"To be honest, not that much," Nate decided.

"If we're still here a month from now, I know your answer will be different. We're from the jet era, the Caribbean singles resort, the microwave oven. No heated car seats, automatic transmissions, no satellite radio, or GPS. No painless dentists, hardly any over the counter medicines."

"You forgot Velcro, credit cards, fast food and Frisbees."

Danny slapped his thigh. "I knew it! You have been thinking about all you're missing! I miss my family and good old three-shots-and-she's-on-her-back Jennifer. And don't tell me you wouldn't miss Brittany, Chelsea and Megan."

"I'd miss it all. But that won't guarantee we can jump back."

Danny glowered at Nate. "My attitude is 'If you don't think positive, it definitely won't happen. Don't jinx us, Nate!"

Nate grunted as he pushed up from the plank placed across the side track. "Maybe my doubting presence is jinx enough. I'm going back to the Wilcox house. Are you coming with me?"

"No."

Nate whacked Danny lightly on the side of the head. "Stubborn. Okay, listen. If you catch the leprechaun, write down the magic formula for getting back on this." He had earlier picked up a dropped bill of lading, to see what it was. He handed the paper to Danny, along with the ballpoint pen from his raincoat pocket. "Stick it under some of these track rocks just inside the mouth of the tunnel. If you disappear, I'll use your directions to follow you."

Danny regarded his friend for several seconds. "Yeah, okay." His mouth opened and then closed.

"What?"

"You'd be all right in this time. You like history. Staying here will kill me."

Nate was simply too tired to debate. He shrugged. "One way or another, I'll see you."

"Right."

Alone in the Wilcox house, Nate sat at the top of the stairs. He was beyond tired and needing to just be quiet for a time to invite sleep. He thought about all the women who had paraded through his life. His sister Whitney's girlfriend, Sabrina, had been five years older than he when she took his virginity on his seventeenth birthday. Time and experience had proven to him that she had been quite skilled at lovemaking and a good teacher. The two bites she provided of the forbidden fruit had instilled an enduring hunger in him. He thought about the succession of female conquests, in prep school, college, at his first job, in his neighborhoods, while gallivanting around the world. In eleven years, the number had run up to more than twice what he could count on his fingers and toes. In another man, the total might have caused immodest pride. In Nate it created a profound uneasiness.

These were not prostitutes or girls so plain of face or poor of figure that they would have tumbled into virtually any young man's bed. Many were beautiful, well educated, intelligent and accomplished. Surely, he thought, at least one of them was worthy of his love. He had been in lust with most, and, for a time, in like with many.

But not one had he loved.

It was his own failing, he told himself. Whether from the poor example of his father's lead and his mother's marriages, or from some missing wiring in his head, he feared he was incapable. He wondered if it was like being colorblind. You could accommodate to life, for example by knowing that the green lamp on a traffic light was the one on the bottom. You could fake the sense by learning that broccoli was green and apples were red. But already, several women had called him on his lacking, declaring their love and hearing right through the insincerity of his responses. Just as he discovered that apples can also be yellow or green, he learned that faking emotion inevitably failed. He had to be honest in relationships. When he was frank, women would take his confession as a challenge, trying to prove that no one quite as wonderful as they had yet come into Nate's life. His warnings up front had not made the break-ups any easier.

In the past three months, although he had yet to tell Danny, he had not gone beyond dinner with an eligible woman. The costs had become greater than the rewards. As if this was not enough of a concern, their constant travel had also begun to pall. He had certainly not abandoned his philosophy of making every second count, but he knew that he also needed to look inward for satisfaction. He wondered if his persistent desire for change was what had brought them through the tunnel.

To a different kind of life, and a different kind of woman.

# CHAPTER SEVEN

In spite of the cacophony of emergency vehicles and time-delay bombs, of the pulsating light of burning businesses and dwellings, and of his personal worries, Nate had at last been able to catch a decent amount of sleep. Danny had not dragged into the Wilcox house until a little after five. Nate elected to let him sleep on. He left a note and promised to return by mid-afternoon.

The powers of youth and rest had largely restored use of his knees. Nevertheless, Nate walked slowly to the Mile End Tube station, studying the damage of the previous air raid. A five-foot-deep hole damaged the street close by the station. He realized that a large, dud bomb had either been dug out of it or else the hole had been the aftermath of an exploded smaller variety. The puddles lying all around indicated that a water line had been pierced but rapidly repaired. One resident garden had been instantaneously harvested by a small bomb, throwing every vegetable out of the yard and stripping a small tree of all its leaves. He saw as well the evidence of incendiary spikes that had either burned out futilely on slate roofs or else had been plucked out by owners or air raid wardens.

If anything, the passengers on the subway train were calmer than they had been the previous day. Nate knew that they had begun to realize the Germans could only inflict so much damage on a city as enormous as London. Over time, he knew, the RAF Spitfires and Hurricanes, guided by radar, would down enough enemy bombers and fighters that the Germans would be the first to lose heart. The bold headline on a tabloid newspaper held by one of the seated passengers read BORE WAR OVER. English humor had once again risen to the fore.

Nate used his knowledge of the various Tube systems to get himself close to the Ritz Hotel. He stopped first at a sundries shop, where he purchased a nail file, a pack of bobby pins, and several other objects of thin metal. When he entered the hotel lobby, he saw with no surprise that it did not appear exactly as it was in the twenty-first century.

He knew that several renovations would be expected in such a swank place over sixty-plus years, even if its furnishings and elegance were intended to seem timeless. In spite of his disappointment at not having found the entire hotel a return time portal, he continued up to the Berkeley suite that he and Danny had moved into two days earlier. He told himself that, no matter how slim the hope, he had to check out every possible reentry point to his own era. He knocked on the door. When he received no reply from within, he took out his newly purchased instruments and tried to pick open the door. It resisted. Nate switched to a credit card from his wallet. He slipped it between the door and the jamb, yanked the door toward its hinges and shoved the rectangle of plastic forward. The door opened.

The suite was rented. A cart with dirty plates and trays stood near the door. In the bedrooms were suits, shoes and suitcases not theirs. His and Danny's belongings had vanished. Nate held the suits up to his frame one by one and found all to be too small. However, the black, patent leather shoes left in the west bedroom were his size. These he slipped into a shopping bag he found from Peter Jones/Sloane Square, along with a dress white shirt and a bow tie. The dozen coins he discovered in an ashtray he shoved into his trouser pocket. Shaking his head with disappointment, he exited the suite and took the stairs down.

Toward noon, Nate changed trains at Tower Gateway to travel south across the Thames. From the Tower Bridge Road stop, he worked his way on foot eastward along the soot-stinking docks, determined to wend from one pub to the next until he found what he sought. There was certainly no lack of drinking establishments. One could not walk for more than two blocks anywhere in the South or East Ends of London, save for a few dense residential areas, without running into one. Some streets might have three within sight of each other. Corners were particularly traditional places to find them. Nate thought of the era he had come from. In spite of the diversions of television and professional sporting events, he realized this one element of the British Isles had not changed much. Except for the trendy and upscale center-city places, public houses were like as not ground-floor extensions of dwellings, serving only a few choices of alcohol and simple food.

He had come to understand that they created a personal choice of "family" distinct from the one a person was born into, with the same clientele frequenting day after day, night after night, year after year. People did not journey far from their homes or places of business to drink or find companionship. Nate counted on these facts for finding near the docks the sort of rough trade characters who could help him with his less-than-legal transportation needs.

Rainbows of oil in the puddles attested to various Southwark night mishaps, as did a line of burned-out shops. Off in the near distance, where he supposed the wending river to be, something continued to burn fiercely.

A watering hole called the Surabaya was open for business. It did not lack for patrons. Most dressed like dockworkers. Nate figured that the wicked Nazi high command and their flying monkeys had put many of them out of work in the preceding sixty hours, and they would be anxious to earn money however they could, legal or not. They occupied all of the decrepit establishment's many corners, every one of which managed to be dark.

Nate stepped up to the bar and laid half a crown on it. He ordered a glass of ale, and when the bartender served it he leaned forward and said, "I'm looking for a special service. I need paperwork to get back to the United States."

"What a coincidence, pal," the man replied, poorly imitating a New York accent. "I have the same need. Have you tried your embassy?"

"They move much too slowly. You have to fill out all these forms, and then they send them back to the States for verification. I can't wait that long."

"Neither can I."

"My documents were burned by an incendiary bomb," Nate said. "I'm not a copper."

The bartender's eyes narrowed. "Who said you were?"

Nate sighed. "Much obliged." He downed half the ale in a few gulps and, leaving the money and the glass on the bar, turned toward the front door.

A hand dug into Nate's right shoulder. From years of practice, Nate captured it with his left hand, windmilled his right under it, pivoted and brought the offending hand and arm into a lock.

"Easy, easy, brother," the owner of the appendage advised. "I overheard your need and wanted to offer my assistance. I don't think you really want to attract everyone's attention, do you?"

Nate let go. The man, who wore an off-the-rack suit and sported a polka-dot handkerchief in the lapel pocket, flashed him a grin.

"That's better. Step into my office." The man turned and made for a secluded table at the back of the bar. When they were seated, the man said, "Alex Bennett at your service." He took a gold cigarette case from his inside jacket pocket and tapped it open. Nate studied his face. His eyes were deep-set and close together. His smile was crooked and formed of crooked, yellow teeth. He sported a pencil-thin moustache. Sitting in a dimly lit corner in a stereotypical dive of a bar, he looked like a villain from Warner Brother's central casting. Nate had met crooked men and women who owed their success to looking innocent and an equal number of thug look-alikes who were the salt of the earth. He neither trusted nor mistrusted the man because of the pub and his looks. Words and body language were what he intended to base his judgment on.

Mr. Bennett offered Nate a cigarette.

"No, thanks," Nate declined. "I like my lungs too much."

Bennett fetched a match from a matchbook with some advertising on the side and struck it. "Suit yourself."

Nate saw no downside to using his own name. He had not existed in 1940 until early Sunday morning. There were no records the man could check. Moreover, he had decided to make use of the identity of his father's father. Nate had been named after Nathaniel Allen, one-time Fuller brush salesman, born in 1915 in the Bronx, on Jerome Avenue near the zoo.

Nate held out his hand. "Nathaniel Allen. From New York."

"I can hear it in your accent. So, you're stuck over here?"

"I am. Actually, we are. My partner and I. His name is Sean O'Shea, from the heart of Boston." Sean was one of Danny's grandfathers, who Nate estimated had been born around 1908, a little too old for the masquerade but within the realm of believability.

Bennett exhaled the first puff of smoke. "Burned out, eh? Let me guess. There's some urgency in getting home," he said in a smooth-voice.

"Now that the Reich has turned its firepower on your country there is."

"Right. Well I tell you, I'm in the import business myself. But I do know a gent who has a printing press. He creates all kinds of documents for shipping. He might have the wherewithal to be of service to you."

"Where can I find him?" Nate asked.

"Oh, in this matter he certainly would not want to be found. That's where I come in. I'm sure this won't be a cheap transaction, especially for two 'authentic' United States passports."

"How much?"

Bennett shook his head slowly. "I have no idea. I'll have to get back to you. Now, where can I reach you?"

Nate shook his head in exact imitation of the other man. "We no longer have an address. It's ashes and soot. Is this your normal hang-out?"

"One of them."

"If I returned tomorrow, would you have an answer for me?"

"I can't promise by tomorrow. The day after, I should say."

"And I assume the printer will compensate your troubles in this regard."

Bennett grinned a crooked grin. "One way or the other, you'll be paying for my services."

Nate nodded and stood. "Day after tomorrow then."

"And a good day to you, Mr. Allen," Bennett wished.

Nate left the pub with purpose. When he turned the block, however, he realized that he had not left quickly enough. Alex Bennett had put a tail on him. The man was not too difficult to spot, since he was unusually small and also wore spectacles that glinted whenever he turned toward the sun.

Nate continued down the road to the next pub. His goal was to ask the same question until he got a second lead. If he could not get back to his own time, he would at least do his utmost to get to the Land of the Free and the Home of the Brave.

The human shadow was competent, which gave Nate hope that he had connected with professional criminal elements at the Surabaya. He kept expecting to lose the man in the street and subway crowds or in changing trains. As the day wore on and the man refused to be shaken, however, Nate was finally compelled to duck into a shop five blocks from the Miles house and to race out the back door.

Nate found Danny still sleeping at three o'clock. Minutes after he roused his partner, a cry went up from outside that another air attack was on the way.

"I can't believe they don't have sirens," Danny muttered as he pulled on his pants.

"No redheaded saboteur appeared, eh?"

"Not last night."

"I've got a fix on forged passports, to at least get us out of the country if all else fails," Nate reported.

Danny grabbed his shoes. "Don't be in such a hurry."

Although the Wilcoxes had an Anderson shelter in their back yard, Nate and Danny ran over to the Miles shelter. They found Millicent switching off the radio.

"They've gone off the air. I suppose to run for their own shelters," she said. "I know that the excuse at night is to give the Jerries no radio signals for their bombers to hone in on." She plopped her light frame on a chair as if she were made of lead. "I wish Penny and Worden were here." She opened her Bible. "Would you like me to read?"

"Please," Nate invited.

She began with the 23rd Psalm and then moved to Isaiah.

The bombers arrived. From the direction of the noises, it seemed that their crews had been given orders to bomb the heart of the city, where both Penny and Worden worked. Millicent's voice and hands shook slightly as she recited. Nate took the book from her and continued reading. The raid was short-lived.

A minute after the last plane engines faded, Mrs. Miles stood up and announced, "I must get supper ready. Worden has so little spare time." She turned toward the two Americans and affixed a glowing expression. "I must congratulate myself on anticipating these events. I laid in a rather prodigious store of goods, and now is the time to begin using them!" And then she was away to the house.

Nate and Danny went into the street to look for unexploded bombs and burning incendiary spikes. They saw Penelope trudging up the sidewalk.

"I'll leave you to your little romance with Mary Poppins," Danny said under his breath, turning toward the Wilcox home.

Nate ignored the barb and closed the distance between himself and the young Englishwoman. "Home early?"

"Yes. I managed to get to the people you suggested I speak with. I couched your idea as my own, and they promised to take it under advisement. My superior gave me the rest of the afternoon off. Said I looked peaked from my ambulance duty and needed rest. Do I look peaked?"

"You look like Sleepy Beauty to me," Nate replied.

"Always playing with words," Penny noted, but she seemed pleased. "I have a dancer's stamina. I need only half an hour to rest and catch my second wind."

"I don't think Hemingway had a second job when he drove," Nate offered.

"Who?"

"Ernest Hemingway. He–"

"The novelist! That's right. He drove an ambulance during the Great War. I read *The Sun Also Rises* and *A Farewell to Arms*, but I can't say I like him. His writing is like meat and potatoes, with no gravies or spices."

"And probably too macho." When Penny's eyebrows knit again, Nate hastily added, "Male bravado."

"Yes, if macho is the word. I like Fitzgerald but not Faulkner. And I adore Mark Twain. Among female American novelists, I like Edith Wharton best. And then Willa Cather. I thoroughly agree with her dislike of materialism and conformism. But I don't like Kathleen Norris. I believe she won't last."

Before Penny could ask for Nate's opinion, he decided to turn the discussion back on her. "I'm amazed you've read so many American authors, considering you're from–"

Penny's expression changed like a stoplight. "I know what you're about to say: 'Considering you're from Bethnal Green.' I suffered the same attitude all through university, often straight to my face," she interrupted with real anger. "I got it indirectly when I applied for teaching positions in the West End. 'How could a girl from the East End be smart enough or well-read enough to teach our children?'" Her free hand went to her hip. "You know, Mr. Gandhi said 'It does not require money to be neat, clean and dignified,' and that also applies to well read and well bred." Her words picked up speed like an express locomotive. She not only clearly felt passionately about the subject but had also rehearsed her words many times, if only in her head. "My father may be East End born, but look where he's gotten himself. As soon as I went to school, my mother opened a children's shop. Nappies, pajamas, prams and so forth. It didn't make a fortune, but they put enough aside so that not only my brother but I as well could attend university. If they hadn't put me through, they could be living in sight of the British Museum!"

While he weathered Penny's rant, Nate compared her in his mind's eye to his sister, Allysia, the last time he had upset her. When she had prattled, "Just between Cammy, Corinne and me..." he had jumped in with, "You mean, 'Just among Cammy, Corinne and me.' Her reaction was "Fuck you! I'm the one with the Ivy League education, so don't correct me, ass wipe." And then pushed him backward over a chair. She was the next youngest among the Allen siblings, three years older than Nathaniel. As an assistant professor of Women's Studies at Goucher, her haircut, her reading glasses, everything she wore and the deodorant she chose not to use were carefully calculated to make provocative statements. Although both women had shown anger toward him, Allysia's and Penny's manners were at opposite poles.

Nate took a step forward and pressed his fingers against Penny's lips.

"Calm down, Miss. What I was going to say when you climbed up on your warhorse was, 'I'm amazed you've read so many American authors, given you're from England.'"

"Oh." Color began to suffuse Penny's cheeks. "Oh," she said again, in a smaller voice. "I'm so sorry."

"I'm not," Nate said truthfully. "I was beginning to think you only had a saintly side. It made me despair of ...deserving your friendship."

Penny looked down at her feet. "That's silly."

"Is it? Not only haven't I read Willa Cather, Edith Wharton or Kathleen What's-Her-Name, but I can't recall reading any Englishmen other than Dickens, H. G. Wells and Arthur Conan Doyle." Nate thought of other names such as George Orwell and E. M. Forster, but he did not know if they had become well known before 1940. In truth, half the novels he was acquainted with he had heard and not read, via books on CD.

"Surely you're being kind," Penny replied. "Anyone who knows Ulysses' wife and who uses 'pusillanimous' in a sentence and pronounces it correctly must be well read."

"How did we get off the subject of driving ambulances?" Nate asked, desperate to be done with literature.

"Hemingway."

Nate started walking, compelling Penny to move as well. "Right. Good old Ernie. He was wounded driving that ambulance, you know."

"Was he?"

"I hope you're watching out for yourself. Especially for the falling shrapnel."

"I'm as careful as I can be, under the circumstances. I picked up a young mother who had taken a large piece of shrapnel in the abdomen last night," Penny divulged in a somber voice. "She was screaming something terrible. And the worst of it was she had a two-year-old who was perfectly fine but who she sent into a wailing panic."

"Did she live?"

"No. She died just as we pulled up to the hospital. I don't know what shall become of the child." She shook her head slowly. "Terrible.

And then I'm the one expected to...."

"What?"

"Enough of that. I'm at liberty tonight..." She looked up at her house. "...and we're home."

Supper was fish and chips, with a salad of lettuce, carrots and radishes from Mrs. Miles's "Digging for Victory" garden. Every spare inch of back yard had been planted. Marrows, cucumbers and turnips rounded out the rows. She was pleased to be drawn out by Nate and announced that she would soon finish her "putting up if the Krauts allow."

Over dessert tea and a biscuit tin full of cookies, Mr. Miles was coaxed to speak of his military service in the First World War. He meandered through tales of his platoon buddies and of their hijinks. He mentioned receiving the Military Medal for service in the Heavy Artillery, fighting at Ypres and on the Somme. But of the particulars of combat, woundings and deaths he was tight-lipped.

"Of course, during that war the French put up a reasonable display of fighting spirit," Worden opined. "This round, we're pretty much all that's left on the Western Front." He fixed his gaze on Danny and Nate. "Since you both work for your government, I hope you can put in a word for the common man here. Aid for Britain and Lend Lease aren't enough. Mr. Roosevelt must convince your people to enter this war."

"It'll happen," Danny broke in. "Just be patient. You don't have any whiskey lying around, do you?"

"Whisky? Sorry," Millicent revealed in an even voice. "We don't drink hard liquor."

Danny waved his hand bravely. "No problem. I don't need it."

Nate kept his gaze fixed on his fork. He knew that Danny could not hold on much longer without distilled fortification. He resolved to find a couple bottles the next day to keep his partner happy.

"I hear that Fat Hermann Göring stood on the cliffs in France, laughing and cheering on his pilots Sunday," Worden reported.

"He said that if a British bomber ever got through the German defenses, everyone could call him Meyer, didn't he?" Nate asked, providing a positive opening.

Worden's eyes twinkled. "Exactly. I guess he should wear a Star of David on his arm just like all the other poor German Jews!" He patted Nate on the top of his hand. Nate shifted his gaze to see if Penny appreciated the remark as much as her father had. She smiled at him.

Worden turned his attention to his wife. "Did you go to the Gas Works today?"

"I did," Millicent answered. "Me and the wheelbarrow. Took me most of the morning standing two-abreast in a block-long queue to get our hundredweight of coke. Everyone is afraid the trains will stop or the works will be blown up. I should have brought my knitting."

Nate thought of the long lines he and Danny had encountered in central London. He wondered how outraged the people of his generation would be under such conditions. He pictured guns appearing by the second day, wholesale riots, road rage deaths. He remembered Penny's words about people in her memory not having bathtubs and bathing in a public park. He recalled clearly a February of his early childhood when heavy snows brought the power lines down for an afternoon and an entire night. His father immediately drove with his behemoth SUV to a hotel with power, muttering about the need to do work and leaving the family behind. His siblings cursed the darkness rather than hunt up candles. His world, without all the electrical and electronic conveniences he had come to take for granted, was reduced to watching the flames dancing in the fireplace after he fought, verbally and physically, with brothers and sisters for sleeping bag space close to the heat.

"Do you know, Mr. Miles, that they've drained the public swimming pool down there? I should think, with all the fires, they'd want to preserve such stores of water."

The flesh around Worden Miles's eyes pinched. "It's to be used as a make-shift mortuary."

"Ah," was all that his wife replied.

"I must go on duty," the ARP warden announced, pushing himself up from the dining table. "Don't forget to cover all the utensils and lid the pots against the dust. You're home tonight, Penelope?"

She looked at Nate. "I thought I'd take Mr. Allen down and show him the YWCA dance."

"Lovely idea. Life must not stop. That's what the Hun would want," Worden preached, "but we won't allow it. There's a shelter right there. Remember: 'Got your gas mask, got your torchlight, alright, goodnight.'"

"Yes, Dad."

"I'll tag along," Danny said, giving Nate a hard look.

"We have only two bicycles," Penelope told him.

"That's fine. I'll run."

"It's more than a mile."

"That's just getting started for me." He snapped his fingers. "Except I don't have my Nikes."

"Have what?" Millicent asked.

"It's American slang for 'running shoes,'" Nate said before Danny could insert his entire foot in his mouth.

"I understand!" Penny said brightly. "The swift goddess of Victory, wasn't she? How very clever."

While Nate and Penelope cleaned up the table and washed the dishes and pots, Millicent made her husband a fortifying flask of tea and a ham and cheese sandwich. Nate stayed in their company while Danny went upstairs for a pair of the dead Ralph's warm-up pants and a rugby shirt. The time for Nate's inevitable speech to his partner about the acceptance of not being able to get home was looming, but he could not deliver it with anyone else present.

The sun hung low in the west when the trio exited the Miles house. Its long, orange rays stained the hundred or so airborne barrage balloons that floated over the eastern reaches of the Thames like a ragged V formation of geese. Nate saw that they had been arranged to interfere with the previous paths of bomber attacks.

Penelope rode a lady's Schwinn, while Nate pedaled a Murray that was a primitive version of an English racer. Penelope's bike had wire baskets on either side of the rear wheel. Into one of them she had fitted an EverReady electric lamp, and in the other she had placed her dancing shoes and gas mask.

A few blocks from the Miles home they passed four little girls jumping rope on an unsullied stretch of sidewalk, two of them intoning the words to "Teddy Bear, Teddy Bear." For a moment, the world seemed timeless to Nate.

"Here's what I'm really looking for," Danny shouted as they approached a pub named the Old George. "Do you know if it's friendly to foreigners, Penny?"

"It should be. A couple of people on our street frequent it. I've even bent my elbow there a few times. But if it isn't, continue west for three more streets and ask anybody where Ye Olde Hope is."

"Will do. You two have a good time."

Nate swung the bicycle in a slow circle. "You know where you are?"

Danny pointed to his skull. "You know me. One time in a place and I'm my own global positioning…" He winced and waved Nate on. Penelope had ridden ahead and apparently not heard Danny's second verbal faux pas of the evening. Shaking his head, Nate pushed harder on the pedals to catch up.

"I'm very pleased you have enough energy left to show me this dance place," Nate confessed.

Penny shook her head back and forth in the breeze created by her forward motion, making her hair swing luxuriantly. One strand fell over her left eye. "I would have to be on death's door to refuse a chance to dance."

"Do you have to serve two out of every three nights for ambulance duty?"

"I'm determined to, until my body tells me I can't any longer, or until the Germans stop bombing."

"It's truly commendable that everyone in your family has volunteered in the war effort."

Penny slowed her pedaling so that she could study Nate's face. "We didn't start volunteering because of the war. We've always done it. Ever since I can recall, my mother cooked meals for the elderly shut-ins and my father delivered them."

"Did you have a car?"

"No. He did it by bicycle. The bicycle you're on, with the baskets behind me. I volunteered as an aide at our hospital until I went off to university. I told you that my mother had a children's shop. It was closed on Mondays, and she laundered several loads of nappies for mothers without families. Don't you volunteer?"

Faced with Penny's expectant stare and realizing how much he cared what she thought about him, Nate said, "I do. I spend a great deal of time seeing that hungry children are fed."

Penny's expression relaxed. "Yes, I knew you would do something like that." An impish grin curled her lips, and she leaned forward over her handlebars. "I'll show you who's more tired. Race you the rest of the way!"

"In the Mood" rolled out of the YMCA building onto the dark street. Depression, rationing, war and death all disappeared at the threshold, dispelled by rhythms that pulsed like blood through young arteries. The sounds of the live band were rich and brassy. The hall was packed to the rafters, and everyone was dressed for fun. Primary colors dominated. Smiles lit the room as much as the sconces on the walls.

Penelope scowled at the scene. "Ever since war was declared, all the dance halls are twice as packed."

"The joint is definitely jumping," Nate said.

"If you think this is bad, you should see the more established dance halls. The Streatham Locarno shoehorns 800 on the floor and almost 300 in the balcony on a Saturday night. The Paramount on Tottenham Court Road hosted a Jitterbug marathon, and I understand they turned several hundred away after the 1400 limit was reached. I know the reason: It's a cheap way to shake off the fears that are winding everyone up like clock springs." She gestured to a chair that had a coat draped over it. "Whoever has claimed this can't begrudge me two minutes." She sat and took her dancing shoes from the same cloth bag that held her gas mask. "Are women in America having trouble getting sheer stockings?" she asked as she opened the straps.

"More from the cost than the availability," Nate replied, guessing.

Penny nodded at the dance floor. "Most of what you see is illusion. The girls pretending white stockings rub wet sand on their legs. Almost every one of them has painted the seams on. You can tell which ones, because their fingertips will be stained. I would never stoop so low." Before Nate could comment, she laughed. "But I use burnt matchsticks to darken my eyebrows, so you can call me a hypocrite."

As she tugged on one shoe, the same tress of brunette hair fell over her left eye. Impulsively, Nate reached over and brushed it behind her ear. The heel of his hand moved across her cheek. It was warm and the softest thing he had touched in years. She stopped tugging and rolled her eyes up, giving him a quizzical stare.

"Don't you like my hair over my face?" she asked.

"I do, actually. It's…dare I say it…quite sexy," Nate replied. "But I like looking at all your face even more."

Penny's lips pursed in a pleased expression. She looked back down quickly.

A young man in uniform strode up to the table just as Penny finished pulling her dancing shoes on.

"Good evening," he said, to both Penny and Nate. "Would you care to dance after you're done fitting your slipper, Cinderella?"

Penny glanced up briefly. "Perhaps later, thanks. I'm with Prince Charming right now."

"And a lucky prince he is," remarked the serviceman. He nodded and was gone.

Nate held his own when slow dancing to "I'll Never Smile Again" and waltzing through a jazzed-up version of "The Blue Danube." However, when the band played a bounce, Nate was out of his depth. He was rescued by the persistent serviceman, who had been hovering like a vulture, waiting for the opportunity. The man was unafraid but not overly skilled. For her part, Penny followed well and made him look good. Nate marveled at her energy and footwork.

When the number ended, the soldier returned Penny to Nate's side. "Lucky indeed," he praised before moving on.

The band took a break, and Penny dragged Nate to the end of a line. "What are we waiting for?" he asked.

"Punch! It's delicious!"

Nate thought of the scores of clubs he had been to in the previous three years. Most were ultra chic with tens of thousands of dollars of fixtures and furnishings. Most piped in the tunes that came and went in a week. Most offered an array of illegal drugs along with a list of liquor and beers that took five minutes to reel off. Most were meat markets, where nothing of self was revealed beyond flesh. The objective there was to be seen and, when seen in the right clothing and accessories and jewelry, to be cool or bad or gas or phat or tits or whatever the in-vogue word-of-the-month was.

He thought of Siddartha Rubenstein, one year out of Barnard College and an editorial assistant at Alfred A. Knopf, chin pressed into her hand, eyes as dead as a Fulton Market fish, looking out on such a place and declaring, "I'm so bored." Now he stood in the bright light of a simple, open space, with fresh-faced youths concealing nothing more than a lack of nylons, happy to drink unspiked punch and then become high on live renditions of the tunes of Glenn Miller, Tommy Dorsey, Count Basie and Woody Herman's Woodchoppers, to touch nothing more than palm to palm and cheek to cheek and to sweat standing up. He gazed into Penny's sparkling green eyes.

"When the war is over, my goal is to save enough money to go to New York and dance at the Savoy Ballroom," Penny revealed as they moved forward on the line. "I read about the Battle of Swing between Chic Webb's and Count Basie's bands a couple of years ago, and it sounded so exciting! Ella Fitzgerald and Billie Holliday sang that night, and Gene Krupa, Lionel Hampton and Eddie Duchin were there! I would have fainted from joy."

When they were two couples from reaching the punch table, a low-pitched moan from beyond the building caused nearly everyone to lapse into silence. Within seconds, it had run up the scale and intensified into a mechanical wail. Sister sounds sang in imitation. Sirens had finally come to London.

No one panicked. Many of the dancers filed out the main doors and moved off apace on foot or bicycle into the early night. Their decisions were welcome, because the dance hall had been packed and there was not enough room in the basement shelter for all who had attended. Penny and Nate elected to stay. With them came another four dozen, as well as the members of the eight-piece band. Almost as soon as they had their bottoms down on one row or the other of the benches, the instrumentalists began playing. Even without the drums and piano, however, the confines of the room made their concerted sound painful. After a time, the many fingers stuck in ears and the shouted conversations convinced the saxophonist and the clarinetist to trade turns playing soft solos of classics in slow, soothing tempos.

The quiet music and the dancers' long, patient silences allowed Nate to reflect on his earlier conversation with Penny concerning volunteering and her family. Well off as they were and with all manner of service people doing their daily labor, no one in Nate's family ever gave to charity or found time to volunteer. They visited churches occasionally on Christmas and Easter but only dropped a few dollars in the plates. Regarding Simon Allen and his brood, Nate was comfortable feeling cold contempt. But it was with considerable consternation that he realized how many of his childhood friends' mothers supported the hospital fete or served on the PTA or organized runs, auctions and bake sales for various causes, how many had given not merely donations but pediatric hospital rooms, pianos for impoverished churches and the like.

The woman he adored and who adored him had always found excuses why her time was taken. He realized with dismay that he had never witnessed her opening her checkbook for a charity. Given his family background, his use of the World Assembly of Churches for his narcissistic lifestyle made him feel all the more hypocritical. Sitting beside Penny Miles, he felt like a fungus blown by fate against a perfect rose.

However long the raid lasted above the cellar, the sirens did not sound the all clear for nearly two hours. During that time, Nate coaxed Penny into speaking of herself at length. She told him of her youth, her education, her first year of experience at teaching, her dance lessons and, finally, her aspirations. He especially drew her out on her apparent fixation with the United States. Beyond New York City, she wished to see Philadelphia, Washington, Chicago, New Orleans, San Francisco and Hollywood. She expressed great respect for Theodore Roosevelt and his campaigning to preserve huge tracts of virgin wilderness for posterity. Her list of national parks to visit included Acadia, Yellowstone, Yosemite and the Grand Canyon. Nate was convinced the Englishwoman from 1940 knew more about his country than the majority of American women he had dated.

At last Nate realized who Penelope reminded him of. Her features were not as delicate nor her eyebrows as arched, but her hair, porcelain skin and emerald eyes were very like those of Vivien Leigh. "What do you think about an Englishwoman playing Scarlett O'Hara?" he asked, while the alto saxophonist played "Tara's Theme".

"Well, if the next choice was Bette Davis, I think they made an excellent selection," Penny responded. "It was April when *Gone With the Wind* arrived here. It played at the Palace, the Empire and the Ritz. We saw it at the Ritz because their screen is so enormous. The color was spectacular! What an age we live in. Think of all the things we have that my grandparents did not. Movies, the automobile, X-ray machines, the aeroplane, insulin. Now, if only the world could learn to get along."

Nate kept her on the subject of motion pictures, sharing tidbits he had picked up about Clark Gable, Leslie Howard, Hattie McDaniels and Butterfly McQueen, mostly from the Turner Classic Movies channel. Every time Penny questioned him about his life, he answered as truthfully as he could, given the time displacement. Always, however, he sought to steer the conversation back toward her life, not merely because it was safer for him but also because he genuinely cared to understand why she seemed so different from the women of his time.

Just before the all clear sounded and after Nate admitted that he lived in a small apartment that was a glorified hook to hang his belongings on between jaunts around the world, he touched Penny's cloth bag and said, "You really can stop toting that gas mask around."

"How can you possibly know that for a fact?" she demanded.

"Because even Adolf Hitler understands that England has chemical warfare agents as well. Even if his bunker in Berlin is too deep for bombs, it's not too deep for air."

"But he's a madman. He clearly doesn't think like a rational human being."

"Trust me on this, Penny," Nate said, setting his hand atop hers.

"I trust your thinking, but I'm afraid I can't stop carrying it, Nathaniel," she replied, looking down at his hand but not pulling hers away. "Only someone who can see into the future has the power to make such as statement as you have. You can't see into the future, can you?"

"No, I can't," Nate answered truthfully. "Only the present and the past."

The night horizon to the east and southeast was again painted brilliant with the glow of hundreds of raging fires. The Germans were single-mindedly concentrating on the docks and the East End industries and commerce. Nate wondered what, after two days and nights of relentless bombing, could be left to burn so brightly.

On the way back to Penny's street, they stopped at the pub where they had left Danny. He was gone. After dropping Penny off at her back door with a goodnight wish and a firm handshake, Nate went into the open-doored Wilcox house. Danny was not there. He assumed his friend was doggedly pacing up and down the train tunnels, in desperate search of the redheaded apparition. He was mistaken.

## CHAPTER EIGHT

Danny dragged into the Wilcox house at a few minutes before four. He tried to sneak in, but the small size of the house and the dry, creaking stairs betrayed him. Nate rolled out of his bed and confronted his partner before he reached the top of the stairs.

"Are you sober?"

"As a judge," Danny replied.

"Did you go to the tunnels?"

"Of course. Where else would I be?"

"And, once again, no redheaded man."

Danny pushed past him, trailing the scent of an unsubtle perfume. "Don't sound so happy about it. Let me sleep."

Nate inhaled deeply, to be sure he had smelled correctly. "I figured today we would find two more pawn shops and get rid of all we can. Passports won't be cheap."

"Fine. Just give me five hours." Danny shut the door behind him.

Wednesday, September 11th dawned dreary and overcast and offered hope the Germans would suspend bombing, even though Nate seemed to remember their London Blitzkrieg had begun with two solid months of uninterrupted attacks. Danny's mood fit the morning. His face wore a constant squint, and after he declared that "I'd give my iPod for a box of Dunkin' Donuts" he seemed content to go through the entire day without conversation. He allowed himself to be led into the Underground and did not question the transfer to another line at Embankment. Only when he emerged behind Nate at Covent Garden did he show any sign of curiosity.

"Are there pawn shops here?"

Nate pointed. "No. But the Savoy Hotel Strand is."

"Are we moving?"

"Not on what we have." Nate straightened the derby on his head and started toward the hotel. "If we're going to pay for forged U. S. passports, we'd better know what the real ones looked like in 1940."

"I wouldn't have thought of that," Danny admitted. "But since that damned train tour was your idea, you should be doing the lion's share of rescuing us."

Nate made no reply. For three years, he had done the lion's share of thinking, planning and negotiating in the partnership. Danny had served well half a dozen times, when muscle and intimidation were necessary during dark deals. In truth, O'Shea's main function was serving as a companion, an affable character who shared the love of travel and of constant stimulation, who did not insist on his own way except when it came to visiting waterfalls or driving exotic sports cars. Not three full days into the extremely challenging, retrograde journey, he was proving an ever-increasing liability, but Nate's sense of loyalty would never allow him to abandon his friend.

"The logical place to find an authentic passport," Nate plunged on, "would be at the U. S. embassy at Grosvenor Square. You know, when General Eisenhower set up his headquarters on the other side of the square, the area became known as 'Little America.'"

"Why do you remember trivial shit like that?" Danny marveled.

"I remember because it's interesting to me. Like the frogs in your railroad tracks. But we can't visit the Chancery building because we don't belong in this time. We don't exist anywhere on paper."

"I don't want to exist here on paper," Danny insisted.

"Right. That's why you're haunting that tunnel. I'm trying to do my level best in the likely case that doesn't work out. The likely case. Where's the other best place to find Americans in London?"

"Getting onto steamships to the States?"

"No. Believe me, Dan, this town is right now filled with Americans intent on staying here. Why? Because there are tons of money to be made. The British need tanks and planes and ships and trucks and medicine and petroleum and on and on. How many civilian contractors went to Iraq after the second conflict, in spite of all the danger?"

"Lots. So where are they in London?"

Nate held out his hand as they came to the entrance of the Savoy Hotel Strand. "We've been here twice," he hinted.

Danny's dour expression lighted. "The American Bar!"

"Bingo."

Nate had had no better idea than Danny had of where to start searching for Americans until Penelope had spoken of Hemingway and F. Scott Fitzgerald. Both notorious drinkers had been denizens of the bar that was famous for originating the White Lady and dry martini.

Nate took a moment after entering the bar to survey the clientele. Since the hour was just past noon, he figured anyone on a stool was a serious drinker. It took him only seconds to pick out his mark, from the man's accent and his loudness. He was talking at the bartender, who was doing his best to ignore the man.

The drinker's obnoxious manner guaranteed open stools on either side. Nate parked himself to the man's right, and Danny took the left. Nate kept his eyes fixed on the bartender, as if desperate for liquid reinforcement. His true intent was to invite the strange American to speak first.

"Howdy do, fella! You American?" Like Nate, his hair was thick and blond. Unlike Nate, he had it slicked down with brilliantine or some other pomade. Like Nate, he was thin. Unlike Nate, he was ugly as an English bulldog.

"I am," Nate replied.

The man held out his hand. "Allan Norman, at your service."

"Nate Allen."

The drinker sat up straighter. "What a coincidence! We're both Allans. A. N. and N. A.! Hah."

Nate pointed past Norman's shoulder. "My associate, Mr. O'Shea."

The paw went out again. "Pleasure, pleasure."

"What work are you in, Allan?" Nate asked.

"Ford. Trucks and engines. What about you?"

Nate elected an industry as far from automotive as he could think of in a moment. "We're with DuPont."

Norman's slightly bloodshot eyes brightened. "DuPont? Our bosses are members of the same fraternity. One World visionaries, right?"

The bartender took Danny's order of a double shot of whiskey, straight up.

Nate nodded for the barman's attention. "World visionaries indeed. What are you drinking, Allan?"

"What else? Dry martinis."

"Another martini for Mr. Norman, and a Manhattan for me. And could you float a sprig of parsley in the center?"

"I'm afraid we have no parsley, sir."

"What's the parsley for?" Norman obliged.

"Central Park." The automotive man laughed for several seconds, clueing Nate to use a lighthearted approach. "Over here supplying trucks for the British cause, eh?"

"No. That's Butler's job. I work with our office in Zürich and our plant in Berne." He looked around the bar, then laid his forefinger to his lips and dropped his voice to a normal tone. "Also with the Vichy plant in Poissy. That's why I drink in the American Bar. I sometimes talk too loud, and I got beat up once in a public house. These rah-rah patriot Brits don't want to understand that the United States is neutral. We're showing enough favoritism to them already. Right?"

"I suppose."

"You better say right, working for DuPont."

Danny set his shoulder bag on the bar, momentarily distracting Norman. In spite of the distraction and the bulge in the man's inside jacket pocket, Nate declined to pick him clean. For one thing, the bartender watched from only feet away. More importantly, he needed more than money from Allan Norman.

"Are you in favor of the Nazis?" Nate asked softly.

"Hell, no! But a buck is a buck. They'll get theirs in the end, but we will continue to chug along no matter what. Even if that socialist Roosevelt forces us to declare war, nothing will change. I know. I've already been given my marching orders on how to maintain the status quo. Countries come; countries go; politicians and governments rise and fall. But business is business."

The drinks arrived. Nate hoisted his Manhattan. "To business!"

Norman downed the last of the drink in his hand and reached for its replacement. "What irritates me is that I'm risking my ass every time I fly into Switzerland, even though it takes forever going the long way. Now the bombs have begun landing here, but the home office in Dearborn won't let me vacate London." He sipped his drink. "They say it wouldn't look good. What the hell do I care if it looks good if a bomb lands on me?"

"You're right. They're really putting it to you," Nate patronized.

"I don't mind flying all over the place, because nobody can really keep an eye on me and how I spend my time. In fact, I love being away from the wife. I've got one in every port, if you know what I mean." He winked conspiratorially and then giggled. "In fact even if they aren't ports. And I certainly don't mind being handed grease money under the table. Just as long as it makes life rewarding and exciting. I'm sure you're in the same situation."

Nate Allen found himself looking into a distorted mirror, and he did not like what he saw. Rather than reply, he asked, "You know what they call it when they mix vodka and orange juice?"

"No, what?"

"A Screwdriver."

"Never heard of it." He looked at the bartender. "You ever hear of a drink called a Screwdriver?"

"No, sir."

Nate realized he was probably talking about a drink yet to be invented. "It's new in the States," he retrenched. "Anyway, what would you call it if you mixed vodka and prune juice?"

"What?"

"A pile driver."

Allan Norman's half-pickled brain took a moment to process the joke. Then he burst into laughter and slapped Nate on the back.

"Good one!" he said. "I've got a million jokes myself."

For the next forty minutes, Nate and Danny swapped stories with the Ford employee while plying him with liquor. When it was clear that the man was having trouble staying on his stool, Nate said, "Is it me, or are these stools uncomfortable after a while?"

"You're right!" Norman agreed.

"You're staying at this hotel, aren't you, Allan?"

"Of course."

"What do you say we get a pitcher of martinis and retire to your room?"

"Sounds like a plan, Nate." Suddenly, Norman's eyes narrowed. "Wait a minute! I've been told London is thick with spies. Spies who talk perfect English. Or American. You tell me: Who won the World Series last year?"

"The Yankees," Danny shot back. "They won the last four years, Allan. If you want to catch spies, you better ask a harder question than that. You tell me now: Which team won the first World Series, and what was the year?"

"I have no idea."

"The answer is the Boston Red Sox, in 1903. Maybe we should suspect you of being the spy."

"Yeah, right." He turned toward the bartender. "Speaking of baseball, where's that pitcher? Har har!"

Allan Norman was out cold ten minutes after entering his hotel room. He carried his passport in the back of his oversize billfold. Nate placed it on a white tray and opened one after the next page as Danny recorded its appearance with the camera in his cell phone. Before replacing the document, Nate counted the money in the billfold.

Norman had seven five-pound notes and one ten. Nate plucked out two of the smaller denomination, sure that the inebriated American would never know what they had gone toward.

"What a lowlife," Danny proclaimed as he stopped to check his appearance in a mirror on the way to the front door.

Nate did not reply.

After finishing their mid-afternoon meal in another of the British Restaurants, Nate asked Danny to empty his pockets and shoulder bag of every bill and coin they possessed. While his partner obliged, Nate said, "I knew the instant old Allan asked about the World Series that we were home free. Good work."

While Nate followed a few college basketball and football teams, he had no interest in professional sports, turned off by the top players' salaries, their behavior and, often, their lack of heart in playing their game.

"You're the walking encyclopedia about history. I'm the Google of sports," Danny said with pride.

Danny not only watched the events but also filled in his free hours viewing reruns of competitive classics and sports quiz shows and listening to radio talk shows that debated athletes, managers, owners and sports history ad nauseum. Suddenly, Nate realized a means to soften Danny's despair if they were indeed stuck in the past.

"If you stay in this time, you're gonna be a millionaire, Daniel," he told his friend.

"Yeah? How you figure that?"

"Who won the 1940 World Series?"

"The Cincinnati Reds. They beat the Detroit Tigers four games to three."

"Who won the NBA championship?"

"Nobody. The first one was in 1947. The Philadelphia Warriors against the Chicago Stags."

"What horse won the Kentucky Derby in 1941?"

Danny's hairline slipped backward a fraction in his amazement. "Holy shit! I know the future!"

"Maybe a billionaire," Nate said. "I remember history because I like it. You remember sports because you like it. But nobody bets on history." He began counting the money.

"But I'd need a nest egg," Danny thought out loud. "I know! We have those eight emeralds."

"We do indeed. But I have a feeling we'll need them to purchase our passports. You might have to actually work for–" Nate's eyes swept over the short piles of coins and bills he had spread over the table. "There's almost two pounds missing." He looked up at Danny in time to see him trying to erase a guilty face. "You met a woman last night in that pub," he said with assurance.

Danny sighed. "Damn. I can't put anything past you."

"Why should you try? We're partners." In spite of his words, he collected all the bills and coins.

Danny tapped his forefinger hard on the table. "I spent the money because I don't agree with you about getting home. Doors don't open just one way. That tunnel or that redheaded man will give us a way back. I'm thinking now, though, that it will be at some fixed, logical time. Like next Saturday night, one week later to the second. Or exactly one month from when we passed through."

"We can't afford to wait around here," Nate argued. "Not on the lack of money we–"

"We can't afford not to wait around here!" Danny shot back. "I can barely stand surviving under these conditions as it is. Even if bombs weren't raining out of the sky, this might as well be the Roman Empire as far as I'm concerned. Christ's sake, I have to pull a chain from a tank in the air to flush a toilet! I hate the taste of wood in my mouth. I want dental floss, not toothpicks. On the other hand, women will always be women. I got me some female companionship so I wouldn't go nuts."

"But did you have to buy it?"

Danny's nostrils flared at the question. "Hey, I have never paid for sex in my life! I bought the place a round of drinks so they would accept me. It was a damned local pub. You know strangers aren't welcome unless they buy. Then this incredible woman comes up to me. Gwen Lamb. Is that a name or what?"

"I'm melting already."

"She's thirty and built like Marilyn Monroe. That super curvy figure."

"You didn't mention the name 'Marilyn Monroe', did you?"

"No. I thought she was from this time, but I wasn't sure."

"Good thing."

"I'm learning. Gwen's old man bought it at Dunkirk, just like Penny's brother. In fact, they were in the same regiment. She lives just around the block from the Mileses."

"And the bereaved Widow Lamb has been awful lonely," Nate supplied.

"Spare me your sarcasm, pal. She has been lonely. It's not like she was on the prowl. She was wearing a black armband. She can't date. It hasn't been long enough. She'd be run out of the neighborhood on a rail if she did. Everybody knows everybody, and everybody gossips. We talked for a while; she told me exactly where she lived, just like it was a signal. Then she moved off, hung around with a couple other women until she finished her pint, and left. I stayed in the pub playing darts for about twenty minutes more. Then I went to see her."

"Just walked up to her front door?"

"Nobody saw. It was about ten minutes into the air raid. The street was clear."

"You never paid for sex in your life, but after you pounded her into her mattress you left her a pound."

"You're starting to piss me off, Nathaniel," Danny said needlessly. "She didn't ask for money. Not directly anyway. She told me how hard it was making ends meet without a husband. And she had just lost her job because of the raids. You think she was lying?"

"No."

"All right. So I left the pound on her kitchen table on the way out her back door. One lousy pound. She was sleeping upstairs. I tell you, she's the best lay I've ever had."

"And still you want to get back to our time?"

"I'll see her a few more times. Then, like you always say, the true excitement will have worn off. And what else do you always say, Nate? What's your life motto: 'I shall never pass this way again.' With any luck, in the next few years she'll become the second best lay of my life, and then the third and fourth. Gimme some of that money."

"For her?"

"Yeah for her. A little, over time. But mostly because it doesn't make sense you carrying everything."

"You'll carry what we sell today at the pawn shops."

Danny looked down to mop up the last of his mutton stew with a crust of bread. "Okay. Just don't let this nightmare we're in start dividing us, Big Fox."

Following their now-traditional supper at the Miles' home, Nate and Danny declined listening to the radio and playing draughts, which both men were surprised to learn was the same as checkers. Worden had a night off from ARP warden duties, but Penny was needed for her tour as ambulance driver. Instead, the Americans went to Danny's adopted Old George pub.

Several of the hardcore patrons were singing "Tipperary" as the two entered the corner tavern. Danny was greeted like he was Old George himself, and Nate grudgingly put down several coins to pay for "pints all around." Gwen Lamb occupied her accustomed place at the end of the bar. Nate assessed her as kewpie doll pretty, but Father Time and the war were working against her. Her platinum blond job betrayed dirty-blond roots. She wore a pencil-thin skirt that made her sit sidesaddle on the bar stool, exposing long, well-turned legs. Her red blouse had huge sleeves and a plunging neckline that showed the generous upper curves of her breasts. Her lipstick and painted nails matched her blouse, working hard to nullify her black armband. She was smoking, and Nate noted that even if she did not have enough money for food, she could afford imported Camels. Penny's speech about stockings caused him to study her legs as well, and he saw that she wore real nylons, although she had a small snag near her ankle and laddering that she had arrested with clear nail polish.

"My goodness, another handsome Yank!" she exclaimed, after Danny made the introduction. "Are you also working for your government, Mr. Allen?"

"I am. And what do you do, Mrs. Lamb?" Nate asked, putting just a little emphasis on her title.

"I was working at the Millwall docks, at MacDougall's Flour Mill. But, of course, it was bombed. They were always warning us not to smoke anywhere around. Did you know that fine flour powder will go up like gunpowder if it ignites?"

"I did know that," Nate admitted.

"A clever one you are. Well, all it took was one incendiary bomb. I'm getting another job next week at a bakery." She shrugged. "Taking the place of a woman who died on Monday night from a bomb. Terrible times, just terrible."

The radio was tuned to dance music.

"Would you care to dance, Mrs. Lamb?" Nate asked.

Danny smiled and sauntered toward the dartboard. He knew that his partner would take care of the woman and simultaneously dispel suspicions among the regulars that Danny and Gwen had something special going on.

The dance was the slow "Moonlight Serenade." Up close to the woman's face, Nate realized that, even given the pub's low lighting and the complete blackout of the previous night's air raid, Danny could only believe Gwen was thirty if he had fallen in love or was needier than he had ever been. He pegged her at closer to forty.

The mood at the pub was upbeat. As Nate listened to the conversations and was, in fact, invited into a couple of them, he realized that this generation had much less than his in terms of material things to lose. They spoke with passion about ideas rather than possessions. They had clearly been pre-hardened to the current situation by the deprivations of the Depression. When talking of defending their country and eventually "beating the Bosch," they wrapped themselves in a buoyant bravado that would have sounded ridiculous in the 21st century but which Nate realized had the same plain-speaking sentimentality as the dialogue in the period's movies.

What was just as alien to Nate was that even though the pub's patrons were blue-collar workers, they spoke with a rich vocabulary and took pride in picturesque turns of phrase. While they all were drinking, none peppered his or her speech with profanity. In his own time, he hardly ever stood in a line or traveled the sidewalks of New York without hearing four-letter expletives filling in gaps in conversation as often as the grating "y'know" and "So, like, he goes." Nate consulted his watch. Midnight was almost upon them. Gwen had left the pub half an hour earlier, in the company of two other women.

He collected Danny and left the pub to a chorus of cheers.

Pedaling the borrowed Miles bicycles through the blackout, Danny and Nate separated at Gwen's house. Nate continued on for several streets, intending to patrol the Underground tunnels himself and see what he could. On the way, he heard the wail of an ambulance siren. Someone had suffered a crisis other than one fallen from the sky. He dropped his feet to the pavement and listened to the siren fade. Then he turned around and headed back toward the Wilcox house.

The second bombing run did not reach London until after one a.m.

## CHAPTER NINE

An early morning rain scrubbed much of the dust from the air and washed London's pavements and buildings. It seemed to Nate as if the celebrated English climate had been ordained eons before to deny the Germans too much dirtying of the capital city. Where the Underground emerged from the earth to become regular train lines, the stations looked much as they normally would. However, as he and Danny traveled closer to the heart of London, they saw how citizens had been allowed at last to stake claims on sections of the platforms and corridors with their pillows, blankets and clothing. Policemen patrolled to insure that the wretched refugees stayed at least six feet back from the platform edges. Workmen carrying tools, loads of lumber and stanchions of metal weaved around the train travelers.

"This sucks, this sucks, this really, really sucks," Danny intoned under his breath.

Nate ignored the comment and studied the newspaper he had picked up from a rubbish basket. News of bombing damage was not expressed in the negative but rather concentrated on what had been missed and how quickly response teams had "put the trouble right." Instead of photographs of bomb havoc, the newspaper featured images of Londoners hard at their jobs or holding their fingers aloft in a V. The caption beneath one photograph of a crowd of Cockney men read, "We can take it!"

Nate led Danny to the Surabaya. They entered and claimed one of its dark corners. Almost an hour passed, with Danny complaining every few minutes about the lack of cell phones and pagers that would have eliminated such a waste of time. When Alex Bennett walked through the door, his head pivoted until he found Nate's face. Then, as quickly as he had entered, he walked out.

"Let's go," Nate said.

Danny got up less quickly. "He didn't look like he wanted to do business."

"He just doesn't want to conduct it here. You have the Webley in your pocket, Big Dog?"

"Three seconds from barking."

"Okay. Let me do the talking."

"Don't I always?" Danny recited.

By the time the Americans emerged into daylight, Bennett was halfway down the street, heading south. He glanced back only once, long enough to assure himself that the two men followed.

Two streets later, Bennett stopped and waited. He dropped his cigarette butt and did not bother to grind it out with his foot.

"Decided to do business, I see," he said as Nate and Danny came up beside him. "Good day to you, Mr. O'Shea."

"Maybe to you, pal, but thanks anyway."

"Here is my place of business." Bennett's hand swept out past a building that had been leveled by a bomb and toward its neighbor, which had its north wall neatly torn off, exposing the first and second floors to what had become a light drizzle. "Curious how chance operates. A high explosive bomb annihilates a building but starts no fire. Carves off one wall of the next building and leaves the rest." He gestured behind him. "Across the street, one tiny incendiary spike burns down three structures, but up the same street three land on a roof and burn out harmlessly. Who knows why. That's my office." He pivoted and pointed to the second story of the building with its façade sheared off.

The exposed floor showed two rooms. The one close to the street had a large desk, completely undamaged, two of its legs positioned almost where the floor joists jutted out. Nate could see two file cabinets against the opposite wall, under the shelter of the remaining roof.

Bennett cocked his head at a furtive noise within the first floor of the building. "Wait here, please." He loped into the piles of destroyed lumber. A few moments later, a high-pitched series of yelps came from the shadows toward the back of the building. Bennett returned, holding a small length of pipe. One end was coated in blood.

"Looters are the bane of society," he declared, dropping the pipe onto the pavement where it clattered and rolled. "If you would step into my office, such as it is."

Just before they came to the stairs, they saw a boy about twelve years of age, lying unconscious among a pile of boxes. A grey sack lay by his outstretched hand. The side of his head was spattered with red blood still welling from a fresh wound.

"He'll live. This way," Bennett called down.

The Englishman made much of pulling two café chairs under the partial roof and wiping the rain from their seats with his handkerchief. "Sit, please! My acquaintance can indeed produce passports for you, and he can do it within several days." He reached deep into his raincoat pocket and pulled out a United States of America passport. He handed it to Nate. "Before we negotiate, I am certain you wish to see the quality of the work."

Nate examined page after page. It looked exactly like the one owned by Allan Norman. He held it out to Danny. Danny declined to take it and glowered at Bennett.

"How do we know that isn't somebody's real passport that you stole?"

"Excellent question, Mr. O'Shea," Bennett responded. "If you'll look on the fourth page, you'll see that the 'official entry stamp' to Jolly Olde England is dated for Saturday next. The gentleman who has already paid for this has business to clean up and doesn't wish to leave for another fortnight. You see, some people have the ability to play with time itself."

Danny exchanged a quick glance with Nate, took the passport, examined the page, and passed the forgery back to his partner.

"All right, we're impressed," Nate admitted. "How much for two?"

"Two hundred and fifty pounds. Each."

Danny threw up his hands. "Is he out of his mind?" he asked Nate.

"That includes my commission," Bennett said calmly. "You're not fools. You've surely priced the competition. I can tell you that what they sell is rubbish and will get you caught. Never mind that their price is lower. You get what you pay for. I'm sure from your expressions that they did not show you the kind of work I can have created for you."

"Five hundred pounds is a small fortune," Nate stated.

Bennett made a dismissing sound in his throat. "If you call that a fortune, then I'm sorry for you. Five hundred pounds won't even buy a decent automobile. You're anxious to return to the United States, where the streets are paved with gold. And, more importantly, where they are not pocked with bomb craters. At least not yet."

"Even if we could raise that much, we'd still need to buy two passages on a ship," Nate told the man.

"Sign on a cargo ship as deck hands if you must."

"There's another way home," Danny argued to his partner. "That's the route we have to take."

Nate shook his head. He was rapidly tiring of his partner's insistence that return via the tunnel was possible.

"I don't know what you mean by another way home," Bennett said, in an off-hand manner, "but I do know there's another way to pay for your passports. Earn them."

The offer did not take Nate by surprise. He had sensed that Bennett had a broader agenda than supplying phony documents.

"Talk."

"There is the opportunity for me and a select few to make enough money to buy a small island nation and issue our own passports."

"Go on."

"Knowledge is truly power, you know. A few men in charge believe that the smaller and less obvious the transport of a great deal of money is, the safer it will be. The payroll for all those in military service along our southern shores will not be delivered this week. In fact, disruption due to the bombings has thrown the pay system into a tizzy. The Bank of England is in the process of printing notes for this prodigious payout, and they won't be ready until around Thursday of next week. At that time, one armored lorry will be charged with the delivery. It will be disguised as a refrigerated van and followed by one sedan carrying four soldiers"

"You want to rob your own country's servicemen?"

"I plan to deprive His Majesty's sailors, soldiers and pilots, as well as government workers in that region, of their salaries. More than 230,000 of them as I understand it."

"Rather unpatriotic of you," Nate said, pronouncing the words with a British accent.

"They'll get their money…eventually. The beauty is that this job requires but four men, and only two risk identification. It would be most beneficial if those two had no records in England."

"If you're worried about identification," Danny broke in, "I'm assuming that nobody is supposed to get hurt."

Bennett leaned against the inner wall. "Absolutely. Killing stirs Scotland Yard like bats from a cave. Losing two-and-a-half million pounds is not so bad for a government in the grand scheme of things. However, their loss would not only get you home but also put a thousand pounds immediately in your pockets and place another twenty thousand in an Irish bank, waiting for you to wire for it once you're back across the pond."

"Doesn't seem like a fair split," Nate said.

"It does when you hear how little you have to do and how little risk it involves."

"So...tell us."

"No, indeed. I really don't know enough about the two of you. I've had eyes and ears out for the past two days checking on your names and Mr. Allen's description, and I've gotten nowhere. In one way that's the best possible news. In another, it could spell disaster if you're working for the authorities. You didn't get into the British Isles with genuine passports. How is it you're here?"

"That's our secret," Nate answered. "You'll just have to keep digging to prove to yourself that we don't exist."

"Rely on it, Mr. Allen."

Nate glanced past Bennett to a break in the cloudy sky. "Do we get our passports right after the job is completed?"

"Before you can blink. Along with your thousand pounds. And it won't be the fresh stuff, because they'll be looking for those serial numbers. I need you to be gone as swiftly as possible once the job is done. The passports and enough money for liner berths will give us both what we desire."

Nate looked at Danny. Danny shrugged.

"Okay," Nate said. "You've got yourself a deal."

"Smashing!" Bennett reached into his jacket and pulled out his wallet. From what appeared to be at least a dozen identical bills, he extracted two and passed them to Nate and Danny. "These are fresh from the Old Lady of Threadneedle Street herself. Consider it an advance and a token of faith up front for signing on."

The currency was five-pound notes. Danny rubbed his fingers back and forth over the minutely raised lettering and figures. "Are you sure your forging friend isn't in the counterfeiting business as well?"

Bennett laughed heartily. "If he was, would I have to rob the Bank of England?" He moved with speed toward one of the file cabinets. He produced a ring with a good dozen keys on it and stuck a small one into the lock at the top of the cabinet. From the middle drawer he pulled out a Graflex accordion camera. He popped it open and perched his posterior on the corner of the desk. Nate's eyes widened at the maneuver. Bennett looked over his shoulder and down at the precipitous drop directly behind his desk. "Ah, yes. Well, I've lived so much of my life on the figurative edge that a literal edge doesn't bother me. Up against a blank wall, if you please. And then you need to provide me your dates of birth, home addresses and so forth."

"I feel like the guys at the St. Valentine's Day Massacre," Danny muttered, as he squared his shoulders and pressed his back against the wall.

"When do we learn about the particulars?" Nate asked, as Bennett took his portrait.

"After I do more checking on you. On Saturday afternoon at two you will stand outside Victoria Station at the triangle of Grosvenor Gardens and Buckingham Palace Road. If, for some reason, that area becomes badly damaged, go instead to Sloane Square and stand in the shadow of Holy Trinity. The Germans have been avoiding the posh districts. I believe they shall continue to do so until the primary targets have been eliminated. Let's snap an insurance shot, shall we?"

Once they were well out of earshot of the ruined office building, Nate said, "Give me that five pound note."

Danny fished into his pocket. "You think it's fake?"

"I know so little about English money of this period, how could I tell?" He studied Danny's, then his. "The numbers are sequential. That would make sense. He said he got them directly from the Bank of England." He handed Danny back his bill.

"I don't care about the money," Danny confided. "What spooked me was what he said about playing with time."

"That had to be a coincidence," Nate assured.

"You think? Ordinarily, I'd agree with you. But consider this: We are a pair of clever scam artists. How diabolical would it be if criminals from another time pulled us through to help them with a heist precisely because we can't be identified?"

"We're not heist artists, Danny. And you are going insane."

Danny shook his large head vigorously. "This whole situation is insane. Meeting him Saturday afternoon will be a waste of time."

"Why do you say that?"

"Because Saturday night we're going to make our own Great Escape via a tunnel. I'm gonna catch that redheaded railway guy and make him send us back to where we belong."

Nate rejected arguing that he had stumbled upon Bennett via his own stratagem and instead said, "And what if your latest theory is right? Then it's Bennett who can get us back."

Danny considered Nate's words. "All right. We go ahead with

Saturday afternoon."

"Thank you. And if none of this works, we figure out how to sail safely back to the America of 1940, and you'll become a multi-millionaire. Who won the MVP for the 1960 Super Bowl?"

"There wasn't a professional football championship until 1967. That year it was Bart Starr. He won the next year as well," Danny recited, trying not to smile.

"Who was the first player not a quarterback to win?"

"Chuck Howley."

"You're golden, pal. Believe me, I'm pulling for the appearance of your redheaded man. But there's no point in just idling around until Saturday night, is there?"

Danny leered wickedly. "Except that the Widow Lamb doesn't begin work again for a few days."

"There will be time enough for her as well. We need to do our homework on Mr. Alex Bennett. For example, learning as much as we can about who rented the second floor of that half-destroyed building. There is no way we're dancing with him without knowing a great deal more. Let's go back to that first pawnshop up in Camden Town. I saw a reflex camera with a long lens for a very reasonable price."

# CHAPTER TEN

On the way back from Camden Town, Danny and Nate foraged at food markets and scavenged a dressed whole chicken, four eggs, two sticks of butter and a can of Mandarin orange slices. Only when they presented their prizes to Mrs. Miles did they learn that chickens were not being rationed. The other items, however, were rare indeed.

"Maybe the reason eggs are so precious," Danny theorized, "is because chickens aren't."

Millicent's laughter cut through the tears that their presents had caused. "There are simply no citrus fruits to be had," she lamented, admiring the tin of tiny orange slices. "Nor bananas. I fear that the entire country shall have scurvy soon, like the Jack Tars of centuries past. That's why I push raw carrots and turnips on this family, even though I despise turnips."

Because they had returned early to the Miles house, Nate and Danny were able to watch Millicent prepare a meal and hear at the same time the depressing particulars of rationing. Each person in a family had a registration number. Because Millicent shopped for three, she had to be able to produce three numbered identity cards. Ration books lasted six months, and the old book had to be turned in to get a new one. Coupons good for a week or two's worth of an item were marked and cut out.

"I have the list memorized," she said as she worked. "We're each allowed four ounces of bacon or ham, one pound of meat, four ounces of butter and two of margarine. Margarine on bread makes me gag, so I cook with it. Four ounces of cheese, eight of sugar, two of cooking fat, two of tea, three pints of milk and three ounces of sweets. It's a terrible burden, especially for us cooks, but I'm of the mind that many in our country will come out of this war healthier than they went in. There's been far too much eating of fatty meats and of chocolate bars." Looking at her spare frame, Nate believed that Mrs. Miles had lived by her tenet long before the rationing. He asked, "What about eggs?"

"Eggs, oh yes! One small egg per person every fortnight. That's what's so wonderful about your gift. And the butter! With some of the sugar and flour I hoarded before we declared war on the Germans, I shall make a splendid cake."

Nate pictured in his mind's eye fifty-thousand-square-foot American markets with perhaps fifty thousand products as he listened to the fact that tinned food was not as stringently rationed. Mrs. Miles mistook his facial expression and hastened to assure that the public got sixteen points each week toward buying anything in that group they pleased. Jams, condensed milk, tinned fish, as well as Spam and powdered eggs from the United States were especially popular. Neither bread nor vegetables were rationed, but exotic vegetables such as tomatoes from foreign shores could not be gotten. Fruits were also confined to those grown in the British Isles.

Dinner consisted of chicken and dumplings, followed by a salad of lettuce and carrots. Mrs. Miles was as good as her word regarding dessert. It was a pound cake with a hint of vanilla, topped by a sugar glaze and three slices of Mandarin orange each. The spread put Mr. Miles and Penny into better moods. Mr. Miles shared his "special intelligence" with the table.

"Epping Forest is a park preserve of about 6,000 acres, just northeast of London," he explained. "The estimate is that 8,000 people have fled to it and are camping out like Robin Hood's Merry Men. Many are from Poplar, Bermondsey, Silvertown, Woolwich and East Ham. Yesterday's estimate was that 45,000 in all have had their homes destroyed. I suppose they're all right for now, but provision must be made when the cold sets in within a few weeks. Meantime, the military are moving in more artillery and concentrating the searchlights on narrower sky paths. That should start to bring down more of those Heinkels and Junker 88s." He scowled. "The blasted heathens have hit several cemeteries. Thrown bodies out into the open. It's not bad enough they slaughter the living; they're desecrating the hallowed dead as well. But the King and the Royal Family are still in residence at Buckingham Palace, so order prevails. Long live the King!"

The group toasted the king's health with apple juice.

Worden elected not to volunteer for ARP duty on Thursdays because "I would be useless for work on Fridays if I didn't rest at least one night." Penny rushed out to her ambulance driver service, leaving Nate and Danny with her parents. The battery-fed wireless radio in the Anderson shelter served as their entertainment. For a time they listened to the jovial rantings of 'Lord Haw Haw,' a traitorous Englishman who broadcast into England to demoralize the citizenry.

"We find him largely ridiculous and just annoying enough to harden our resolve," Worden pronounced. "But that doesn't mean we won't hang him high when the war's over."

At that moment, Lord Haw Haw was saying, "There is a store in Liverpool owned by the Jews at the bottom of Brownlow Hill. They are members of the international Jewish conspiracy to control the world. Others Jews in this conspiracy were Sigmund Freud, who tried to confuse us about our thinking with his ridiculous theories, and Karl Marx, who poisoned the world with the pseudo-utopian farce of communism. Isn't it interesting that a man who calls religion 'the opium of the masses' was able to fool so many Russian peasants into thinking that they would ever be equal to their commissars? They have simply traded a tyrannical tsar for a nest of tyrants. Fearful of incurring the hatred of those people they live beside but with whom they never mix, the Jews seek to put up others like shields in front of them, to advance their control. They cannot hide from the ever-widening vengeance of the Third Reich! Very soon there will be an empty pool of Jews in Liverpool."

"Cheeky blighters," Worden exclaimed. "It's not bad enough to bomb us, but now they announce precisely who they'll bomb. It will be interesting to see if they can do it."

"It's interesting enough if there are actually Jews at the bottom of that hill," Danny added. He had rested his chin on his interlaced fingers and was leaning close to the apparatus, apparently captivated by the notion of radio for something other than rock music.

Later in the evening, they dialed the BBC to "It's That Man Again," followed by "Name That Tune" with Violet Carson at the piano. Predictably, Danny and Nate were terrible at guessing. In the middle of a new tune, the sounds went dead.

"Bother!" Millicent said with exasperation. "The accumulator's run out of energy."

Nate consulted his wristwatch. "I think the thing to do is to catch some sleep before the night raid begins." He stood. "Thanks much for your continued hospitality."

Mrs. Miles crossed to him and pecked him on the cheek. "Thanks to both of you. You've made us feel safer. You've also helped fill in the void of our son's death."

"In spite of all your complaining, you're starting to accommodate to this time," Nate observed to Danny as they entered the Wilcox house. "You actually enjoyed those radio broadcasts."

Danny waggled his hand. "They weren't bad. But they won't take the place of HDTV, Tivo and Blue Ray. I'm more than ready to go home this Saturday night. I wonder if we'll find ourselves back on September 7th or jumped ahead to the 14th. That will take some explaining to everyone looking for us. Not to mention the hotel bill!"

Nate held his tongue. He looked up into a sky strewn with enough cumulus clouds to mask the nearly full moon. The Wilcoxes had not installed their Anderson shelter as well as Worden Miles had. The space was damp, with a coating of water on the floor from the day's rain. The pair elected to dare the Wilcox house unless the intensity of the night bombing became such that it would be folly not to run to the shelter.

Nate turned off the house's gas and climbed the stairs holding a lit candle. He rid himself of the grit and dust of the day with a thorough sponge bath and then exchanged his smelly clothing for a nightgown that Mr. Wilcox had left behind. He climbed into a soft bed with cool sheets. The darkness and silence were unlike that of any major city he had ever slept in. Under other circumstances, they would have relaxed him and coaxed him swiftly to sleep. But, working in the world's major cities and in the overpopulated 21st century, the darkness and silence were unnatural, alien. He realized the days were slipping by with no guarantee of resolution. Not since his youth had he ever felt such lack of control. He despaired that Danny's hopes were anything more than a pipe dream, and he deeply mistrusted the smarmy Alex Bennett.

Nate still lay awake when the bombers arrived. Their sounds grew progressively closer, and they seemed massive. Nate dashed into Danny's room and roused him from his usual sleep of the dead. They reached the backyard shelter just as several bombs whistled down into Bethnal Green. No high explosives impacted on their street. Nate surmised that the Germans had anticipated a concentration of barrage balloons and anti-aircraft batteries newly massed around the docks and had altered their targets to areas north and west. At least 150 bombers flew close enough to the district to distinguish their individual engines.

Every fifteen minutes, they risked darting outside to check the Wilcox's and Miles' roofs for incendiary spikes. Nate saw with dismay that the clouds had perversely disappeared, and what would soon be called a "bomber's moon" was providing excellent illumination for the darkened city.

All clear sirens sounded after ninety minutes, but the clatter and wail of emergency vehicle bells and sirens went on long afterward. Danny and Nate returned to the Wilcox bedrooms. Within minutes, Danny's snores ripped the air like a chain saw. Nate closed his door, but he still could not find sleep. In the middle of the raid, a thought had occurred to him. Because it was truly terrifying, he did not share it with his partner. With the possible exception of the ambiguous Nostradamus, no one from the past had ever successfully predicted the future. The clear implication was that anyone else who had shared the fate of Danny and Nate and been whisked back in time had not lived on in the past long enough to communicate their precious knowledge.

Nature or the same fate that had put them in a wrong time had invariably and permanently corrected the error in short order.

## CHAPTER ELEVEN

Among the streets hit on the south side of the Thames the previous night was the one where Alex Bennett had his office. A day later, the sheered-off building lay as flat as the one beside it and the burned-out ones across the street. The desk and two chairs had either been blown apart or consumed in the ensuing fire. The two file cabinets were charred black and half-buried under bricks.

From the inhabitants of the buildings remaining on the street Nate was unable to find anyone who could tell him who had done business on the second floor of the now-flattened structure. Nor did any of them recognize the name Alex Bennett. He retreated from the area and retraced his circuitous route back to where Danny stood in a narrow alley directly across from the Surabaya.

"Any sign of him?" Nate asked.

Danny stepped aside to give Nate a better view of the pub. "No. I hope we didn't buy that camera for nothing."

"Maybe he went in before you arrived," Nate speculated.

"Now you see why I suggested we bring Gwen with us. She was willing enough."

"We have no right to drag your Mrs. Lamb into this."

"We could have given her half a crown. She could have walked in there and been out by now. Hell, she might have been able to get him to take her back to his place."

"And that would be all right with you?" Nate asked.

"Oh, she would have found some excuse to leave before her virtue…whatever she has left…was compromised."

"Well, she's not here," Nate said, tiring of Danny's ifs and mights.

"What else can we do?" Danny said, shifting his weight impatiently. "It doesn't take two of us to stand in this alley. Maybe he's listed in the telephone directory under Alex Bennett, even if it isn't his real name."

"Where do we get a directory around here?" Nate countered, looking up at a sky strewn with fleecy clouds, like lambs wandering a vast field. "Not in the pub. No, like it or not, we have no place better to be. This is called surveillance, Danny. Cops do it all the time."

"Which is why I'll never be a cop. I thought bouncer duty outside a club was boring. At least I had the freaky clientele to stare at. This was a bad idea to come out today anyway. Friday the 13th? Watch a bomb land right at my feet."

"A bomb could just as well have landed in the bed you were so loath to get out of," Nate pointed out. As well as the dark, Daniel O'Shea counted several superstitions as fears. Triskaidekaphobia ranked in his book with walking under ladders, breaking mirrors and spilling salt.

Danny reached into his shoulder bag and pulled out his iPod. "I had to put in my spare battery this morning. Thank God it's an extended life version. If we're still here when it runs out, you will not want to be around me."

Nate looked down at the Exakta SLR camera that hung from a strap around his neck. Beyond the fact that the camera was not digital, it was strange to him in many other ways. The viewfinder was meant to be looked at straight down. Both the shutter release and the film advance were on the left sides. The shutter release was on the front of the camera and not the top. The pawnshop manager had explained that the owner had sold the German camera in a fit of patriotic zeal, and that no other Englishman had wanted it, in spite of a good price. Its main virtue to Nate was that it came with an 80mm Tessar long-range lens. The manager seemed to know his cameras, and he was very amused to have Nate imagine there were such things as 150 or 200mm SLR telephoto lenses in 1940. The 80mm bayonet-mount lens was the best available to the private citizen for bringing a subject closer. The inner-London street was typically narrow, and the equally narrow alleyway was dark enough for someone spying on the Surabaya to stand within 75 feet of its front door. Nevertheless, the lens could not deliver a shot better than a man's full length at that distance.

Forty-five minutes dragged by, with Danny muttering intermittent complaints on either side of his retreat to relieve his bladder against the back alley wall. As he adjusted his iPod headphones, Nate pushed him back into deeper shadows. Nate snapped a photo, flipped the film advance lever, and snapped another.

"Was that him?" Danny asked.

"Yes. I just hope the shutter was fast enough to keep his face sharp. Darned clouds had to mask the sun"

"Shouldn't we follow him?" Danny asked, urging Nate forward with his free hand.

"Let him get a good distance. We do not want to piss the man off."

They lost Alex Bennett after one street. All they knew was that he had headed farther south, in the direction of Tower Bridge Road. They could not be sure that he had not taken the Underground, whence he could move off in any direction. He was not, however, on the northbound platform when they arrived.

When the Americans emerged onto Piccadilly Circus to bring the film to the only location they knew for developing, they saw that the heart of the city had borne the brunt of the previous night's bombing. One large building was only scarred in the front, with a section of its sidewalk badly damaged from a bomb impact. Three doors down, most probably from the same rack of bombs, a building was still smoldering, its insides burned away so that it seemed like the skeleton of a devoured beetle. Another multi-floored structure had its façade partially stripped away and looked to Nate like the back of a child's doll house, with much of the interior furnishings still intact. With so much film still unexposed, he captured half a dozen images.

While he advanced the film, the high-pitched noise of fighter engines came rapidly close. A Messerschmitt roared low over the city. Nate swung the camera up, even though he figured he was too late to capture the image. But the plane raised its wing flaps and began to climb rapidly, staying in the frame. Nate pressed his finger to the shutter release. At that instant, a Spitfire also came into the shot. As Nate looked from the viewfinder and glanced up, the British fighter dipped its left wing and went into a climbing turn.

"The Kraut is probably trying an Immelmann," Nate speculated.

"A what?" Danny asked.

"A dogfight maneuver. A half loop and then a half turn to right his plane. Yes, there he goes. It's a quick way to reverse direction." Nate captured another shot, even though he knew the planes would be tiny. "But the RAF pilot is right after him. I'll bet the German was doing photographic reconnaissance of last night's hits."

Behind them, ack-ack guns opened up. Another Spitfire zoomed in from the west.

"He'll be lucky to get home," Nate reckoned.

"So will we." Danny gave his mate a shove. "Especially if we stand out in the middle of a London street. Let's get the film developed."

Rush developing required two working days. Yet again, Danny railed at the primitive conditions. This time the annoyance was the inability to produce one-hour, double glossy prints.

"Not to mention making digital 8x10s on your own HP All-in-One," Danny added.

Nate insisted that they stay in the West End for a time, walking up Charring Cross Road and along Oxford Street. His head shook constantly at the degree of destruction. Enormous buildings had been gutted. Stretches of smaller structures were flattened. Bricks, concrete, cinder blocks and twisted steel lay in rough piles across roads. An elevator shaft stood open to view. Dust and ash swirled with every gust of wind. Great pools of filthy water lay in recently excavated holes. Sewers appeared half-exposed. The remains of roofs hung off their buildings like cardboard flaps from carelessly opened food packages.

On the streets, the buses and trams had stiff wire screening recently installed to protect the riders from flying debris. Burned-out vehicles had been dragged from the roads. Shop windows were either boarded up or crisscrossed with wide rolls of shipping tape. One plucky owner with nine large panes of glass, three high and three wide, had created a tic-tac-toe game from the taping. Several Union Jacks flew prominently. Workers in half a dozen different uniforms swarmed like ants, putting right as much as possible as quickly as possible. And everywhere, the British citizen moved on about his or her business, embodying that uniquely English word, "indefatigable."

"How many people from our time get to walk through the Blitz?" Nate marveled.

"Only two that I know," Danny replied without enthusiasm. "What do we do when we get back those shots of Bennett?"

"Nothing, unless he tries to double-cross us. We can't be bringing them to the police now; they'd want to know who we are and why we're doing it. We can't use your Mrs. Lamb to do it either. If the police are indeed looking for Bennett, you told her about the Surabaya. They'd have it out of her before you could say 'Bob's your uncle.'"

"I would never say that," Danny affirmed.

Nate smiled. "If he delivers those passports to us, we don't want him arrested until we're safely in the States."

"So you're telling me we have to trust him."

"No. We listen to the rest of his spiel. If it sounds too crazy or too dangerous, we're back to square one."

Danny thought about square one for half a block. "Since we can't do anything else, let's check the tunnel. Maybe we'll get real lucky."

Nate resisted sighing. "Why not?"

The Friday evening supper at the Miles residence was bubble and squeak, freshly cooked vegetables and potatoes plus leftovers from the previous days, fried up in a large pan. Since bread was not rationed, Nate and Danny had bought two loaves, both of which were consumed by the end of the meal.

According to Worden Miles the living gazette, on the 11th the RAF had lost 29 fighters while taking down only 25 of the enemy. The news was being suppressed. During the summer's fighting, British fighter pilots had downed two German planes for every one they lost. Worden worried that a new version of German planes might have gained the edge with larger engines or more maneuverability.

Nate looked around the table. Aside from Danny, who mopped up his plate with gusto as if he had not a care in the world, everyone else looked close to tears. He knew how disheartened he felt after viewing the destruction in downtown London and could only begin to imagine the Miles family mood. No army across the whole of Europe and North Africa had stopped the Nazi war machine. Worden, Millicent and Penny had every reason to expect that Hitler would invade. They would hardly believe that the madman would all but abandon his air war against England within a few more months. As he had done in the Underground, Nate was compelled to offer some hope.

"It will all work out fine, Mr. Miles. They'll be overextended very soon. They've gobbled up too much. Think about how difficult it is to hold onto North Africa, Greece and everything in Europe but Italy, Spain, Switzerland and Portugal. I predict that Hitler will make the fatal mistake of attacking Russia next year. He badly needs oil and gas. When he does, the same thing will happen to him that happened to Napoleon. Russia is just too big, and it has too many tough people. The Nazis have hit their high-water mark. You just have to keep on keeping on."

Danny had stopped chewing and pointed to his partner. "Yeah, listen to him. This guy is a real student of history."

After the meal, Nate and Penny walked into the back yard with the dirty dinner bowls, to deposit their few remains onto the compost heap. While Nate scraped, Penny went to the gateway trellis and examined the Tudor rose bushes whose tendrils wound in and out of the wooden slats. Most of the petals lay on the ground, as if a wedding had recently been performed in the yard.

"You must be right about the dust and soot," she said in a sad voice. "Usually the blooms last until first frost."

"They're wild and strong," Nate offered. "They'll be back next year."

"But will I?" Penny did not wait for a reply but bent and scooped up a handful of the fallen petals and brought them to her nose. When she inhaled, she immediately sneezed. "They smell like ash." She took several steps toward wilted flowers on tall stalks that had big leaves.

"I don't recognize them," Nate confessed.

"They're hollyhocks. Dying as well. Ah well. They've made their seeds. Mum will tuck them in a sack for next year. The growing season is all but ended at any rate."

"Nevertheless, it's sad to see beautiful things die," Nate said at her side.

Penny leaned toward him and whispered, "Let's go dancing again."

"When?"

"Tonight. This is my night off."

"All right," he replied, profoundly pleased. The tips of her long hair touched his neck and drew goose bumps. "The YWCA?"

"No. It's too noisy, too crowded and they don't play the best music."

"Then where?"

"I have a side-door key to the school where I'm supposed to be teaching. The gymnasium is a perfect place."

After supper, Nate changed into the dress shirt and grabbed the patent leather shoes he had stolen from the Ritz Hotel. He left his blazer and grey slacks behind as well, wearing the suit he had purchased earlier in the week. While he could not bring himself to use pomade, he wetted his hair, parted it down the center, and combed it back, trying for the Robert Redford look in *The Sting*.

The school was not far distant. They pedaled there side by side in the last rays of sunlight, avoiding glittering bits of window glass blown into the street from the overpressures of a nearby bomb burst. When they reached the primary school side door, Penny pulled something that jingled from out of her dance bag. Nate saw that it was the large safety pin with the medium and small keys that had been inside the piggy bank. After she unlocked the door, he carried the bikes inside to a small, antiseptic-smelling corridor. Penny peeked outside, making sure no one had seen them enter the school. Nate noted that she made sure to lock the door from the inside.

Penny had secured a Coleman kerosene lantern in one of the wire baskets of her bicycle, alongside a vertical stack of records. In the other basket were two pairs of dancing shoes and her gas mask. She had changed her skirt and blouse at the house. Her replacement skirt was a dark blue wrap-around of light material that reached within two inches of her ankles and swirled easily with her movements.

"You hold these," Penny directed, of the records and lantern, after Nate had exchanged his street shoes for the shiny dress pumps. She opened a nearby door with the smaller key. From inside the space, she called out, "This is my own personal storage closet. Where did you get those shoes?"

"They're mine," he lied. "They were among the few things that survived the bomb that blew up the place Danny and I were leasing."

"Not a scratch on them! Then this evening is truly meant to be, isn't it? Light the lantern, will you?" Penny reemerged into the hallway weighted down by a suitcase.

"What's that?" Nate wanted to know.

"You'll see. This way." Penny led Nate around a corner to a small gymnasium with a polished oak floor. The outside wall had more than fifty panes of glass extending the length of the gym, high up like church clerestories. The glass had been covered by black squares of a cardboard-like material.

Penny set the suitcase down on the lowest row of an opened bleacher, unlatched it and flipped back the lid.

"Whoa!" Nate admired. "An RCA Victor portable!"

"I suppose you're right," Penny granted. "It's just another gramophone to me. I only care that it works. You look at it like it was an antique. It's but a year old."

Nate thought how to cover his surprise. "We've developed far more sophisticated replay systems where I work."

"Really? You're not telling me something you shouldn't, are you?"

"You trust me; I trust you."

Penny turned the crank several revolutions. "It doesn't produce a bad sound, considering it's a wind-up and the horn is built right into the case. They turned off the gas and electricity," she explained. "I expect it will get cool later, but it will feel fine if we keep moving."

"You taught here last year," Nate wanted to understand.

"Part of the year. After many of the children returned from the countryside. I work here and at another local school teaching those who have special problems reading. I also teach a bit of dance to round out my contract. My part of the curriculum wasn't supposed to begin until the first of October. That's why I was still working at the—"

Nate shook his head, causing Penny to stop in mid-sentence. "That's more information than you should tell me."

"I have a feeling that, somehow, you already know where I work. By the by, it was most kind of you to share your thoughts on Russia at supper. I worry about my parents' nerves. They put on such a brave front that even I don't know precisely how they're feeling." She offered her thanks in a quick, offhand manner, wanting Nate to accept without discussion.

While Penny adjusted the lantern flame for maximum illumination, Nate studied the recordings she had brought along. He had never held such old platters. Their weight surprised him. Each black disc was protected by a brown paper sleeve, but each sleeve also had a circle cut out of the center so that the labels on either side could be read without removing the recording.

"Seventy-eight revolutions a minute," Nate said to himself, marveling at the swift twentieth-century evolution of technological innovations that had led to thirty-three-and-a-third, to tape, to CD and beyond.

Penny straightened up. "What's that you say?"

"For records that go around so fast, you'd think the fidelity would be higher."

"Fidelity?" Penny laughed. "You do know the big words, don't you? What interests you there?"

Nate passed her the third record in the stack. "This one."

"'Dancing in the Dark.' Quite appropriate."

Nate was at the same instant thinking the identical words. His thoughts, however, were not on the dim gymnasium. They went instead to the illegal dance Alex Bennett had offered him and Danny and how unnervingly unenlightened they were about the details. Being out of his time also meant being dangerously out of his ability to control.

Penny set the lantern in the exact middle of the gym floor, where its glow reflected in a rich gold off the lacquered oak. Beyond twenty feet in every direction, darkness held sway. They found themselves cocooned in a cozy hemisphere made purely for two.

While Penny rotated the needle up, set the record on the turntable and finished winding the machine's main spring, Nate said, "I have ten moves in my foxtrot vocabulary. Let's see how many I use.

"I wonder if the names are the same as we have."

Nate ticked off the steps on his fingers. "Forward basic, back basic, feather step, natural turn, hesitation, promenade, three step, closed impetus, side sway and…." His pinkie stayed up. "Uh-oh. My mother would kill me. Wait! Reverse turn with feather finish!"

"Your mother taught you."

"Yes." His words about the phonograph had reminded him to censor the mention of television and soap operas. "She was on the stage briefly."

Nate's soap opera almost-star mother, who had endured years of acting, singing and dancing preparation, had used Nate as her dancing partner from the time he was nine, ostensibly to "keep myself ready for my comeback." She had taught him the foxtrot and waltz, as well as a few tango and tap steps. Her life had been so filled with raising Nate's stepsisters and in decorating her husband's elbow at a myriad of events that any time she devoted solely to Nate had been precious to him. So he concentrated on being good at dance. He was also proud of his mother's beauty, and saw in her eyes how much she loved him when she praised his footwork and told him how handsome he looked.

"How interesting! Was it in music hall?"

"Something like that. Shall we?"

Vivienne Allen had used "Dancing in the Dark" as one of the numbers she practiced with her son. Nate recalled that it was the standard thirty-two bars in length but not the classic A-B-A form. His mind reached back ten years to reconstruct the routine.

When his mother was dying and obsessed with reminiscing, she spoke on several occasions to him about the wonderful ability of the human mind to jump back decades in an instant. "Time does not exist in here," she had said, pointing to her head. After her death, Nate was acutely aware whenever he made mental jumps. He wished, by closing his eyes and reconstructing the sights and sounds and smells of Zimbabwe, he could magically put himself and Danny back a week. But even if he had the power, he would not have closed his eyes for anything until he had finished this dance.

"Let me hear it once," Nate requested.

Penny lowered the steel needle. The rendition was purely orchestral. The record had been played many times and softly hissed and popped.

"'…'til the tune ends. We're dancing in the dark,'" Nate sang softly. His eyes closed, remembering.

"You have a lovely voice!" Penny complimented.

Nate swayed and moved slightly to the rapidly reconstructing choreography. "Don't sound so surprised."

"Go on!" Penny encouraged.

"'Time hurries by. We're here…and gone.'" The particular appropriateness of the words chilled Nate as he glided alone. He stopped.

"What's the matter?" Penny asked.

"Nothing. I've got it. Start the song again."

Nate led Penny close by the lantern during the introductory measures. As he executed foot passing actions, heel turns, glides, weaves and fallaways, giving ample warning of his intent, she followed him expertly. He realized that she was both trained and talented enough to dance professionally. Other women from time to time had assured Nate they could foxtrot, young prep school ladies at formals, women at the swank children's weddings of his father's associates, even a ravishing economist who professed to be highly skilled and who dragged him to a ballroom dancing club. They were all mistaken. Nate had been taught that even the most basic patterns incorporated a myriad of subtle torso, arm, neck and head elements beyond mere footwork. If one did not understand concepts like axis of rotation, weight connection, spotting and top line, there was no chance of true grace. Penny understood at least as well as he did. She took her cues not only from his words but also from his eyes and hand pressures. She never looked down or faltered.

By the fourth playing, the couple moved like a veteran team, gliding slow-slow-fast, turning, opening and closing in near-perfect synchronization. She was an excellent height to be his partner, less than two inches shorter than he. She wore what his mother called "character shoes." They had a slight heel and a flexible strap across the instep. Most of her height, however, came from being long-legged. Because the foxtrot often moved the partners in tight, tandem motions, he could feel the press of her thighs against his. He sensed that she was slender without being skinny. He labored not to tense, but her look was absolute ease. A faint smile played across her lips and her eyelids were slightly lowered.

Nate would have been happy to repeat the same dance a dozen times, but after the third repetition, Penny broke from him and moved to the phonograph.

"Time to rewind?" he asked.

"Yes, that. But playing a record too much in a small amount of time is bad for it," she declared as she bent and cranked the handle.

Nate sat to catch his breath. "Why is that?"

"It has something to do with the movement of the needle heating the material and warping it."

A noise came faintly into the gymnasium. Penny's head swung around quickly. Her eyes grew wide with alarm.

"Was that a door?" she asked.

"It sounded like something fell over down the hall. I'll check."

"No! Oh. Yes, go."

Nate walked to the double doors and pushed through them. The building was completely dark. He heard nothing. He returned to where Penny stood, her hands squeezed into nervous fists.

"Could you lose your job over this?" he asked.

"I don't believe so. Perhaps I'd merit a reprimand."

"What about your father and mother? Would they approve of their daughter entering a place illegally to dance with a stranger?"

"You're not a stranger."

"I can see from your face and hands that this is not something you're accustomed to doing, Penny."

"Well, it's something I've thought of doing before but always lacked the courage. I'm developing more courage of late, and I really wanted to dance. I need to dance, and you…"

Nate sat and looked up at Penny with a slight tilt of his head. "I'm the mysterious partner from somewhere far away."

"Exactly." Penny flipped her head back, rallying. "I have no regret, even if we are caught." She pointed to the records. "Now, did you see anything else you like?"

Nate began to understand the allure of the moment. To such a sheltered young lady, breaking into a school and dancing with him was a new height of danger and romance, a declaration of daring and free will. A freedom from the shackles of war-ravaged London. He was happy to indulge her innocent fantasy. He reached to Penny's waist and gently pulled her down on the bleacher seat beside him. "I see something I like very much: You," he answered.

"That's very nice of you to say."

"It's true."

"I knew you could dance well," she said, looking into his eyes without blinking. "Just like I knew about you doing volunteer work."

Nate wanted to kiss her, but did not want to be misunderstood. He was not here to stay. The only way to lessen the disaster of being yanked out of his time was at least traveling back to the neutral United States. Toying with Penny's affections, even to indulge her fantasies, he told himself, would be worse than cruel. Some light flirting and the dance had to suffice.

"The foxtrot is named after a guy named Fox," Nate commented, to break the spell. "Some time just before the First World War."

"You're pulling my leg."

"No, honestly...although that's a tempting invitation. It's one of those things named after its inventor. Like the guillotine, silhouette, macadam roads."

Penny's plucked and darkened eyebrows rose with surprise. Then a mischievous expression filled her face. "And the crapper. What? The highly educated Nathaniel Allen doesn't know about him?"

Nate paused for moment to compose his words. "No. I've heard of him. He invented the toilet. I was just...a bit..."

"Put off by the very proper Penelope Miles speaking of such a thing. Oh, Nate, I can be naughty. I brought us here, didn't I?"

Nate smirked. "And you nearly jumped out of your skin at that noise. I highly doubt that you've had much practice at being naughty."

"Not practical practice. But I've been lively inside my head," she insisted.

Nate thought what a lovely head it was. He felt improper stirrings.

Penny added, "You're not quite as erudite as you might believe. Thomas Crapper did not invent the flush toilet. Actually, it was invented around Shakespeare's time. Mr. Crapper was a clever plumber who popularized the notion of sanitary households. A vogue was established when he installed toilets for British royalty in their palaces and hunting resorts."

"And gaming clubs," Nate added. "Thus the origin of the expression 'a royal flush.'"

Penny rolled her eyes. She turned and selected another record. "You already know that I am a great fan of Fred Astaire and Ginger Rogers. My all-time favorite dance routine is in their film *Top Hat*. Do you know which one I'm speaking of?"

"I can't recall," Nate honestly replied.

"Shame on you! You really don't spend much time at the cinema, do you? It's 'Cheek to Cheek.'"

"Ah, yes," Nate remembered. "That dress with the feathers."

"Which kept flying in Mr. Astaire's mouth. He hated the dress, you know, until he viewed the result."

"Surely you don't think I could begin to approach the footwork of Fred Astaire," Nate defended.

"Why not?" Penny countered with conviction. "I saw that film six times and committed the routine to memory. I've been praying for you and your dancing shoes every night for years." She traded discs on the turntable.

Nate stood. "This will teach you to be careful what you pray for. Don't drop the needle just yet. Let's walk through the first moves slowly."

"We can't do the exact routine, because the tune was chopped apart to their needs. But I know every eight measure sequence, so I've modified it to fit this recording."

"Is it orchestral?"

"Yes. Just the accompaniment."

Nate walked toward the light. "I know the tune: 'Heaven…I'm in heaven. And my heart beats so that I can hardly speak…'"

"Wonderful!"

"I don't know the next lines." He continued by humming.

Penny stood. "I told you I can be naughty." He thought she was blushing, but he could not be sure in the yellow light. "I can't teach you your steps unless you can see my feet. So…." She reached to her waist and unhooked her skirt.

Underneath, she wore form-fitting, black shorts that came halfway down her shapely thighs. The material looked like silk, but Nate supposed it was made of one of the synthetic products newly developed in that era. They had little cuffs, and the waist was so nipped in that Nate imagined he could encircle Penny's middle between his thumbs and middle fingers. He realized he was staring at her beautiful figure and suddenly looked up.

"You…have these…in America," Penny stammered, registering Nate's beguiled stare. "I know it. Eleanor Powell dances in them."

Nate waved his hands. "No, no. It's…. You're right. I was just looking at the material and wondering how you can't get nylon stockings here but you can get these."

Penny nodded. "I've had them for three years. Saved me ha'pennies." Having survived the awkward moment, she quickly turned and grabbed her shoe bag. She sat and began the process of changing to her tap shoes. "While I'm putting these on, show me a shuffle toe, a ball change and a couple of shuffle hops."

Nate demonstrated his knowledge.

Penny's lower lip went out slightly in appreciation. "You've mastered the time step, all right." She stood and walked up to his right. "You know what the bridge in a song is?"

"In this one, it's "Oh, I love to climb a mountain–"

"Right. This is the jazz tap section of the piece. We dance in unison, side by side, so let's start there. The steps are not as simple as what you just did."

"It's Fred and Ginger," Nate replied. "I didn't think they would be."

They worked for half an hour getting down the eight plus eight bars. This time, Penny supplied the music with a series of bahs and dums. Her voice was pretty but not on a par with her dancing. As if the tap footwork were not difficult enough, her long, bare, shapely legs and her athletic torso and posterior in the tight, silken shorts kept distracting Nate. The bridge ended with a languorous dip, where Nate had ample time to stare deeply into his partner's eyes. The first time he did it, Penny blinked. The second time, she smiled. The third time, she looked mildly alarmed. She pressed herself up and moved away from him.

"Let's have an interval," she suggested, fanning herself with her hand. "It hasn't gotten as cool as I thought it would."

"I need taps on these shoes," Nate decided, in the awkward silence. "You don't happen to have an extra pair, do you?"

"I think I might."

"With you?"

"No."

"Then for next time."

Penny turned to face Nate. "You mean you'd be willing to do this again?"

"Absolutely. I'm having great fun. But I'm no Astaire. The real question is: Would you be willing to do it again?"

"Yes…I would." Penny slowly raised her left hand. "Let's work on the beginning now. If you recall, Fred sings the song first, simply holding her, swaying and executing a few turns. They're among other dancers. Then he promenades her away, stage left, over a bridge to an open area."

"I'm getting the picture."

"Basic ballroom position." She extended her left hand and came in close enough to allow him to place his left flat against the small of her back. "This recording has two measures of pick-up, using part of the bridge tune. Then on the first 'Heaven,' we do a reverse turn, a glide for me, followed by six alternating twirls and counters, you first." Between her confident knowledge of the routine and her expert teaching, Nate picked up one after another of the steps until he had roughly mastered the thirty-two measures.

"I'm starting to flag," he confided.

Penny's eyes pleaded with him. "We're nearly there. I'll guide you through the places where you're lacking. Let's at least string together the opening and the bridge."

Hands in pockets, Nate shrugged his acceptance. He was rewarded with a sunburst smile that made his chest tighten. Penny rushed to lower the needle on the recording.

"Ready?" she asked, as she fairly raced to him to arrive on time.

"Ready."

The happy music echoed throughout the gymnasium. Penny came into Nate's arms. They stepped tandem in intricate patterns across the floor, their long, thin figures reflected in the high, golden polish. For a magical minute, they moved with every bit as much sophistication and elegance as the music. Even though the beat from measure to measure disproved it, time seemed to Nate to stand still. Then they ran out of rehearsed moves. The music bounced on, but the two remained holding the sensual line of the dip.

Nate knew that Penny desired his kiss. Her lips were languidly parted. She stared up at him with expectation. The music pulsed on. He could feel the forceful beating of her heart through her rib cage and knew it was from more than the exercise. He pulled her up.

"Powerful stuff," he said softly. "It can really put you in a romantic mood."

Penny nodded.

Nate let go of her waist, shook out his hands, and turned toward the record player. "That was good."

"Yes," she agreed. "Lovely."

Nate walked slowly into the darkness, pacing around the edge of the light, listening to the song end. "What's my grade, teacher?"

"You passed."

"Not superior marks?"

"It needs work…from both of us."

"Then we'll do it again, soon." Nate stopped moving. He looked at Penny, whose back was to him. She had turned her head to catch him over her shoulder. "Do you have something less complicated?"

Penny crossed to the phonograph and replaced "Cheek to Cheek" with a song Nate had never heard called "Together at Last." She was not making his resolve easier.

They came together, she following him in a series of box steps and other simple moves.

"Who else do you dance with besides your mother?" Penny asked as the music rolled on.

"Debutantes. Senators' daughters. Old wives that millionaires hope to get rid of."

Penny laughed. "This time you are having me on."

"Why should I lie to you?"

"You're telling me you're a somebody back from where you come."

"Everyone is somebody," Nate evaded. "'Back from where you come,' eh? That is the sort of arrant pedantry up with which I shall not put!"

Instead of laughing at the line he had stolen from Winston Churchill, she rested her head against his shoulder. "You enjoy being a mystery from far away."

Without being able to stop himself, Nate tightened his hold on Penny. "No. I enjoy very little about myself," he said, realizing how sincerely he meant his words.

The kerosene lamp began to flicker, threatening to plunge them into darkness. A moment later, the music stopped.

"Somebody's trying to tell us something," Nate said. "We'd better get back before Adolf's nasty lackey come knocking. The moon is full tonight."

Penny bent for the lantern. "Next Monday?"

"It's…" Nate stopped himself from using the word 'date'. "It's good for me." He grabbed the record player and his street shoes and hurried to the storage room.

On the way back to their street, Nate and Penny talked of cuisines. Her favorites were Italian and French. She had tried Chinese only once and professed to enjoy it. Indian cooking she claimed was too sharp for her tongue, even though she enjoyed some spices. Nate remembered that American foods such as pizza, cheeseburgers, fries and Buffalo wings were all in the future, along with the fast-food franchises that had spread around the world like a plague. The neutral subject carried them to the Miles' garden gate. Penny unloaded the wire baskets, and Nate stored the two bicycles against the side of the house. When he turned, Penny stood on the slate of the garden path. She extended a formal hand.

"Thank you ever so much for indulging me, Nate."

Nate took her hand, lifted it and pressed it lightly to his lips in the continental manner. "Thank you," he responded, "for being you."

## CHAPTER TWELVE

Danny stumbled into the Miles's tiny, post-construction upstairs bathroom and bumped into Nate, who had just finished shaving.

"I gotta pee," Danny mumbled. "What time is it?"

"Almost eight."

"Jeez. It's only been four hours since the all clear. After three hours in that shelter, what are you doin' up so early?"

"Going downtown."

"Why?"

"To sell more of the stuff." Nate left Danny and closed the door behind him. He crossed to Danny's borrowed bedroom, set his shoulder bag on the bed, zipped it open and began rummaging.

"Now what are you doing?" Danny asked from behind him.

"I just told you. Selling more of the jewelry. If you don't find your redheaded man and Alex Bennett proves too dangerous, we need money to get out of this country."

"Lots of money. Emerald money as well," Danny pointed out.

Nate emptied the bag of Danny's iPod, his flashlight, spare batteries, cell phone, a padlock Danny kept with him for foreign gym locker rooms, and other personal items, as well as the Webley pistol. "It may come to that."

Danny moved his belongings off the bed. "Why now? The pawnshops are open at two and three and four. What's your rush?"

Nate would not say that Penelope Miles was his rush. She was heading to her job to put in half a day, as so many Londoners did on Saturdays. "I'm awake."

"I'm not. I'm going back to sleep. You don't need me."

Nate did not need and, in fact, did not want Danny with him, but instead of admitting it and causing disharmony, he said, "I know where to find you later on."

For this remark Danny sat up. "Don't look for me at Gwen's house. It's awkward enough for me to get in there."

Nate picked up the shoulder bag. "Not Gwen's house, dummy.

We're due to meet Alex Bennett at two o'clock outside Victoria Station, at the triangle of Grosvenor Gardens and Buckingham Palace Road. You would have forgotten, wouldn't you?"

"No." Nate knew he was lying. "Not once I've had some sleep. I'll meet you there." Danny collapsed back onto the bed and pulled the pillow over his head.

As they ate breakfast, Penny asked Nate, "Did you and Daniel come over on the *Eastern Prince*?"

Nate continued to spread strawberry preserves on his toast. "Why do you ask that?"

Penny punched him lightly on the shoulder. "Don't answer my question with another question. We both know that was the first ship bringing us armaments from the United States. It set sail four months ago. I was just wondering how long you've been in London."

"Not as long as that."

"I won't ask when you're going home, but I worry if it's too soon," she disclosed, the furrow between her eyebrows attesting to the truth of her words. "The German wolf packs are sinking everything on the seas. Last month, Hitler announced a total blockade of the British Isles. Even ships flying neutral flags are being sunk."

"I know."

"They sank the French liner *Meknes* in July, and France is a neutral country under their thumb! They must have known the liner *Arandora Star* was carrying German and Italian prisoners to Canada. They sank her anyway, just to be sure she wouldn't carry any armaments back to us. No one is safe from monsters who would kill their own so wantonly."

Nate set down his knife. "Are you saying you personally don't want me to leave?"

"I want you to be safe," Penny evaded.

"Safe in London?"

Penny rose from her chair. "Bring your toast with you if you're coming. I shall be late."

Nate had three goals for his Saturday. The first was to see about ship sailings. The second was to purchase another roll of film and take photos of war-ravaged London and its brave inhabitants. The third was to pawn more of the jewelry. He knew that *The Times* ordinarily published shipping news, but he could find nothing. He went to the address of the Cunard Line. Through the cobwebs of memory, he remembered that almost all Cunard-White Star liners beginning with the letter 'A' had been destroyed during the two world wars. Several had been sunk by torpedoes, one bombed in a harbor and one by a mine. He also, for no good reason, remembered that the *Aquitania* had not only served in both wars but had survived.

Nate spoke with a man at the Cunard Lines front desk. The desk clerk was infinitely polite but ultimately unhelpful.

"There are no passenger liners departing anymore from London, sir," the man said. "Not since the third of July. Nor from Southampton. The piers are being targeted by the Luftwaffe, and nothing can get out of the Thames estuary anyway, due to the U-boats."

"I understand," Nate said. "But liners are still leaving the British Isles. In convoys, correct?"

"That's right. Out of Liverpool or Belfast, Ireland. I don't know how much longer we can keep Liverpool open, with the recent bombings there."

"When does the *Aquitania* next sail?"

"She is not scheduled. We are not, in fact, posting schedules far in advance, due to the war."

"What an annoyance!" Nate said with extra emphasis.

"Indeed. There used to be seventy-eight separate routes out of England to ports of the world. The number has been drastically reduced, because everything requires destroyer or submarine escort."

"I might be a spy in off the street," Nate acknowledged, registering the man's guarded demeanor, "but I'm not. I'm just a very unhappy American citizen, anxious to get back to New York."

"I understand. We have nothing sailing to New York within the next fortnight. However, there are other lines, you know."

"Who?"

"Ellerman's, for example." The clerk consulted a list. "Oh, bad luck. Their *City of Benares* just left yesterday, bound for Canada. You might have caught a train home when you landed. I take it you don't work for your government."

"No," Nate said straight-faced, reversing the lie he had been telling all week. "I'm a private businessman."

"Pity. If that were the case, I'm sure they would make the arrangements for you." The man sniffed and looked up at the ceiling. "I suppose there must be aeroplanes hopping back and forth. You know, stopping at Iceland or Greenland."

"Do you mean from Heathrow or Gatwick?" Nate asked.

"Gatwick? That was a private field to the south, but I believe it's closed. I've been told that the RAF has put up a tent at Heathrow and that your country's planes land there."

Nate tucked the information away in his mental file cabinet, thanked the clerk and moved on to his next order of business.

As with everything else, film was in short supply. The price was sufficiently high that Nate could only buy one roll in good conscience. The shop owner allowed him to load it in the shop's back darkroom. He immediately went out onto the streets, looking for the best shots of Londoners "carrying on," of crews restoring damage, of "cheeky" signs of defiance against the Nazi regime, and of the worst bomb aftermaths. He knew they would be a spectacular prize if, by some slim chance, Danny was correct and it was possible to return to their own time.

At one particularly devastated corner, six men shoveled debris into a dump truck of good size. Nate stepped around to the far side, opened Danny's bag and took out the tunnel crash victims' wallets and clutch purses and all other items with identification. He looked around to be sure he was no being observed and tossed the belongings into the dust-choked truck bed.

In order not to repeat his dead English aunt story, Nate was forced to travel to two districts of London and visit the pawn shops where Danny had sold. He managed to unload all but two watches and one man's wedding ring, which he tied around a cloth handkerchief to keep it from being lost. For some reason, the shop owners were in a more generous mood than in previous visits. Nate calculated that he received almost one quarter of the new purchase values of the items. Nevertheless, the total did not elevate their combined money anywhere close to the asking prices of the passports. It was clear that, by one shady means or another, more dealing would have to be done.

Nate worked his way toward Victoria Station, timing his walk so that he would arrive at ten minutes before two. He stood at the appointed triangle north of the station and soaked in the ambiance. He particularly observed the passing fashions. Even the most stylish men were not as well clothed as average men sixty years later, who would be wearing their modern fiber blends impregnated with wrinkle- and stain-resistant chemistry. Derbies and bowler hats were standard, as were the "brollies" that protected their owners from the rain.

As one of the major confluences of London, Victoria Station resembled a human beehive. Londoners emerged from the dark entrances very much like the little social insects. Trolley-busses and omnibuses clogged up in lines, waiting to disgorge and absorb scores of passengers. Most of the omnibuses were still the famous post-box red, but some had been painted a concealing drab olive brown. Further congesting the area were the lines of those pathetic creatures waiting for space in the deep Underground shelter at the station. From across the wide street, Nate saw his partner pushing peevishly through the crowds. He waved.

An air raid claxon began its stepwise climb through an unearthly scale. Its cry was immediately imitated by several others, like metal land beasts screeching out the warning of the imminent attack of great metal birds. Nate gazed reflexively into the sky. He pulled the camera from the shoulder bag and slipped its strap over his head.

"Come on!" Danny cried, from halfway across the street. "Let's get into the shelter!"

Nate pointed with the camera toward the enormous station. "Look at it! You'll still be only halfway to safety ten minutes from now."

"What do you want to do?"

Nate began his answer by loping down Buckingham Palace Road toward Lower Belgrave Street, forcing Danny to follow.

"I know my history. You know I know my history. The Germans target the large railway stations, to disrupt transportation. Victoria Station is a prime target. Alex Bennett knows that, too. He told us to meet him at Holy Trinity Church if there was an attack."

"No. If the station got destroyed," Danny corrected on the run. "It's still okay."

"He'll be at the church," Nate insisted.

Danny glanced at his wristwatch. "It's all the way over at Sloane Square. We've taken a taxi from Victoria Station to Sloane Square."

Nate banged Danny's bag into a hurrying pedestrian and apologized over his shoulder. "It's about a mile and a half. You're the big-time runner."

"Fuck!" Danny lengthened his stride. "I'm a jogger, not a miler. And you sure can't go that far without stopping."

The city's sirens wailed at full power. People poured out of buildings with closed lips but anxious eyes to reach air raid precaution shelters. Barrage balloons rose quickly, two, three, four thousand feet and climbing.

Within another minute, Nate had fallen fifty feet behind his friend. "Go left!"

They turned off Belgrave Street onto Chester Row. Danny slowed his pace to allow Nate to catch up. "Seven minutes from sirens to bombs. It's already been three. Dig deep, brother."

Not long after, Nate began to make puffing sounds. His sentences became ragged. "We're away…from the station now. This is residential. They don't…target houses on purpose. Especially…in the daylight… when they can see. Houses aren't strategic. Stop!"

Danny pulled up and turned. "Are you out of your mind?"

"No. Out of breath." Nate came to a halt near the western limit of Chester Square Park. While his lungs heaved, he lifted his camera, checked the shutter speed and dialed down the lens aperture for the midday sky. "We'll be okay," he said, looking as assured as his words.

"We're out in the open, for Christ's sake!"

To the east, batteries of anti-aircraft opened up.

"Here they come!" Danny said, in a voice an octave higher than usual. He looked around. In the upscale neighborhood, shoulder to shoulder, white-walled townhouses stood like Dover's cliffs. Unlike Bethnal Green, their front doors were closed. Many first floor windows had wrought iron bars over them. Except for the lush vegetation, the park in their center might have been a prison exercise yard. Danny pointed to the end of the park. "There's a church."

Nate started off again, with long strides. "Not the right one."

"But it's shelter."

"Maybe not. I know for a fact that St. Paul's survived with almost no damage, and I'm ninety per cent sure Holy Trinity did as well. I toured it last year." Nate picked up his pace as he heard the first of the high explosive impacts. "It was built just before the turn of the century, as a mixture of Gothic cathedral and the Arts and Crafts movement. It had the original stained glass windows when I toured it, so what's the chance it was hit during the Blitz?"

"Elementary deduction, Sherlock," Danny granted. "But we're still a long way from there."

Three Boulton Paul Defiants roared overhead from the west, moving so quickly that Nate did not have time to lift the camera. Nate knew from reading as well as from television programs and movies that the German bombers would come in tight formations, wave after wave, in the order that they had lifted off from one or several foreign airfields.

The early Henkels, Dorniers and Junkers had topside, belly and nose machinegun turrets, but no defense on their tails. The RAF fighter pilots would make a first strafing pass from whichever direction they arrived and then circle around to attack from the bombers' vulnerable rear. The Germans would have Messerschmitts and other fighter planes hovering above and behind, to drop down on the British interceptors from positions of tactical advantage. If the British could muster enough planes and had enough warning, they would send in their own reserve wings to surprise the German escort fighters in turn. Nate mused that it was Indians versus wagon trains with the occasional last-minute rescue by the cavalry, except in three dimensions and at hundreds of miles per hour.

Nate knew that, with London so large and offering so many viable targets, the non-strategic upper-crust neighborhoods were statistically good places to be during a raid. On the other hand, dogfights, anti-aircraft, even wind could push something moving at 250 miles per hour half a mile off course in a matter of seconds. He had only hoped to run and jog two-thirds of a mile away from Victoria Station and then find a sanctioned shelter somewhere between the station and Holy Trinity. And then he realized that the rich were not about to allow public shelters in their exclusive neighborhoods. Block after block passed without even a shelter sign. The only high-percentage sanctuary he could think of was Holy Trinity.

The first waves of bombers dropped their loads well behind where Danny and Nate ran. A group of four, however, flew directly overhead, with their bomb bay doors only beginning to close. Nate paused and snapped a photograph of their wake. Hard after them came two Spitfires. Moments later, a pair of Messerschmitts followed. The scenario was exactly as it had been described in books and shown to Nate in computer recreations. He took another snapshot and then started off again after the receding figure of Daniel O'Shea.

The din of more and more planes, impacting bombs and anti-aircraft flak spurred the pair on until their hearts were near bursting with the strain. Finally they came to the end of Chester Row, where it met Holbein Place. Nate chanced to look up at the increased noise in the sky just above. He saw five German bombers several thousand feet up, with bomb bays open. More importantly, he saw the silver glint of many explosive bombs plunging in their direction. As their demoniac whistling came into his ears, he grabbed Danny from behind and hauled him down. For only an instant, they lay on the pavement. Then Nate half stood and dragged Danny up and past a low, iron gate. Immediately beyond, there were stone steps that the pair half tumbled down toward a basement door.

"Close your eyes! Cover your ears!" Nate shouted as he flattened himself to the alcove at the bottom of the steps.

The string of high explosives passed over their heads at about four hundred feet and continued their plummet westward, not falling straight down but moving on a vector imparted by the air speed of the bomber that had released them. The first bomb landed a block distant, in Sloane Gardens. Its brothers landed at half-second intervals, creating a line of havoc. The explosively compressed air caused Nate and Danny to struggle for breath.

Several seconds after the first bomb annihilated itself and everything within a fifty-foot radius, hunks of wood and slate and glass and brick rained down on the two. Soon after, a dense cloud of dust descended. Nate unzipped the bag, pulled out the handkerchief, and transferred the ring to his finger. A shallow puddle lay in a depression of the lowest stone step. Nate soaked up half the water and clapped the cloth over his nose and mouth. More clumps of debris hit the ground all around them.

"Give me your handkerchief!" he commanded. He repeated the procedure. In spite of his precaution, the finest dust penetrated the cloth and threatened to choke the men. Within twenty seconds, their upper sides were completely covered in a grayish-yellow cerement. "Stay low!" Nate shouted, as yet another plane roared by.

From somewhere within hearing range, a woman began screaming. Her shrieks went on for almost a full minute and then stopped as abruptly as they had started. At last, Nate could see farther than the limit of their tiny, open shelter. He rose to one knee, testing his health.

"Let's keep moving," he told Danny through the cloth. Each time he blinked, grit irritated his eyes. When they came up to street level, he could peer far enough through the swirling haze to see that a bomb had leveled a pair of neighboring buildings on the opposite side of the street. Somewhere beyond, a fire could be heard devouring, and thick, black smoke swirled inside the more general, pale brown storm of dust.

Nate lifted the camera and removed the lens cap. He focused on the destruction and captured it with his third-from-last frame of film. When the mirror spun once more to allow viewing, he realized that he was looking at a bare arm and hand rising out of the pile of debris. He jogged across the street and cautiously made his way over heaps of materials to the appendage. When he reached out to test for a pulse, the weight of the arm came onto his thumb and middle finger. What had been a part of a living woman now was completely detached. Shocked, Nate allowed the limb to drop.

"Gross!" Danny said behind him. He pointed. "Get her rings. She doesn't need them anymore." On the left hand's ring finger were a wedding band and an engagement ring with a solitaire cut diamond that Nate judged to be more than a carat. Given the neighborhood, he was not surprised.

Nate thought of his distaste for touching the bodies in the wrecked railway car. And yet he had been able to remove their valuables. This time, he could not. He straightened up and shook his head.

Danny bent, took the limb in both hands and began yanking on the circles of gold. "It creeps me out, too, but Gwen could really use this kind of help."

Nate opened his mouth to chastise his partner, to tell him that they badly needed more money to escape the living nightmare, and that he had no business thinking about anyone else's plight. Again, he could not do it.

Several more fighter planes streaked over from the south. Emergency vehicle bells and sirens approached.

"Hurry up!" Nate urged.

"Got 'em!" Danny cried out in triumph and then stood. "Which way?"

Nate pointed north. If so much dust had not filled the air, they could have seen the edge of Sloane Square. Nate's mind eye saw it clearly enough. The area had been one of his main hangouts on previous trips in his own time, between its chic shops for him such as Kenneth Cole and Hilfiger and places like Gucci, Prada, Fendi, Dior, Giorgio Armani, Boodle & Dunthorne, Cartier, and Tiffany & Co. that attracted the smart, rich young women. He knew the square and Sloane Street would not be the same as in his era, but he also knew that the dates proudly displayed on many stores during his time proved that they had plied their upscale trade in the district since Winston Churchill was sucking on something other than his cigar.

They walked as quickly as their lungs would allow, given the small amount of air penetrating their clogged handkerchiefs. When they came into the open square, Nate looked to the west and realized what the bombers had been targeting. The Duke of York Barracks, which fully occupied an enormous block, was on fire in two places. Tongues of flames from a couple of other fires licked out above the tops of the nearby buildings. A time-delay bomb exploded within the barracks, shaking the entire square.

On its corner, the steel frame of the revolutionary "curved curtain wall" of Peter Jones still stood, but the store's great stretches of glass had been blown out. Through the dust, sunlight managed to catch the millions of glass slivers and make some of them sparkle.

"Son of a bitch!" Danny yelled through his handkerchief.

Nate picked up his pace. "Keep moving!" He pointed. Towering Holy Trinity stood unscathed just a few buildings north of the square. To Nate, it looked like an ochre and cream version of Pisan wedding cake architecture, where important buildings were fashioned of alternating layers of colored stone. The enormous, Gothic-arched stained glass window that faced the street was intact.

Unbidden out of Nate's primed memory popped another fact of the war. Three years hence, when the Germans would launch weak reprisal raids against London with only twelve or sixteen bombers at a time, the citizenry would become so cocky that few would flee to the shelters. Instead, they would come out for "a look/see" and even have the temerity to walk up to searchlight and gun crews and make suggestions as to what they should be targeting. Such luxuries were many ruined buildings and many sacrificed lives off.

The dust had penetrated up Sloane Street but was swiftly settling to a waist level fog. Nate and Danny beat the caked dust from each other's suits and then ducked into the giant house of God. They found themselves not alone. More than one hundred people stood or sat inside, many huddled against the massive pillars that held up the roof.

Alex Bennett stood alone in a corner almost as dark as the one he frequented in the Surabaya pub, inviting comparison to a cockroach. When he spotted Nate and Danny, he gave a little nod. They crossed to him. His suit, which was a different one from the one he had worn the first two times Nate met him, bore no trace of dust.

"How the hell did you get here so fast?" Danny wanted to know.

"I was coming to Victoria Station from this direction," Bennett answered. "I dashed in before the bombers arrived."

"Good for you," Nate said, brushing off the arms of his suit jacket. Bennett consulted his wristwatch. "I congratulate you on only being ten minutes late. I trust the show outside has redoubled your desire to return home."

"You have no idea, man," Danny said, wiping his eyelashes clean.

Bennett crooked a finger. He led the two Americans through an archway and to a locked door. "Post a watch for me, will you?"

While Danny imposed his frame between the sanctuary and the door, Nate studied Bennett's lock-picking skills. The man had a ring of very professional and impressive tools. Within fifteen seconds, he had the door open.

The staircase beyond wound upward through one of the church's front turrets to a loft. When walked out onto it, the men found themselves alone and looking down on the collegiate-style sanctuary.

"I assume from the fact that you're here that you're still with the plan."

"Assume away," Nate said. "And you're here because you have found nothing bad about us."

Bennett smiled broadly as he reached into his jacket. His hand came out holding a Webley Mark I pistol, a gun that held seven bullets and which packed a much bigger punch than the weapon Nate had relieved Jack Eastwood of. He took a step backward.

"I've learned nothing good about you either. Which forces me to do a little more investigating on my own. Please be so kind as to prove to me you're unarmed. First step apart. Thank you. Now remove your jackets and place them here. Then face that wall."

The pair did as they were told. While Bennett's attention was distracted patting down the jackets, Nate made his left hand into the shape of a gun and raised a questioning eyebrow at Danny. Danny shook his head slightly, signaling that he had not brought the Webley .32 with him.

"I assume you're looking for hand guns," Nate said.

"Assume away," Bennett answered, imitating Nate's phrase and voice.

"It's hard enough for an Englishman to get a gun. How do you think we could?"

"You could be part of His Majesty's Security Service, that's how. Hold very still, or our solid friendship could have a sudden hole in it." Bennett patted down each man's back and trousers with great caution. He then moved on to the shoulder bag. Nate listened to him rummaging through it.

"All right. Turn around, gentlemen. Sincerest apologies," he said insincerely. Bennett's suspicious attitude seemed mollified. He held up the two wristwatches he had removed from the bag not with a question on his face but rather a look of amusement. "Is this how you've been surviving, nicking time pieces?"

Danny shrugged. "A living is a living."

"Rest assured, if you compel me I can use two other men. I must be convinced of why you walked into the Surabaya."

Nate said, "We need passports. We smuggled something into England, and we can't manage to smuggle ourselves out."

"What was it you smuggled?"

"Uncut emeralds."

"If that's true, why can't you afford to pay the price for the passports?"

"Because our fence has disappeared. We're still holding onto the stones, and we don't know how to unload them otherwise. You wouldn't know, would you?"

Bennett's tongue circled the inside of his mouth as he considered the story. He shoved the bag toward the Americans and gestured for them to put on their jackets. "You don't happen to have these emeralds on you right now, do you?"

"Of course not. What about a source for unloading them?"

"Sorry. Not my racket."

"They would more than pay for the passports."

"The printer won't be interested in gem stones. Do you think it wise to wander around London with no identifications at all?"

"Why not?" Nate returned. "We don't exist, remember?"

"Sit!" Bennett returned the pistol to his shoulder holster. He sat as well but at a safe distance from the two Americans. "I may have told you that I believed this operation would take place on Thursday next. It has, in fact, been moved up to Tuesday night. What is involved is a relatively simple strike on an open country road between here and...let us just say for now...there." He fetched a pack of one of Salmon & Gluckstein's more expensive brands from his jacket pocket and tapped out a single cigarette. His gold cigarette case had disappeared. "The military escort must be separated from the armored lorry. You two will be seen, if only for a few moments, by the driver and guard. You will not speak. If you must, you had better have a passable English accent. You will unload the money. It will be stacked on four pallets." He produced a book of matches, struck one and applied it to the cigarette. "I will supply a heavy-duty trolley, so it shouldn't be much trouble at all."

"A what?" Danny asked.

"A hand truck," Nate translated.

"Trolley, bonnet, windscreen, lorry," Danny muttered with annoyance.

"I hope one of you has driven on the left side of the road before."

Nate thought of Danny on the motorways of England, accelerating well past the seventy-mile-per-hour limit in a rented convertible XK Coupe, one hand on the wheel, the other playing with the shift like it was a woman's breast.

"We both have," Nate said.

While the Englishman talked, Nate realized that, along with his crooked smile and crooked teeth, he had a crooked pinkie finger on his right hand. It had evidently been badly broken. Nate wondered what the situation had been that he had not gotten good medical attention to set it.

"Excellent. My partner will drive our lorry away. You two will be provided a car that has been stolen that day. Its number plate will be switched for one that's expired. You will also be provided a map. You must toss it away the moment you know where you are."

"That's difficult these days, with the road signs removed," Nate pointed out.

"True enough. I'll also provide a sheet with prominent buildings, intersections, landscape features and so on."

"We get our passports on the spot," Danny made sure.

"Indeed. I want you out of my country as quickly as possible. You also receive one thousand pounds each in old bills and coins. Finally, I shall give you a bank name and account number, which you must memorise. The account will receive over a period of six months the remainder of your earnings. It will be jointly opened in the names on your passports. Unless you wish other names." Bennett's attention on Nate's face increased, searching.

"No. Those are fine," Nate granted. "What about guns?"

"You will be provided hand guns. I trust I need not tell you that they are to be used only in the direst situation, such as inability to escape in any other way. As far as I am concerned, this plan is so well constructed that no gunplay need happen. However, I am also not such a fool as to disbelieve that "the best laid plans of mice and men aften gang astray," he finished, using a Scottish burr.

"So, where do we meet on Tuesday night?"

"At five o'clock in the afternoon, you will leave from Trafalgar Square on the Tube line that takes you to Sloane Square. Beginning with Victoria Street, you will get off your train at every successive stop and wait on the platform for the next train. You will do this, if need be, all the way to Chelsea."

"We get it. You need to know we're not bringing company with us," Nate confirmed.

Instead of answering, Bennett said, "A man will eventually come up to you and ask how to get to Brighton. He will then expect you to show him at least one emerald. My man will then move off. You follow him."

The sounds of someone climbing stairs came into the loft. All three men looked in that direction.

A man wearing clerical garb and a faint smile appeared. "Excuse me. I don't know how the door got opened, but you're not allowed up here."

"Is God throwing us out?" Bennett asked in an overloud voice, exhaling a puff of smoke.

The reverend stiffened at the reply and the gesture. "It's a rule. Just as not smoking is a rule."

"I thought you only had ten rules. This is too good a fag to put out," Bennett returned, tapping the ash onto the floor. "Besides, I intend to smoke in the hereafter, so it's practice. We're not disturbing anyone, Your Worship."

"Nevertheless—"

"You're disturbing us."

"Sir, I should not like to summon a policeman."

Bennett dipped his head toward the outer wall, beyond which alarms clanged and wailed, and yet another plane roared by. "And I'm sure the very busy Bobbies feel precisely the same as you." He stood. "I'm glad I'm not some peasant seeking sanctuary. Bloody ecclesiastical parasites." He brushed past the flabbergasted cleric.

Dipping their heads apologetically, Nate and Danny followed.

"I love to yank the tails of so-called men of God," Bennett confided over his shoulder as he descended.

The man's stock lowered another point in Nate's book. "Is there anything else we should know right now?"

"Only that I'm depending on you Yanks. Don't disappoint me. Tuesday at five, then."

When they reached the back of the church, Bennett continued through the doors without saying farewell. Nate debated trying to follow him. He realized Danny was not at his side. When he turned, he saw that Danny had dipped his dust-choked handkerchief in the font near the entrance.

"What are you doing?" Nate asked, appalled. "That's holy water."

"All the better." Danny swirled the cloth around his face and smiled.

By the time the interview had ended, so had the raid. Dust continued to drift up Sloane Street, and smoke drifting down from the square made breathing doubly difficult. The square was clogged as well with emergency vehicles.

"I'm sure they hit Victoria Station, or at least dumped bombs in that area," Nate told Danny. "Let's hoof over to the South Kensington stop."

"I don't trust that Bennett," Danny declared.

"And how is that different than several dozen guys we've dealt with in the past?" Nate asked.

"You mean 'in the future.' Those guys didn't have British accents. What's all this about the guard and driver seeing our faces? Hasn't he heard of ski masks or stocking masks?"

"It sounds to me like we're being set up as fall guys," agreed his partner. "We're going to need every bit of wit and nerve we've got Tuesday night to get those passports."

"No, we won't," Danny replied. "We're going home tonight, via tunnel."

The rail system was chaos following the daylight raid, which had been a large one. Danny and Nate were not able to return to the East End until after five o'clock. Nate could not convince Danny to stay away from Gwen Lamb. Danny's rationale was that he had the two rings he took from the dead woman's hand and needed to give them to Gwen before he left 1940 England "for all time" that night.

Nate continued on to the Wilcox house. He removed his suit, beat what dust and grime he could from it, and sponged it. Even though his blazer and gray slacks were not in the best of condition, he put them on. He realized that he still wore the man's wedding ring he had shoved on his finger when he needed the handkerchief to shield his face. He washed out the handkerchief as well and hung it over the Wilcox's bathroom sink. He went into the main bedroom and rummaged through the dresser until he found Archie Wilcox's handkerchiefs. He slipped off the ring, tied it onto the borrowed handkerchief, and placed it in Danny's shoulder bag, which he had carried since parting with his friend.

For reason of safety, he deposited the shoulder bag, which he had loaded up with Danny's belongings, the camera, Webley pistol, empty Altoids tin, two men's wristwatches and the tied wedding ring in the Wilcox Anderson shelter. He realized with great annoyance that Danny had taken out his iPod and cell phone. He wondered if his partner would be dumb enough to demonstrate them to Gwen Lamb.

Among the other items in the bag was a sack of toffees that Nate had purchased "under the counter" from a merchant on the walk away from Sloane Square to the South Kensington station. His stomach growled from having missed lunch. He opened the sack and took out three toffees. He had intended the entire sack for the Miles family, but now that he had opened it he was embarrassed to present it sloppily retied. Instead, he filled his hand with the cellophane-wrapped delights, crossed through the backyards and knocked on the door to the Miles kitchen.

"Who is it?" Penny's very feminine voice inquired.

"Candy man," Nate announced.

Penny opened the door. She did not appear as pleased as he had hoped. In fact, she looked ill at ease.

"Hello, Nate."

"Wizard!" exclaimed a deep voice from inside. "I get to meet the mysterious Nathaniel Allen from America."

Penelope's expression did not relax. She pulled the door open all the way and stepped back.

Nate took advantage of the silent invitation and walked into the kitchen. Seated at the table was a man wearing an RAF uniform. He stood. Nate found him to be about an inch smaller than his own height. He wore the impressive, gray clothing well. His hair was a brownish-red, and Nate wondered if this and his first name indicated some Irish heritage. Like Penny, his teeth were white and straight. He extended his hand.

"Pleased to meet you."

"Excuse me for being rude," Nate replied. He turned to Penny. "Hold out your hands, please." She obliged. He transferred the fistful of sweets.

"Toffees! They're my absolute favourite. They must have been dear."

"What? No flowers as well?" the serviceman asked. There was only the slightest hint of joviality about the remark.

Nate felt his face begin to heat up. "I had the opportunity to purchase them, and the Miles family has been so good to me—"

"I understand," Penny's suitor broke in. "They're a wonderful lot, the Mileses. Certainly a family I wouldn't mind being part of." He looked down at his still-extended arm. "I feel like a railway crossing gate."

"Sorry," Nate said. He put his hand into Brendon's and received a crunching greeting. He looked down at the large fingers that surrounded his and saw that the man chewed his nails.

"Brendon Danvers."

"I've heard a good deal about you."

"Same here."

"Supper will be in half an hour," Penny interjected, in a small voice. "Mum's obviously caught in some line. I'm about to start it."

"Am I still expected?" Nate asked.

"Yes, indeed. Bangers and mash."

"Penny's engaged," Brendon declared.

Penny glanced at Nate with doe eyes.

The pain in Nate's chest could no longer be credited to the coach crash. Too much healing time had passed, and he realized he never felt it unless he was around Penelope and there was some threat of her attention being denied him. This time it felt like the stab of a long, thin knife.

"Tonight, we're going to the cinema," Brendon added, glancing with some confusion at Penny.

"Wonderful," Nate hastened to say. "What's playing?"

Penny said, "*The Private Lives of Elizabeth and Essex*. It took its own time getting here. I suppose it wasn't a priority on anybody's ship. I've been a bit dubious of seeing it, since Bette Davis is playing Queen Bess. But that handsome rogue Errol Flynn is Essex. I understand she didn't want him, but he's excellent." Penny's words tumbled like an avalanche. "It's in colour."

"I'd ask you along, but I only have this one night free," Brendon explained, placing a proprietary arm around Penny's waist. "Awfully, sorry, but I'm not willing to share her."

Nate focused on the large hand curved around the swell of her hip. "Understood."

"We won't have Mr. O'Shea to supper?" Penny asked.

Nate pictured his friend with Mrs. Lamb at that very moment.

"He's trying to stay on top of some work."

Penny slowly nodded. What was on her mind was on her face, and

Nate saw that she had heard about Danny and Gwen. The sordid secret was known by the whole neighborhood. Nate had not been the one who betrayed it; he had become too careful and accomplished a liar over the past decade. He remembered a time when he had been proud of such ability.

"Then we won't expect him."

"No. You're busy with company and supper." Nate moved to the door. "I'll come back in half an hour."

Nate ate his meal with speed, because Brendon Danvers was inquisitive to the point of rudeness. The only respite Nate found was in turning the table and besieging the man with his own questions. He found that Brendon and Penelope had "met at university" and that the young man had a degree in mechanical engineering. His family lived in Guildford. His father was a farmer, and his mother had organized not only the local quilting group but the reading improvement society as well. They had yet to meet Penny.

During the back and forth, Penny noticed that a bit of rain had begun to fall. She excused herself to take the laundry down from the line. Mr. Miles arrived in the middle of the meal, sat beside his wife, excused himself for being late and mercifully interrupted Brendon's inquisition with his "insider's intelligence."

"You won't believe it, but the Germans did actually manage to bomb out that Jewish business on Brownlow Hill in Liverpool! The only explanation for such ability is that they must have a strong network of spies throughout the country."

"I'll wager you're right, sir," Brendon sang out, keeping his gaze fixed on Nate.

Worden spoke for a minute more on the subject. Then he switched suddenly to the day's air raid. His face lit up as if the triumph were personal when he reported that, in spite of being heavily outnumbered, the British pilots had shot down fourteen German planes, equal in number to their own losses. The total of bombers in the day mission was more than 100, but apparently at least 20 had faced such furious attack that they had diverted to secondary targets.

"They're throwing everything they can at us, in preparation for their landing." Brendon said with assurance.

"They are throwing everything," Nate agreed. "But days like today will prove to Hitler that he no longer has the strength, in the air or on the ground, to take England." He noticed that Brendon was shaking his head and had lifted his hand, about to offer an argument. Nate's composure snapped. The desire to squash the serviceman became more than he could control. "It's called 'Operation Sealion,' and it's about to crack. Hitler made a fatal error in not giving priority to the replacement of planes. Now the number of losses will prove it's too late. The invasion will be aborted."

All three mouths around the table fell slightly open.

"I can't say any more," Nate told them.

"Why are you here?" Brendon's question sounded more like a demand.

"I wonder that myself, Lieutenant Danvers," Nate replied. He looked at Worden and Millicent Miles. "If you mean in this house, it's because of the incredible generosity of this family."

At his last words, the three seemed to relax. Penny returned. In her hands were only a bed cover and a couple linens. Nate recalled that Monday and not Saturday was washday at the Miles house. He could feel his eyebrows furrowing with puzzlement.

"Just airing a duvet and some muslins," Penny explained. She erected a too-wide smile.

"I asked her to set them out," Millicent verified.

Nate also realized that Penny had been gone more than three minutes. His radar told him that something was not right.

Millicent set down her napkin. "I'm sorry we have no dessert."

"We have toffees…thanks to Mr. Allen," Penny announced.

As soon as Penelope announced that she and Brendon had to rush to make the cinema on time, Nate took it as the cue to excuse himself from the Miles house. He collected the shoulder bag from the Wilcox Anderson shelter, went into the house for his and Danny's raincoats and left to fetch his partner. Too annoyed by both Danny's indiscreet philandering and the succession of unexpected events at the Miles home to care about appearances, Nate walked right up to the Lamb front door and knocked. When he got no reply, he knocked again, this time for five seconds. He stepped back onto the pavement so that he could be seen from an upper window. Not surprisingly, a curtain parted.

Two minutes later, the front door opened. Gwen Lamb greeted him cordially and without embarrassment, although she was all but naked in a diaphanous peignoir.

"Did Danny give you a surprise?" Nate inquired.

"He did indeed." Gwen giggled like a coquette from the Opera Comique. "It's the first time I've been given a wedding and engagement ring without a proposal."

Nate said, "I believe you accepted his proposal quite a while ago." She winked in reply, beneath insult. To wipe the smug smile off her face, he said, "Did he also tell you he pulled them off a dead woman's severed arm during today's raid?"

"Yes, he did," Gwen replied airily. "I admire his nerve." Danny had evidently met his soulmate.

"His pluck," Nate corrected, expecting the woman would not recognize the double entendre.

Danny clomped down the narrow steps of the little house. As he descended, he zipped up his trousers. He did not look happy.

"Time to go 'you know where,'" Nate told him, before Danny could say a word.

"It's not even eight."

"But we need to get in place, Daniel," Nate insisted. "Don't we?" He held up the shoulder bag and Danny's raincoat.

"'Oh Danny Boy,'" Gwen sang merrily, in a nasal tone, "'The pipes, the pipes are calling.' Wherever you're going, Lover Boy, hurry back."

Danny gathered the voluptuous woman into his arms, planted a steamy kiss on her lips and squeezed her bottom.

"He won't be back tonight," Nate warned Mrs. Lamb, "so you might want to rescue the evening and visit the pub. I'm opening the door."

The partners departed quietly into the gathering dusk. It was not until they were half a block away that Danny said, "Just because you're not getting any from your prim Miss Miles—"

"Not another word!" Nate's voice had an edge like katana steel. His angry eyes punctuated the command.

Danny walked on for several moments. "Fine. We'll be history to both of them in a few hours. This is the night we catch our ride back to the twenty-first century. It had goddamn well better be."

Danny shook his flashlight for nearly a minute before they started over the muddy tire ruts that led through the open field to the tunnel ladder system. The ladders and platforms were slippery in the rain.

Their decent to the bottom was of necessity slow. With night and clouds above them, no diffusion or reflection of light from above came into the tunnel. As soon as they rounded the bend away from the few station work lights, the tunnel became as dark as a mile down a coal mineshaft. Nevertheless, Danny kept the beam pointed barely ahead of their path to deny warning to anyone in front of them.

"Get your light ready, too," Danny instructed, as he reached into the bag for the pistol. "I'll be damned if we lose him this time."

They walked silently side by side, until they stood at the junction with the main line.

"Where do you want to wait?" Nate asked, his English "torch" in one hand and a length of pipe borrowed from the field above in the other.

"Right across from those rungs," Danny replied, nodding.

The sound of a train approaching from the east came into the Tube. Nate and Danny placed themselves just out of the field of its headlight and watched as it rushed by. A few minutes later, Nate found the plank of wood they had perched on days before and moved it so they could rest on the ground.

Thirty trains passed, twice from both directions at the same time.

After ten o'clock, noises of another air raid came down faintly into the tunnels from the opening in the ground. Little by little, it increased. From where they sat, they could barely distinguish the difference between anti-aircraft and bomb concussions. All they knew was that the noise was furious and continuous.

And then it was silent.

"Listen!" Nate commanded with hope.

"It stopped." Danny did not sound impressed.

"No. It stopped suddenly," Nate corrected. "Like maybe we jumped into another time?"

Danny shot up from his haunches to listen. "Damn! Could we be that lucky?"

As if in mocking reply, the explosions began again. The silence had lasted a little under thirty seconds.

"Fuck," Danny said softly, letting himself slowly back down onto the plank.

"Engaged!" Nate exclaimed.

"Now what?" Danny asked.

"'Two nations separated by a common language!'"

"Have you gone totally nuts?"

Nate pointed his light at Danny's face and switched it on. Danny grabbed the light and turned it off. "Don't do that!"

"'Engaged' in England also means 'busy.' He was telling me that he and Penny were going to the movies. He felt threatened and wanted me to butt out."

"He who?"

"Brendon Danvers."

"Oh, that helps me a whole lot."

"Penny's serviceman boyfriend."

Danny was silent in the blackness for several moments. "You were really upset when he used the word 'engaged'? Christ! Nathaniel Allen has finally fallen in love, hasn't he?"

"No."

"Hasn't he?"

"I like her a lot – unlike you, I've managed to keep it under control."

For almost a minute, all that could be heard was the breathing of the two men. Then Danny said, "No, you haven't. Penelope Miles is a symbol of this time for you. You like this time, in spite of all the bombs, and she's the nicest part."

"I'm trying to be a realist in dealing with this time," Nate corrected. "I have to admit that I don't share your faith in our salvation via this cold tunnel."

"Nah," Danny's voice came back. "You like it. Unlike me, you hate your family and don't miss them. You've got nobody to go home to. For an excitement junkie who speaks English, loves war history and really digs London, this has to be the best out of all possible times and places."

Nate did not contradict his friend.

Convinced he had at last won one of their arguments, Danny lapsed into a prolonged, smug, verbal silence. The only noises he made were occasional teasing noises in his throat.

Nate did not hear Danny's taunting. He was too engrossed in remembering a poem he had once selected to memorize when required for twelfth grade English. It was called "Miniver Cheevy" and was by an American poet of the early twentieth century whose works fitted Nate's sardonic, disillusioned attitude in his senior year. The poet's name was Edward Arlington Robinson.

> …Miniver loved the days of old
> When swords were bright and steeds were prancing;
> The vision of a warrior bold
> Would set him dancing….
> Miniver mourned the ripe renown
> That made so many a name so fragrant;
> He mourned Romance, now on the town,
> And Art, a vagrant.

Nate privately admitted his fascination for the past. He was not ignorant enough to mistake that what he treasured were illusions, partial truths that neatly avoided the accompanying ills of other times. But, sitting in the near-total darkness, he also had to admit that he sometimes enjoyed the predicament he and Danny had been dumped into. He had not reflected enough to be able to point his finger at every individual incident that thrilled him, but he did know that one very important piece of the puzzle was, as Danny had so aptly pointed out, Penelope Miles. He accepted the truth and began humming "Dancing in the Dark" within the surrounding blackness. "Shut up," Danny hissed.

The air raid lasted less than forty minutes. Nate wondered if the evening rain clouds were the cause of the light attack, if someplace other than London such as ill-fated Coventry had been targeted instead, or if this was indeed the long but sure descent from the highpoint of the Battle of Britain. His thought lasted but a moment, and then he focused on remembering Penny Miles in her dance shorts.

Nate felt and heard Danny stand and stretch. Another train rumbled down the tracks from the heart of London, pushing a bright beam of light ahead of it.

"What?" Danny screamed with outrage.

And then the train's noise blotted out the rest of his words. It sounded its horn in warning as Danny stepped forward and made his presence known. Having no more reason to hide, Nate stood as well and peered at and into the passing cars. Everything was vintage 1940.

"I don't believe it! No, no, no!" Danny ranted as the train passed. He snapped on his flashlight and dashed across the pair of tracks. Nate followed slowly. "What's the matter?"

In answer, Danny bent to the track bed on the far side of the tunnel. When he straightened up, he held a red bandanna.

"He's mocking us. The bastard's toying with you and me." Danny dropped the kerchief, his shoulders sagging. Nate had never seen his friend look so defeated.

## CHAPTER THIRTEEN

Nate did not bother to wake Danny. After spending the major portion of the night with him in the tunnel and not finding the notorious redheaded man much less a way back to the twenty-first century, he could not tolerate listening to one more syllable of self pity. Danny would never have agreed to accompany Nate on his latest adventure at any rate; agnostic was too passive a word to describe the anti-religious attitude of the grandson and son of devout Roman Catholics. Daniel O'Shea possessed no faith in any god.

In contrast, Nate's mother and father had been twice-a-year Christians, attending local churches with connected members on Christmas Eve and Easter Sunday morning. The only other times they set foot into a church or synagogue was as invitees to a wedding or bar mitzvah. Nate had attended the non-denominational service at Kirkpatrick Chapel on the Rutgers campus two or three times a semester with dorm mates. The main attraction for him was the choir singing and organ music. He maintained an open mind concerning faith but did not feel a need for ritual communion. In the war-torn London of 1940, however, he felt a strong need to witness a church service and the congregants who worshiped.

When Nate knocked on the Miles's back door and asked Mrs. Miles if they were attending church, she looked as if he had asked her instead if she saw horns on his forehead. Her head jerked back and her eyes went wide.

"Yes, we are," sounded Worden Miles's voice from the kitchen. "Do you care to come with us?"

"I would very much like to."

"Then come have some breakfast. We don't leave for another forty minutes or so."

The last of the bacon Nate had bought was served up, along with something unnamed that tasted to him like Southern grits. Two precious grapefruit had been purchased "under the counter," and a half of one was offered to Nate. No inquiry about Daniel O'Shea was made, and

Nate was not about to broach the subject on his own.

Penny had descended only moments before breakfast was served. Although she was polite, she seemed even less enthusiastic to see him than during Brendon Danvers' visit the previous evening. He hoped there was a simple explanation, such as accumulated exhaustion from the long past week.

"How much longer do you think you will be in this part of London?" she asked, in the middle of his oration about attending chapel services at his university.

"Not more than another week, I expect," he replied. He looked for disappointment on Penny's face, but she merely nodded.

The Anglican church lay a brisk walk from the Miles house. Its south-side wall had been blackened by thick smoke from the detonation of a nearby high explosive bomb, but otherwise the structure looked sound enough.

The sanctuary was three-quarters filled with fresh-scrubbed faces, the men in suits, the women in dresses, hats and gloves. Clearly, the Miles family was no stranger to the place, because they were greeted or nodded at many times. They took their place in a pew halfway down the left side. The opening hymn was "Oh God, Our Help in Ages Past."

The celebrating priest conducted the Act of Penitence, Kyrie, Gloria, the Collect and readings with a face so devoid of expression except for his moving lips that he looked to Nate like Japanese anime. Only when he ascended the pulpit to deliver his sermon did he take on a personality. His speech had an informal tone, and he leaned forward on his elbows and spoke his words as one might chatting over a fence to one's neighbor.

"Today, my Christian friends, I would like to speak on civilization. A bishop considerably older than I recently made an observation to me. He said, 'You know, outside it may be zero degrees centigrade and snowing. But inside a house, the furnace keeps it a cheery twenty degrees. But in the kitchen, the icebox keeps the food at five degrees so that it won't spoil. That is civilization.' He said it with a wink in his voice, and I understood that he was joking. But many others would not think so. They fully equate a nation's degree of being civilized with the latest advances in its technology, its national output and the count of possessions in each home."

The middle of the priest's sermon defined civilization in varying terms, including the original Latin 'civicus,' which could mean 'community,' 'culture,' and 'courteousness.' He dwelt upon how the German people, with their poetry, drama, music and their pioneering industries, considered themselves the pinnacle of civilization. He compared this to a Christian definition. Then, after a pregnant pause, he came to the meat of his sermon: the Blitz that had so dominated London life in the week past.

"In former centuries, warfare had rules. Nations that called themselves civilized did not target civilians as the Germans have done so mercilessly and methodically in Poland, Czechoslovakia, the Netherlands and now Britain. What has made men like Adolf Hitler and his lieutenants so fearless of committing atrocity after atrocity against their fellow man? Is it a natural consequence of the Age of Enlightenment, of Science, of the Machine? Are these not all bites of the apple that grows on the Tree of Knowledge, seeming so pretty to the eye and delicious to the tongue but containing the seeds of our separation from God...and of our ultimate destruction? Is the world we find ourselves suffering in not the result of an ever-increasing belief that man is God and accountable only to the scoreboard of who wins and who loses? Is this not what Nietzche's 'superman' means, an 'Übermensch' who owes nothing to his creator, if indeed that creator ever existed? Did not Darwin's survival of the fittest theory justify in the minds of Godless men the capitalist manifesto that greed is a good thing and fosters progress? Do you not feel pride and hubris falling from the skies just as much as the bombs?

"It is said that the devil hath the power to assume pleasing shapes. We laugh at our ancestors believing in the kinds of demons and the hell preached in medieval times. We think 'How quaint' when we view the imaginings of the apocalypse by painters like Hieronymous Bosch. We know there are no such devils and demons. But we fail to see the devil in the freedoms without moral restraint that modern times allow. We tell ourselves with great pride that we are not like the Germans, but are we not losing our souls as well? Is it simply that we are losing our fear of God, sense of humility, love and compassion for one another in a more 'civilized' manner? When we beat the forces of evil arrayed against us...and we shall...let us determine to analyze the causes of two world wars in the space of less than half a century. For if we do not, my Christian friends, then may God have mercy on us all, the winners and the losers."

Nate looked surreptitiously around for the third time, reading the faces and body language of the congregants. He saw no one as visibly shaken as he felt. If there was a reason why he should be hurled back in time, the lesson of the sermon seemed to make the greatest sense. With despair and elation simultaneously welling up inside him, he realized why he had to travel constantly, to seek out new thrills and companions, to feed his addiction to excitement. He had flung himself relentlessly in all directions because he had no moral compass. His values were superficial and put on from the outside like expensive, flashy suits. He had reveled in his cleverness to flaunt the rules of society and get away with it. He had cared nothing of the misery of the peons forced to mine the gems he smuggled. He used charity and volunteerism as a front. He thought of himself and his pleasures first, second and third. Compassion, community, courteousness were also-rans in the pointless race that was his life.

The remainder of the church service flowed as a blur to Nate.

Afterward, the Miles family respected his silence and conversed among themselves as they strolled home. When they were yet two streets from their house, the air raid sirens began their wail. Nate noticed that all those coming from church, the Miles family included, picked up their pace but refused to run in an undignified and panicked fashion. For his part, Nate broke into a jog. He needed to be sure of Danny's safety.

As he had feared, Danny slept through the siren warnings. With only two minutes remaining out of the seven between first siren and first bombs, Nate had Danny up and pulling on his trousers.

"I'll check to see that the buckets and trough are filled with water," Nate told him. "Make sure you've got your bag and everything that belongs to us."

"You go ahead," Danny directed.

Nate went down to the Wilcox outdoor shelter and deposited all his belongings inside. Then he walked out with a wooden basket and calmly and methodically picked and stowed the fresh marigolds, the lettuce and the radishes that grew in the dirt that covered the roof. He did not venture to safety when the barrage balloons rose to their limits. Nor did he retreat when the anti-aircraft guns opened up and dotted the sky with smoky, black mushrooms. He stood his ground as the first planes came into view and counted their massed numbers. He realized that this was the battle royal, one of the last great attempts of the Luftwaffe to force Downing Street and Parliament to sue for peace. The sky was filled with aircraft, both British and German. From his distance, it looked to him like the fourth plague of Moses. When Nate spotted the silver glints of the bombs falling, he at last moved into the shelter and battened the door.

Danny sat at the little table, playing solitaire.

"It's called 'Patience' over here," Nate remarked, as he removed his jacket.

Danny moved a card up. "Yeah, they would. Living in England in 1940 takes a lot of patience."

"I went to church this morning."

"No shit."

"That's right. It was no shit," Nate told him.

"Why would you do that?"

"I wanted to see if I could pick up clues why more than half this country attended church in this time, and in our time only two per cent of those who claim to be Anglican attend regularly."

"It's the same reason there are no atheists in foxholes."

"No. Before the war the numbers were way up."

"It was the Depression then."

"And before that?" Nate asked.

"Another world war. And before that, people were ignorant and still in the power of the churches."

"Ignorant?"

"Yeah. They believed in God."

"They also believed in community, and kindness, and volunteering. Funny how the decline in those and failing attendance at churches go hand in hand, isn't it?"

"Don't look at me. Where's that damned ten of spades?"

"When is the last time you volunteered for anything?"

Danny rocked back on two legs to regard Nate. "When was the last time for you?"

A bomb landed nearby, rattling the shelter.

"Jesus!" Danny shouted, falling backward out of the chair.

"Why are you crying for God when you don't believe in Him?" Nate asked, not having flinched.

Danny jumped up. "It's just an expression, ferchrissake. What's your problem?"

Another bomb landed, even closer, and then a third. The kerosene lantern glass cracked.

"You know what I saw in the congregation?" Nate said.

"No. Educate me," Danny spat back.

"I saw about twenty per cent of those in the pews nodding off or staring vacantly. They were there out of habit, afraid not to be seen, sure that the sermon didn't apply to them."

"You bet. Hypocrites wasting their time. They were always part of the numbers."

"But the rest were listening. Some nodded their heads. A few even had tears in their eyes."

"Tears? What was the sermon about?"

"Civilization."

A series of basso thumping noises penetrated the shelter. A fourth bomb thundered through the neighborhood.

"Fuck me! That was close!" Danny shouted. He whirled on Nate. "I'm not gonna ask any more. I know when you're lecturing me, when you think you're so superior."

"I do act that way, don't I?"

"Constantly."

The bombing continued, but the explosives landed increasingly toward the center of London. Nate reached for the crossbar and lifted it.

"What do you think you're doing?" Danny demanded.

"I'm volunteering." Nate opened the door and walked into the garden. It was peppered with incendiary spikes, flaring like Fourth of July sparklers. He pivoted and studied first the Wilcox house and then the home of the Miles family. Both had burning spikes on their roofs.

Nate ran to the ladder stored against the back wall of the Wilcox house. He wrestled it upright. The ladder was short and reached just below the eave line. Cursing the stupidity of inadequate tools, he grabbed a trowel from the basket under the back steps and then climbed. He shoved the trowel under his belt, grabbed the eave with both arms and swung his left leg over. His movement caused the ladder to slide away and land with a clatter.

"Dan!" Nate shouted as he fought to get his entire body onto the roof. Another squadron of bombers approached, bedeviled by RAF fighters. Nate could see the individual lines of tracer bullets flashing in the midday sky.

"What?" his partner's voice sounded from inside the shelter.

"The ladder fell."

"So get back in here!"

"I'm on the roof!" Nate stood in a stooped position and cautiously walked toward the five flaring incendiary spikes that had almost burned down to the level of the shingles. One by one, he knocked the sticks into the garden.

A screaming noise came from the sky to the east. Nate glanced in the direction of the swelling noise and saw a Messerschmitt fighter heading directly for him. He threw himself over the ridgeline of the roof. Multiple lines of bullets tore into the back wall and the roof. Nate felt a pain like a hot knife in his left side. The plane screamed past. Nate rolled over and examined his shirt. Two holes had been torn in it. Around the openings expanded circles of blood. Wincing, Nate pushed his forefinger through the front hole and explored. He felt the ragged flesh of the wound. It was about an inch-and-a-half long but superficial. When he pressed it, the pain made him cry out. He came up on his knees and looked over at the Miles roof. Several spikes had burned fiery depressions in the shingles.

Nate thought about trying to jump across to the other roof. It lay only six feet distant, and slightly downhill as well. The pain in his side dissuaded him.

Danny exited the shelter, ran like an Olympic sprinter toward the house, and grabbed the ladder. He set it upright and dashed back toward the shelter.

"Goddammit, hold it for me!" Nate yelled.

"Are you okay?"

"Yeah. Hold the ladder!"

Moving as swiftly as he could and doing his best to ignore the spasms of his wounded muscles, Nate climbed down. He looked at the Miles house and saw that the roof had caught fire.

"Mr. Miles! Your roof!" Nate cried out.

Another fighter buzzed by at low altitude. Danny and Nate threw themselves prone, but it was a Spitfire

Nate jumped up, grabbed the ladder and threw it over the low wall that separated the two properties. Worden Miles had just emerged from their shelter. Wiser now, Nate placed the short ladder on the top of the back steps. It reached over the eave. He climbed. Gritting his teeth against the agony that had flamed through his side when he rolled onto the roof, he stood and realized he had lost the trowel. He moved toward the two smaller fires and extinguished them with his shoe.

"Here!" Worden cried from the ladder. He held a length of hose up. "There's no pressure from the tap. I'll put this hosepipe in the stirrup pump straight away!"

"Straight away" was more than half a minute before water began burbling from the end of the hose. By that time, the two fires that remained had eaten their way through the roof, into the rafters, and onto the upper side of the second-floor ceiling. Nate was startled by the heat of the flames. Moving up to the holes as close as he dared without receiving burns, he trained the weak stream of water on one until it seemed out, then raced to the second. Mercifully, although the raid went on as thickly and desperately as before, the vector of the bombers had changed. The air space above the house was clear.

Shaking his head in frustration, Nate saw that the last fire had taken hold inside the attic. The water stopped. Mr. Miles shouted that he had exhausted both his buckets. Nate directed him to fetch the water from the Wilcox garden. While he stood helplessly on the roof, he heard noises from below him, inside the house. They were sharp, like the falling of an axe.

"Ready again!" Worden shouted up. Somehow, the middle-aged man had dragged the large galvanized trough half filled with water out of the Wilcox garden and through his own garden gate. Nate heard the frenzied sound of pumping. To assist, he put his mouth to the hose and sucked. Several seconds later, the water arrived. He crept as close to the smoldering hole as the billowing smoke would allow and trained the hose down.

The sounds of building materials tearing and snapping came up from inside the house. From several streets away sounded the clangs of a fire apparatus.

"God, what has she done?" Millicent Miles's voice came up through the hole in the roof. "She's summoned the Auxiliary Fire Service!"

"Step back, Mrs. Miles!" The second voice below Nate belonged to Danny O'Shea. The sounds of destruction continued.

Millicent began coughing. "Bloody hell!" she exclaimed. It was the first curse from any member of the family that Nate had heard.

Up the street rolled a taxicab and a pumper with its own supply of water.

"That's the lot of it," Worden Miles called.

Nate's stream of water failed. He let go of the hose. It snaked down into the garden. He straightened up and watched the three men working from the fire engine. Another two men with hooks on poles and wearing wet, ungainly clothing and Wellington boots clomped into the house. Gawkers began appearing from neighboring houses. A pair men came into the back yard through the gate and conversed with

Worden about offering help. They all went around the front and inside the house. When Nate saw the firemen getting ready to train their hose on the roof, he retreated to the unharmed side of the roof, just above the ladder.

Over the increasingly distant din of the air battle, Nate heard someone in the neighborhood cheer. He looked up to see that a German bomber had been badly crippled. Its tail had been shot apart, and it was losing altitude and executing an uncontrolled turn that would put it directly over the Miles house while still at about two thousand feet.

Nate was transfixed by the imminent death of the bomber and whoever remained inside. He could not look away as its whine became greater and greater. He saw that the swastika under one wing was pierced with bullet holes and that the nose turret had been badly damaged as well.

From the open side hatch dropped a solitary German airman. He barely cleared the craft when he yanked on his ripcord and opened his parachute. The speed and direction of the plane caused the figure to plummet toward the street behind the Miles home.

Nate worked his way down the ladder as fast as his wound would allow and hurried across the garden and through the gate into the street. The descending bomber crewman was heading straight for him. He had come near enough for Nate to see that his face was blackened with soot. Perhaps a mile away, the deep, furious sound of the bomber meeting the ground tore through the air, a different concussion and explosion from that of the bombs.

Two older Englishmen appeared from seemingly nowhere. One held an axe and the other brandished a sledgehammer. They barked words at each other to work their blood into a greater boil for the task at hand.

A sudden gust of wind blew along the street. The instant the German's feet touched the asphalt, the wind caught his trailing chute and yanked him onto his back. He was dragged half a dozen yards. Nate ran to catch up with him.

"Nicht töte!" the young German cried out. "Ich bin kein Feind."

"What's the bastard saying?" one of the white-haired Englishmen demanded as he swung his axe up menacingly.

Nate studied the very German face and saw that its owner could not have been older than twenty. A sudden image of a World War II cemetery he had visited in Luxembourg came into his consciousness.

He remembered the ultra-orderly rows of white crosses and stars of David for the Americans and British boys, most of whom were between eighteen and twenty-two, and the rows of black crosses for their German counterparts. And none of them, Nate realized with a shudder, was dead yet. "He's asking for you not to kill him. He says he's not your enemy."

"Hell if he isn't," growled the second man, raising his sledgehammer.

Nate stepped in their path, holding up his hands. "Are you as bad as they are? Do you want to live with the blood of an unarmed man on your hands?"

The old men lowered their weapons.

Two middle-aged men wearing khaki jackets and cloth caps and carrying World War One vintage Lee-Enfield rifles jogged around the corner. When one spotted the parachute, he shoved a whistle in his mouth and blew for all he was worth.

"Home Guard!" his partner shouted. "Step away from the prisoner!"

The German had come up on his knees. At the sight of the rifles, he raised his hands.

Nate hastened to the top of the parachute, which threatened to haul its wearer down the street. He stepped on the cords, bent and began rolling up the billowing silk.

"Nicht schiesse!" the German cried out.

"He says 'Don't shoot,'" Nate translated.

Nevertheless, the two Home Guardsmen pointed their rifles at the weaponless airman. They seemed more nervous than he did.

"Nick Sheesuh, eh? I thought he recognized you, Nick!" one of the old men called to a Home Guard. Everyone but Nate and the downed German laughed. The tension was partially dispelled.

The Englishman named Nick jerked his rifle in an upward direction. The German stood and shrugged out of the parachute harness.

"We held him for you," the second of the old men declared. "You want us to help you march him somewhere?"

One of the Home Guards looked up at the sky, still dotted with anti-aircraft explosions. Planes of various shapes and sizes could be seen in the distance.

"No. Get into your shelters like you're supposed to," the Guardsman replied. He turned to Nate, who was gathering the parachute into a tight mass. "And who might you be?"

"Nathaniel Allen."

"Nate!"

Unobserved by all, Penny had appeared at the bottom of the street. She broke into a run. "My God! You're wounded!"

"I thought the German shot him," one of the old men divulged. "He was the first one here."

"I was strafed," Nate told the group. "It's all right."

Penny had clearly heard as she closed the final distance. "Nobody who's been shot is all right. Hello Mr. Standish, Mr. Dichter."

The Guards doffed their caps at Penny.

Penny hooked her hand under the crook of Nate's arm and turned him toward the Miles garden gate. "Come with me! What have you been up to?"

"Putting out fires and capturing Germans," Nate was happy to report as he walked. "And I also got you yards and yards of silk! Do you sew?"

"Yes."

Nate had been careful to carry the parachute on his unwounded side, to prevent his blood from staining the precious silk. "Then here's the material for your Ginger Rogers dress."

"That's lovely of you, but never mind the dress. Set that down and take off your shirt!"

Nate unbuttoned the front of her brother's shirt, and Penny simultaneously worked open the buttons at the wrists. She carefully peeled the shirt from his shoulders and examined the wound.

"You see? Not too bad," Nate said brightly and with maximum bravado.

Penny grimaced at all the blood. "It wants stitching."

Throughout London, planes continued to skirmish, bombs exploded, anti-aircraft guns kept up their pounding din, and smoke filled the September sky. But in the Miles back yard, a charged silence set in. Nate looked at Penny's worried expression and knew he loved her without reservation.

"I must go on duty myself now," she said, running her fingers down his flank. "With all the terrible injuries there are bound to be, you wouldn't be treated for hours. I've learned how to sew it up neatly. Come inside."

"It's chaos in your house," Nate said.

"No. In the shelter." Penny took his hand and led him the few steps into the steel enclosure.

"You went for the Auxiliary Fire Service," Nate said.

"When I couldn't raise them on the telephone."

"Your mother didn't seem happy about it."

"She's been hearing tales from my father about how they charge in like elephants, doing more damage than good. From their point of view, they need to put out fires quickly, or one house might end up burning down ten." Penny guided Nate gently onto a seat. "One moment. I need to go in the house and fetch some alcohol."

"Do you have rubber cement? The kind that sticks paper together?"

"I think we do."

"Bring that, too." When he saw the confusion on Penny's face, he added, "I'll show you. Just get it."

Left alone in the shelter, Nate set to wondering what he would do regarding Miss Penelope Miles. After yet one more abortive night in the railway tunnel, he was completely convinced that he and Danny could never return to their own time. He also remembered his grim thought about no one long surviving such a time jump to tell the world about it. In spite of having just eluded death by inches, he was nonetheless convinced that the odds were he would not outlive the month, much less the war. If by some miracle he did, he believed it best to get to the United States to be among those who spoke American English. Such a task would have to be done without getting on government rolls, because soon enough men his age would be drafted into the U.S. military to serve in this same war. Given his conviction that Death actively pursued him, he was not about to commit the ultimate irony and aid the Grim Reaper by doing what he knew to be right and volunteering for service. He would find other ways to serve his country and England. Returning to the British Isle in fewer than five years was therefore all but impossible. Both the need to avoid death and to gain distance strongly suggested that he leave the woman alone and not complicate her already frazzled life.

And yet, now that he admitted to himself how much he loved her, his realizations pained him worse than the wound in his side. He decided that he could make no admission of his love, put no pressure on her. On the other hand, if she voluntarily confessed that she loved him, then he would do everything in his power to stay alive and with her.

"Alcohol, rubber glue," Penny announced, returning to the shelter.

"I'd like to see your nurse's diploma first," Nate said.

"If I were you, I'd rather ask to see my needlepoint." She smiled as she reached for a curved needle in the Miles first aid kit. It had already been threaded. "Needles to say…this will hurt."

"Ouch."

"Yes, my jokes can sting worse than bullets." She pressed a piece of sterile cotton to the mouth of the alcohol bottle and tipped the neck. While she gently swabbed the wound, she asked, "Is the Wilcox house safe?"

"I knocked several fire sticks off the roof. Repairs will need to be done to patch the bullet holes."

"You got this on the Wilcox roof or ours?"

"The first."

"So you were outside while planes were strafing. And then you climbed down wounded, set the ladder against our roof and put out our fires?"

"Somebody had to do it. Don't start at the edge of the wound, Penny. You only need to put three stitches in the center."

"But the edges will heal ragged."

"That's what the glue is for." Nate knew that hospitals in his time had picked up a triage trick from late twentieth-century American battlefield medics and were routinely using superglue to close wounds more neatly than suturing. He was willing to try the same with rubber cement.

"My family owes you a great debt for saving the house," Penny said.

"Yes, it does." Nate watched with pleasure as Penny digested his cocky words. "And you shall be the one to pay me back." Now her head pivoted up, expectantly. "You had last night off from your ambulance driving. When are you next off?"

"I served extra duty the previous Monday if you recall, so I only have tonight and then I'm at liberty tomorrow."

"Excellent. I believe we already made a date to finish our dance." Penny's expectant look dissolved. It was not, however, replaced by a smile. "Yes, we did. Tomorrow night at the school. But you won't be able to dance with this wound."

"Oh ye of little faith. The bullet just ripped the skin open."

While Penny finished her sutures and Nate did his best not to wince, he thought of the two frames of film remaining inside the camera. "I know you're in a hurry, and this seems trivial with blood all over me, but I'd like to take a picture of you when you're finished."

Penny's head jerked up. He hastened to add, "Standing in front of your house with the holes in the roof. Wait right here!"

"I look a fright," she called after him.

"Nonsense," he said as he gingerly swung his leg over the low picket fence that separated the Miles and Wilcox back yards. "I'll be two shakes of a lamb's tail." He entered the shelter, dug through the shoulder bag for the camera and then hurried out.

Penny stood near the house, looking ill at ease. He expected her to be primping, but she had not found a brush nor gone after make-up.

"I'm only shooting you with a camera," Nate teased. "Don't you like yourself on film?"

"No."

He curled his fingers to coax her toward him. "In a few years, you'll be glad I captured this. Stand right there!"

Penny stepped forward without comment.

Nate adjusted the aperture and shutter speed. He moved the advance lever. The camera's tension was easier than it had been the previous day. He worried that throwing himself down the stairs near Sloane Square had damaged the internal workings. On the outside, however, the instrument looked fine. He looked down into the viewfinder.

"Give me one of those million dollar smiles."

"We deal in pounds."

"Then just say 'cheese.'"

Penny obliged. Nate begged a second shot, to finish the roll.

"Now that's done," Penny said, squinting from the sun. "Show me how to apply the rubber cement, and then I really must change into my uniform and be off."

"Fine. Be off with you then." In spite of the hot pain in his side, Nate felt happy. At least, he told himself, he had captured her image.

Smoke had damaged the inside of the Miles house far more than fire had. Even that damage, along with a bit of water staining, was limited to the walls, furniture and belongings on the second floor, so that the entire first floor could still be used. Nate and Danny insisted that the Miles family transfer what they had salvaged to the Wilcox upstairs. The Americans elected to take up residence in the Wilcox shelter.

Although he had received his share of praise for his efforts, Danny remained in a foul mood. The first time he found himself alone with Nate, he related that he had calculated being ten thousand calories short of nourishment across the week they had been stranded. For his own sanity, Nate suggested that Danny visit Gwendolyn Lamb. Danny admitted that Gwen had told him not ten minutes after he presented her with the two expensive rings that they had been together far too much and that she could not see him again until at least Tuesday night. Tuesday night, however, Danny and Nate would be robbing the Bank of England. It guaranteed that Dan could not enjoy her physical charms again until at least Wednesday evening, when she returned from her new job at the bakery. In effect, Danny had been placed on two diets simultaneously.

The day raid had been enormous and generalized. From standing both on the roofs and in the gardens, Nate could clearly see by the towering columns of smoke in every direction that massive destruction had been wrought on the capital. Toward four, the smoky skies were silent. Even the alarm noises faded. Four hours later, another raid began. It was nearly as enormous as the first. With the fading of the sun, the magnitude of the hundreds of raging fires could be appreciated. Nate knew that the next trip downtown would reveal London as he had only previously viewed it in iconographic book images. He thought of the priest's sermon and of Hieronymous Bosch's image of hell, and then he thought of the famous passage from Christopher Marlowe's Faustus:

Hell hath no limits, nor is circumscribed
In one self-place; for where we are is Hell,
And where Hell is, there must we ever be.

# CHAPTER FOURTEEN

The heart of London was more devastated than Nate had imagined. Useless strategic targets such a tobacco shops and bookstores were ruined. There was no evidence of precision bombing but rather one general purpose of grievously wounding the will of a people. Yet again, it had not happened. Still, the inhabitants of the great city went on about their business with grim resolution. Nate was acutely aware that this was not a war where soldiers were sent off to foreign lands as proxies for the nation's ostensible agenda. Everyday citizens shouldered and shared personal responsibility to their nation.

Working side by side the night before, separating what could be saved from the Miles home and what could not, Nate had asked Penny to articulate her mood. "I'm frightened," she admitted. "But I must not allow fear to dominate me. I have an obligation to my family, my colleagues and to my country to bear up and carry on."

Nate thought of his own generation and the one that had raised him. They numbered the type of person who sued after opening a hot cup of coffee between her legs while driving. Worse, they were the jury who awarded millions to the dimwit. They were the generations who consumed billions of Oxycontin, Lortab, Valium, Tylenol, Advil and other pills because Madison Avenue assured them "You haven't got time for the pain." They were the kind who paid a thousand dollars a year to a gym and drove a quarter of a mile to use it. None of them could have functioned under such hardships as Nate witnessed.

To the young man who had crisscrossed the planet for years, it appeared that the entire "civilized world" of the twenty-first century had lost the steersmen of their ships. Not just him but nearly everybody in his generation and the one before it seemed to have lost their moral compass. Everyone in his era knew their rights, but few wanted to hear anything about responsibility. In the London of 1940, the buildings were damaged but the people were whole. In the London, the Paris, the Berlin, the New York of his era, the buildings were whole but the people were damaged.

Nate was relieved to find the photography store intact. He paid for the roll he had had developed and for the small prints. He saw that his first shot of Bennett had been clear enough to identify the man by. He was pleased by the half dozen shots he had taken of London and noted with particular pleasure that his photograph of the Spitfire pursuing the German fighter could be blown up to something worth framing.

Nate took the Exakta camera from around his neck and handed it to the shop owner. "There's an exposed roll in there. Would you unload and develop it?"

"One moment, sir."

The man disappeared behind a thick black curtain for only a few seconds. He reappeared wearing a furrowed brow. "There's no film, sir."

Nate looked at the open-backed camera in the man's hands. "That's impossible."

"I'm afraid it's true. Perhaps someone in your family unloaded it…as a favor to you?"

"I'm single."

"Then I don't know what to tell you."

Nate pushed past the man and the curtain, into the small darkroom.

"Please, sir! What are you doing?"

The bench had no roll of SLR film. Nate whirled around and faced the owner, who had poked his head through the curtain. Nate pulled him into the darkroom and ran his hands up and down the man's flanks, feeling for the film.

"Here, here! What's the meaning of this?" the shop owner demanded.

"It's very important film," Nate said, although he knew of nothing he had taken of value on the roll. The fact of the film's disappearance was what unnerved him. "Very sorry. Clearly, someone wanted it, and I have to begin narrowing the possibilities."

"Well, it wasn't I who took it," the man declared, straightening up and thrusting his chest out with patent umbrage.

"I know." Nate grabbed his camera and the developed film and prints he had paid for. "A thousand apologies." He left the shop moving as quickly as he could.

In the smoky, acrid air, Nate paused and pondered who the culprit might have been. He could not imagine that Danny had anything to do with the theft. He doubted if Danny could open an SLR camera. His partner had shown no interest whatsoever in Nate's picture taking. His only fixation was the tunnel. At the moment Nate stood outside the photography shop, Danny was somewhere in the Tubes. His revised plan upon waking was to explore the tunnel beyond where he and Nate had waited, to catch the redheaded man unawares.

That left the Miles family the most likely suspects. The film advance had indeed felt empty when he took the pictures of Penny. Again, Nate could not fathom what the motivation for any of them to take the roll would be.

And then Nate remembered that the camera had been in the bag when Alex Bennett frisked them. In the middle of the sidewalk, Nate held up the camera and pressed the back release. It opened with no noise. It would have been unlikely but possible for the man to have opened it, yanked out and pocketed the film. Given the man's need to know precisely who Nate and Danny were, it made sense. From his point of view, stealing or destroying the records etched on the silver nitrate stock might have saved him from prison.

Thoughts of Bennett and the camera led to the developed photographs. Nate held them up to the daylight. A daring thought came to him. He knew that it might prove a problem later, but he had to know if Bennett was the inside man at the bank.

Nate walked to The City, the financial square mile in the center of London. On Threadneedle Street sat the Bank of England. It was an impressive amalgamation of structures. On the street level and against the sidewalk was a two-story, gray barbican that reminded Nate of the palazzi of the banker families of Renaissance Florence. Above this towered a white edifice that looked like a combination of a wedding cake, the front of the Supreme Court Building and a French Baroque palace. It took him some time to find the entrance for employees. He walked in wearing a broad smile.

A gentleman in a three-piece suit greeted him. "Are you looking for the public entrance, sir?"

"No." Nate held up the better photograph of Alex Bennett. "The other day I met an employee of your bank and took his picture. I'm from America, by the way. As a representative of our government."

"Good for you."

"I'm in the neighborhood today on Lend Lease business, and I thought I'd pop in and see if I could give him this copy. Do you recognize him?"

The bank employee gave the photo a cursory glance. "This is a very large establishment, sir."

"The biggest! You don't recognize him, then?"

"Can't say as I do."

"I've forgotten his name. It was something like Bennett. Do you have a list perhaps?"

The man took the photograph from Nate's hand and examined it more closely. "No. I've been an employee of this institution for twenty-one years, and I have never seen this face."

"Pity."

"Is that a public house he's standing in front of?"

"It is. Don't officers of the Bank of England bend an elbow from time to time?" Nate inquired.

"Can I be of help in any other way, sir?"

"Nah. I'll just be pushing on. 'Cheerio', 'Pip-pip' and all that rot."

Nate pivoted smartly on his heels and walked out the door.

When Nate returned in the late afternoon to the Wilcox house, heavy-laden with a crate of groceries, he found Danny sitting out in the garden. He sunned himself in the one space that was not shaded by drying laundry.

"Still no redheaded maniac, eh?"

"When I do catch him, I'm leaving you behind," Danny said without opening his eyes. "You and this war deserve each other." Nate declined to share information about the missing film with his partner. He did not want to give Danny yet one more excuse to back out of the robbery. Instead, he told about his fruitless visit to the Bank of England.

"The man at the door basically said that he knew everybody," Nate finished. "So I have to guess Alex Bennett is an outsider. Which means the insider supplying the information is the driver of the armored truck or the shotgun rider."

"Yeah?"

"The first thing the police do after bank robberies is look for the insider. Do you think maybe Scotland Yard and the Metropolitan Police are pretty good at sweating the truth out of people?"

Danny shifted on the chair. "Not as good as us Americans. They're far too civilized to torture or threaten. They probably just bore them into spilling their guts by droning on about fair play and God and king."

"However they do it, they're good at it."

"Which means the inside man has to disappear really well after the heist."

"Or die."

"Bennett said he wanted no gunplay."

Nate set his crate of food on Danny's lap. "What the hell do you think he'd say to us? 'By the way, guys, I'm blowing away the driver because he's the inside man. You two don't mind being accessories to murder along with robbing the Bank of England, do you?'"

"I see what you mean."

"And if he'd kill one, what's two more to him? Especially two who have no identities?"

Danny grabbed the crate and straightened up. "So you're saying we should not show up tomorrow night."

"No. We need those passports. We need money. You weren't a Boy Scout, were you?" Danny's frown provided the answer. "I didn't think so. Nevertheless, you will be prepared. We have that little Webley, fully loaded."

"And if he frisks us again?"

"Thank God you like to wear your shirts large. The gun is little and thin. You will hang it against your chest, from a piece of string tied around your neck. You saw how he patted you down. He felt sides and back but not front."

"True."

"How badly do you want to be a millionaire, Daniel?" Nate asked.

"I wouldn't mind at all."

"Finding the redheaded man looks more and more like a long shot. You need seed money for all those sure bets you're gonna place. And you told me yourself that there isn't as much to bet on in this era as there will be in the Fifties and Sixties. You need lots of cash to live on until then. Otherwise, it's stuck in 1940 England or America and poor until you're middle-aged. For you, the worst of all possible worlds."

Mrs. Miles exited into the yard through the Wilcox back door. Nate snatched the crate from Danny's lap and marched it up to her.

"Good afternoon, Mrs. Miles! Since it's washday, I tried to buy things easy to prepare."

Millicent smiled faintly. "Thanks much." She accepted his crate of provisions and walked into the back street and around to her own house.

"She looked tired," Danny observed.

"Preoccupied," Nate judged. "Maybe she was looking at us and thinking of her dead son."

Danny stretched like a cat. "Yeah. They say the worst thing in life is outliving your children."

At supper, Mr. Miles was uncharacteristically quiet, as if picking up the mood of his wife. In spite of Nate's prompting, he spoke nothing of the progress of the air war. Instead, he talked of inflation.

"It only makes sense," he said.

"With items in such short supply," Millicent spoke up.

"I mean look at that..." Worden's hand flew in the general direction of the kitchen counter.

"Toaster," Millicent supplied without looking up from her food.

"Exactly. I'm glad we purchased it when we did. I saw it for twenty shillings more just the other day."

A lull settled around the table.

"Aren't you taking Nate out dancing tonight, Penny?" Worden asked.

"I am."

"And how will you be spending your evening, Danny?" her father inquired.

"Oh, hoisting a few at the Old George pub."

"Right then. You young folk don't need to hang around entertaining Mother and me. Off with you all!"

Once again, Penny unlocked the door to the school closet that had been reserved for her alone. Nate gently pushed her back so that he could lift the heavy portable record player and carry it into the vacant gymnasium. They set the kerosene lantern once more in the center of the floor and turned it up to full illumination. Once again, it created a bubble of light resting in velvet blackness for their intimate dance.

"How long will it take to make a copy of that Ginger Rogers dress from the parachute silk?" Nate asked.

Penny removed her skirt and stood in her abbreviated dancing shorts. "Not long. The trick will be working without a pattern. Mum's a wizard with a sewing machine. She'll do most of the work."

Nate stood transfixed, staring at Penny's excellent figure.

"Wind the machine," Penny directed. She sat on the bleacher and selected the correct record.

"Shall we get into it by reviewing as much as we already rehearsed?" Nate asked.

"All right." Like her mother and father at supper, Penny seemed to have lost her perpetual spark of energy. Nate credited her mood to the horrific previous week. He expected that she would perk up as soon as the music coaxed her to forget the cruel reality beyond the gymnasium walls.

The sounds of "Cheek to Cheek" echoed off the walls of the large enclosure. Penny put herself in Nate's arms. Unlike his expectations, they did not execute the front end of the piece flawlessly. Both he and she made missteps. Several were caused by his stitched wound, either from him wincing or her being too conscious of it. She reset the phonograph needle on the shiny, black platter and strode back to where Nate waited.

The second time they were markedly better. Neither smiled, concentrating on remembering the constant change of patterns. Nate looked forward to the long, low dip at the end of the first section, where he would bend his face close to hers. When he did, she smiled softly but showed neither the shyness nor the desire to be kissed that she had on the first occasion. He decided to at least brush her lips with his. Before he could, the music moved on into the bridge.

When they came to the end of what they had rehearsed, Penny held up her hand in an arresting motion. "Listen to it!" The orchestra played on. "Two forte sections, just like in the motion picture," she pointed out. Sixteen measures later, the music came to the double bar. Nate moved to upend the needle arm.

"Right," Penny said, standing like a dance instructress. "A forte section of four measures. It opens with a lift to the right and then this series of steps in parallel unison." She demonstrated and then held out her hand.

The minute Penny was satisfied that Nate had memorized the section, she moved to the next. Spins and counters were followed by another forte section featuring quick steps. The piece finished with three lifts and a variety of dramatic poses. They had to forego the lifts because of Nate's side. However, he would not allow her to omit the last, fully extended dip. Coming out of it, they moved "upstage" together, where she was supposed to recline against the wall and he to stand at her side, cross-legged with his fingers interlocked in a relaxed and self-satisfied pose.

With Penny counting the beats and measures out loud, they worked through the sequences three more times, each time leaving out the lifts.

"Let's take a break." Nate sat on the bleacher, giving Penny no opportunity to object. She decided the time had come to try the dance wearing her lightweight skirt. She hooked it up and twisted it round her waist until it hung as she desired. She put herself down beside him and stared into his eyes.

"What are you thinking?" he asked.

"Have you been to Japan?"

"Yes."

"Anywhere else in the Orient?"

"Hong Kong, Malaysia, Burma." He made sure to use the last country's old name.

"Anywhere in Africa?"

Nate thought he knew the point behind Penny's questions. He struggled to remember what places he had enumerated in past conversations. "Egypt. Ethiopia. Rhodesia."

"What about the Middle East?"

"Nowhere," he lied.

"Australia or India?"

"No."

"But England several times. You must travel constantly."

"Well, you know what they say: 'I shall never pass this way again.' You have to squeeze all the excitement from life you can as quickly as you can."

Penny looked down at her hands. "That's not what that saying really means, Nathaniel. The full quotation is: 'I shall pass this way but once. Therefore, any kindness I can show or any help I can give, let me give it now for I shall not pass this way again.' It's exactly the opposite of what you're saying. One focuses on selfishness; the other focuses on charity."

Every event since he arrived in the London of the Blitz seemed to impinge upon this moment. It was as if someone or something wanted to be absolutely certain that he had learned his lesson, and Penelope Miles had been chosen as the unwitting examiner.

"What if one derives excitement from traveling in the cause of charity or other good works?" Nate asked her.

"I was hoping that was the case with you. And Daniel, naturally."

The pinch relaxed around Penny's eyes. Nate felt himself drawn into their green brilliance. "I recall you have a rather long list of places and things you want to see in America."

"True. I want to visit Italy and Greece, as well. And certainly the Holy Land."

"Not Paris?"

"That's a hop, skip and a jump once the war is over."

"I see. My excuse for constant travel is business. You're just bitten by selfish wanderlust," Nate riposted.

"But I'm anxious to travel because I know I also want to settle down. To have at least a bit of a useful career and then a family."

"I want to settle down someday, too," Nate heard himself say.

"'Want to' and 'get to' are two different things. Some never do."

"It's true." Nate thought of the capuchin-cloaked bone man with the long sickle tracking him and eliminating the mistake of his being in 1940. He chastised himself for having any thought of possessing Penelope Miles much less a pipe dream of settling down with her. And yet the desire was nearly overwhelming. He thought that he knew what was making Penny look sad of late. She had at the same time been considering him as a permanent partner, but she had unhappily accepted that his lifestyle precluded such a possibility. He badly needed to shift the conversation. "*The Private Lives of Elizabeth and Essex.* Did you enjoy the movie?"

"Oh, I suppose it was all right as drama. To tell the truth, it was annoying for anyone who knows history. You should see it and tell me what you think."

"I'll add it to my list. What did Brendon think?"

"He's not a critical person. Unless it comes to torque pressure." She laughed at her own joke and touched her arm just below the elbow, as if remembering his touch.

Nate tried to recall the size of the night raid on Saturday. The unremitting attacks were beginning to blend into each other in his head. "Were you able to see the entire movie?"

"Yes. The bombing was light and not near the cinema."

Nate listened to the silence. The darkness hung around them like thick, black theater curtains. He set his hand lightly on hers. "I worry about your safety, going out at night."

"We all should worry," she replied. "But, ultimately, there's only so much we can do to stay safe, unless we want to crawl down into the Underground and live like rats. Without a crystal ball we can't know what will be targeted or where the bombs shall land."

Nate knew Penny was right, at least in her world of sensible rules. But he remembered three instances from the lecture of Reggie, the tour guide, on the ill-fated ride through the Tubes. He was not about to allow this woman he increasingly adored to come in harm's way in cases where he knew the future.

Nate put his forefinger under Penny's chin and lifted her face slightly. "Listen to me very carefully. I've had several premonitions. Don't ask me how or why, but my omens almost always come true. I have seen in my mind two station disasters in London from these German attacks. Stay out of Marble Arch Station until the end of this month. Then don't stop at Trafalgar Square in October. And when the Bethnal Green station's deep level shelter is opened, never, never, never go into it during an air raid! Especially down any of the spiral staircases."

Penny stared at Nate for a long time. He watched her expressive face roll through a series of emotions, from surprise, to fear, to wonderment, to distrust. He pulled his finger back.

"It's all right," he assured her in a soft voice.

"Is it? How can you know about our radar installations? Why are you so sure the Germans will never use gas against us? How can you know where and when bombs will fall?"

"Some people receive rare gifts," he answered. "That's all I can say."

"You really aren't a spy, are you?"

Nate laughed. "Gott bewahre! Sei entspannt, Schatzi!"

Penny's eyes grew wide. "You're frightening me."

"I'm sorry. Bad joke. I took German in high school." He was about to say "That's as close to Germany as I've ever gotten," but since it was not true and there was the smallest chance she might see through his lie, he refrained. Still she did not look entirely reassured. "Let me tell you a story.

"On an autumn day like today, a young Frenchman was walking through the Bois de Boulogne in Paris. He saw a young woman sitting alone on a park bench. She wore sunglasses. He sat next to her and tried to strike up a conversation about 'amour.' She remained silent. He thought: 'I'll bet she is shy.' He leaned over and pecked her cheek. She did not react. He murmured a few more sweet nothings in her ear. She declined to reply. 'Perhaps a little more physical passion,' he thought and kissed her on the neck. She seemed cold to him. So he decided to pull out all the stops. 'This woman really needs heating up,' he said to himself, and he grabbed her by the lapels of her coat and planted a torrid kiss on her lips. Just then, a gendarme came running up the path. 'Don't touch that woman!' he screamed. 'She had a fatal heart attack and I was summoning an ambulance!' 'Thank God!' replied the young Frenchman. 'I thought she was German!'"

Penny tried not to smile and failed.

Without further warning, Nate grabbed Penny by her shoulders, turning her face toward his. He kissed her fervently. She allowed it, and he increased his pressure. Still she did nothing to stop him. Her lips were soft and warm and yielding. His brain was becoming intoxicated with her to the point where he feared he might lose his equilibrium and slip off the bench. Regretfully, he pulled back. She looked at him as if he had asked her to multiply two six-digit numbers.

"And that proves that neither of us is German," he explained.

"That was the cheekiest way to steal a kiss I have ever heard of," she proclaimed, but without anger.

"What's the name of the perfume you're wearing?"

"It's talc."

"That sounds Persian."

Penny giggled. "No, silly. Talcum powder."

Nate was stunned. The simplest, least expensive toilet article, combined with her natural scent, smelled like heaven to him. Without articulating into words, a memory flashed through Nate's mind of Jessica Chambers from Upper Saddle River, New Jersey and her $600-an-ounce Missoni Missoni perfume that did not smell half so wonderful to him as Penelope Miles did sitting next to him on a gymnasium bleacher.

"Don't ask me again if I'm a spy, or you'll suffer the consequences," he promised.

Penny's eyes narrowed. "Are you a spy?"

"You asked for it." This time he cradled the nape of her neck as he brought his lips to hers, his fingers penetrating the wealth of her hair. His other hand slipped down to the small of her back. Her lips parted. He felt the tip of her tongue. Then he heard her sigh. He let the moment burn deep into his mind, so that he would never forget it. This kiss was not a preamble to deeper intimacies, as with past women in his life. It was but a tantalizing peek through the keyhole to the Garden of Delights to which only the most romantic and clever of lovers gain access. And yet he knew it would forever be the most important kiss in his life. He also understood, with mingled ecstasy and despair, that nothing more was possible between them without many future events going right.

Slowly, gently, without leaving her lips, Nate coaxed Penny up from the bench. At last he drew back. His hand trailed from her neck along the line of her jaw over her collarbone and shoulder, along her arm down to her hand. He gripped it firmly as he lowered the needle once more to the recording.

The introduction was just long enough to bring the couple to the middle of the room. They swayed and twirled through time, ebbed and flowed effortlessly with the line of the melody, two bodies stringing together seamless moments of perfection like pearls on a priceless necklace, the most refined yet passionate of lovemaking, the most pristine metaphor. When at last he lowered her into the final dip, he touched his cheek to hers and then brushed it feather-light with his lips.

They moved to the dark wall and took their final poses. The music stopped. Only the light susurrations of the last groove of the record repeating disturbed the charged silence.

"We must do this again," Nate said.

Penny searched his dimly lit eyes. "Must we?"

"Definitely. It isn't 'Cheek to Cheek' without the lifts. When are you at liberty again?"

"Thursday. Will you be healed by then?"

"I think so."

"And will you still be here?"

"I will if I can. I want to be."

"Then Thursday."

"Meantime…" Nate took Penny in his arms and began humming the melody to "Dancing in the Dark". He moved her expertly around the room, within the hazy territory between darkness and light.

# CHAPTER FIFTEEN

At precisely five o'clock in the afternoon, Danny and Nate left from Trafalgar Square on the subway line that ran to Sloane Square. All the while they descended, Nate worried that this would be the day Trafalgar Square was crippled by an air attack. At the next stop, Westminster, they got off the train and walked up and down the platform. No one awaited them. However, sharp-eyed Danny noted that a little man wearing a buff-colored winter stadium coat had also left their train from one coach back and disappeared into the crowd pushing toward the platform exit. Just as the sound of the next train approaching on the same track came down the tunnel, he had reappeared. He waited until Nate and Danny crossed into one of the coaches and then moved with speed to enter the same car before the door closed.

As the train heaved and squeaked toward Westminster Cathedral, the diminutive figure changed his place, putting himself directly beside the pair.

"You gentlemen wouldn't know what train to take to get to Brighton," man said softly. He had an accent Nate had never heard in Britain, substituting the hint of a 'tch' for 'g' in 'gentlemen.'

Nate studied the man's face. His wire-rim spectacle frames supported glass thick enough to make his eyes significantly larger. His skin was fish-belly pale. The extreme smoothness of his skin contrasted with the rough blue-black areas where he had shaved not long before. He had a pug nose, just enough to hold up his glasses. Above the wire rims were two abbreviated eyebrows. Nate could tell nothing about his hair, hidden under a bowler hat, except that it was brown. His expression was one of expectation. He looked neither dangerous nor meek.

"You're going in the wrong direction, mate" Nate replied. "You need to get to Waterloo."

When the man continued to stare hard at him, Nate was not surprised. This petite person had had plenty of opportunity to memorize Nate's face. He was the one who had followed him back to Bethnal Green after the first time he met Alex Bennett.

"I'm to look at a stone," the man persisted.

"Brighton has cockle shells, not stones," Nate returned.

The man waited. He looked at Danny, who stared him down.

The little man exhaled his exasperation. "Have you got the stone or not?"

Danny moved close to the other men so that a protective triangle was formed in the middle of the coach. Nate pulled the Altoids box from his coat pocket and flipped it open, exposing one of the smuggled emeralds. It was surrounded by rough British toilet paper, the kind that caused Danny to curse every time he was forced to use it.

The man nodded. He looked up and down the length of the car. "When the train stops, wait until everyone gets off, then exit."

"Minding the gap," Danny finished.

Nate tucked the tin away. "That doesn't mean anything to him. Then what?"

"Go out on the street and head toward Westminster Abbey. Walk counterclockwise around Parliament Square without stopping." Having said his piece, the man pressed through the standing passengers toward the other end of the car.

When the train pulled into the Underground station, Nate and Danny waited as directed. They left the train and moved through the pathetic mounds of humanity camped on the platform, up from the deep hole toward daylight. No one appeared to be following them. The little man had stayed in the train.

As they walked, Nate informed Danny about the former role the little man had played.

"Okay, so that explains how he recognized us. Then Bennett will have to pick us up."

"Not necessarily."

"Why not?"

"Because Bennett took photographs of us for our passports."

Danny snapped his fingers and then thumped the side of his head. "Right."

Only upon their second perambulation of the park did a black sedan pull up beside them.

"This is it," Nate said to Danny.

"I'll let you do the talking, Big Fox" Danny intoned good-naturedly.

They climbed into the backseat and the car moved with speed away from the great abbey.

"Good afternoon," Nate greeted in a friendly tone.

The man behind the wheel was not Alex Bennett. He merely nodded.

"How long is the trip?"

The man glanced in the rearview mirror. He wore no hat, betraying a bald head. He had a bull neck and a badly deformed nose and cauliflower ears, strongly suggesting he had been a prizefighter in his youth. He looked to be about forty. He blinked often, as if the grit of the London air bothered his eyes. "Long enough."

"I don't recognize this brand of car."

"1932 Wolseley 9."

"Where are we headed?"

"To the money."

Nate waited for the driver to volunteer more, but he was laconic to a fault. His attention was entirely devoted to the road ahead and to his rearview mirrors, which he consulted regularly. Nate settled back into the big sedan's leather seat, and Danny mimicked him.

They crossed over the Thames via Westminster Bridge and stayed on Westminster Bridge Road long after Nate lost his bearings. They detoured several times, compelled to do so by the colossal damage created by more than a week of constant bombing. Not far from the great river, the south side lapsed into tight housing, then hovels, then slums.

One set of passing homes reminded Nate of the style lived in by Gwendolyn Lamb. He was not about to mention her name in front of the stranger at the steering wheel, but he asked Danny, "So, you really fancy that widow, don't you?"

"I do. And she told me she has never been treated better...even by her late husband."

Nate lowered his voice another few decibels. "I'm not surprised, between what you pack in your pants and what you've shelled out from your pants pockets. You know, those two rings could have paid our way to the States on a steamer."

"It would have been blood money."

"All the gems we've ever dealt for have all been blood stones, Daniel."

"Those, yes. Because we spent the profits on ourselves. I tell you, Nathaniel, it felt a whole lot better spending it on Gwen than any money I squandered on me."

A few weeks earlier, Nate would have insisted that the profit from the rings go to their well being. But he had changed. He saw Danny's point of view; the woman was in her own way as bad off as they were. His challenging words, therefore, had merely been to see what Danny would say. Trying to hide the fact of his new-found magnanimity, he stared poker-faced at his partner. "Are you trying to tell me I tricked you into a terrible life, that I didn't lay it out honestly right up front?"

"Not at all. You were perfectly honest, and I joined with my eyes wide open. That's the amazing thing about you. You're right up front about being the most selfish bastard I know. You tell the ladies, and they take it as a challenge. You even work at fooling yourself by saying 'As long as I don't hurt anyone else, it's okay.' But just taking is not what it's about. You sell excitement, right? I have never been so excited as when I saw Gwen's eyes after I gave her those rings, when I heard her chatter about what they can do for her."

"I'm the most selfish bastard you know," Nate echoed, feeling pained by the superlative even though he knew it to be the unvarnished truth.

"That doesn't make you a bad person," Danny hastened to say. "It just doesn't make you a good person." He turned his face away. "Maybe it doesn't make you or me persons at all. People are supposed to care about each other. I didn't take much from those times I was dragged to church, but I did get that. Hell, I'm not telling you anything you don't know. That's why you haven't been enjoying our glamorous life so much the past several months, isn't it? That's why you keep talking about not hurting people, like you did after we finished our deal in Zimbabwe." He glanced at the back of the driver's head. "It's why you've been acting like a knight in shining armor to a certain family." He shrugged. "That and the long-legged incentive with the green eyes. I'm only being honest, like you. So don't be mad at me."

"I'm not mad," Nate assured.

"Good."

For the better part of a largely silent hour they negotiated the semi-ruined city to the limits of London and into the gradually shifting open spaces of towns, then villages and, finally, countryside. The sun sank toward the horizon. Only twice did they catch sight of a few formations of German planes skimming over the cityscape, and these both had attracted considerable RAF attention.

From the constantly shifting position of the lowering sun, Nate could tell that they had traversed the rolling landscape in many directions. It was as if the driver wandered aimlessly. Nor did he seem to be in a hurry. Nate grew increasingly anxious at their helpless position. He thought of the worst situation he and Danny had ever faced. It had been in Columbia the previous year. They had accompanied a massive delivery of food to a Catholic mission in a remote village. A gang of guerrillas had been alerted and waited in ambush. The convoy was lost and all the soldiers and drivers shot or captured. Danny and Nate had chosen to ride in the middle truck, knowing the usual pattern of attack on convoys. The pair had carried well-stocked satchels. Their two M11 machine pistols were more fearsome than any other weapon in the fight and had cowed the guerrillas in the initial minute, allowing them to escape.

A detailed topographic map of the region and a handheld GPS locator allowed the Americans to navigate through the dense jungle and along a mountain stream with assurance. When they at last reached a good-sized village, they had money to rent a room and a satellite phone to call for rescue. They knew that the safety and comforts of a major town lay only one hour away. Not one of these advantages was available in 1940 England.

After more than twenty minutes of travel among back roads and increasingly dense stands of foliage, Danny sat up.

"Hey, pal, do you have a name?" Danny asked the driver. Nate was about to assure their silent chauffeur that he and Danny did not really wish to know anyone's name, when the man spoke.

"John Bull."

"John Bull," Danny repeated. "I think I know–"

Nate shot him a withering look. Danny lapsed once more into silence.

"We do need to understand the plans for the evening…Mr. Bull," Nate said. "Are you the one to deliver them?"

The baldheaded man looked into the review and side mirrors, as if making sure one last time that they were not being followed. Then he pulled into a dirt side street off the two-lane road and parked. "I can tell you the general information. Mr. Bennett will give you specifics and answer any questions." Nate recognized a Birmingham accent. "We drive to an isolated part of the route where the bank lorry and their follow-up sedan will travel. They should pass the first intercept point at between eight-twenty and eight-thirty. We will isolate the car and lorry from each other. When the lorry reaches a house by the road where you will wait, it will have to stop. One of you will hold the driver and guard prisoner while the other transfers the four pallets of cash from one lorry to the other. Mr. Bennett should arrive in this sedan about thirty seconds before I am ready to leave. He and I will drive the lorry away. You two will use this sedan to return to London. You should be across the Thames before eleven, barring any interference from our German visitors."

"And provided the maps are decent," Nate added. "We're not at all familiar with the countryside of southeast England." The driver said nothing. "Who gives us the maps…you or Mr. Bennett?"

"He does."

"Why don't we all wear masks?" Danny blurted out.

"Ask Mr. Bennett." The driver consulted his watch. He seemed in no hurry to bring the engine back to life. "Ahead of schedule," he declared.

"Guns?" Nate asked.

"Ask Bennett," the man said peevishly. His eyes continued to blink rapidly. "I'm catching a few winks, if you don't mind."

Nate had tried to memorize several of the buildings and landmarks along their route until he recognized a farmhouse and realized they had driven in at least one circle. He, too, settled against the door, rested his cheek on his forearm, and closed his eyes. Due to the hot pain of the infected bullet wound in his side, he could not relax enough to sleep. The margins of the wound that had only been held together with rubber cement had opened. He was fairly certain it had happened while dancing with Penny, but he had no regret having taken the risk.

The words 'no regret' triggered another memory. Nate thought about a conversation he had had with Daniel O'Shea not too long after they met. It was a major reason why Nate had decided to recruit him for his team. Danny had informed Nate that "I have no regret killing those two Muslim soldiers" with rifle fire during the first Iraq invasion. Nate had never seen his partner do worse than knock out an adversary with his fists. However, from those two episodes and from Danny's handling of the M11 in the jungle, Nate had little doubt he was still capable of killing without hesitation. He opened one eye and saw that Danny had crossed his hands over the nearly imperceptible bulge of the Webley that depended by the trigger guard from the cord under his shirt front.

What gave Nate added hope that the heist was exactly what Bennett had described was the driver's unfriendly behavior. If the man had been overly pleasant, Nate's suspicion of a set up would have been redoubled. As it was, he was convinced that Bennett would fail to come through with all of his promises.

Insects began their evening songs. Twenty minutes after closing his eyes, the man behind the wheel returned from the apparent dead. He backed into the empty road, dropped the shift into first, and eased down on the accelerator pedal. Soon, they approached a rather large town that had a river running through it, a church with a prominent tower, a town square with a central fountain, shop fronts within two-story brick buildings, and many charming homes and gardens, all blanketed by the long, crawling shadows of dusk. Much as the British government had tried to disguise road signs to confuse possible invaders, the shop and restaurant proprietors were not about to lose business by removing their signage. Nate read that they had entered Sevenoaks.

When they exited the town, Nate saw by his watch that they were heading east. Rather than drive toward the main highway, the driver veered off down a dark lane. The road made a sharp turn to the right and then, shortly thereafter, to the left. Darkness swiftly closed in, reducing lines of trees to flat, black silhouettes against a purple sky. In another minute they were once again in natural countryside. The driver let off on the accelerator and allowed the car to move at the speed of a quick jog.

Out of the newborn darkness loomed a parked lorry. It was not especially large, but it commanded attention by its crimson-painted exterior. It had twin rear doors, which stood open. A man faced into the truck back, wriggling something large out. The driver of the sedan tootled his horn. The engaged man turned. Nate saw that it was Alex Bennett. He wore coveralls and a soft cap with a snap brim. Both articles of clothing were jet black, so that his face and hands seemed to hover disembodied in the early nightfall. Bennett struggled to carry a bar of metal about five feet long and a third of a foot wide. Its color was matte black.

"Right on time," Bennett grunted through his crooked smile. A cigarette glowed between his pursed lips. "Give me a hand!"

Danny and Nate climbed out of the back of the sedan. Bennett laid the long, metal contrivance down at right angles to the length of the road. He already had placed on the ground an opened cloth toolkit meant to be wrapped up and tied when not in use. From two of its pockets he selected hammers and handed them to the Americans. Out of a coverall pocket he withdrew half a dozen metal spikes.

"Nail it fast into the roadway," he directed, as he rushed to the lorry, slammed the doors shut and drew down the latch.

Wincing from the wound in his side, Nate bent to the task. He saw that the thing they were securing to the roadway was in fact made of a number of parts. The two main ones were the length that lay against the road and an equally long piece that looked like the business side of a very long and crude saw. Every two inches, a sharp tooth rose from the shank. Both lengths of metal were joined by hinges and a set of hinge pins. Bennett had laid down the hinged side so that it faced the direction of traffic. Once they had nailed the contraption to the roadbed, Bennett attached a flexible length of steel cable to the shoulder side edge. This he hooked onto a foot pedal.

"Gimme a fag," the driver said to Bennett.

Nate glanced up in time to see Bennett tap one cigarette from his pack and then hand over a book of matches.

Where Bennett had stopped his lorry stood a sizable tree that grew very close to the road. It became clear to Nate that the plan was for the man to hide behind the tree. Once the Bank of England lorry passed and just as the following sedan arrived, he would mash down on the pedal with both feet. This would twist up the hinged metal teeth so that they punctured any tires passing over them. The teeth were not so long that they would shred rubber but long enough to penetrate each tire with at least two holes. A bump would probably be felt, but it would not be so great that anything more than a thin tree branch would be supposed to have been run over. Within half a mile, all four tires on the sedan that held the four soldiers would be flat.

While Nate and Danny worked, "John Bull" drove the sedan the three had arrived in up a dirt path that lay at right angles to the country road. He executed a K turn. A gathering of evergreens hid the black machine from view. He jogged back. The cool night air and his forward motion made the cigarette in his mouth glow fiercely.

Alex Bennett relieved Nate and Danny of the hammers. He bent to his tool kit and tucked them away. From two of the slots he withdrew a pair of high-powered pistols.

"Those are American," Nate noted.

Bennett shook his head as he handed them over. "They are Browning 1935s, but they were made in Belgium. They're some of the last weapons shipped out before the Germans overran them."

Danny pressed the magazine catch release and slid his clip out. It was filled with thirteen 9mm bullets. Nate imitated his partner, feeling the weight of the lead, powder, primer and casings inside the spring-loaded clip.

"Only if something goes terribly wrong," Bennett warned. "Please, don't even load the chamber."

"Why shouldn't we be wearing masks?" Danny demanded of the operation leader as he snapped his magazine back in place and ignored Bennett's plea.

Bennett dipped his head in deference to the question. "You know, I was thinking at the outset that it would be clever to have the guard and driver describing two blokes who don't exist on any record in the Isles. But then I realised they could have one of those police sketch artists draw you two well enough that you might be recognised from a post office poster. So I did bring along balaclava helmets for you as well as us. They're in the front of the lorry. Happy?"

"I'm wetting my pants with joy," Danny deadpanned.

"Lovely. You've gotten the plan from my associate?"

Nate repeated what they had been told.

"Exactly. The sedan car carrying the soldiers should have shredded its tyres to the rims within half a mile." He tapped the asphalt with the toe of his shoe. "From the weight of four passengers, it will stop dead. The place where the bank note lorry will be stopped is a bit over a mile from here. Even if the soldiers are trained runners, it should take them at least five minutes should they elect to pursue in the dark on foot. Everything has to move like clockwork. Do you understand your parts?"

"How will the bank truck be stopped?" Danny asked.

"The road is narrow. We park this lorry directly across both lanes. There's a stone wall blocking one shoulder, and the other one is so muddied up that passage around is impossible."

"You said the bank truck will be disguised as a refrigerated van."

"Exactly. The bank's supposedly clever ruse is the reason they are comfortable using only one civilian sedan to follow it."

"But the truck will be armored."

"Absolutely."

"Then your inside man for this heist must be the driver," Nate said with assurance.

"Why not some bank clerk on Threadneedle Street?" Bennet asked.

"Because, otherwise, an innocent driver and guard would simply sit tight inside the impregnable truck and wait for the soldiers to arrive."

"Why couldn't the guard be the inside man?" Bennett probed.

"Because an innocent driver would stop the truck if the trailing sedan blew its horn. Or if it got ahead, when the driver saw the roadblock, he'd back the truck up toward the soldiers. You don't have the vehicles to block both back and front."

Bennett took the butt of his cigarette from his mouth, dropped, it and ground it out. When he looked up, he wore his crooked smile. "You're cleverer than Dick Whittington's cat, aren't you?"

*And good at catching rats as well,* Nate thought. Aloud he said, "So the driver stops the truck and hops out, leaving the door open for us to outnumber the guard?"

"Exactly."

"And late tonight, when the guard tells the story of the stupid and cowardly driver, you don't think they'll squeeze your inside man until he leaks?"

Bennett did not seem shaken by the question. "The driver comes with us. We tell the guard we're taking the driver as a hostage."

While neither the baldheaded wheelman nor Bennett had been caught in outright lies, neither had told the whole story until Nate drew it from them. Nate's well-tuned warning mechanism tripped into high alert. He glanced at Danny. Danny's face had hardened to the inscrutable expression Nate had come to know was his reaction to a potentially dangerous situation.

"Lorry!" the baldheaded man shouted.

"Move off the road!" Bennett directed, pointing to the darkness beyond the tree.

Nate and Danny followed Bennett to a clump of trees, where they squatted down. The man who called himself John Bull remained by their lorry with his hands in his pockets. He took a long drag on his cigarette and exhaled a plume of smoke.

The truck that rattled and wheezed down the road was mid-1920s vintage. It was of the stake variety, piled high with bales of hay. It stopped next to the crimson lorry.

"Trouble, mate?" the driver inquired.

"Yeah, but I patched it all right."

"Good on you! I'll be on my way, then. Cheerio!"

The stake truck gears meshed and it began to move. A few moments later the vehicle backfired, sounding like it was not far from dropping by the side of the road itself.

"Neither of us has operated a hand trolley," Nate disclosed to the leader as he moved toward the secured rear doors of the lorry. "If this is such a split-second operation, shouldn't somebody show us how to do it now?"

Bennett stepped in his way. "Let's not have someone else drive by with all of us here. My friend up in the cab will work it; you two watch the guard and driver and give a hand if needed." He bent to pick up his kit of tools and then turned toward the tree.

"What about our maps?" Nate asked.

Bennett turned with an apologetic mien. He reached into his coat and jacket and pulled out a printed map and a folded sheet of paper with notes written on it. "Thanks for remembering. Saves us another fifteen seconds at the farmhouse." He passed the two items to Nate. "That should do it."

"Not quite. Our passports."

Bennett shook his head. "That and your two thousand pounds will only take five seconds. I'll keep them until you fulfill your part of this bargain. Off with you now!"

The baldheaded man was already seated on the driver's side of the red truck's bench seat, waiting.

"There's not enough space for the three of us in here," Nate told him. "Open the back, and we'll ride in there."

"It's only about a mile," the man said, looking extremely annoyed. "Squeeze in."

Nate climbed in first and was sandwiched between the two bigger men, with his right thigh pressed hard against the shift. As they pulled away, he realized that the war aided the robbery considerably. Illumination inside every building and from streetlights that might guide German pilots had been blocked out. In the process, the British people also operated outdoors in pitch blackness at night. The two slits through which the headlamps shone barely allowed the road to be distinguished. Spotting the metal trap on the country road would be impossible. Likewise, the truck guard would not be able to see that the sedan no longer followed them.

The taciturn driver executed a hard left turn soon after starting off. The placement of the metal trap was well planned, because the sedan would be having problems with failing tires by this stretch of road. If it honked its horn, the nearby copse of trees and bushes would absorb most of the sounds. Moreover, when the sedan driver tried to negotiate the sharp turn, one or more of the damaged tires might peel off the rims.

After the left turn, the road became perfectly straight. They passed a long hedge wall on the right, followed by a decaying wooden fence. Seconds later, a stone wall began on their left. Not long after, the dim headlamps picked out the mass of a farmhouse that lay near the road. Its windows were predictably black. But as they slowed to within feet of the place, Nate saw that the windows had neither shades nor paint on the panes. The shutters were decayed or missing. Weeds grew in profusion around the front path. It was clear that the place had been abandoned.

"John Bull" turned the lorry into the pebble-covered farmhouse driveway and pulled it just barely off the narrow road.

"Where are our ski masks?" Danny asked.

The driver's eyebrows knit in confusion.

"What you call balaclava helmets," Nate translated.

The man pointed to the glove compartment. Danny extracted the three black knit headpieces that covered all but an oval around the eyes.

"It should be another ten minutes," the driver announced. "Leave 'em off for now."

"Whatever you say, boss," Danny replied. It was a sentence Danny used with people he did not like. He threw open his door and hopped out. Nate followed in slow motion, making sure he remained in the line of the passenger-side rearview mirror. He watched Danny snap the cord that held the Webley pistol around his neck. As Danny continued to the back of the lorry, he chambered the pistol and pushed it into his left raincoat pocket.

The baldheaded man opened his cab door and whistled for the Americans. Nate now took the lead, so that Danny could extract the pistol if necessary without being seen.

"Should we open the back to save time?" Nate called out over the idling engine.

"Wait until the lorry blocks the way," the driver replied.

Danny turned and listened. "Something big is coming fast!" he warned.

"Get off the road!" called the driver.

While Nate and Danny moved toward the dark farmhouse, their truck eased across the middle of the road. Nate noted that the name stenciled in black against the broad field of crimson on the side panel read "Reddington & Sons/Reigate."

Danny and Nate pulled the black knit masks over their heads. From the far side of their lorry came the driver's barking voice. "Kneel like you're working on a wheel!"

When the red truck rolled to a stop, Nate knelt. Danny remained standing and alert.

The bank truck emerged from the darkness with pace. The headlamp beams were not strong and only cast a thin line of light fifty feet in front of the oncoming vehicle. It was almost upon the blocking machine before it applied its brakes hard. At almost the instant it stopped, the driver's door flew open.

Nate stood up beside his partner. The bank truck driver, dressed in a grey uniform and wearing a    cap, backed out of the cab. In one hand he held the truck keys. With the other, he reached for the holster on his belt. Before he could unsnap it, a shot rang from inside the bank truck cab. The fumbling driver sprang backward onto the road.

"Bloody hell!" he shouted. "He shot me!"

Nate and Danny squatted as one. They drew their Browning pistols. Nate pointed at the wounded driver, and Danny kept his weapon trained on the passenger side of the bank truck.

The passenger door opened, and a man wearing a uniform identical to the one worn by the driver leapt from it and began running toward the blackness of the field opposite the farmhouse. Danny raised his pistol but hesitated.

A shot cracked through the air. The guard spun from the impact of the bullet. A second shot hit him squarely in the chest. He crumpled to his knees and fell face forward onto the muddy shoulder of the road. He did not try to break his fall, indicating that he was unconscious, if not dead.

From the side of the Reddington & Sons lorry strode the baldheaded man. His extended pistol smoked. "So much for no gunplay," he declared as he passed the Americans, who were just rising. He kept walking until he stood above the face down, unmoving body of the bank guard. He pointed his pistol and fired point blank into the back of the guard's head.

On the opposite side of the bank lorry, the wounded driver screamed and cursed in pain. Nate and Danny cocked their Browning pistols and aimed them at the man. The baldheaded man rushed in and shot the driver twice. The body jerked with each hit, then lay still. One of the bullets had caught him just below his left eye.

"John Bull" looked at Nate and Danny. "Bloody mess. Now is the time to open the back of our lorry. You can put away the guns. Nobody else to shoot."

The partners pocketed their pistols and moved to the back of the truck. Danny shoved up the latch and turned it. They each took a door and swung it wide. A small overhead light burned inside. On the compartment floor lay a long metal ramp. Beside it was the hand fork lift. Behind both lay four pallets covered by tarpaulins.

"You've already got something in here," Nate said, turning.

The baldheaded man stood five paces from them, with his weapon again aimed.

"Just because you don't have anybody else to shoot, I might," he said. "Use the trolley to get those four pallets out. Quick!"

Danny stepped on a metal lorry stirrup to move up into the compartment. He climbed into the left side, so that his left hand was hidden from the murdering driver. He lifted the back end of the ramp and fed it down toward Nate. Nate pulled the ramp toward the baldheaded man. When he was within two long paces, he twisted and pretended to trip on the ramp. He fell awkwardly in the driver's direction.

Just as Nate hit the roadway, a blast echoed out of the lorry compartment, followed by a second. Nate rolled away, preparing to jump up and tackle the driver if necessary. As he stopped his movement, his eyes found the bald-headed man. An expression of abject astonishment filled the man's face as he glanced at the two holes in his upper chest. In slow motion, he swung his face and gun arm up. Another explosion from inside the truck produced a small hole just above the bridge of his nose. His head jerked back. His body followed, crumpling to the road so that his rear end hit first. Then he twisted to his right and lay still.

As Nate stood, Danny extracted the Browning from his right coat pocket, cocked it, pointed it at "John Bull", and squeezed the trigger three times. Nothing happened. Danny did not show surprise. He squatted next to "John Bull," thrust his hand into one pocket after the next, and emptied them of all contents. When he was done, he picked up the man's pistol.

Nate meantime jumped into the back of the Reddington & Sons lorry. He ripped away the canvas tarpaulins and looked down.

"Let's get these onto the road, pronto," he directed his partner.

Danny hopped up into the compartment. "Jesus! They already

have millions in here!"

"Hurry!" Nate encouraged.

"I don't understand."

"I'll explain later. Quickly, Dan!"

They moved the four pallets down the ramp to the road with maximum haste. Nate took the keys and unused pistol from the dead bank driver. He unlocked the back of the bank truck that bore the signage "Dunn & Bradburn Select Meats/By Appointment to His Majesty." Inside, they found four pallets stacked with packs of sealed and banded five-pound notes. The pallets were identical in size and color to the four they had left on the road.

Within another three minutes they had the pallets switched. Nate shoved the metal ramp back into the crimson lorry and secured the doors as Danny climbed into the cab.

The lights of an approaching car appeared from the far side of the roadblock.

"Bennett!" Danny said in a strident voice as Nate swung in through the passenger door. "What do we do?"

"Sideswipe him," Nate directed.

Danny put the lorry into reverse. Just as the car came to a stop, he dropped the transmission into first, tromped on the accelerator, and bashed in the front right corner of the Wolseley 9 sedan. Nate heard the headlight housing smash. Danny plowed past with no injury to the truck, its high bumper having absorbed the impact.

"Do we stop?" Danny asked.

Nate ripped off his mask and swiped at the rivulets of sweat running down his face. "And risk getting killed? For all we know, he has a machinegun."

"But he has our passports!"

"Are you sure? Did you see them?" Nate asked.

"I'll bet he does. What if we had demanded to see them when we were back at that tree?"

"You're probably right. But he's not about to hand them over now."

Danny drove the lorry at a moderate pace down the all-but-invisible country road. "Where the fuck am I headed?"

"I think east," Nate answered, unable to read his watch in the dark cab. "Other than that, I have no idea."

"Use your map."

"Good thinking. Now all I need is light."

"Speaking of light, there's one following us!" Danny reported.

"Wait until he's right behind us. Then tromp on the brakes."

"He's not getting that close."

"Shit. We should have taken out both his lamps."

Nate hunted across the dashboard until he located an interior light switch. When he consulted the map, he learned that they had driven from the farmhouse in the correct direction. Only one left turn was necessary to bring them to a highway that led directly west for about twenty miles. Nate used the compass of his watch to confirm their heading.

Traffic on the four-lane highway was heavier than Nate would have expected, especially with trucks. The crimson truck was never out of sight of other vehicles at any moment. A number of them flaunted the law and burned full headlamps.

"This darkness is disorienting," Danny remarked. "I can't see Bennett. I think he's hiding behind the truck riding our rear."

Nate grabbed the crank handle on the door and began lowering his window. "Yeah, it won't be easy for us to get lost with this red mastodon. Stick your arm out the window and wave the trucker ahead. Then lower your speed."

Danny whipped the mask from his head and tossed it at Nate's feet. "Isn't the usual technique to try to lose the pursuer?"

Nate took both masks and tossed them out the passenger window. He looked back. "Maybe the unexpected will work better. Get ready to sit on your brakes for two seconds."

"Gotcha."

Danny waved his arm and eased his foot off the accelerator. Because of the darkness, the driver of the truck directly behind reacted late. He had just enough time to swerve right into the fast lane. The instant the trucker cleared the lane behind, Danny tromped on his brakes, making his tires squeal. The next moment, the Wolseley kissed their sturdy rear bumper. The collision caused the Reddington & Sons truck to veer into the fast lane. Danny overcompensated the steering wheel several times, fishtailing the vehicle back and forth down the highway.

In the same moments, Nate squeezed his trigger finger as quickly as he could and emptied the bank truck driver's pistol at the front end of Bennett's car.

"Go!" Nate shouted, his eyes riveted to the action at the rear.

The truck straightened out and accelerated. The struck car seemed to be gently bumping up and down, and the distinct noise of a pushed-in fender rubbing against its tire could be heard. Rapidly, the car lost speed and receded into the blackness.

"That did it," Nate reported. His voice would have conveyed more joy had the wound in his side not pained him so much. He thought he felt a trickle of liquid running down that side and wondered if it was perspiration or blood.

"And there go our passports," Danny said, putting space between each word.

"Were you willing to shoot him in case he had them?" Nate asked. He wiped the empty pistol clean of his prints and tossed it out the open window.

"Shoot that son-of-a-bitch?" Danny said. "Hell, yes! His plan was to kill us all along. Wasn't it?"

"I think so." Nate unbuttoned his shirt and pulled it to the side. The wound was seeping blood on both edges. His rubber cement treatment was a fiasco. He would need at least two more stitches on either margin. He pressed his handkerchief hard against the wound.

Danny glanced in his side mirror, unaware of his partner's discomfort. "I have my theory of what just happened. Let's hear yours."

Nate never enjoyed discussing complicated situations with Danny. Over the years of their partnership, he had learned that simplification was always the best way. "All that's important is that Bennett wanted both the guard and driver dead, and he needed a couple of bodies to blame it on. If our bodies were virtually unidentifiable, all the better."

"Makes sense. That's how I figure it. And he couldn't depend on the innocent guard sitting still very long after he knew the car with the soldiers was no longer following."

Nate wondered where Danny was going with his notion, but he declined to ask.

Danny added, "That's why he needed two fall guys. The money in the back of the van had to be moved quickly…before the soldiers caught up."

"Right," Nate said with emphasis, as if punctuating the thought.

"But I don't get the money in the red truck. Did they already do another heist exactly like this one last night or today? And why were we supposed to swap it into the bank truck?"

"Because it's phony money," Nate said. "Counterfeit."

"What?"

"Do you still have that five pound note Bennett gave you?"

"I think so."

"I know I have mine," Nate said. "We'll check later."

Danny set the fingers of his left hand, clawlike, against the crown of his head and massaged his scalp roughly. "Wouldn't you know I guessed it the instant Bennett gave us those two bills! I thought I was kidding. I don't get it. Why go through the trouble of printing four pallets of money and taking the time to trade it with the real stuff? Why not just rob the real pound notes?"

"To make the robbery look like a botched job, so the police won't work hard looking for anyone else beyond the bodies at the scene. If the counterfeit pounds are well made, nobody would be the wiser." Nate popped the magazine from the Browning Bennett had handed him.

Danny banged his palm against the steering wheel. "I can't drive and think this deep."

"Then concentrate on your driving," Nate counseled. He unchambered the top bullet, examined and hefted it. "No primer. No powder. When you weighed your magazine it didn't feel different, because I bet there are twelve real ones underneath. Same here. Can't get to them if the first casing won't blow back. By the time we both went for the guns they gave us and found out they wouldn't fire, we'd have been ventilated." He shoved the useless bullet into his pocket.

"All that driving and death, and we still need passports," Danny fumed. "But brother, do we have money!"

Nate's heart still beat hard and, it seemed to him, erratically. His head and throat ached from the tension of the terrifying past minutes. In contrast, Danny's breathing was regular and his voice calm and even. Nate marveled at his partner's ability to recover from what would have shocked a normal man into a catatonic state. He was relieved to hear that Danny had apparently given up on the redheaded man escape theory. He thought about the dead driver. "What did you take off of 'John Bull'?"

In reply, Danny dug into his pockets. He produced a wallet, several coins and the book of matches Alex Bennett had given him. The wallet had a driver's license in the name of Rufus Greest. His address was on Poplar High Street. Nate knew Poplar to be one of the East End villages that had received the most bombing attention. He studied the matchbook. On the cover was imprinted the name "The Royal Standard" and the address 42 Harpers Road. He opened the cover.

Only four matches had been removed, and undoubtedly two of them had lit the cigarettes of Bennett and the baldheaded driver less than an hour earlier. At the rate Bennett smoked, he probably had picked up the book earlier in the day.

"This truck is like a matador's red cape," Nate said. "We have to ditch it as soon as we can."

Danny steered the truck into the fast lane. "How much money is in the back?"

"Bennett said it would be two-and-a-half million pounds."

"How much is that in dollars back in our time?"

"About a hundred million, I think."

"Jesus. And it's all ours."

"Not as long as Bennett's still alive."

The line of Daniel O'Shea's jaw hardened. "Yeah."

Nate pointed. "Finally, a sign to London!"

Danny pointed the truck toward the highway off ramp. For a time the two men drove in silence, churning their own thoughts.

"We could dump the money at Gwen's place," Danny volunteered. Nate could not imagine the gay divorcee keeping her mouth shut about so much money, much less sitting tight on it. After three years of harebrained suggestions, Danny had set a new record.

"No," Nate said, in his best Final Decision voice. "That could get her killed or at least sent to prison if something goes wrong."

"Then where? The Miles family is in the Wilcox house since the roof fire. What about inside the Miles house?"

Nate counted to five. "Moving that much money into a house would take us hours, Dan. We'd be seen. The truck would be seen. And then Worden, Millicent and Penny would be arrested."

"Well, we're rapidly running out of places," Danny said impatiently.

Nate knew that his partner had finally said something smart. Nate had a place, but it would not be without danger or large expenditures of time and effort. "Keep driving," he said. "I'll keep thinking."

"Don't you always?" Danny replied.

The smell of London came to Nate before the sight of it did. Westerly winds blew the ash and soot of a thousand recent fires toward the continent. Nate consulted his watch. The time was a little before ten o'clock. They had yet to get across the Thames. They guided themselves toward the river by the unfortunate fact of a number of fires lighting the horizon. At least one night raid had already occurred. By trial, error and luck, they found their way to Lower Road, which

Nate knew ran into Broad Jamaica Road.

"There's a sign for a tunnel!" Danny pointed out, letting his foot off the accelerator pedal. "That's the safest way to the other side."

Nate squinted at the sign. "Don't turn! It's banned to trucks."

"Damn. Probably because a Nazi terrorist could load a truck with dynamite or fertilizer and take out the whole tunnel," Danny speculated.

"You're thinking about the wrong end of the century," Nate replied, using the interior light and the London map. "The reason is probably because it's old and too narrow or low for trucks. Keep going along this main road. We'll have to take Tower Bridge, King William Street, or Southwark Bridge."

When they had skirted two detours and neared the Tower Bridge, another wave from what was the busiest bombing night since the Germans began the Blitz swooped in over the city. Nate and Danny were alerted first by the sirens, then the banks of crisscrossing searchlights, and finally those barrage balloons that had not been shot down during the previous ten days and nights.

"Find someplace safe to stop," Nate said. "We can't risk crossing the bridge during this."

"Safe?" Danny echoed. "Are you nuts? We're a few hundred feet from the river!"

"Look for residences. Nothing higher than two stories, so a building won't fall on us. That way is south. We have about five minutes."

The streets were all but deserted. No speeding vehicles challenged them for the road. Danny guided the truck toward gaps in the city skyline. After weaving from street to street, he at last put them on a small one that ran between shoulder-to-shoulder tenements. It lay at the northern tip of the area called Elephant and Castle. Two hundred feet ahead, the street made a sharp left turn to run around a three-story warehouse. Nate figured they were no more than a thousand feet south of one of the main bombing routes, but he did not share the frightening fact with his partner. A high-roofed moving van had been parked on the left side of the one-way street, which contained not one other vehicle. Danny headed to the stretch of street behind the van.

"No. In front," Nate directed. "The German planes will be coming in from the east. That van can shelter us."

"'Shelter us?' Why not park behind a Japanese rice paper screen?

I've said it before I'll say it again," Danny intoned. "This sucks, this sucks, this really, really sucks."

"Hey, chill out," Nate counseled, in a soothing tone. "You just iced a guy who wanted you dead from less than twenty feet. This is–"

"He didn't have a plane, bombs and machineguns," Danny snapped back.

Nate gave Dan's shoulder a gentle push. "Just pretend you and I are the first ones on a very realistic Universal Studios ride."

Danny was neither amused nor reassured.

The Bofors 40mm and other anti-aircraft guns opened up, punching holes through the sky, creating bursts of light, and leaving mushrooms of smoke only visible when the searchlights swept through them. From having just finished a serendipitous tour of the Bermondsey and Southwark areas, Nate knew they sat on the boundary line of the German targets. Block after block just to their north had been virtually leveled. The debris of building materials lay in heaps waiting to be disposed of. Each gust of wind raised a curtain of smoke and dust. In the distance, a flaming, deflating barrage balloon drifted earthward.

Within seconds, the district immediately around the truck became the temporary focal point of the entire war. The air was choked with airplanes and light and artillery. The noise was so great and terrifying that both men pressed their hands to their ears. They hunkered down in their seats and craned their necks upward to stare out the top of the windshield at the activity.

One, two, three, four German bombers passed above them like an armada of airborne dreadnaughts. The last had both engines on fire, trailing smoke, flame and sparks. Fighter planes harried their wakes. The telltale whistling of a series of bombs filled the air, growing louder, more high-pitched and shriller by the second.

"Brace yourself," Nate said, curling over into a fetal position.

"I love you, man," Danny said in a small but sincere voice.

"I love you, too, you Big Dog," Nate returned.

The block behind and in front of the truck turned into hell. The first bomb landed in the intersection three hundred feet back. Another landed only forty feet behind the moving van, making it jump off the ground. As the third bomb plowed into a narrow alley a hundred feet ahead of the red lorry, the street behind heaved and buckled from the severing of a gas line. The explosion rattled Nate's teeth and rocked the truck back and forth. The moving van's metal frame groaned from the

pummeling delivered by pulverized roadbed. A fourth bomb hit the
street at the top end. It did not explode, but its impact popped a
manhole cover high in the air and caused a water line to erupt. Beyond
the newborn geyser, a fifth bomb pierced the warehouse wall that faced
the truck. A five-foot circle of brick disintegrated instantly. The bomb
exploded a millisecond later, blowing more of the wall outward. Course
after course of brick disintegrated and collapsed onto the street. On the
other end of the thoroughfare, intense gas line plumes ignited
everything within fifty feet, blocking escape to the rear. Nate peeked up
from the bench seat. From the destruction caused by the three
detonations, he knew the plane's rack had contained 50Kg bombs. The
100Kg variety would have leveled both sides of the street and killed
him and Danny.

"We gotta get out of here," Danny yelled, starting up the engine. In
two places, the windshield glass had been cracked by flying debris.
Otherwise, the lorry had survived with nothing worse than scores of
dents.

"You can't go back," Nate said, looking at the gigantic torch fed by
the ignited gas line.

"Do I dare drive past that warehouse?" Danny asked. The
extremely buckled wall looked ready to collapse.

"You can't even if you want to," Nate decided. "There's a hole in
the street and piles of rubble."

"Then let's take some of the money and run."

"Drive forward."

"Why?"

"I see an alley. Drive forward, Dan!"

Danny eased the truck out into the center of the street, heading
toward the warehouse, whose face dripped individual bricks like
perspiration. The alley lay on Nate's side of the truck.

"Steer left now," Nate directed.

"Good idea. I'll just guts my way to the other end."

"No! Wait. What's that?"

Nate did not expect Danny to consider that there were not yet any
steel-belted radials with puncture sealant. He knew that the war era's
tires, with thin skins and inflated inner tubes, burst with the slightest
provocation. He opened his door and hopped out. The feeble truck
headlights had revealed a hole where an unexploded bomb had buried
itself in the dirt. The impact crater was two feet in diameter. As Nate
moved along the alley, he discovered at his feet a ragged square of

wood that had once been a sign on the outer warehouse wall. He picked it up and saw that it was about three-quarters of an inch thick. The unpainted side had four long bolts protruding through it. He turned the bolts away from his chest and walked toward the hole.

The alleyway was made of dirt with a pair of deep, compacted ruts running the length of it. Other than weeds crowding the edges, the passageway was clear. The bomb had burrowed into one of the ruts so deeply that the top of its copper tail fin protruded exactly as high as the surrounding dirt mound. The encircling ring where the dirt had been blown out exposed the top third of the unexploded weapon.

Nate approached cautiously. The bomb's inner works were ticking. His heart felt like a well-used boxer's speed bag. The bomb was a time-delay demon. Nate believed he remembered from his history lessons that they could be set from five minutes to an hour. If it was disturbed, by something such as a truck driving directly over it, it could annihilate everything around it in a moment.

The truck's horn sounded within a concentration of ack-ack explosions to the south. Nate looked skyward. A Messerchmitt fighter skimmed the horizon, heading straight toward the Thames. It approached on a direct line with the alley. Nate dropped into a tight ball and clutched his thin shield of wooden armor over his head and torso.

A fusillade of machinegun fire ripped along the alleyway, but the space was so narrow that the bullets tore into the roofs of the houses on either side.

"Son of a bitch! Twice!" Nate screamed, shaking his fist at the receding German machine. It was bad enough when industries, transportation lines and government buildings were targeted, but for two fighter pilots to go out of their way to target one man was beyond belief to him. Then he thought perhaps it was the same pilot. And then he thought of no man stepping back in time ever successfully predicting the future. He thought of Death's swift and certain involvement in correcting the unnatural situation. The era of the scythe was over; the day of the machinegun bullet execution had arrived.

Nate was trying to command his shaky legs to stand in spite of his cascade of thoughts when he heard a sizzling sound to his right. A hunk of exploded anti-aircraft shell buried itself in the alley. Nate threw his wooden shield up again. Several more pieces of shrapnel landed, one of them striking the wood so hard it nearly knocked the panel out of Nate's hands. He held the shield up for another few seconds by the bolts, all the while terrifyingly aware of the ticking of the bomb beside him.

Nate carefully laid the panel down over the hole, making sure that none of the bolts brushed the bomb. Over the raucous cacophony of noises filling his world, he heard the wood make a scraping sound as it touched the tail fin. Nate winced. He set down the panel and ran for the collapsing warehouse.

"Hey!" Danny called.

Nate slowed. "What?"

"Where are you going?"

Before Nate could answer, the parked moving van's petrol tank ignited from the fierce heat of the gas line break. The van disintegrated, blowing pieces in every direction. Just beyond the rear fender of the red truck, the van's radiator flew by with a humming noise.

"Just sit tight for one more minute!" Nate yelled. He dashed with overlong strides toward the warehouse. It had begun to burn inside.

The street was now a holocaust at either extreme. He avoided the bomb crater near the open manhole but was still soaked by the fountain of water from the ruptured line. He gathered four among many fallen bricks, straightened up and started into a run. Behind him, the last of the wall tumbled down with a boom that sent Nate springing a foot in the air. The bricks slipped from his hands. A new wall, formed of dust and tiny bits of brick and mortar, rushed toward him from behind. He absorbed the pain of a hundred shards of mortar and brick striking him. Just before the dust enveloped him, he caught a breath. He returned for the bricks, blindly grabbed them and started off again through the watery curtain that soaked up the dust and sent it falling as mud onto the street.

Nate's dash back to the unexploded bomb required fewer than fifty strides. In that short span he congratulated himself on having avoided death six times. A rack of smaller bombs had prevented instant cremation. He had eluded a direct hit from one bomb when he made Danny park the truck ahead of the moving van. His choice had prevented falling shrapnel from piercing him by using a wooden panel as a shield. He had stopped to humor his partner, which saved him from being killed by a flying radiator. Finally, he had selected bricks far enough from a collapsing brick wall to avoid being crushed. He wondered how few men had ever faced so many deadly situations within three minutes and survived. His elation was soberly tempered by the realization that Death's arsenal was limitless.

Nate brought the bricks to the hole and laid them down, two along the front and two at the back. When he lowered the panel, it sat slightly above the bomb's tail fin. Thinking about the proverbial cat fresh out of lives, he considered retreating down the alley and letting Danny unwittingly drive over the bomb alone. He decided he could not do it. He ran back to the truck and swung inside.

"You have to move slowly, and you have to run your right tires directly over that piece of wood," Nate directed. "I mean absolutely straight."

"No sweat," Danny said.

Nate drew in a slow, long breath as Danny dropped the shift into first. The truck eased forward. Foot by foot it advanced, until it was almost on the wood.

"Stop!" Nate ordered.

"What?"

"I'll get out and direct you from in front. Then, when the cab goes over the hole, I'll watch the back tires."

"Fine. Let's just hurry, shall we?" Danny said through clenched teeth.

Nate squeezed out of the confining space and sidled to the front. When the truck tire passed onto the panel, the wood bowed slightly. Nate tensed. The tire passed over without mishap.

Rather than waste time squeezing along the open inches between truck side and wall, Nate jumped on the bumper, the hood, the cab top, the compartment roof and then swung down behind. His vision momentarily swam with a brilliant red as the pain from his wound shot up his side, through his neck, and into his skull. When it subsided and he could see again, he realized that the rear tires were wider than those in front. By distributing weight, they would prevent the wooden panel from sagging.

"Go, go, go!" Nate called out. He jogged down the alley directly behind the rolling truck and climbed in only after it had exited and turned onto the next street.

"You are a mess," Danny observed of Nate's wet and dusty suit.

"You have no idea," Nate said. For the past minute, he had been fighting the urge to add his bladder's liquid to his trousers. The bullet wound hurt twice as bad as when he received it.

As Danny accelerated along the undamaged street, the time-delay bomb went off with a roar focused and intensified by the narrow passageway. The alley mouth erupted behind them with brilliant light, as if a thousand flash bulbs had exploded at once.

Danny's foot tromped involuntarily on the gas pedal. "What the fuck was that?"

"There was a bomb in that hole," Nate admitted.

When the truck reached the end of the street Danny stopped the truck and glowered at his partner.

"What other choice did we have?" Nate asked.

"We could have walked out on foot."

"Holding maybe twenty thousand pounds. Now we have two-hundred-and-fifty-thousand pounds."

Danny depressed the clutch. "With no place to put it."

"I have a place," Nate assured him.

The German attack stopped ten minutes before the Americans drove over the Thames. They navigated into Stepney, an East End district southeast of Bethnal Green. It was a pocket of poverty without squalor, largely occupied by recent Jewish refugees. Lying closer to the river than Bethnal Green and just beyond the docks, it had taken a terrible collective beating since the onset of the Blitz. Every second street was blocked off to traffic. By wending back and forth through the swaths of destruction they eventually reached Mile End Road. They drove east, realized they were headed in the wrong direction, reversed themselves and found Cambridge High Road. From this point, they knew their way. Danny drove to within a street of the one behind the Wilcox house. He parked and jogged silently to the Anderson shelter for his shoulder bag. He returned with the bag's main compartment empty, except for his gym padlock and his and Nate's flashlights.

In another five minutes, the badly scarred, red-paneled truck was parked halfway between the unfinished Bethnal Green deep level shelter entrances, in front of the wooden fence with the two slats they had wrestled loose on their first night in wartime.

For the last fifty minutes of their maneuvering, the skies had been clear of bombs, AA shells, searchlights, flares and airplanes. Fires, however, continued to light the cityscape. The city stunk of the smoke of consumed buildings and the expended cordite of thousands of anti-aircraft shells. Ambulances, fire trucks, relocation vehicles and construction crew vans raced back and forth, in and out of blankets of blackness. No one paid any attention to the truck Danny drove.

"How many packets of money are there?" Danny asked, for the third time.

"Five thousand in all," Nate answered, trying not to sound as irritated as he felt.

"That seems like too many."

"No. One-thousand-two-hundred-and-fifty packets per pallet. Four pallets."

Danny's face screwed up in concentration. "One hundred bills to each packet. Times five. 'Cause they're five pound notes."

"Correct."

"Five thousand times five hundred...."

"Is two-and-a-half million."

"And we have nothing except my shoulder bag to get them down into the shelter. Not even a rope to lower the bag."

"'tis a problem," Nate agreed. "Great wealth causes great headaches."

"And I know you're feeling like shit from that hole in your side."

"I can help."

Danny sighed and opened his cab door. He grabbed the shoulder bag and stepped onto the deserted street.

Nate eased gingerly out of his side of the truck, wanting nothing more than to stop moving for a few days. By the time he reached the rear Danny had the doors opened and had jumped inside.

"Fill your bag as full as you can," Nate directed.

"Twenty-eight, twenty-nine, thirty," Danny counted. "Why do they have to make their paper money so large? That's all. Crammed as I can get it. At that rate, it's how many trips?"

Nate rolled his eyes at the question. "The answer is: Lots. Throw me half a dozen."

Danny bent to the top pallet. "What are they wrapped in?"

"Cellophane."

"I thought so. I'm amazed they had it all the way back in this time."

Nate began singing softly and without any of the élan the composer intended. "You're the purple light/Of a summer night in Spain."

"What are you doing?" Danny asked.

"'You're the Nation'l Gall'ry/You're Garbo's sal'ry/You're Cellophane.'"

Danny handed six clear-wrapped packets to Nate. "Great. You know a song with the word 'cellophane' in it."

"It's a Cole Porter classic. Let's go." Nate led the way through the narrow opening in the fence. "You should be ashamed of yourself not knowing such a famous song."

"Bullshit. Nobody our age from our age but you knows stuff like that," Danny protested.

"That's not true. But so many are like you that it's a crime."

"Songs aren't important," Danny affirmed.

"Wrong. 'The Star-Spangled Banner' makes grown men cry. 'Deutschland Über Alles' got eight million Germans to volunteer to die."

They came to the edge of the gaping opening.

"What's a hole in the ground called, Daniel?" Nate asked.

"A tunnel? A tube?"

"No."

"The Underground."

"No."

"What already?"

"A grave." Nate shook the packets of money he held. "Who says you can't take it with you? This is what is called grave humor. Comic relief for the hours of terror we just went through. Like the grave-digger scene in Hamlet."

Danny transferred the bulging bag to his other hand. "I hate it when you get in these weird moods. We're gonna need more than comic relief after climbing down and up these ladders all night. I don't think I have the energy for more than five or six trips, no matter how much it's worth to me."

"We're only climbing down and up once," Nate said. Without further preamble, he tossed his six packets, one after the other, down the eighty-foot drop.

Danny watched them sail into the gloom. "Shit! Won't they bust apart?"

"Sealed cellophane?" Nate answered. "I hope not. The stuff is thick. Spin 'em, so they land with a twist."

For at least the tenth time since the bombing stopped, Danny sighed. He opened the bag and tossed his packets down into the darkness.

"Bon voyage." Who says you can't take it with you into the grave? It will be waiting for you on the other side," Nate assured. They did not stop for a break, even during two more bombing attacks. With Danny stuffing extra packets in his pockets and Nate increasing his individual load to ten packets, after three hours they still had not removed all the stacks of five-pound notes from the second pallet.

"Let's stow what we can," Nate advised, looking down into the nearly black abyss. "Then we'll drive the truck to the safest back alley we can find and finish the job tomorrow night."

Danny was drenched in perspiration and breathing hard from the constant rush back and forth. "Yeah. What else can we do?"

Nate said nothing more. Even after removing his raincoat, he had been sweating more than his partner. He knew with dread that the beads drenching his body were not merely from labor. He had a fever. His wound was infected.

Carefully, they descended to the rough track spur. They found four packets split open, but the bills had not flown far. They collected these first, filled the shoulder bag and moved up and into the bomb shelter. Nate showed his partner the electric panel closet, hidden behind the door with the padlock flanges. He reminded Danny of what Worden Miles had said about the construction being abandoned. Unless they had very bad luck, the place would be ideal for hiding the money for weeks, if not months to come.

"You think it will all fit in here?" Danny asked.

"Maybe just," Nate estimated. "Let's start stacking."

Another three hours were required to shuttle and stow what they had thrown over the cliff. When they had finished, Danny slipped the padlock over the flanges, snapped it shut and spun the dial.

"What's the combination?" Nate asked.

Danny gave him a hard look. "You're not gonna run out on me, are you?"

Nate laughed. "Sure I will. I'll carry it all on my back at one time."

"It's right to 10, twice left to 5, right to 15."

"Easy." Nate started walking back toward the ladders. "Now for the climb up."

Danny followed behind, swinging his flashlight beam back and forth. He made a noise like a horse blowing his lips together. "Jesus, what a workout! After everything else tonight. I can't remember ever being this tired. I'm too bushed even to look for that redheaded bastard. Are you sure you can make it up the ladders?"

"I don't have a choice."

"Do I look as bad as you?"

"I hope not."

Dan nodded toward Nate's flank. "You been losing a lot of blood from your wound. It must have opened up."

"It did. And I have a fever."

"Not good. Not in this day and age."

Nate thought about the discovery of sulfa drugs just before the war and how many more wounded Allied soldiers than Germans and Italians had been saved because of them.. He despaired, however, of getting any. If they were in England, he had no document identity to walk into a hospital and ask for them. He reflected that it would be a supreme irony if the bombs, bullets and shrapnel of the Blitz did not get him, but some bacterium in existence since dinosaurs walked the earth and sure to be around long after mankind disappeared would serve as the Grim Reaper's executioner.

"I have penicillin, if you think it will help," Danny volunteered.

Nate stopped walking and turned. "How do you have penicillin?"

Danny held up the shoulder bag. He flipped back the top and unzipped the flat, plastic pocket built into it. It was clearly meant to protect something like a magazine or newspaper from wet clothing, but Danny had found another purpose.

"It's part of my survival kit. I've also got those Band-aids with the stuff in the gauze."

"The kind impregnated with Neosporin?"

"Right. And a little tube of ointment for pink eye. And anti-malaria pills. Christ, with the backwater places we do deals in, you gotta be ready for anything. I have halogen for dirty water..."

Nate figured Danny meant halozone, a good water purifier. Dirty water in a glass was easy to fix in comparison to dirty beasties in the blood stream.

"Six Vicodins for pain, like a toothache," Danny continued. "And, let's see, in this little baggie I have seven penicillin pills. You remember in January when I lost my voice and had that terrible sore throat, and the penicillin wasn't working? That doctor in Hong Kong prescribed something stronger."

"Zithromax."

"Yeah. It did the trick. Well, I saved the rest of the penicillin for a rainy day. Here."

"God bless you, Daniel! You are a genius. Keep them in your bag until we get to the top. And give me two of those Band-aids as well."

"Will do." Danny took the lead and lengthened his stride, invigorated by the praise. "We gotta hide the truck real good. You said Bennett had somebody tail you right into Bethnal Green?"

"Yes. That runt with the thick glasses who met us in the subway."

"Him. Yeah, I'd like to put a bullet between those beady eyes. So, we have to hide the truck…and not around here."

"I'll do that."

"We will do that." Danny waited for Nate at the bottom ladder. As he started to climb, he said, "We're really stuck in this time, aren't we?"

"I'm afraid so, my friend."

"But now we have a hundred million dollars, and I know the history of sports for the next sixty-odd years."

Nate did not speak for several seconds, concentrating on climbing each rung of the wooden ladder. "I figure we return most of the money to the Bank of England."

"What? Then why are we doing all this work?"

"Hear me out. We write to them and offer to return it, in exchange for citizenship and a one per cent finder's fee. They reply via a legal notice in one of the newspapers."

"A lousy million?" Danny complained.

"Remember your infallible ability to predict the future, Daniel. We do need to become citizens of some country, don't we?"

"Let me think about it." After several more rungs, Danny sighed yet again. "Oh, hell. Whatever you decide. I always end up letting you do the thinking."

"And letting me do the talking."

"Don't I always?" Danny said, good-naturedly reciting his part of their running joke. "We have that book of matches Bennett handed his dear, departed crony, from The Royal Standard pub, as a clue to finding him. Do we turn that and the photo of him over to the police and let them do the searching?"

"Probably."

"I see! We're moving the money so that if the bank doesn't go for the deal, we keep it all."

"You've got it."

"No, we've got it."

They reached the first platform and paused.

"It'll be morning soon," Danny estimated.

Nate pressed the illuminator on his watch. "You're right. Then rosy-fingered dawn will come creeping over the western horizon just as you tumble into your cozy bed in the Wilcox's lovely steel shelter. You can sleep the sleep of the dead."

Danny put his hands around the next ladder. "Let's stop talking about graves and death, shall we?"

Right after they cleaned the majority of dirt from their bodies, Danny used the first aid kit from the Miles shelter to cleanse Nate's wound and stitch its outer edges. Because the tear in the flesh was infected and very tender, Nate first poured a shot of whiskey over the wounds and then sent three more down his throat, along with a penicillin capsule. The makeshift anesthesia did little to lessen the pain, so that Nate was forced to bite into a rolled-up newspaper to keep from screaming. The antiseptic-impregnated bandages finished their battlefield surgery.

Too late, Nate felt the whiskey numbing his brain. He sat on one of the shelter's folding chairs with his shirt off, enjoying the coolness of the night air on his heat-radiating skin. He said, "See if you still have that five-pound note Bennett gave you."

Danny grabbed his wallet. He had shoved the note in carelessly, so that it was wrinkled. He smoothed it out on the shelter table. Nate laid the note Bennett had given him beside it. He then broke the seal of the one packet of pounds he had taken from the truck before they hid the rest. He peeled the first two notes from the top of the neat stack and placed them next to the other notes.

"Right now a magnifying glass would be helpful," Nate said. He held one Bennett note and one Bank of England note up under the suspended, naked light bulb. His eyes swept back and forth, back and forth.

Danny breathed heavily on his shoulder. "It's bad paper, right?"

"No, it's very good paper. They're both rag, but it looks like this is phony money. Let's compare the other two." When Nate was finished, he said, "The design of this money is so simple to copy it's a sin."

"Everybody uses coins," Danny observed. "Maybe paper's so rarely used that the engravers didn't feel the need to work hard to protect it."

"Good point. Look here on the seal. This cloud dips down a little lower on the Bennett notes. I suppose this is the allegorical Britannia sitting on her throne. In the fakes, her lips are not quite as full."

"Yeah. You're right."

"Also, the crosshatching on the right side of the beehive is lighter. But if I didn't have a reason to suspect, I'd never find such subtle differences," Nate admitted. "This is quality work. Expensive work. Especially the paper and the watermarks."

"Why commit a big robbery," Danny remarked, holding up one of Bennett's gifts, "when they could have passed this stuff?"

Nate set down the pounds and glanced at his friend. "Another good point. This whole business is very strange." He winced and grunted from having twisted his torso.

"Worry about it in your dreams," Danny advised. "You've got to beat that fever."

"One last task," said Nate. He moved to his blazer, which was draped on a hanger that hung on a length of stretched rope. He removed the blazer and set it flat on the table. He took the Altoids tin from his trouser pocket and opened it, exposing the emerald lying within the rough toilet paper cushion. Then he sat.

"One of our nest eggs, in case everything else goes wrong," Danny said.

"Then let's put it back in its nest." Nate lifted the right sleeve and grabbed the bottom brass button with the thumb and first two fingers of his right hand. With his left hand, he fastened onto the upper half of the button. He twisted it counterclockwise. The surface rotated. After three more twists, it separated from the bottom threads, so that the brass-coated lead looked like a tiny shield with an anchor insignia. Because the button was overlarge and the lower half extra deep, the uncut gemstone fit with a bit of space inside it. Soft wax packing kept it from rattling. Nate replaced the cover and screwed it carefully on. Then he wiped his hands clean of the wax and any lead that might have flaked off.

"We're gonna make this work out all right," Nate assured Danny. "I promise."

Danny, who had stripped off his clothes and tumbled into his cot, merely nodded his head and closed his eyes.

# CHAPTER SIXTEEN

Nate sat on the steps of the Wilcox home, watching the street. Danny had elected to do a perambulation of the Bethnal Green district, both to work off the jitters of the previous day and to purchase some needed items. Nate's assignment had been to beat his infection and fever with penicillin and rest.

Nate found that many clearly apparent but easily overlooked facts could be learned by simply sitting and watching the immediate world pass by. He confirmed again how much more often people of this time walked and rode bicycles and how few persons were overweight. He observed that neatness and proper dress, even when cleaning, were important. He saw how, in spite of the constant precipitation of dust and soot, someone was out in front of each home bright and early to sweep and neaten. He recorded that every neighbor was important enough to greet and to share a little conversation with. Health, pride, civility and community were well, in spite of the multitude of wounds inflicted on Londoners by the war.

The most poignant moments of the day occurred when a male in his late teens motorcycled up to the house directly across the street from the Miles home. He wore the uniform of a postal telegram boy. In the front window of the counter row house was proudly displayed a flag with the insignia of the RAF. Worden Miles had mentioned several days earlier that the son was a fighter pilot in the British air force. The hair stood up on the nape of Nate's neck. He rose from the steps and went into the kitchen, where Millicent was scrubbing a pan.

"I believe some bad news has arrived across the street," he told her.

Mrs. Miles hurried to the front door with her tea towel in her hand. "Oh, heavens! How horrible!"

The door of the house opened. A woman who looked to be about Millicent's age answered. The instant she saw the young man, she let out a cry.

Millicent hurried down the steps to offer comfort. Nate knew that the Miles family was the only other one on the street to have lost a son to this point. The young man removed his cap and handed over the dreaded message. A few moments later he was back on the street kick-starting his motorcycle, on his way to desolate another family.

As Nate basked in the welcome late-morning heat of the sun, feeling as well the touch of the breeze on his fevered skin, the street came to life with the bad news. Within minutes, women carrying baskets emerged from their homes and converged on the one directly opposite where Nate sat. Some twenty minutes later, a young woman wearing a jacket with a miniature RAF wing lapel medal, which Nate had been told were called "sweetheart badges," strode onto the street. Tracks of tears streamed down her face. As she walked, she tortured a handkerchief between her hands. She, too, disappeared into the mourning house.

Nate listened to the Miles house. He heard nothing. And yet a man was upstairs, ostensibly working on replacing the destroyed section of ceiling. Nate had first seen the man when he emerged from the Wilcox shelter. The supposed construction worker was dressed in white coveralls and looked out Penelope's window. It was not a glance. He seemed to have taken up a position there. This caused Nate's inner alarm system to switch on, but he tried to chalk it up to the possibility that the demand for construction laborers in London was currently so great that only a lazy one could be found.

Nate wandered to the front of the Wilcox house. From its stoop, he observed a man standing near the red post box on the corner. The man disappeared for a minute and then was back, carrying a newspaper. After thirty minutes, he had not moved. He never looked at Nate. From this, Nate knew he was being watched. He found it highly unlikely that he could be linked to the armored truck robbery so quickly, unless Alex Bennett had found out previously where he and Danny were hiding, had been arrested and had confessed and elected to cooperate. Even so, if officers of the law had not marched up to the house by this time, he knew that he and Danny had little worry until they again went near the money. The equivalent of one hundred million dollars missing was no small matter, even for the Bank of England. The police would not risk Nate and Danny being arrested without first taking the opportunity to follow them to where the money had been stashed.

Millicent Miles was the second woman to leave the home of the RAF pilot. As she climbed the steps toward Nate, she said, "Rose has enough company right now. My thought is to offer sincere condolences, make sure she understands I'm here, and then leave her to do her first grieving alone. That's how I wanted it."

"Would you care to sit for a minute with me, Mrs. Miles?" Nate asked.

Millicent turned and eased herself down, flattening her apron as she sat. "Don't mind if I do. These steps are getting lower and lower," she observed wryly after uttering a little groan. "And how is that wound in your side?"

"Infected," Nate revealed.

"Let's see."

Nate unbuttoned the left-behind work shirt he had borrowed from Mr. Wilcox's closet. He pulled the material back and twisted toward the light.

"I can't see much with those fancy bandages on," Mrs. Miles told him.

Nate figured the antiseptic Band-aids had done their best in the past few hours, so he gingerly tore them off. The margins of the wound were swollen and bright red.

"Nasty work. That Nazi bugger." Millicent pushed herself up with a grunt. "Wait right here."

Banging began upstairs. Within two minutes, Mrs. Miles returned. She held a clean rag and a brown bottle containing hydrogen peroxide. She again sat beside Nate and gently daubed the liquid onto the wound. It bubbled and foamed.

Nate knew that Millicent had to be privy to the purpose of the man in her house, if not also the one down the block. He decided to draw her out.

"Do you have any rich relatives?"

"Me? Not a one."

"What would you do if, out of the blue, someone left you ten thousand pounds?"

"Mercy. I'd replace my pots and pans." Penny's mother seemed content to leave it at that.

"You wouldn't move your family out of Bethnal Green?"

"I suppose I would…for reasons of safety. We're just too close to the German targets. But I would miss my friends and neighbours, the shopkeepers, the postman. I would very much miss my church."

"Wouldn't today be a good day for such news?" Nate persisted. "With your house so damaged? Wouldn't you like more?"

"More of what? Material things? Not really. You can only wear one set of clothes at a time, and I have several. You should only eat and drink so much. A radio twice as expensive doesn't deliver entertainment twice as good. Money doesn't buy friends either. Not true ones."

"You could give some of the money to Penny, so she could travel as soon as the war is over."

Millicent still showed no sign of linking the robbery and Nate with his conversation. "I suppose that would be a blessing. But if I had a wish between ten thousand pounds in my lap and that this war could be over, there would be no choice about it. There! At least the surface is thoroughly clean. You'll have a rather ugly scar for life, I'm afraid." Nate was not worried. Aside from the fact that the scar was under his shirt, he figured he would have it re-cut and stitched by a good cosmetic surgeon once such a creature became common. In the meantime, he would have an impressive story to tell. He tucked into his memory the determination to try to patent the superglue stitching process as soon as the product came on the market. Failing that, he would at least buy all the stock in the company he could.

"What about your shirts? Are they stained with blood?" Mrs. Miles asked.

"They are. I have them soaking, but only so much will come out."

"Then fetch them for me." She held up the bottle of hydrogen peroxide. "A liberal treatment with this should do the trick."

Nate decided on one more stratagem for reading Millicent Miles's mind

"It doesn't sound like you're getting your money's worth out of that fellow upstairs," he observed. "He spends most of his time looking out the window."

The woman's face hardened, and a veil seemed to lower over her eyes. "I think he's afraid of the Luftwaffe paying another visit to our house, and I don't blame him." She pushed up from the step and entered the house.

Left alone again, Nate firmed up his opinion that the two men watching him had nothing to do with the robbery. Nevertheless, they were not at all a good sign. Someone on the street, perhaps even a member of the Miles family, had found the prolonged presence of two non-Englishmen who came and went at very odd hours too much not to report. But Nathaniel Allen had played dangerous games before, in countries with far less sense of fair play and proper jurisprudence than in England. If the authorities had not closed in, it was because they had no probable cause on which to act. He was sure that, with England's critical dependence on the United States in these war-torn days, few Americans were being arrested. He closed his eyes and concentrated on enjoying the sun's healing rays before the next air raid.

Danny returned to the shelter at a little after three o'clock. His protracted hike through Bethnal Green had yielded two identical canvas satchels, each of which could transport as many as forty packets of pound notes. Inside one of the satchels were two tightly wrapped coils of stout rope, each measuring 100 feet in length.

"Did you remember to buy my writing tablet?" Nate asked.

In reply, Danny took from the same sack a manila envelope that contained 50 sheets of three-hole-punched, lined paper and several legal-sized, white envelopes.

"Couldn't find exactly what you asked for," Danny replied. "This is 1940, remember?"

"It will do fine," Nate assured him.

"I took one of the envelopes and a stamp and mailed your letter," Danny reported.

The letter had been addressed to the editor-in-chief of *The Times of London*. In it, Nate carefully laid out the facts that the money left in the Bank of England armored truck was counterfeit and that the original money was safe. He supplied one of the photographs of Alex Bennett and described in great detail the little man with the pug nose, white skin and thick eyeglasses. With all other participants at the country road massacre aside from him and Danny dead and unable to testify, he brazenly swore their innocence regarding the murders. He went on to modify the truth further, claiming that he and Danny had been tricked into helping unload illegal trucks in exchange for access to identity documents. He stated that, for reasons of political conscience, he and his partner were in England without identities and wished to be granted British citizenship. In exchange for this and a one-percent finders fee on the original money, they would return the two-and-a-half-million pounds and offer witness against the other men.

Having picked up important concepts of law from his father and from personal readings, he spelled out how the newspaper needed to serve as the official record for the government and print wording that did not allow the agreement to be abrogated once Nate and Danny turned themselves and the money in. As soon as formal acceptance in agreeable language was printed in the newspaper, the senders of the letter would visit Scotland Yard.

"I did like you said," Danny added, "and put it in a post box as far from here as I walked."

"Good. Now it's a matter of waiting." Nate picked up the other four postage stamps Danny had purchased and studied them. On each stamp King George VI's bust faced to the left, with a crown suspended over his head. The innocuous-looking pieces of glue-backed paper were yet one more reminder to Nate that he was in another time. The oldest of the five Allen children, Simon, Jr., had collected stamps since he was ten. He owned a copy of the stamp Nate stared at. Nate recalled learning from his brother that virtually every stamp in England had the current monarch's image on it one way or another, but that in the United States it was illegal to display on postage the likeness of anyone living. No person, not even the adored Franklin Delano Roosevelt, deserved such official adulation in the land where all men are created equal. 'Two nations separated by more than a common language,' Nate thought. And now he was preparing to live the rest of his life in this new world, separated from all that was familiar by time, distance, fashion, culture and a hundred other factors. Only his knowledge of what lay ahead and his acquaintance with Penelope Miles provided comfort.

"I got the Mileses all the food I could cram in the other sack," Danny proudly announced. "Delivered it already. It came to two pounds, six pence, but we don't have to worry about money anymore, do we?"

Nate shook his head. He stretched his side and reassured himself that the swelling of his wound had eased.

"How are you feeling?" Danny asked, sitting down next to his friend and taking his own visual assessment.

"I believe your penicillin saved me from a real bad time," Nate honestly replied. "I still have four pills left, but I can already feel that disgusting taste in my saliva. It's well into my system. My fever seemed to break about an hour ago. We'll see tonight, when fevers always seem to spike."

"Are you strong enough to help me unload the rest of the money?"

"Fortunately, yes. We can't leave that truck out, no matter how well we hide it." They had found the back wall of a burned-out processing building standing, near a yard filled with all manner of glass bottles waiting to be recycled. The wall and piles of glass completely hid the truck from view, and there would clearly be no work done at the place for some time to come. Nate added, "Even if nobody tries to break in, it could all go up in flames with the next raid."

"So you just hung around today?" Danny asked, as he pulled off his shoes and socks.

Nate related the story of the telegram boy arriving across the street. He did not, however, tell Danny about the men watching him. For one thing, he knew such news would unnerve his partner. Danny did not have the disposition to sit tight and tough out situations. He was a take-the-bull-by-the-horns person, and his kind of solution was not possible in this instance. Further, Nate wanted to test Danny's powers of observation, to see how much time would elapse before he recognized the stakeout himself. Across three years Nate had tried to sensitize his partner to such situations, but Danny sometimes forgot to be observant, especially when he had much on his mind.

Because they needed to spend at least five more hours transporting the money down to the deep level shelter, Nate had no trouble convincing Danny to catch a nap. They awoke to Mr. Miles tapping on their shelter door.

Supper began as always, with a prayer. As they joined hands, Nate volunteered with a grace he had once read and which had stuck with him.

"God of pilgrims, we give thanks for a table where we can tell our story and sing our song." Peeking out of one eye at Penny's bowed head, he decided to add his own four words. "And dance our dance."

The entire Miles family praised the sentiment. However, Penny and Millicent lapsed into silence directly after a discussion of the death of their RAF pilot neighbor. In contrast, Worden Miles returned to his ebullient, talkative self after a few days of near-silence.

"I heard the official estimate of the numbers taking up residence in the Underground. Seems there are just over 100,000 on the platforms and in the, uh…"

"Deep level shelters," Millicent smoothly supplied.

Worden nodded his thanks.

Nate noted that this was not the first time one Miles elder had finished the other's sentence. He reflected as well on his former observation that husband and wife looked more like brother and sister. He remembered reading that, perhaps because of shared environments, attitudes, diet, et cetera, two people would naturally grow to look like each other. He smiled at the thought and at the couple, thinking that they were like comfortable slippers, left and right, well broken in to perform one task. Nate decided he wanted the experience of something that comfortable in the rest of his life.

"A total of 140,000 Londoners have been left homeless in less than two weeks," Worden went on, shaking his head. "I also learned that ten per cent of the bombs that land are outfitted with delay fuses. The Hun really play dirty."

"They'll get theirs," Danny promised, through a mouthful of biscuit. "Hey, Mr. Miles, did you ever hear of a pub named The Royal Standard?"

"I have indeed," Worden replied. "It's quite famous. It's the oldest freehouse in the country. About 900 years if I recall."

"That means it was built before the Tower of London," Nate reckoned.

"True enough. But it's not in London. It's in, uh, Beaconsfield."

"How far away is that?" Danny asked.

"If you hiked it and back, you'd wear out the soles of your shoes. It's halfway between here and Oxford."

Nate estimated forty miles. It seemed unlikely that the man who called himself Alex Bennett hailed from such a distance place. However, Nate did not put it past the cagey character to carry the pub's matchbook precisely to provide a false clue to his residence.

"Why are you asking?" Worden asked Danny.

"Oh, somebody recommended it to me, but he didn't say how far away it was."

The electricity failed without warning. While Penny brought two candles to the table and lit them, speculation on the cause of the outage ranged from a normal repair to bomb-damaged lines to expectation of an imminent air raid.

"Collin over at the presses shared an interesting note I hadn't thought of," Worden Miles said, returning to his verbal journal once the candle flames were flickering. "Did you know the smaller bombs whistle or scream? You can tell if it's going to be large if it chugs through the air. And he also told me that what makes the incendiary spikes burn so hot. The critical ingredient is either magnesium or phosphorous."

Nate glanced at Danny, who only half listened, intent instead on packing down seconds of the generous meal set before him. Nate wondered why his partner was not as astonished as he that the recently tight-lipped Mr. Miles once again fairly hemorrhaged information. With the supposed carpenter positioned all day upstairs at the Miles house windows and the other man perpetually reading the newspaper at the corner, the likelihood that someone thought he and Danny were spies was extremely great. Worden seemed to be going out of his way to supply interesting but ultimately non-strategic information in the hopes that Danny and Nate would betray how they were passing such facts on to the enemy. Based on recent changes of behavior, Nate was betting that Millicent or Worden Miles had blown the proverbial whistle on the two foreigners who arrived from nowhere and came and went at all hours.

"Interesting," Nate responded, playing his expected role, when Worden ran out of breath.

"There were three raids by the time I left work," Mr. Miles continued. "Seventy bombers. Nineteen were shot down. Twelve RAF fighters were lost. The balance is tipping our way. They dropped far more tonnes of incendiary spikes than high explosives today. My thought is that they know they got most of our factories. Now they're concentrating on burning the rest of London to the ground, trying to break the will of the common citizen."

Nate set down his fork. "I'm sure you're right."

Mr. Miles rattled on, delivering a long list of the major buildings damaged or destroyed in the heart of London over the past three days. While he spoke, Nate looked at Penny, who sat directly across from him, apparently lost in private thought. In the soft glow of the twin candles, with her porcelain skin shining and her long hair let down, she reminded him of several paintings by the seventeenth-century Frenchman Georges de La Tour. One he had seen in Amsterdam's Rijksmuseum, one in Washington's National Gallery of Art and one in New York City's Metropolitan Museum of Art. He remembered that they all featured the same female model. In each she wore a light-colored, flowing blouse. She posed in front of a single candle, surrounded by umber darkness and looking pensively into a mirror. He reflected that that woman from another time had apparently also beguiled him.

Nate was in love for the first time, and he knew it. He knew because he had no reservations; there was nothing Penelope Miles needed to do or know or be before he gave his heart. He knew he would forgive her anything, even rejecting him if it made her life better. If he was now given a choice between returning to his own time or staying with her, he would stay.

Worden choked briefly on a bit of food he had not chewed well enough in his haste to continue talking. He waved away the table's solicitation. "I'm fine. On the home front, there's more interesting news. Yesterday evening there was an attempted robbery in the countryside between Sevenoaks and Maidstone."

Millicent tsked her reproof. "Such a shame that we English can't be civil to each other while the Germans are at our throats."

"True enough, Mother. But listen to this: It was an enormous payroll from the Bank of England, in The City, to Fort Clarence, in Maidstone. Fort Clarence is the headquarters of the Home Guard, don't you know."

"I know nothing of Maidstone," Millicent admitted.

"Nor I," Penny said, returning from her reverie.

Worden straightened up in his chair, happy to play university don delivering his lecture. "It's been a place of strategic import for centuries. Now, with the Germans just across the Channel and poised to invade, it's even more important. I saw a photograph today. The place was built to look like a medieval castle. Moat, portcullis and so forth."

"How did the robbery fail?" Penny asked.

"They're not sure, if I read between the lines. At any rate, the money is safe. Three men died. Two from the bank and one robber. They are certain at least one other would-be robber is at large."

Danny had stopped eating during this news and briefly looked up. Nate felt his partner's eyes but refused to connect with them.

"Let's see…what else? Oh, yes. Last night a German U-boat sank a liner called *The City of Benares.*"

This time Nate choked and was slapped several times on the back by Danny.

"So sorry," Millicent apologized. "I must not have cut the beef small enough."

"No. My fault," Nate said. "Listening when I should be chewing." He saw Penny watching him with mild alarm. He offered her a reassuring smile.

"The ship was ferrying a goodly number of children to Canada," Worden went on. "First report is that many have drowned."

The sinking of this exact ship, mentioned by the clerk at the Cunard desk when Nate was seeking passage, hammered home just how unsafe was any attempt to get to the United States early in the war.

Nate redoubled his resolve to carve out a new life, at least for the foreseeable future, in England.

"And, finally, one of today's bombers dropped a large bomb on Marble Arch station. It killed twenty persons."

Penny's head jerked up. She swallowed the food in her mouth with difficulty, narrowly avoiding becoming the third person at the table to choke. Her eyes had grown more enormous than Nate ever remembered. She stared at him for just a moment, and then shifted her focus to her father.

"Were you there today, Penny?" her mother asked.

"No. No, I avoid all the stations when the air raid sirens sound."

"Good thinking," Millicent decided. "They must be prime targets." She took in a fortifying breath, as if to let the table know enough sorrow had been discussed. "Let me tell you all about Penny's new silk dancing dress."

As Mrs. Miles spoke within the intimate circle of candlelight, Nate remembered that all three of the de La Tour paintings had something else in common. The young female subject held the top half of a human skull with no sign of revulsion. Instead, her grasp of the gruesome object seemed tender. On viewing each of the paintings, Nate had wondered if it was meant to represent the symbolic future facing even the most beautiful young creature or if it was instead the literal skull of the man she loved, representing not being able to hold onto what one most adored.

Following the meal, Penny and her mother rushed over to the Wilcox house. Millicent had been fashioning the dress there, and her daughter needed to endure a last fitting before changing into her Ambulance Service uniform. Directly after dessert, Danny rushed out the front door trailing apologies. Mr. Miles hastened off to his warden duties, leaving Nate alone. Without being asked, Nate washed the dishes, cups, utensils and pots. The Miles's portable radio had been moved into the kitchen, and Nate had it tuned to the BBC. Judy Garland singing 'Over the Rainbow' was followed immediately by Vera Lynn singing 'They'll Be Bluebirds Over the White Cliffs of Dover,' and Nate understood the common theme of hope. The refusal of an entire people to wallow in self pity humbled him.

When Mrs. Miles entered the kitchen, she paused with surprise. "Are you feeling better then?"

"Yes. Considerably," Nate said truthfully.

"This wasn't necessary."

"But it was," he insisted. "I'll dry. You put everything away."

Millicent carried the cups to the cupboard. With her back to Nate, she said, "Did you not say last week you wouldn't be long in this area?"

"I did, yes. But our plans have been somewhat delayed." Nate set down a dish. "I hope we haven't overstayed our welcome."

"Anyone who saves my house from fire can hardly overstay his welcome."

"But..." Nate coaxed.

Mrs. Miles arranged the cups. "With Ralph gone, we only have Penelope now. Every day she's becoming more taken with you."

The declaration and its implications thrilled Nate, in spite of its obvious negative couching. He hastened to reply, "Believe me, Mrs. Miles, I would never do anything to hurt your daughter."

"Not on purpose leastways."

"I understand what you're saying. I can tell you that I have also not purposely led her on."

Finally, Millicent turned and regarded Nate. "And that is undoubtedly the reason you appeal so to her. She has always longed for the less accessible, the more exotic. For example, we have encouraged her to favour Brendon Danvers. He's polite, well brought up, well educated, with a clear future ahead of him. And he fancies Penny a great deal. But he's just too ordinary for her. She chases the challenge."

"And now it's me."

"Most definitely. You are, to say the least, a great mystery." She smirked. "Young women always favour the dangerous, rebellious young men. The smarter among them, however, realize these men are not for home or family or stability. They eventually settle for someone more reliable."

"I won't lie to you, Mrs. Miles," Nate said, setting down the dish he had just dried. "I have never been so taken with a woman as I am with your daughter. She is uniquely special. But I also am not in command of what will happen to me in the next month or two. I promise to maintain enough distance until we leave so that she isn't hurt. Perhaps in a few months, I can come back here and try to establish a different, better relationship."

Mrs. Miles seemed tremendously relieved. "I hope you can, as well. I thank you for your candour." She looked around the dimly lit room.

"I'll deal with the rest. Why don't you have a lie-down? I understand tomorrow night you are expected to dance. You need to renew your strength."

Nate took a step forward and planted a light kiss on Mrs. Miles's cheek. She smiled faintly when he pulled away.

Just after dusk, a legion of German bombers descended on London. Bethnal Green, however, was not their target. Nate had long since learned to ignore anything that did not attract the anti-aircraft fire from Victoria Park. He slept through part of the raid and directly after it. He only awoke when Danny pounded on the shelter door.

"Who is it?" Nate grumbled.

"Guess."

"Adolf Fucking Hitler."

"And how do you know I don't have Queen Elizabeth with me?"

"Because she isn't–" Nate unlatched the door, opened it and peered around, making sure no one stood near his partner. "Because she isn't queen yet, Daniel. Haven't you been paying attention? Her father, George, is still on the throne."

"What the hell do I care?" Danny answered, pushing past into the dark shelter. He grabbed the box of wooden matches and headed right for the kerosene lantern. "I'm American."

"Not if we get British citizenship," Nate said through a yawn.

Danny lighted the lamp. "Yeah, well, I've been meaning to talk to you about that. If I was the British government, I wouldn't give citizenship to two guys who helped rob their official bank. No way. So maybe we try for American citizenship."

"The United States of America doesn't grant citizenship to criminals."

Danny grinned. "But what if our condition to the Brits was the finder's fee and just shoving us out of their country without saying what we did? I am now holding the ace card to guarantee that."

Such a pat show of confidence was rare in Nate's partner. Daniel had fully attracted his attention. "And how did you come by this card?"

"By using the information on the back of Bennett's matchbook."

"The Royal Standard?"

"The same."

"There is no way you went to Beaconsfield and back in a few hours."

Danny grinned like the Cheshire Cat, as he slowly shook his head back and forth. "How many homes of hot wings are there outside of

Philadelphia? I figured if The Royal Standard is the most famous pub in England, how many copies must there be in London?"

"How many?"

"Two."

"And you hit pay dirt, you bloody genius," Nate praised.

Daniel sat at the table. "Remember, the address was right below the name? There it was, sitting on the street corner, big as life!"

Nate's warning system snapped on. "You just barged in and asked for Alex Bennett?"

Daniel reared back his head in offense. "Please! Am I not your partner? Of course I didn't barge in. I sent Gwen."

Nate erected his passive façade. "Gwen. Interesting."

"Sure. In case Bennett was sitting there." Danny slapped Nate on the knee. "And wait until you hear this: I gave her the other photo you took of him standing in front of the Surabaya. This way, number one, she already knows him if he's there. In which case she turns around and strolls out, and I wait for him to emerge with my gun in my hand. number two, by her having the photo there was no need to use the phony name he gave us."

"Go on."

Danny's grin became even bigger. "Here's the best part. Just before she walked in, Gwen stuffed a throw pillow under her dress. With her coat buttoned tight around it, it made her look seven months pregnant. Great, right?"

"Inventive."

"Thanks. So she waddles in, takes a good look around, doesn't see him. Then she waltzes up to the bar and shows the…" He held up his forefinger to show how much he had learned. "…publican the picture. 'You see this?' she asks the man, sticking out her swollen belly. 'This was caused by this man. As you can see, he is not exactly a loyal patron of this here pub alone, so you don't have to be loyal to him either. He's a liar, he is, and I need to know where he lives.'"

"And the man told her."

Danny sat back in his seat and crossed one leg over the other. "You are not going to believe what he told her. He said, 'If you have a complaint against Detective Adams, you had best take it to the Southwark Borough Police on Borough High Road.'"

"Jesus Christ," Nate exclaimed.

"My words exactly."

"No wonder he had access to guns."

"And criminal helpers," Danny added. "And why he could be wandering around during the day. The Surabaya is in Southwark – his beat."

"He must have had Saturday afternoon off, so when he meets with us he leads us away from his stomping ground, over to the West End."

Nate wanted to kick himself for not having suspected earlier. Multiple clues had been staring him in the face. The man's demeanor stunk of detective. His brutal handling of the looting twelve-year-old boy without any fear of consequence was a perfect example. The frisking in the church was another. The professional set of lock-picking tools and his skill with them at Holy Trinity was a third. The fourth was the Webley he had flashed inside the church. Nate recalled with chagrin how he had told Danny on the roof of the Cockspur Street car park that Webleys were the gun of choice among London's Metropolitan Police. The fifth clue was that Bennett was not truly concerned if Nate and Danny were members of the police. He had clearly checked that out through internal means. The proof of his lack of concern was that he had the two produce the emerald in the subway at the last minute, to confirm their stories. If proof had been so important, he would have insisted on seeing the emerald himself and at least a full day earlier.

Danny could not wait for Nate to respond to his last words; he had too much good news to share. "Thinking quick, Gwen says, 'Alex's real last name is Adams?' The barkeep goes 'Lady, if your story is true, you've really had the wool pulled over your eyes. His first name is Giles.'" Danny threw his hands wide, as if expecting to be hailed the hero.

Nate had all he could do to maintain his composure. Danny's story was like a shop fire, growing worse by the second. "What else did Gwen do to disguise herself?"

Danny's arms lowered. "Nothing. Why should she? He doesn't know her."

"True. But, thanks to that runt with the thick glasses who tailed me the first day I visited the Surabaya, Giles Adams knows the neighborhood where we've been staying."

Danny's bright expression dimmed. "Why should he link her to us?"

"Oh, no reason. Unless he has been sleeping with a blond, big-titted woman with a Hackney accent! What's to stop the detective from sending a cop or two as crooked as his smile into Bethnal Green to find her? And from her direct to us?"

"Hackney's a big place. She'll come with us when we leave. We'll be gone in a day, right?"

"Now we must be. Are you that smitten, to have her as baggage?"

Danny shrugged half-heartedly. "For a while. She doesn't have much to hold her to Bethnal Green. Her old man's dead. She lives in a rented house. She lost her good job. The bakery job is only until something better comes along."

"Like you."

"Right." Danny leaned closer to his partner. "Listen, if the government goes for our deal, my half of the fee is half a million bucks, right?"

"No. Twelve-thousand-five-hundred pounds," Nate corrected sternly. "You've got to begin thinking in this currency and this time."

"I will. Let's say we run off to Bath for a year. I liked Bath. At the end of the year, I could give Gwen a thousand pounds of my money. That's...."

"Forty thousand dollars," Nate said wearily.

"Yeah. Enough to set her up in a little shop."

Nate was at least relieved to be hearing no more of the redheaded railway worker or Danny's plans to return to the twenty-first century. What he was not happy about was the information Danny was attempting to hide with his patter.

"What else happened at The Royal Standard?"

"Nothing."

"What else, Daniel?"

Danny looked toward the end of the shelter, as if salvation sat waiting there. His cheeks puffed out. "Before Gwen came out again, a guy left the pub. He was moving quickly."

"What did he look like?"

"He was wearing a policeman's uniform."

"Wonderful."

"Big deal. It only confirmed what the bartender had said. The guy was hurrying to warn a detective friend in his precinct."

"So now both Alex Bennett and Giles Adams are aware that we know who they are."

"They're the same guy, Nate."

"Right. Where is Gwen right now?"

"We parted company about three streets from here. This afternoon she got a message. Her mum wasn't feeling so well, and she's spending the night with her."

"Did you happen to mention to the merry widow your plan about taking her away?"

Danny shook his head slowly. "No."

Nate saw that Danny was lying again. He figured that, in anticipation, Gwen was having a last fling and getting what she could out of some other local boyfriend before she flew the coop with the American rooster. He hoped he was right. In either case, mother or boyfriend would keep Gwen Lamb safe for the night.

Nate stood and ran his right hand lightly along his side, feeling his wound. There was only slight pain and a lingering heat. The day of rest, pills and hydrogen peroxide had done wonders. He looked down at Danny, who wore a dejected expression.

"That was excellent sleuthing, Big Dog," Nate told him, knowing Danny needed the bone to be thrown.

"Thanks, man."

"An ace card indeed. Now we have that information to trade, as well as the money and our testimony."

"Maybe he'll run," Danny offered. "That would be really good."

"It would," Nate agreed, even as he thought that the chance of Detective Giles Adam leaving London without his hundred million was about as likely as the two of them jumping through time again.

Nate worried what else Danny had missed at The Royal Standard. His partner had yet to spot the surveillance team watching them.

The night was filled with the best efforts of one race of people trying to throttle another. So many bombers flew over London, in so many squadrons, that Nate wondered with sudden shock if he and Danny had not entered or even caused a new reality. In his imagination, Hitler had decided against invading eastward for the Russian oil and gas fields but rather had elected to conquer the British Isles. The only good he could think that came out of the huge and prolonged raid was the total city blackout that allowed him and Danny to climb boldly over several fences before exiting to the street several houses above the Wilcox residence. When Danny asked why they were taking the more difficult route, Nate had replied that he did not want the Miles family to worry about them leaving their shelter during an active air raid.

Even as racks of bombs and bundles of incendiary spikes landed within blocks of the Bethnal Green station, where they once again parked the truck, Nate and Danny set to work. Nate had decided that living in London during the Blitz was like accepting a job mining coal. The danger was so commonplace that eventually the only way to handle it was to adopt a fatalistic attitude and ignore it.

"If this bombing prevents us from unloading all the money," Nate said as they moved through the fence with the first load, "then we dump the truck with what's left."

Danny grunted his disapproval of the idea as he carried two bags to Nate's one. Needlessly, he added, "You just watch me leave a single pound behind!"

"We're taking a big chance having the truck sit out on a street for hours," Nate argued. "Our detective friend is probably expected to serve in his own borough during raids, but perhaps not. And it was out there half the night yesterday. Sooner than later, somebody official is going to get curious about a truck from Reigate sitting in London."

"That's what we have firepower for," Danny replied. "I figured that was why you had us bring all the guns."

The last thing Nate wanted to do was engage in gunplay. "Not at all. If you'll recall what I put in my letter, we are supposed to have been merely beasts of burden to move the money…just like we're doing right now. But we are holding onto two guns with barrel rifling that corresponds to the slugs in the bodies of the bank driver, the guard, and sweet, old 'John Bull.' We cannot be caught with those guns on us, Dan, and we are not going to play Bonnie and Clyde and go out in a blaze of glory." Nate decided it was easier to hug his satchel to his chest as he walked through the rutted field to the open cliff face.

"Okay, okay. But we will keep the Brownings."

"I'd rather not, but we'd be stupid not to have protection. At least they weren't fired. Let's keep it that way."

They came to the top of the ladder and scaffolding complex and looked down. The area directly below was stygian black. Only beyond the opening in the ground, inside the station area, did a scattering of work lights continue to blaze on the walls.

From his sacks Danny took the two lengths of rope he had purchased.

"Whatever you're trying is going to take a long time," Nate warned, thinking of the many supposed shortcut roads Danny had gotten lost on over the years.

"But this will prevent the packets from bursting open. Watch."

Danny tied the ropes to either handle of one sack. Nate carried the sack to the edge of the cliff and let it down. When Danny had lowered it no more than twenty feet, one of the handles snagged on a rock outcropping. In freeing it, several of the packets spilled out. The friction of the ropes along the cliff caused more trouble. Finally, when the sack sat at the bottom, Danny jerked on one of the ropes. He yanked it up and down, but because the sack sat in total darkness, he could not see the result of his effort. When he hauled the sack up, he found that three of the packets had resisted being dumped.

"Probably held in by the ropes," Nate speculated. Without waiting for a reply, he took several packets from his satchel and spun them out into the abyss. "Old ways are the best ways."

The shuttle process to empty the truck took more than three hours. During that time, three waves of bombers, accompanied by the deadly aerial acrobatics of friendly and enemy fighters, flew over the Bethnal Green area. Twice, bombs landed close enough to illuminate the neighborhood in surreal black and white. Danny and Nate did not stop.

The work was so mechanical that Nate was able to inventory through every woman with whom he had ever experienced more than a casual relationship. He concentrated on cataloguing their strengths and weaknesses. Collectively, they possessed a great number of good qualities. None in is estimation, however, could tip the scale as well as Penny when it came to weighing positive against negative attributes. When Nate was finished with that exercise and still faced a full pallet of money, he switched his thinking to himself. He analyzed how his values had changed of late and how much the changes had been due to Penelope Miles. Even though she was still impossible to pursue, she had become a beacon to him, a guiding light on which he fixed, a goal beyond all the immediate ones of survival, identity and wealth that he would fight to attain. At last his compass had a direction, and it felt amazingly good.

The moment they finished ferrying the last packets, Nate trudged painfully back to the truck and climbed into the cab. He waited until an Emergency Services truck roared by, and then brought his engine to life and turned on the feeble headlight beams. Since Detective Giles Adams knew that he and Danny hid somewhere in the Hackney district, it was unnecessary to drive the truck too far away. He headed west for four streets, turned into a side street and stopped when he found a repair truck garage. He parked the crimson-sided vehicle in the farthest spot from the street and left the key in the ignition. Using his handkerchief, he wiped the key, the cab and the inside of the back compartment as clean as he could. Then he checked the dark street and began his walk back to the field that lay between the Bethnal Green shelter entrances.

As he walked, Nate became aware of a human shape modifying the flat line of the front wall of a tenement. Nate stopped and pressed himself into deep shadows. Unmoving, he observed the figure, who was unaware of his presence. The droning of aircraft and the pom-pom bursts of anti-aircraft masked all subtle street noises. Nate saw that the person was thin and held a crowbar in his left hand. He wore a dark jacket whose lines suggested a windbreaker. Nate watched as the man shoved his right elbow through the glass of a first-story window. He continued observing as the figure reached through the hole, unlatched the lock, forced up the sash and then wriggled inside the house. A burglar was using the air raid to invade a home that Nate expected had been abandoned for the safety of someplace outside London. He thought of the Miles and Wilcox residences and their doors left trustingly open. He put himself in the place of the owners of this home and thought how he would feel in returning from avoiding slaughter by the Third Reich only to discover that one of his own countrymen had looted his possessions.

Nate left his hiding place, crossed the street to the front door of the invaded house, and pounded on it with the butt of his flashlight "This is the police! Come out of the house with your hands above your head!" he called out in his best authoritarian British voice. For good measure, he banged on the door once more. Then he walked down the stoop steps, shined his beam back and forth, up and down through the house windows, and strode away as if hurrying for reinforcements. He had no idea whether or not he had prevented the burglary, but at least he knew he had not witnessed it and done nothing. I won't pass this way again, he thought. So there's one act of kindness.

Within fifteen minutes Nate was back at the top of the ladder system. Two minutes later, he was down on the unused station track, shining his flashlight back and forth. Hundreds of packets of pounds lay all around him, but his partner was missing.

"Danny!" Nate called out in an urgent but restrained voice. He heard nothing. His flashlight found the two satchels gone. He filled the shoulder bag and walked toward the station.

Danny came through the foyer toward the platform, softly singing. Nate knew he was listening on his iPod to Aerosmith's "Bone to Bone", because he heard the words "Coney. Bone to Bone, Bone to Bone screamin'. Coney. She be screamin' Coney."

Danny thrust his hand into his pocket when he spotted Nate's shadow.

Nate clamped one hand around Dan's wrist and thrust the other up in a warning gesture. "It's me. Damn it, take off the headphones!"

"Sorry."

"You were trained by the best army in the world and you served in combat, Dan," Nate scolded. "Until Giles Adams is behind bars and we have our pardons, consider that we are in danger twenty-four hours a day. And save your precious battery."

Scowling from guilt, Danny stowed the iPod and headphones in a pocket. "All the old money is still there. No footprints around except ours."

"Good. Where are the Webley and the revolver we took off 'John Bull'?"

"I left them at the bottom of the ladders. What are you gonna do with them?"

"When we get tired of moving money, I'll show you."

An hour later, when they had cleaned up all the broken packets and moved a considerable amount of the rest of the pounds, rain began to fall in a drizzle.

"Now's a good time to take a break," Nate said, picking up the two pistols. "Did your uncle ever tell you how often they dig up track and lay down a new bed?"

"A new track bed? I think they just replace the stones that disappear." As if to make his point, Danny kicked at chunks of granite laid between the railroad ties. The top stones did not move. "They had to replace rotting ties before they made them from concrete, and they had to replace the rails pretty often when the locomotives were powered by steam, but not the rip rap."

Nate started walking toward the main line. As Danny went on about the roadbed, Nate was again impressed by his partner's depth of knowledge and use of railroad jargon. He had always known that when Daniel O'Shea wanted to learn a subject he learned it. When he applied himself, he was never less than competent. A large factor in his apparent simple-mindedness was laziness. His willingness to let Nate do the thinking had worked well in another world and time, so neither man felt a need to change the arrangement. Nate had already had ample demonstration that the demands of 1940 were beginning to fray their friendship. He determined to demand more from Danny for Danny's sake, to tutor him into increasing independence. He made a pact with himself to work harder at being tolerant. In spite of his shortcomings, Daniel O'Shea was the best and most loyal friend he had ever known.

For that he alone he was owed.

"Why would steam trains wear down track any faster?" Nate asked, sure that Danny would have the answer.

"Because the driver arms shove hard on only a part of the stroke. Steam engines are giant pistons. Diesel driving wheels turn smoothly."

"But down here is electric, so it's all smooth," Nate guessed.

"Which means the rails last a long time. The stones could be here until a major renovation. Decades."

"Good to know. Thanks." Nate stopped some fifty feet before the turnout switch. That section of track surely needed periodic attention. He knelt between two ties and began scooping out the chunks of rough stone.

"You're burying them here?"

"One of them. Just putting your wisdom to practical use." Nate cleared away enough stones so that the pistol would lie under two layers. If the top layer was moved, the weapon's black surface would still conceal it from all but the most minute scrutiny, even in bright light.

"My wisdom?" Danny grinned. "I get the idea. Give me the other gun."

Nate handed the smaller Webley over and watched for a moment as his partner followed his flashlight down the track. Before positioning the murder weapon used by "John Bull," he cleaned every surface with his handkerchief. What stones were left over when he covered the gun, Nate scattered around. He noticed that he could identify the place now, because many of the turned, gray stone surfaces were without dirt, soot and grease. He flipped a couple of them and then decided that nature and time would take care of the rest. He rose and walked down the track toward the main line.

When Nate caught up with Danny, his partner still held the gun they had taken from Jack Eastwood in the car park. He was instead engaged in swinging his flashlight back and forth, up and down the tracks.

"Still hoping to find the redheaded man?" Nate asked.

"Shit, yes! We could bring all of the pounds we could hold in three sacks back with us. Think what unused old money would be worth!"

"He's not showing, Dan."

"I know."

Danny set his light on one of the railroad ties and laid the Webley beside it. He began clawing out pieces of stone. Nate shone his light down toward the track turnout. Left with nothing to do, he idly counted the ties from the guardrails to where Danny worked. The number was twelve.

"Here," he said, handing down his handkerchief for Danny to wipe the weapon clean. He watched as Danny replaced the stones. Again, about half were conspicuously cleaner than the rest. He decided not to bother his partner with the triviality.

They returned to their work and, within a mist of rain, moved the last of the Cellophane-wrapped packets. It was past three when Danny snapped the padlock shut on two satchels and all the money less the one packet they had taken the night before. He spun the dial and gave the lock a yank to be certain.

"And now we wait for a reply in the newspaper," Danny said, picking up his shoulder bag.

"And now we wait."

"How long do you think?"

"I'm sure they don't want to wait any longer than we do." Nate winced from the strain that the night's labors had put upon the wound in his side. He touched his shirt and was relieved to find that at least it had not reopened. He felt warm from their activities, but he did not feel the heat of fever. All that was left to do was climb the precarious eighty feet to ground level and then hike back to the Wilcox shelter. "Let's start climbing, my friend. I want to be in my bed before Hitler's bomber crews are in theirs."

# CHAPTER SEVENTEEN

Nate did not awaken until almost ten o'clock. He was amazed to find Danny out of the shelter. Normally, his partner moved like a doped-up corrida bull in the morning, banging against surfaces, making snorting noises, shaking his head from side to side to clear the cobwebs. They had no tasks to do. Gwen had gone to her bakery job. There was no excuse for Danny to be gone. Nate sat bolt upright. A sick feeling passed through him, from head to bowels. He had not specifically told the ex-Marine to stay away from Detective Adams.

Nate dressed hurriedly and rushed into the Wilcox house. Danny was not there. When he knocked on the Miles back door and was admitted by Millicent, she informed him that she had seen Danny walking through the garden gate, dressed in his raincoat and cap. She was surprised that he had not stopped in for breakfast, as was his habit. He had left, she reported, about half an hour earlier.

"You're dancing tonight…in spite of your wound?" Millicent said.

"If Penny wants to."

Millicent's eyebrows elevated slowly. "It is all she spoke about this morning. I received strict orders to have her dress finished, even if the Wehrmacht storms the beaches. And I am to ask you if I can have your suit with the stripes, to sponge clean." She made a sarcastic sound in her throat. "It's so wonderful to be needed."

"I can clean my own suit," Nate said.

Mrs. Miles waggled her fingers. "Your assignment from the princess is to make your dress shoes shine. You'll find blacking and a polishing kit under the sink."

Nate took the polishing kit to the shelter and spit-shined his stolen shoes to a fare-thee-well. If he could do nothing else for Miss Penelope Miles, he determined to give her a fantasy dance evening she would remember the rest of her life.

When he had finished, Nate took a slow walk around the block. The workman inside the Miles house had disappeared. However, the man at the post box was again in place, reading his newspaper. Nate sauntered past, giving him an opportunity to speak. The man said nothing. Nate smiled at him.

In response, the man nodded sharply and entered a beat-up sedan. An Emergency Washing Services van passed. Several pedestrians and bicyclers went by. Nate turned his back on the sedan and walked down the street.

Nate found a second surveillance man in the street behind the Miles house. The plainclothesman had busied himself polishing a car. The two unmarked cars comprised half the private vehicles on the local streets. Nate recognized that surveillance in a residential neighborhood was a very difficult proposition, but he also knew that it could be accomplished with more subtlety than was being displayed. He wondered if it was not merely a show to frighten him and Danny away. Whatever the reason, men were watching, and that was not good. If they moved in, Nate and Danny would be helpless. He had already determined that this must be their last day in Bethnal Green. He strolled into the Wilcox back yard via its gate and entered the Anderson shelter.

The packet of lined paper Danny had purchased the previous day lay on the table. Nate propped the shelter door open for light. He moved the table close to the doorway, sat and took up his Cross ball-point pen. His purpose was a detailed note to Penny. It would say nothing of his feelings. Not directly, at any rate. Instead, his care for her and her future would be expressed through directions.

Nate glanced up at his blue blazer, which hung from its hanger on the rope stretched down the length of the shelter. He counted the buttons, to be sure they were all there, two on each cuff, four down the front.

*Dearest Penny,* he started in a compact version of his handwriting. *I know that you would have a special and happy life without what I write here, but this will ensure it and more. Cut the eight buttons from my blazer. Inside each is an emerald. To get at the stones, turn the top of each button counterclockwise. Obtain several appraisals for them and then sell to the highest bidder. These stones are for investment.*

*Once the war is over, visit America. It is, indeed, the land of opportunity. Over the coming decades, invest in the equities listed below. Hold onto each equity at least until it has split three times. When one of these companies first appears, sell a good percentage of stocks you own that have plateaued and invest immediately and heavily in the new one. Do not worry about any of these losing value unless I put a date behind it (by which time it should be sold). Do not hesitate to buy prudently on margin.*

Nate realized that he had already omitted information he needed to impart. He resigned himself to creating a rough draft and plunged into a non-chronological list of sixty-seven blue chip companies. Among the better-known names were IBM, AT&T, Polaroid, Kodak, Walt Disney, Boeing, BellSouth, MacDonald's, Burger King, KFC, Coca-Cola, PepsiCo, Sea-Land, Merck, Pfizer, Bristol Myers, Squibb, Johnson & Johnson, UPS, Fed Ex, Time Warner, Toys R Us, Wal-Mart, Verizon, Sprint, Home Depot, Weyerhauser, Microsoft, Hewlett-Packard, Dell, Gateway, Cisco, Yahoo, Sony, AOL, Bank of America, Citigroup, Wachovia and SunTrust. From reading books like *Barbarians at the Gate*, he knew something about the hostile takeover and merger and acquisitions frenzy of the 1990s, and he began his list with RJR Nabisco.

Then he detailed the difference of how those buys and sells should be transacted and which brokerage houses participated and reaped windfall profits. He was not intimately versed in the year-to-year trends of the stock market, but he knew of the October 1987 crash and the September 2001 post-WTC plummet. He advised pulling out a month earlier and re-buying each time, after the collective market index had dropped and then leveled.

When he finished collecting all his crystal-ball-like wisdom, Nate recopied his notes onto the front and back of a single sheet of paper. As best he could, he listed the companies in the order in which he believed they had emerged.

Because he had not eaten breakfast, Nate was famished by noon. He walked over to the Miles back door and knocked. No one answered. The door, as always, was unlocked. He entered and found no one there. He returned to the shelter and fetched both copies of his letter to Penny. He climbed to her bedroom and stopped at the doorway, memorizing the space. He closed his eyes and inhaled. The lingering odor of smoke had covered the delectable scent of talc, which saddened him. He removed the thumbtacks from the photograph of Fred Astaire and Ginger Rogers dancing and neatly hid the rough copy of the letter beneath it. Then he replaced the photo exactly where it had been on the wall. As he stepped back to judge his work, he thought of how the British called thumbtacks 'drawing pins.' "'Two nations separated by a common language,'" he intoned. He and Penelope

Miles were separated not at all by language but rather by time and fate.

Because of the sack filled with food that Danny had splurged on the day before, Nate did not feel too guilty for raiding the refrigerator. He dined on a couple slabs of ham, some cheese, a roll and a salad made from the pickings of the Miles's and Wilcox's gardens.

On one wall of the kitchen was installed a telephone. Nate had only heard it ring once. It had been someone from the pressroom of the printing company Worden worked for, asking a last-minute question about registration. When he hung up, Worden related that they were one of the few families on the street who had their own telephone. His work as a warden had necessitated that it be kept. Now as he chewed, Nate stood and crossed to the telephone. He saw that its number was written on a piece of cardstock under the hook. He looked around for a slip of paper to copy the number. He was surprised to find nothing at all in the kitchen or living room. In desperation, he tore off a little of the bottom corner of his neat letter to Penny. Using his pen, he carefully noted the succession of digits and then tucked the slip of paper into his wallet. On his way out the door he picked up his suit, which Mrs. Miles had neatly laid over the back of one of the chairs.

A chemist's shop three streets from the Miles residence sold newspapers. After stowing his suit in the shelter, Nate took a slow stroll to the shop to purchase *The Times*. He noted that the newly polished sedan followed him at the distance of one block. When he entered the shop, he bought a new tin of Altoids as well. As he received his change, he realized the shop had a public phone booth in the rear. He took out his pen and copied the phone number on the opposite side of the slip of paper that held the Miles information. He went out in the sunshine that peeked between clouds and read the paper, hoping against hope that the swiftest of replies to his letter might have been made. He found nothing.

When Nate returned to the Wilcox shelter he found Danny stretched out on his bunk, with his bare feet hanging over the rail.

"Where have you been?" Nate asked.

"Trying to buy nine millimeter bullets for you and me. The way I was trained, one magazine of ammunition isn't enough to guarantee the win."

"You didn't have any luck," Nate stated.

"You're right. In a country at war, you'd think they'd be lying around on the ground like mushrooms." Danny rolled his eyes.

"People didn't even know where to tell me to look."

"This is a civilized country," Nate told him.

"So is ours, but we have guns up the wazoo."

Nate declined to debate with a man literally and figuratively lacking ammunition. "You didn't go across the river, did you?"

"No, of course not. I'd consult with you first." He raised his forefinger. "But I'd love to put a slug through Detective Adams' slimy skull."

Nate ignored Danny's murderous bravado. "How did you come back here?"

"On foot. Just like always."

"Front or back entrance?"

"Front. Through the house."

"Did you happen to notice a car parked up on the corner?"

Danny's eyes drifted to the side. "Uh, yeah…maybe."

"There's another one on the back street."

"Cops?"

"They're not ice cream trucks, Danny."

"What do we do?"

"We have to leave Bethnal Green."

"Right now?"

"No. Tonight." Nate went down on one knee, reached through the duckboards, and removed the drain grate.

"That's good. But late, okay? After Gwen gets home from work."

Nate twisted his hand into the dark pipe. He removed a rock and then reached in again for the stack of pound notes that he had fitted into the pipe's curve.

"After dark. During an air raid."

Danny glanced down at *The Times* lying on the table. "No reply from the government yet, right?"

"It's too early."

"I figured."

Nate remembered Danny's lie, that he had not told Gwen about leaving London. "So, you're convinced the bereaved Mrs. Lamb will be inclined to traipse after you to the hinterlands?"

Danny grinned. "Oh, yeah."

Before leaving the Wilcox shelter to eat, Danny wondered aloud what "The Last Supper" would be. When Nate saw what Millicent Miles had prepared, he knew that she was thinking of it as the same thing. Six genuine eggs that Danny had secured from his favorite black market stall were extended with a mixture of powdered eggs, and the resulting omelets also featured grated cheese, a dash of freshly ground pepper, and a few pinches of fresh onion. The last of the green vegetables from the Wilcox-Miles victory gardens were combined with part of the store of carrots and onions that were expected to last for at least a few more weeks. Parsley potatoes appeared in abundance. Roly-poly pudding rounded out the fare. A week earlier, Danny had waxed rhapsodic over "good, sweetened iced tea." The presence of a pitcher of the drink indicated to Nate that they were at least in Mrs. Miles's good graces.

All talk of the Blitz, death and destruction was assiduously avoided. Instead, the assembled five traded jokes. Nate knew hundreds but did not like to put himself on display as a comedian. His style was to tell a joke if an appropriate situation could be enhanced by it or if he wanted to make a serious point in a lighthearted manner. Danny, at the opposite extreme, reveled in holding court and shotgun-blasting humor. His specialty was Irish jokes, and his piece de resistance was the bald excuse for a succession of groaning one-liners called "An Irish Mother's Letter to Her Son." Nate endured it one more time before raising his notorious modern watch and announcing that he and Penny should leave to dance before the nighttime fury of the Luftwaffe descended on London.

Penny had excused herself halfway through the storytelling. Nate sat on the steps and waited for her to come out of the bathroom. A bushel of jokes and ensuing laughter drifted from the kitchen while he waited. When Penny appeared, she dressed in the same dance skirt and blouse she had worn for the first two sessions, but she carried a carpet bag with her as well. Nate stood and ascended to meet her. As he took the bag from her hand, he complimented her on the alluring make-up job she had done with rouge, lipstick and mascara. He saw as well that she had woven her hair into the same pattern of braids across the top of her head that Ginger Rogers wore in *Top Hat*. Of this change he said nothing.

Again, they took the bicycles from the yard. Penny's rear-fender, wire baskets were filled, and a large, open wooden basket had to be hooked to the handlebars of Nate's racer to hold the carpet bag and his belongings. A temperature inversion was closing in on London, and a light fog had begun to settle over the streets, giving the neighborhood a dreamlike quality.

As they pedaled toward the school, Penny said, "I've told you about the places I'd like to travel to. What's still on your list?"

"Dubrovnik, Yugoslavia," Nate replied. "I hear it's very beautiful and far enough out of the way that it isn't overrun with tourists."

"Where else?"

"There's a Greek temple at Segesta, Sicily that's supposed to be in amazing shape."

"Is that all?"

"Not by a long shot. I want to stand at the tip of Tierra del Fuego, to swim among the Maldive Islands near Ceylon. I want to sail among the Pine Tree Islands in Matsushima Bay, northeast of Tokyo. There are hundreds of miniature rock islands, with only a few weathered trees clinging to them, like natural bonsai displays."

"Why did I know that your list would be so much more exotic than mine or anyone else I know?" Penny asked.

Nate let the question hang in the air.

While they waited at a corner for a pair of trucks to pass, Penny said in a rush, "I owe you an apology. My entire family does."

"For what?"

Penny offered an exaggerated look of contrition and said, "I told my father what you had told me about the radar installations. He said that such things were not batted lightly about in the halls of Washington any more than they are in London. He said that he was afraid you and Danny were spies."

Nate was not surprised. "But I reminded him that he had found us and not the other way around."

"Yes, I know. That made no difference to him. He thought you two were simply looking for any good English family to stay with, so that you could blend in. He thought you had offered me the suggestion on the radar stations because the Germans already knew where they were. What you told me would only serve to lower my family's defenses."

"I can see how he might think all of this," Nate granted. "So, two men from some government office were sent to watch Danny and me."

"Actually, four, I believe. The government is quite confused that they can't ascertain who you two are, but they feel you are genuinely American."

"That's good."

"You're telling people you work for DuPont Chemicals, but you don't. You investigated a man who works for Ford and who our government suspects is a spy. At the American Bar."

"Who told you that?"

"My father."

"One of the men watching us told him this?"

"No. The man my father reported you to. He's an acquaintance in MI5."

Nate needed no more explanation to understand what had happened. Thanks to his extensive readings on World War II intelligence networks, he knew that British security services had been woefully unprepared for the conflict. Their worst efficiency was in investigating the legions of persons on the island who might have been German or Italian spies. The organization was, in fact, so badly mishandled that it was in near-collapse around the very time in which Nate now found himself. When British agents saw two anonymous Americans working on another American, they assumed it was the O.S.S. investigating their own citizen on foreign shores. They were happy to step back and allow an operation that might embarrass Ford into closing its factories in Switzerland and France. Suddenly, the scales of divine justice seemed to tip in balance. The bullets and bombs Nate had dodged had been equaled by the chance good fortune of finding big-mouthed Allan Norman at the American Bar. The need to know what a 1940 U.S. passport looked like had kept him and Danny free.

"Are you American spies?" Penny asked.

"We certainly look like it, don't we?" Nate replied.

"I wish you would stop answering me with questions. It's no answer at all." Penny clenched her teeth and flinched, as if she expected Nate to strike her. "I need to apologize personally because I stole the film from your camera."

Nate nodded, immensely relieved to have the mystery solved. "And when they developed the film they found nothing of a compromising nature."

"Apparently."

Nate's only real regret was losing the chance to capture Penny's image, but he declined to tell her.

"Dad was still suspicious until you divulged this German Operation Sealion. He now agrees you must be an American agent on the highest level. He thinks that Daniel is your bodyguard."

"What does your mother think?"

"Mum always felt you two were good chaps. She works more by feelings than logic."

The statement caught Nate off guard, until he remembered how well Millicent Miles sheltered her own thoughts.

"You evidently believed we were bad guys for a while," Nate prompted.

It took Penny several moments to speak. "I didn't suspect you of spying. I was angry because when I went into that bag for the camera, I saw a wedding ring tied to a handkerchief. I tried it on. It was clearly too small for Mr. O'Shea's fingers, so that left you."

"But I haven't–"

"No," Penny interrupted. "You've been a perfect gentleman. That eventually led me to believe you have it as part of a disguise, for when you are required to be married."

"I swear it is not my ring," Nate assured her. "I can't say anything more about it."

"I understand." Penny looked left and right and saw that the street was empty of vehicles. "Can we go before I completely melt from embarrassment?"

Once again, Penny used her keys to unlock the school's side door and her personal storage closet. After they brought the bicycles inside, Nate carried the record player into the gymnasium, set the Coleman lantern at the center of the shiny, oak floor, and lit it. He returned to the bicycles for his clothing and the records. From his pocket he withdrew the neatly handwritten instructions to Penny he had put on the single sheet of paper. His finger moved accidentally across the bottom, and he felt the rough corner where he had torn off the piece to write down the Miles phone number. He folded the paper and looked through the recordings. He had seen one that was particularly appropriate. It was "We'll Meet Again", recorded by Vera Lynn. He inserted the sheet behind the record and moved the song to the bottom of the pile.

Penny had taken her newly completed version of the *Top Hat* dress into the girls' lavatory, along with her torchlight. Nate heard no sound of her returning, so he stripped off his jacket and shirt and slipped the dress shirt on. His wound did not hurt at all, but he felt a tug from the strips of surgical tape he had covered it with, to be sure there would be no tearing of stitches when he lifted his partner. He stepped into the highly polished formal shoes and draped his tie around his neck. It had been a long while since he had tied a bowtie, and he hesitated.

"Allow me," Penny said, appearing at the gymnasium doorway. She took a step forward.

"Stop!" Nate commanded. "Don't rush. Make the entrance the dress deserves."

Penny let down the arm she had used to push back the door. She squared her shoulders, rolled them back and drew in a breath. Her chin elevated a notch, accentuating the length of her bare, elegant neck. There was no question that this young woman who never put on airs nevertheless knew well her physical assets and how to show them with maximum effectiveness. She glided into the room, never taking her eyes from Nate's.

Nate felt the familiar, exquisite pain in his chest. For the first time, he felt as well a lump in his throat. The silk dress, dyed a soft green, fit Penelope's long, shapely form perfectly. It swayed and swirled with easy grace as she moved across the floor.

Penny stopped at arm's length from Nate. He smelled her talc. She smiled at the clear message of beguilement his entire body betrayed. She extended her right hand to his left.

"Here," she said softly. In her open palm were tap cleats for his shoes.

Nate took the two pieces of metal and turned their tiny teeth upward. He knelt and placed them precisely where he wanted them on the tips of his shoes. Then he stood and secured them with his weight. Penny had elevated her face another few degrees. Her eyes held a patent challenge for his comment.

"You are the most beautiful creature I have ever seen," Nate said honestly. Before her smile grew too large, however, he added, "But I don't like your hair like that. It's breathtaking, but the style is Ginger Rogers and not Penelope Miles. Don't move."

Nate walked behind Penny, studying the complicated weave of her hair. He came in close to her and began the process of letting it down.

"I don't have a brush or comb," she worried.

"I do. I made sure to bring a comb when I saw what you'd done." Nate came closer, so that his breath could be felt on the back of her neck. His elbows caressed her shoulders as he worked.

"I love your hair," he told her, inhaling so that she could hear. She made no reply, but he felt her begin to tremble. He berated himself for his words and actions, even though he genuinely meant and felt every one of them. The line between making this woman he loved feel radiant and falsely seducing her was razor fine. Such a dance was as unrehearsed for him as it was for her. She deserved a night of electric passion, but she also deserved to understand that it was for this one night only and it could not be consummated.

Nate drew the teeth of his comb gently through her hair, again and again, moving from side to side with a critical eye as he did. Finally, he tucked the comb back into his suit pocket.

"Finished."

Penny turned. As if choreographed, one strand of hair fell across her left eye, exactly as he and she both liked it.

"And now it's my turn to do you," Penny said, reaching for the ends of his bowtie. "My brother favored bows, and he had me do this all the time." Penny concentrated so hard that her eyes crossed slightly, giving her the added allure of a Siamese cat. Nate took in their emerald sparkle and then glanced down at the silk dress, to see how well its tint complimented their captivating color. He caught more than he expected of the upper swell of her breasts in the dress's décolletage.

"Are you being naughty?" Penny asked, halfway finished tying the bow.

"Sorry."

"Don't be. I like your attention."

Nate knew that the song filling his head came from the war era, but he was not so informed that he knew if it existed on September 19, 1940. He decided that he didn't care. He began singing the Jimmy Dorsey Orchestra tune.

"Those cool and limpid green eyes,
A pool wherein my love lies,
So deep that in my searching
For happiness I fear
That they will ever haunt me.
All through my life they'll taunt me.
But will they ever want me?
Green eyes, make my dreams come true."

Penny drew in a sharp breath. "I've never heard that before. It's beautiful."

"It's you."

"And is that the way you feel?"

"You mustn't ask that."

"Because you're going away?"

"Yes."

Penny's eyes lowered. Her lips pursed. She tugged the tie tightly into place.

"Would you like me to come back?" he needed to ask.

In answer, Penny hugged Nate and laid her cheek against his. "I don't believe it's possible."

Of the hundred different replies Nate might have imagined, he was not prepared for this one. "Why not?"

"Because you won't be allowed."

"Who won't allow it?" he persisted.

Penny turned her lips to his ear and whispered. "God."

Given her religious upbringing, Nate was not totally astonished by Penny's answer. What confused him, however, was that her words were a conclusion of determinism and not free will. His entire life had made him a poster child for free will, but when he understood that he had been thrust back into 1940 he began to believe that at least major events in human life were determined, by God or some other supernal, unknowable power. Whatever thinking was behind Penelope Miles's words, her response suited his need. He determined to make no direct reply.

"Let's dance," he said, taking both her hands in his and drawing her away from the light. "The entire song without the record. Sing it softly to me!"

They began with assurance. Nate adjusted for the sweep and swirl of Penny's dazzling dress. When the tap segment arrived, the gift of her taps allowed him to hear his footfalls and time the steps exactly to hers. They continued on, to where the three lifts occurred. Nate thrust her into the air once and twice. But when the measure arrived for the third lift, he came around behind her and drew his body close to hers. From the lifts and now from pressing the front of his thighs to her taut buttocks, he realized that she wore only the thinnest of underwear beneath her silk dress.

"There are three lifts," Penny said, after she gasped and recovered from the pressure of his body against hers.

"In *Top Hat*, he said. "Three lifts for Fred and Ginger. We are Nathaniel and Penelope. We must make this dance truly ours, if only for several moments."

Nate had anticipated the possibility of objection. Instead, Penny instantly said, "How?"

Nate borrowed a step from a comedy number he had participated in during high school. Now in a completely different context, he counted on it looking as sensual as anything could on a dance floor. Talking Penny through it beat for beat, they moved as if welded together back to front, forward, then stutter-step and forward again. As their momentum slowed, he spun her around so that she faced him. His left foot braced back far enough to absorb her motion and to allow her to extend her line. Her cheek went neatly against his neck. Her breasts pressed against his chest.

"Got it?" he asked.

Penny's eyes smoldered. "One more time."

The moment the repetition was finished, Nate said, "I'm sure we know the ending. Now let's add the orchestra."

Nate set the needle down. At last, after three grueling rehearsals, their version of "Cheek to Cheek" became not a succession of steps but one organic creation. Their bodies were as unerringly in tune as the orchestra. When Nate caught Penny's eye, he winked. She grinned from ear to ear. Their ballroom steps dovetailed seamlessly; their time steps were sharp as freshly cut glass. They both knew absolutely that they were meant to dance together.

The couple finished the last, languorous dip. Nate drew Penny up from it with an effortless motion and led her back to their final positions. The music ended, and the soft, infinitely repeated hissing of the last groove proved that their frozen pose only pretended to defy time.

Nate took Penny's hand, raised it to his lips and pressed there a pristine kiss.

Penny's chest rose and fell from the exertion of the dance, but she did not gasp for breath. She blinked several times as she gazed into Nate's eyes.

"You can't say it, can you?"

In spite of the spell in which Penny held him, Nate refused to tell her he loved her. If he did, she would undoubtedly confess the feelings that her mother had spoken of. After such a mutual confession, she would expect him to stay beside her. He knew he would, risking his life and possibly hers. If he could not prevent her from initiating a declaration of love, every act he performed from that moment would be to bring them together as soon as possible.

"I cannot," he replied with bitter regret.

Penny nodded sharply. She led him to the bleacher bench and

invited him to sit by first seating herself. She drew in a long breath.

"You're an angel."

Nate expected that Penny's statement was prologue. She was abandoning convention, swallowing her pride, and beginning her confession of love with an expression of endearment. When she did not continue, he realized she was being literal.

"What…makes you think that?" he was barely able to ask.

Penny laughed ruefully. "What doesn't? I consider myself smart and a woman of the twentieth century. Up until last week, I barely believed angels were real. But now, the overwhelming evidence admits no other explanation. Even more astonishing, there are two of you!"

"Go on."

"Nathan-iel and Dan-iel," she pronounced carefully. "Every one of your kind has a name ending in i-e-l or a-e-l. Gabriel, Azrael, Mikael, which of course we pronounce as Michael. I suppose they're the equivalent of masculine and feminine in humans. Both mean 'from God.'"

Nate had never thought of the coincidence of both his and his partner's names ending in the same letters. In a flash he saw that her misunderstanding was useful. It could provide him the excuse for leaving that he needed until he was free to return and begin anew. At the same time, however, feeding her fantastic theory prevented him from returning to her, unless he later convinced her that she had allowed one of the more whimsical elements of religion to cloud her thinking. Fanciful as her belief was, it was no laughing matter to him.

"Neither Danny nor I have wings," he argued, both to keep the conversation going and curious to hear her answer.

"Archangels supposedly do. Seraphim, cherubim, dominions, principalities as well. But again and again in the Bible, angels mix with men and men show no fear. Often, no suspicion. A pair of angels visited Lot for two days and walked around with him. Oh, this is ridiculous that I'm telling this to you. You are meant to look just like we do, precisely so you won't frighten us. You need us to hear your messages."

"Because angels are just messengers."

Penny looked at him with exasperation. "Now that I know you, I don't think that. But 'ang-iel' means 'messenger from God.' History proves your main purpose for existence is to deliver God's word to mankind."

"Telegrams in human form."

Penny nodded. "You came to deliver a message of hope, because I'm so very frightened."

"I have found you no more frightened than anyone else," Nate said, meaning every word.

Penny squeezed his hand. "Don't try to confuse me. That's because when I'm around you, you take my fear away. But when you're not with me, I'm as terrified as I was before. I'm so much more petrified than my father or mother...or any of the people I work with. My brother was bravest of all, and I'm so afraid of betraying his memory by acting like a coward."

"You are not a coward."

"I am! Under my thin façade, I'm worse than a two-year-old child. You think Mrs. Wilcox could scream? But I know I must carry on with grace and dignity. I can't shoot a rifle or fly a plane. So carrying on bravely is my duty to my country, my tiny part in winning this war. And you've given me ever so much more confidence that I am not holding myself together for nothing."

"You aren't."

Penny labored a smile. "Here we are in Angle-land, the land of the angels. The Greeks and Romans saw our fair hair, fair skin and light-colored eyes and assumed we were angels. We're certainly not. But you are."

"Just because I've delivered a few speeches of hope."

"No. That's not the only reason. Because you can't produce a real identity. Because you've traveled the world far more than anyone who looks your age possibly could. Because you have no time for trivialities like cinema. But you are good at music, aren't you? Because it's the language of the spheres, the universal language, they say. You certainly can dance. I wouldn't be surprised if you, Danny and fifty more like you can dance on the head of a pin. You wear clothing that barely wrinkles. You wear a watch impossible for any nation to make. You know that gas masks will never be needed. You tell me accurately about bombs landing days, months, or years in advance. The only thing that truly amazes me is that you swore you could only tell the past and present. Can angels lie?"

"I do have knowledge of the future," Nate admitted, "but only to a limited extent. I am not omniscient."

"Of course you aren't. Only God is. But you also get through locked gates, don't you?"

"So can any good thief."

"Are you telling me that's what you are?"

Trapped, Nate answered, "No. I'm more than a thief."

"Can you tell me when this war will end?"

Thinking of Death and not God, Nate replied, "I can, but I don't think the rules allow."

Penny nodded. "You see? I shouldn't have asked. You've given me ever so much already."

"It's not one thousandth what I wish to give you," Nate said earnestly.

"Make love to me," Penny said in a rush.

Nate felt his heart stand still. He had never in his life wanted to hear those words more, nor never feared hearing them more. "Penny... I can't."

"You are able to lie then," she said with conviction. "The Bible states clearly in Genesis, right between Cain and Abel and Noah, that angels found the daughters of men beautiful and lay with them and created extraordinary children."

"That was a long time ago."

"Daniel has no trouble bedding Gwen Lamb."

"How do you know he's not just serving as her guardian angel?" Nate riposted. "She's a recent widow in need of comfort."

Penny rolled her eyes. "Comfort to Gwen Lamb means either a drink or sex. Your partner is not a pint of ale! Do you love me, Nathaniel?"

"As much as existence itself."

"And I love you, whether human or angel."

Nate thrilled at the sound of her words. And yet he knew, with the robbery and his lack of identity hanging over his head, her confession was not enough to guarantee a magical happy ending. Titanic emotional forces tore at his brain. They made him want to rip her dress from her tantalizing figure and take her on the hard oak floor and simultaneously flee as fast and far from the temptation of her as he could get. His anguish compelled him to pull her to her feet.

"Dance with me," he said firmly.

"Make love to me," she pleaded.

"I have been making love to you."

"No, as a man and a woman make love."

Nate pulled Penny toward the records. He shoved the stack aside so that he could get at the bottom one.

"Nathaniel, answer me."

"I am answering you. Dance with me!" He let go of her hand and traded the records. Then he set down the needle and led the stunned Penelope Miles into the middle of the cavernous room.

Penny recognized the song even before the first word was sung.

"No!" she protested in feeble anguish against Nate's chest as he gathered her tightly to him.

Vera Lynn's dulcet voice began "We'll Meet Again."

"We'll meet again,
Don't know where; don't know when,
But I know we'll meet again
Some sunny day.
Keep smilin' through
Just like you always do,
Til the blue skies chase the dark clouds
Far away."

After the bittersweet song ended, Penny stood like a rag doll in Nate's arms and petulantly professed interest in nothing else she had brought along. Nate slipped "We'll Meet Again" into its sleeve, careful not to crush his letter. While he cared for the record player and the lantern, Penny changed back into her blouse and regular dance wrap. Nate muttered his frustrations into the vast and uncaring space. They had come so far this evening, but he could not allow it to go any farther. Only time, wits and good luck could rescue their relationship, and he had shared all the words of hope with her that he could. Nate removed his bowtie and exchanged his shoes, and still Penny did not reappear. He loaded all the baskets, returned the Victrola, locked the storage room door, and moved the bicycles into the night.

At last, Penny emerged from the dim hallway. He expected her face might be puffy from crying, but it was not. In spite of her own self doubts, he knew that she was made of stern stuff, capable of controlling more than her fear of death. He loved and pitied her for her strength. She nodded her head as she threw her leg over the woman's Schwinn, indicating that he should take the lead.

Nate chose the route back that skirted the edge of Victoria Park. The night air had not grown colder. If anything, he believed it had warmed a bit. The fog rose well above their heads. They had just reached the northwest edge of the park when the air raid sirens began to wail.

"Oh God, oh God!" Penny cried out. She stopped pedaling.

"We can make it back to your shelter before the planes arrive," Nate assured.

"Why not just stand here?" she asked him. "Survival is pure luck."

"That's not true. A shelter offers a much better chance–"

"Yes, yes, fine!" Penny pushed feebly at her pedals for one rotation and then stopped. "I'm sorry. I can barely make my legs work. Perhaps it was the dancing."

Nate knew better. He had not done enough to give her hope. *I've been too busy thinking only about myself and my problems*, he berated himself. He touched her gently on the shoulder.

"Get off your bike. We'll take shelter in the park."

"Where?"

"The rose garden. It has thick, high walls. And the anti-aircraft batteries are a few hundred meters away. The Germans know to avoid the area by now."

Penny dismounted. Nate led the way on foot down the length of the park canal boundary, across the bridge, and toward the garden.

"I'm sorry," Penny apologized. "It's all becoming too much for me, the work six days a week, worrying about my parents and the house, driving at night. I don't merely drive that ambulance. When the men carry in the wounded, I'm expected to clean the back. It's always covered in blood. Often entrails. Bits of ripped flesh. I could easily be lying in the back of a similar ambulance tomorrow."

Nate heard in his mind the prolonged screams of the woman near Sloane Square. He saw the image of the severed arm. "No, you won't!" he insisted.

"Can you absolutely guarantee that?" Penny demanded. "No, of course not. You came to bring me hope for the future, but I'm so drained by the present I can't find the energy to hope."

They reached the garden gate. Nate turned.

"Is that why you want me to make love to you?"

"Yes! I'm twenty-two years old, Nathaniel, and I'm still a virgin. You know I'm not the sort of woman who would give herself to just anyone because she was growing older. But you came into my life…and I love you. I need more. Right now. If I died tomorrow, at least I would have fully experienced love…spiritual and physical love."

The sirens grew louder and more insistent. The searchlights started sweeping the dark skies above the fog.

Nate set his bicycle against the outer wall. He took Penny's bike from her and balanced it beside the racer. Then he took her in his arms and kissed her as he had never kissed a woman. She moaned into his mouth and lifted her hand to run her fingers through his hair.

"Watch carefully," Nate told her, gently pushing back. He reached into his pocket and pulled out his keys and knife. He selected one of the knife features, inserted it into the big lock and jiggled it up and down. Within five seconds, he had the gate open.

"Is this how an angel gets through a locked gate?" he asked her. Penny did not answer.

Nate pulled her into the garden. The distant sound of planes came through the opening in the wall. Nate took Penny squarely by the shoulders and looked her hard eye to eye.

"You're going through a gate that can never be re-entered," he said. "I promise you that I will do everything a man or an angel can do to return to you. But promises cannot always be kept."

"I understand."

"If I never return, what will you have to give your husband?"

Nate's question did not daunt Penny. "I will give him my fidelity from our wedding day forth. I will give him children. I will honor and obey him in sickness and in health. And, hopefully, I will love him half as much as I love you." She touched her hand to his cheek.

Nate kissed her again. She took his hand and pressed it to her breast. He began to explore. The thin cloth of the blouse and her undergarment could not conceal the heat of her rising passion or her body's excitement. She laughed deep in her throat, a sound of pure joy. He pulled her toward where he remembered a large expanse of moss lay, between two beds of thorny roses. Penny pushed him down. Every rose petal had fallen, but their lingering life essence emanated sweet, delicate scents.

A nearby, powerful searchlight beam cut through the fog and played diffuse light down the path, allowing Nate to read the ignited fire of lust in his soulmate's eyes. She began unbuttoning her blouse with haste.

Nate reached up and imprisoned her hands. "No, love. Slowly. Savor every moment. I know this dance. Let me teach this one to you." He kissed and sucked on each of her fingers. He gently dragged his teeth across the fleshy part of her thumbs. He slowly insinuated his fingertips under the collar of her blouse and drew it down and off her shoulders. As he did, he lightly kissed each bit of exposed skin. He found the vigorous pulsation at the base of her throat and pressed his mouth there. With his thumbs and forefingers, he lifted her brassiere straps from her shoulders and kissed those places. The backs of his fingers drifted around the porcelain curves down her arms, coaxing the material off her breasts. He kissed and then he suckled while she trembled in silent expectation.

"Oh, Penny," he said. "If you ever regret this, blame me. I'm so afraid that what I've done to you is wrong."

Penny closed her eyes and concentrated on his touch. "If you did anything wrong, it was doing everything right."

The night lit up with fire.

The raid lasted almost an hour. As Nate had predicted, no planes came close to Victoria Park. They made love again and again until they quivered, from ecstasy, from the evaporation of their exertions, from the cool bed of moss, and from the cooler night air. Penny could only be persuaded to dress when Nate said, "We are out later than we promised. The raid will worry your parents. Don't feed their fears." While she pulled on her undergarments, he said, "Make me two promises."

"Anything, my dearest dear."

"You know I must go tonight. I will leave my blazer behind, in your safekeeping. Place it inside something to protect it, and keep it in your shelter."

"Because you'll be back for it," Penny said with assurance. "What's the second promise?"

"If I haven't returned within two weeks, take out that recording of 'We'll Meet Again' and play it on your home machine. But you must not play it before then!"

"Yes, Your Majesty." Penny set down her clothing, rose to her knees, and tugged at Nate. "But only if you will do one thing for me."

"And that is?"

"Dance with me…one last time."

The only way Nate was able to convince Penny to separate from him in the Miles back yard was to suggest that her mother was watching for her from one of the dark windows. She gave him a parting peck on the cheek and hurried into her house.

Nate took only enough time to set the contents of the baskets just inside the kitchen door. He concealed the record sleeve containing his letter in the middle of the stack. Then he walked out to the back street and set off through the fog toward Gwen Lamb's duplex.

The rented house lay dark. Nate knocked on the front door, and knocked again. When he got no answer, he walked around to the back door and repeated his actions. He grew angrier by the second, wondering where he, she and Danny would spend the night, knowing that fewer and fewer hotels or boarding houses would welcome new clients at such a late hour.

Nate returned to the Miles house and borrowed the English racer, calculating in his ever-darkening mood every extra minute lost. He berated himself for being selfish and needing one last dance with Penny. He knew it was not safe for him, Gwen, or Danny to linger in Bethnal Green. He thought he knew precisely where the two barflies would be. He pedaled the ten blocks to the Old George pub, counting on recent memory to guide him through the landmark-concealing fog. When he came close to the establishment, he noted a large sedan parked on the opposite side of the street. The hazy figure of a man stepped from it and jogged across the open space and into the bar. Nate coasted the bicycle to the pub, leaned it against a wall and stepped inside.

Nate blinked at the sudden change to brightness. When he opened his eyes again, he saw the man who had just entered walk up to the bar. It was the diminutive character with the thick spectacles who had met them in the subway and who had tailed Nate back to Bethnal Green. In his right hand he held his keys. In his left, he clutched two U. S. passports. He raised the hand with the passports to attract the attention of the pub keeper, but he stopped in mid-gesture. His head swung sharply to his left. He let his keys drop as he thrust his hand into his pocket.

Danny, sitting at the bar four seats from where the little man stood, pushed himself into a standing position.

"Nate! Watch out!"

Warned, the little man flung his hand from his coat pocket. In it, he held a revolver. Before Nate could react, the muzzle of the weapon struck him hard in the temple and sent him to the floor.

The pub erupted with noise.

Shaking his head to clear the stars that filled his vision, Nate struggled to rise. He saw the little man pivot to face the back of the bar. He glimpsed Danny fumbling inside his jacket. Then he lost sight of his partner as Gwen Lamb screamed, hopped off her barstool and interposed herself between the little man and Danny.

A shot boomed.

Nate saw the instantaneous hole appear in Gwen's neck. She lurched away from the bar, exposing Danny.

A second shot exploded in the room, where patrons all around dived for the floor or behind anything that might offer protection. Now upright and planting his hands on the floor to stand, Nate saw Danny jitter from the impact of the little man's bullet. The big American did not go down, however. In his right hand appeared his Browning pistol. With the grimmest expression Nate had ever seen on his face, Danny swung the gun upward and squeezed off three shots. Between the swift reports sounded one more from the revolver of the little man.

Both shooters fell at the same moment. The little man's wire-rimmed spectacles sprang from the bridge of his nose as he struck the floor. He landed directly in front of Nate. Two of Danny's slugs had found his chest. The third had hit him on the left side of his forehead. Nate tottered to his feet and lurched toward his partner.

Gwen Lamb sat on the floor holding her throat. Blood spurted from between her soaked fingers. Her yellow print dress was splattered with red. She gave Nate a pitiful look of confusion, then toppled over. Danny writhed on the dark wood floor. When Nate kneeled beside him, he said, "My iPod battery…died this evening. This place…just isn't for me, Big Fox." He reached out and squeezed Nate's hand. And then he was gone.

The front and back doors of the pub burst open as patrons fled into the night.

Nate stood and moved with speed toward the front. On his way out, he bent and scooped up the passports and the little man's keys. A screaming woman collided with his rear end and nearly knocked him over. He recovered and staggered out the door and into the fog. He grabbed the bicycle, wheeled it across the street and secured it to the metal trunk attached to the rear of the car. As quickly as his legs would allow, he entered the driver's side and sat down. Only then did he pause.

Nate's breaths came and went in ragged bursts. He felt hot tears spring from his eyes. He held up his hands. A swimming image of two quivering fists appeared. One hand clutched the passports. The other held a ring of six keys. Nate set the passports on the seat next to him and methodically worked his shaking fingers over the keys until he located the one for the ignition. He looked through the windshield and into the mirrors to see if anyone rushed toward the car. He was alone.

Across the street, the door of the Old George stood open. A rectangle of dark yellow light burned into the gauze-shrouded night.

Nate started the engine, engaged the first gear, let up on the clutch and eased away from the gruesome scene. He steered around the corner and accelerated, but he did not bother to switch gears. The transmission whined from the increased speed. Above its noise came the too-familiar sound of London's air raid sirens.

The fog beyond the glass and the fog of his shock caused Nate to become lost within a few streets. He steered the sedan car over to the curb, parked and shut off the engine.

Detective Giles Adams was most certainly still at large and in search of two-and-a-half million pounds. Just as Danny had hit pay dirt by visiting a pub in Southwark, so had Detective Adams's henchman in Hackney. Anywhere in London the method of investigation made perfect sense. When Nate was in the twenty-first century and visiting London once before, he had used the internet to uncover interesting pubs. The search allowed a radius to be set from any locale. Within the three-mile diameter of where he and Danny had stayed, there had been 675 pubs. If anything, the neighborhood pub phenomenon had been greater in wartime London. Since the little man had been able to tail Nate from the Surabaya into Bethnal Green two weeks earlier, it stood to reason that by visiting no more than a couple dozen drinking establishments and showing Nate and Danny's photos he would learn exactly where and with whom Danny was staying. They had indeed waited too long to escape the neighborhood.

Nate thought about the little man. Alex Bennett had not seemed like the central casting version of a cop, but the man with the spectacles was even more unlikely. For one thing, he should have been too tiny to pass a minimum height and weight requirement. For another, his terrible eyesight should have excluded him. For yet another, he was definitely not from London. Nate thought back on his accent. It seemed English, and then again it did not. Nate remembered the strange 'tch' the man had pronounced. And then he realized which nationality used that sound.

German.

## CHAPTER EIGHTEEN

One of Nate's ancillary theories to his life credo was that nothing worked more against a person's ability to act than fear. Fear to him was a natural trait to have and to express, but after acknowledgment it immediately had to be suppressed. He entered the London of 1940 with the normal human fear of death, of seeing it and coming close to it. The coach crash, the severed arm and the murders on the country road, however, had gradually helped him to master that fear well enough to continue functioning. What he had never had to deal with, had never considered how to deal with, was operating in danger without Daniel O'Shea watching his back. It was worse than being naked. It threatened to paralyze him.

Nate was stunned to find that coping with Danny's death was almost as painful as the death of his mother. Unlike his mother's passing, it had happened so quickly that Nate had had no time to prepare himself. He felt as if one of his limbs had been figuratively torn from his body. He had driven several more blocks on pure adrenaline, but then his strength failed him. Once again, he pulled to the curb and sat staring at the nothingness of the fog. He felt like someone was tightening barrel stays around his chest. Only when bombs and shrapnel began to fall close by was he able to rally.

By means of the compass in his watch and by recognizing several landmarks, Nate took himself back to the Miles's neighborhood. He left the car one street distant and wheeled the English racer along the deserted pavement, ignoring the constant explosions from the Victoria Park batteries. He entered the Wilcox back yard via its gate, leaned the bicycle against the stone wall and went into the Anderson shelter. Methodically, he collected every item except Danny's clothing and his own blazer. The blazer he left hanging facing the door, where it could not be missed. When he came across the blank sheets of paper Danny had purchased for him, he sat down and used his pen to create a large heart with the initials NA and PM inside it. He connected the initials with a plus sign. No words could possibly mean anything in comparison to what they had shared in the rose garden. Instinctively, he felt that the simpler the expression of love, the more effective it would be.

Nate tucked the remainder of the paper, the envelope and the postage stamps into the shoulder bag. He searched under the bunks for any item that might have been dropped. He elected to leave behind his dress shirt, shoes and bowtie, as symbols that he would not be using them with anyone but Penny.

For several moments Nate debated driving to another district and sleeping on the wide bench seat in the back of the sedan. Then he pictured a patrolling policeman waking him and demanding to see the car registration. He was certain it was stolen and that its license plates were from yet another car.

Nate began his walk back to the sedan. When he reached the Miles's garden gate he paused. He knew Penelope slept only a few yards away, inside the shelter next to her mother. His heart felt like it would rip from his chest, refusing to separate from the woman he so loved. He strained his eyes to pierce through the night and fog, memorizing the place. Finally, after exhaling a slow sigh, he moved on.

As if by its own will the car stopped at the repair garage where Nate had left the red heist truck. He pulled into the driveway and saw that the truck was still there. The street was not a main thoroughfare and, in fact, had suffered a bomb crater since he had concealed the truck. He had needed to steer carefully around the roadblock to enter the street with the car. He figured it was as good a place as any to stow it until the next morning. He grabbed Danny's bulging shoulder bag, tucked his spare pants and shirt under his arm, and took Danny's flashlight in his hand. Shaking the light to generate power, he staggered up the street. He easily located the house where he had seen the burglar enter on Wednesday night. The broken front window had not been patched. He walked down the alley and to the back door.

Nate was not surprised to find the rear door unlocked. His shouting, pounding on the door and shining the light into the windows had evidently caused the burglar to flee out the back. Nate entered cautiously and locked the door behind him. He found himself in a cramped kitchen. He moved forward through the house and called out.

"Hello? Is anybody here?"

He received no answer. He saw by flashlight that, while each room was furnished, almost all small items had been removed. The electric lights did not work; nor did the gas stove. The tenement house had been shut down. Like Mr. and Mrs. Wilcox, the residents had evidently found someplace safer to live.

Nate climbed the stairs to the second story and found two bedrooms. The back one had two windows opening onto a porch roof that he could use to climb out onto and roll down if escape was necessary. He went into the front bedroom, yanked the bed close to the windows and looked down into the foggy street. In spite of being dog tired, he forced himself to stay awake. He feared that an alert neighbor might summon the police to investigate another break-in to the deserted tenement house. About five minutes into his vigil, the shadow of a man wearing the same kind of shallow tin hat Worden Miles wore on his Air Raid Precaution patrols strolled down the street through the fog. Every few seconds, the man switched on his torchlight and then just as quickly shut it off.

Nate pondered his future. If he wanted, he had a passport to flee the British Isles and all the pounds he could carry or convert. The rest he could bury for exhumation on a return visit. But his desire was to stay with Penny. He longed to take her from London, to the northern extremes of the island where life was infinitely safer. He knew how Millicent felt about leaving even her immediate neighborhood much less London. He was certain Penny's super-patriot father would never abandon either of his jobs. Therefore, Penny would never leave. Unless he married her. If allowed, he would make her his wife as soon as possible.

He had no reservations about happiness with her and could think of no personal reason for delay. But the conviction among the Miles family that he acted in England as an American spy would no doubt allow nothing beyond engagement until the end of the war. Staying near Penny meant that Nate had to tough out his proposition with the government. He had to lie low and wait at least a week for their response. If by then he found none in *The Times*, he would hand-deliver a second version to the Bank of England and wait another week. If both acts failed, then he very well might need to hide in England at least until the U-boat wolf packs had been annihilated, move the money and then return to the United States until VE Day.

No matter what, Penny had to be convinced to wait for him.

Nate felt himself falling forward. His eyelids shot open. He caught himself before striking his head on the windowsill. He realized he could not sit on guard any longer. He thought about taking his Browning from the shoulder bag for protection and then decided that he could not shoot anyone to effect an escape. Such an act would land him in prison for certain. He lay down on the bare mattress and placed the bag at the head, to serve as a pillow. A minute later he was asleep.

The sound of a downstairs front window frame creaking brought Nate back from oblivion. When he identified the source of the sound, he figured it could only be the burglar from Wednesday evening, daring a return visit. Nate eased himself off the bed. Faint noises from the first floor indicated a thorough sacking of the house.

While the intruder moved up the noisy steps, Nate eased behind the half-open bedroom door. He stood patiently until the burglar came up to the threshold. He heard the person lean forward to peek through the crack on the hinge side of the door, to make sure no one waited there. Nate, however, stood sideways just behind the door. He waited until the figure entered the room and then executed three karate moves that had the person flat on the floor and unconscious within a matter of seconds. In one hand, the burglar held a swag sack made from a pillowcase; in the other he held a crowbar. He was thin and wore a windbreaker, proving to Nate that it was the same person.

Acting quickly, Nate took out one of the lengths of rope Danny had saved from his abortive attempt to streamline the transfer of money to the deep level shelter. He flipped the burglar over and tied his legs together. Then he secured his hands behind his back. As the man revived, Nate dragged him into the bathroom and up onto the toilet. Cutting another section of rope, he fashioned a slipknot noose, fit it loosely over the man's head and around his neck and tied the other end to the toilet pull chain. Finally, he used the last of the rope to lash the man's torso to the pipe that led down from the flush tank fixed high on the wall. The room was so dark that Nate could not make out the intruder's age or features. Nor did he care.

"Who are you?" the man asked.

"Your executioner," Nate said, "unless you behave." He went to the shoulder bag for the roll of surgical tape and returned to the bathroom. He ripped two strips off and crisscrossed the man's mouth.

"I badly need sleep," he said, as he undid the burglar's belt and yanked down his trousers and underpants. "If you need to relieve yourself, you're all ready. Otherwise, don't make any noise, or I'll come back and put a bullet into your brain. And, yes – there is a noose around your neck. If you start struggling and try to free yourself, it will tighten and strangle you. I will let it happen. I suggest you stay awake until I return from my rest…however long that may be."

Shortly after dawn on Friday morning, Nate had to remove the intruder hurriedly from the bathroom to service his own needs. When he emerged, he found the man still lying on the floor, ankles tied together and hands secured behind his back. He saw that the man was about his age but poor concerning personal hygiene. His breath smelled; his teeth showed visible decay; a layer of permanent grime was embedded around his neck and in his hands, and he stank of old perspiration. Nate left him lying half naked, with his trousers still around his ankles. He reached down and ripped the tape from the man's mouth. To his credit, the character did not cry out.

"What's your name?" Nate asked.

"George Perkins. What's yours?"

"George Washington."

"What do you intend to do with me, General?" the man asked in a cockney accent.

"I'm thinking on it, George. I tell you what: I'm going out to fetch some food. I'll get enough for both of us. If you're still here when I come back, we can talk about the future."

"I can't believe I'm saying this, chum, but I think I need the bathroom."

Nate checked first to be sure the ropes were tight. Then he hauled the man back into the little room and dumped him on the toilet seat. The rope he had used to tie around his waist he then used to join the outer doorknob and the banister rail.

Nate did not leave the tenement immediately. He instead used the lined paper, envelopes and stamps to create four identical letters. In these he explained in detail the payroll burglary, the counterfeit money left behind, the shooting of Danny and the little man, the little man's German accent and Detective Giles Adams's part in all of it. When he was finished, he took his letters with him to a local shop where prepared food and newspapers were sold. He purchased editions of all three available newspapers. To his great disappointment, *The Times* did not contain a reply to his coded name. He found the addresses to reach the three editors-in-chief, and addressed the envelopes. The last envelope he addressed simply to Robbery Division/Scotland Yard/London. Then he found a nearby box and posted the letters.

A red telephone booth was clearly visible a block away. Nate jogged to it and asked the operator to connect him with the Southwark

Borough Police. When a woman answered, he put on a neutral English accent and asked to speak with Detective Giles Adams. He was informed that "Detective Adams was on the job late last night and is not expected in until noon." She asked if there was a message.

"Yes. Tell him I will call again at ten minutes past twelve."

"And who shall I say has called?"

"The fellow from Reddington & Sons, with the crimson lorry."

"Crimson lorry. Very well."

There was no such thing in the local neighborhood as carry-out coffee or tea, much less Extreme Mocha Mountainside Latte. Nate heard in his mind's ear Danny's predictable rant. Swallowing a rising lump of sadness, he counted himself lucky to have secured half a dozen fresh rolls, some cheese and several apples. He found George still inside the bathroom, although the man had managed to loosen his bonds somewhat. Nate pushed the bed across the room to the wall near the door. He took out his Browning and shoved it under his belt. Then he dragged George across the front bedroom and under the windows, where he propped him up. He released the main knot binding the man's hands, set down a roll, a section of cheese and an apple on the floor, and sat on the bed.

"What makes you a thief?" Nate asked the man, as George worked at freeing his hands.

"Accident of birth. Bad luck. The damned Nazis."

"Let me guess: Your steady job was bombed out," Nate said, not believing it.

"I got no steady work, but the Nazis bombed out the day work, too."

"You hate the Germans?"

"The Nazi Germans I do."

"And if I told you they had delivered counterfeit pounds to England to ruin the economy, would you be willing to help stop them?"

The man's cunning eyes betrayed the working of his mind. "Yeah. Sure."

Nate reached into his suit jacket for his wallet. He displayed the thick wad of pound notes. The man's eyes bulged.

"This is the real stuff. I'm an undercover American agent working with your government. The reward for helping to bring these men to justice is one thousand pounds."

"A thousand?" the man exclaimed.

"And not upon conviction," Nate emphasized. "Merely upon arrest. You get it the same day."

Nate stood, peeled five five-pound notes from the stack and walked up to the burglar. "What's your real name, George?"

"It's George Perkins. I swear on me mother's life."

Nate bent and held the money up to George's eyes for a moment. Then he tucked the bills into the man's right windbreaker pocket. "A token of good faith and an advance for your help." He straightened up and dug into another of his jacket pockets. He first produced his own fake passport and held it up to the man's face. Then he did the same with Danny's passport. He opened it to Danny's photo. "This was my partner. The Germans killed him. I'm very unhappy about that."

"I understand."

"I need a temporary partner to take his place. As I said, it pays one thousand pounds. Are you particularly busy tonight, George?"

George's eyes drifted down to look at the Browning tucked under Nate's belt. "Not particularly."

At noon, Nate loitered beside the telephone booth. He watched an old woman step in and dither with her purse for a while, trying to find exact change. Her time inside the booth, all totaled, last five minutes. Nate stepped into the vacated booth and bought time by pretending to speak for several minutes. After consulting his watch, he dialed the precinct phone number and again asked for Detective Giles Adams. He was connected in short order.

"We're rapidly losing personnel, Detective," Nate stated as soon as Adams identified himself.

"I wonder if you wouldn't mind calling me again in ten minutes. Call at this number." Adams recited the sequence twice, did not wait for Nate to speak but hung up immediately.

Nate stepped out of the booth and allowed two Londoners to make their calls. Then he entered it again and dialed the new number.

"Mr. Allen," the familiar voice answered after the first ring.

"Mr. Alex Giles Bennett Adams."

"And I still don't know precisely who you are."

"It never mattered. What matters now is that your two men are dead – and so is my partner. I figure we're both down to just each other...unless you wish to bring Scotland Yard or some of your brother detectives into this."

"No, indeed."

"Where was the counterfeit money made?"

"Why don't we speak in person?"

"Only after we agree on several important matters. Firstly, that we do not need to kill each other. I don't know if you ever planned for the armored truck driver to survive the robbery, but if you did you have three fewer persons to split the take with. I am not a greedy man. I have all two-and-a-half million pounds safely hidden. Secondly, for seven-hundred-and-fifty thousand of those pounds, I will walk away and never bother you. You must make the same promise."

Adams let a silence hang for only a few seconds. "I believe you have the passports."

Nate knew that Adams was letting him know how tapped into police intelligence he was. Clearly, a detective from Southwark could obtain a report of murders in Hackney within half a day. "That's correct. I'm no longer paying for them."

"I must say that this is a most welcome proposition indeed. Far too much blood has been spilled. Where and when do we meet? "

"In Bethnal Green. At the corner of Wilmot and Finnis Streets. Eight o'clock this evening. Be alone, or I'll take it all and throw you to the dogs in the bargain."

"Mr. Allen!" Adams said with haste.

"Yes?"

"So much can go wrong in this city, what with all the air raids, transportation breaking down everywhere and my professional duties decided by others. Give me the number you're calling from. I shall check in with you again at seven."

Nate thought for several moments.

"There's no risk to you," Adams said, reading his mind. "I'm not going to trace the location of the phone and set the police on you. Neither would I have you shot with a high-powered rifle. I would lose my millions. Accept this for what it is: A prudent precaution."

Nate knew how he would handle the situation. "Fine." He delivered the phone number.

"Stay well, Mr. Allen," Adams wished. He hung up immediately.

Nate returned to the tenement with food for lunch. He did so by walking boldly through the front door that he had unlocked. He brought the bag upstairs with the Browning in his hand and cocked. He found with relief that the rope still tied the banister and the outer bathroom knob together. The second he undid the rope, the door swung open a fraction. Nate sidestepped backward and raised the pistol.

"Don't shoot me," George told him. "I'm coming out with me hands over me head." He swung the door back very slowly and stepped into the hallway. Not a vestige of the ropes that Nate had thought would secure him again remained on him. "I got loose about ten minutes ago. Now, if I wanted to leave I could have kicked this flimsy door down. I stayed to show you I'm truly interested in your proposition."

Nate backed into the rear bedroom doorway, keeping the pistol raised. "Fair enough. Let's go downstairs and have some lunch."

George ate like he had not dined in a week. The only thing that kept him from chewing were the questions emerging from his understandable curiosity. Nate had no proof of his theory about the counterfeit money, but he confected an enormous plot to ruin the British economy. He resurrected his persona as an American spy and told the man about many true Nazi atrocities, including the murder of the insane and crippled and those of their own people born with birth defects. He related the wholesale extermination of the intelligentsia of Poland and Hungary and went on to speak of the methodical gassing and burning of gypsies and Jews. Anything Nate could think of to turn a hard-core criminal into a patriot he dragged up. For his part, George seemed genuinely shocked, but his questions kept returning again and again to the money. Nate resigned himself to it.

"I have a solemn promise from the man I'm dealing with that he is coming alone to pick up his share of the money, but there is no honor among thieves," he told George.

"Absolutely," the man agreed, oblivious to the fact that he was simultaneously condemning himself.

"You are my protection. My plan is to make sure this other man and I are both unarmed before I reveal where the money is. Then I will bring him to it. You will be waiting with this gun." Nate held up the Browning. "Do you know how to fire it?"

"No."

Nate painstakingly showed George the steps and then repeated them.

When George had shown that he understood, he asked, "You trust me enough to give me your gun?"

"I have to, George. Just as you have to trust what I've been saying."

"That's true. I got no proof." George's face screwed into a look of discomfort. "But you're the first person who's trusted me in a really long time. I want you to know I appreciate it. And I won't let you down."

At seven o'clock precisely, the outdoor telephone rang. George Perkins stepped from the shadows of a nearby alley, opened the booth door and lifted the receiver off its cradle.

"Whoever is calling, you dialed the wrong number," he said without preamble. "This here is a public booth."

"Who are you?" Giles Adams demanded.

"I'm trying to make a call."

"Is anyone else standing near the phone?"

"Yeah. A guy with blond hair. He has to wait his turn."

"This call is for him," Adams said with annoyance.

"Don't get your knickers in a knot, chum. Hang on!"

Since the phone rang, Nate had been observing the street and every window and rooftop that looked on the booth. He saw nothing out of the ordinary. He stepped out of the alleyway and crossed to the phone. George handed it to him and stood close to the booth, offering protection and playing his part of the impatient caller.

"Sorry," Nate said into the phone. "He was just walking into the booth when I turned the corner."

"Change of plans," Detective Adams said without acknowledging Nate's words.

"What kind of change?"

"The kind with wavy, long, brown hair and green eyes."

Nate's felt his entire torso convulse. "Go on."

"I told the chief of detectives for Hackney that I was working on a case with a man who fit your description. He called my boss and got me free to work up in Bethnal Green. Trawling pubs turned out quite poorly for my associate last night, but I had the most amazing luck this afternoon. Everybody knows everybody in these neighborhoods, you know. They also know everybody else's business. It's been so nice of the Miles family to keep you and Mr. O'Shea safe all this time. And that

Worden Miles is such a talker, isn't he? He even told me about first meeting you and Sean…sorry, it was Daniel, wasn't it?"

"You have Penny?"

"She seems to know so many intimate details about you. I asked her if you had been with her to any storage places where you might have hidden something. She was quite embarrassed and confided that you and she had been to her school when you shouldn't. Something about a storage closet. She volunteered to take me there for a look round."

"You think I'm going to give you all the money?" Nate asked.

"Not at all, not at all! I just want to stay alive and out of prison, and Miss Miles is my insurance. But getting back to Worden Miles…he tells me you and Daniel appeared through a fence near the unfinished Bethnal Green station. That's quite close to the intersection of Wilmot and Finnis, isn't it? Why don't we meet there instead?"

"Eight o'clock."

"No, be there in fifteen minutes," Adams ordered. "I'd hate for Miss Miles to meet with a disfiguring injury while we're waiting."

Nate hung up the phone and spun out of the booth. "Let's go!" he yelled.

"Everything all right?" George called out, running after him.

"It will be if we hurry."

In order to insure a quick escape from the locale, Nate had taken the sedan out of hiding and loaded it with all his belongings. He rounded the corner, dashed to the car, threw open the driver's side door and stabbed the key into the ignition. George climbed in the other side.

"I won't need to actually shoot him, will I?" George worried.

"No."

"Good."

Nate gave the engine lots of petrol and rocketed away from the curb. The distance to the Bethnal Green deep shelter station was only a matter of blocks, but the auto saved them precious minutes.

"You're a good guy just like you say, ain't you?" George inquired in a meek tone. "Not just a fancy thief."

Nate thought of his years of smuggling, of effectively stealing better lives from the hundreds of peasants who worked the gem fields, mines and hillsides, of willingly allowing food to be diverted from thousands who needed it most. All so he could live "fancy." He wondered if the sum total of good works he could do in the rest of his life could balance out so many sins.

"I'm a good guy," he assured.

"Then, for once, so am I," George decided.

The rough man's face looked so genuinely serious that Nate almost wished he could trust him. If that were the case, he would not have needed to replace the bullet without the powder in the top of the Browning pistol's magazine shortly before driving to the outdoor phone booth.

They reached the long fence between the shelter entrance buildings and jumped out of the car. Nate held back the loose boards so George could duck through the space. Then he followed. He led the way down the ladder and platform system, scrambling so fast that he nearly lost his grip and fell thirty feet. When he reached the bottom, he encouraged George to hurry. Without waiting for the scruffy character to get to track level, Nate ran toward the main tunnel. Enough daylight remained for him to find the half overturned stones of the pistol he had hidden between the track ties. He knelt and dug it out. He checked to see that it was in good working order, advancing the cylinder chamber by chamber. Satisfied, he gestured to the just-arriving George to follow him into the station. He brought him past the circuit breaker panel closet and into the side of the shelter that contained the uncompleted sleeping and bathing chambers.

"It shouldn't be much longer," Nate said. "You hide through that door."

"It's black as sin."

"That's the idea." Nate pressed the Browning into George's hand. When George failed to draw back the hammer and point it at his face, Nate ached to confess to giving him a gun that would not fire. Reason and experience, however, had told him that "once a thief, always a thief." And yet had he not changed? Amazingly, his new attitude had apparently converted George Perkins, a man who had thought of himself as bad. His dilemma was now that he could not admit not having trusted the man without destroying both George's belief in Nate and his confidence in the plan.

Nate said, "Count slowly to twenty when you hear us outside in the foyer. Then come out with this gun raised. Point it straight at the face of the other man, and don't be afraid."

Nate had added the last phrase because George indeed looked like he again needed a functioning bathroom.

"A thousand-pound reward," Nate reminded him, to buck up his courage.

"Right."

"I gotta go. Hide now!"

Nate did not wait to see if George had obeyed his command. He ran out of the hallway, through the foyer and down to the platform. He followed the work lights to their end and sprinted back to the ladders. Marshaling his strength, he climbed.

Although he had never killed, Nate knew that Giles Adams had to die. Once the man saw where the money was hidden and how impossible it was to move it quickly, he would concluded that both Nate and Penny had to be silenced. They could not be allowed to leave the station alive. A week earlier, Nate would not have been sure he could kill; this day, with Penny in danger, he had no doubts.

Nate reached the top of the ladder system and had just stepped onto the rutted dirt path when the boards of the fence moved. Penny crossed from the pavement into the field. She moved awkwardly. Nate saw in the dying sunlight that her arms were secured behind her. She wore an expression of extreme anguish.

"It's all right," Nate called out to her. "I'll handle this. Everything will be fine." By his last words, he hoped to keep Penny from daring any unsuccessful action that might get her killed. He wanted her to believe that her angel or at least the American spy was fully capable of saving the day.

"I assured her as much," Giles Adams said, stepping through the fence. He smiled. Then he raised a revolver.

Nate jerked his weapon upward and pointed it.

"Right," Adams said. "We've established that we're both armed. But I wouldn't dream of harming you before I saw the money."

"It's below."

Adams gave Penny a gentle shove, so that she began walking toward the excavation opening. When he came close to the edge, he said, "That's quite a hole you put it in."

"With a great number of places for concealment," Nate said.

"Is this the only way down?"

"Unless you can get a train to stop at an unfinished station or convince the subway authority to open one of those shelter entrances." He nodded to his left and right.

"I see. Lead the way."

"Penny can't climb down without her hands free."

Adams dug into his pocket and produced a small key. He inserted it into the handcuff lock, which sprang the cuffs open. Adams pocketed the key and the cuffs. Penny faced Nate with expectation.

Nate wanted to stare into her magnificent eyes, to assess how much pain and abuse she had taken, and to comfort her. But he knew the greater need, and he counted on having limitless time in the days and years to come. He kept his focus fixed on Adams.

Penny wore an ankle-length black coat with a napped-in waist.

"You can't climb down wearing that coat, Penny," Nate told her. "It's too dangerous."

Penny nodded, shrugged out of the coat and let it fall to the ground.

"Now will you lead the way?" Adams asked with impatience.

Nate stepped onto the top ladder and offered cautionary directions as the trio descended. He had altered his plan to shoot the policeman turncoat in the back the instant Penny touched track level. He saw with dismay that Adams kept his weapon trained on her at all times. When he was still several rungs up, Adams surprised Nate by jumping down and to the side and landing like a cat, with his revolver pointed again at Nate's chest. He grabbed Penny and moved her in front of him. Once again, he snapped the handcuffs on her wrists.

"The money was made in Germany," Nate said.

"That's right. It takes the backing of a major world power to produce the quality of forgery you saw."

"Two-and-a-half million pounds will hardly harm the Bank of England," Nate asserted.

"True. But what if the Empire is flooded with them? Australia and India and the Bahamas? It was a test. If the pound notes could be passed successfully in the mother country, then they could pass anywhere. The sun never sets on the British ruination." He smiled his crooked smile at his own witticism.

"Your little friend with the Coke-bottle glasses was German, but you're English. What's your excuse for treason?"

"I'm English, but I'm also highly rational. Please keep moving, Mr. Allen. The Germans have taken over all of Europe, and rather easily I would say. The milquetoasts like Neville Chamberlain did all they could to see that we weren't prepared to resist such power. Hitler will be in London by Christmas."

"No, he won't. He has an appointment with several Jerry cans of petrol behind a bunker in Berlin."

"Dream on, Yank. You think I'm the only Englishman who agrees with their theories? They count us among the Aryan races. They don't want to conquer us; they merely want us off their backs, so they can do the job the bleeding hearts are too cowardly to accomplish."

"Wiping out the lesser races."

"Exactly. Before the human cockroaches overwhelm us with their numbers."

"Between your service to the Reich and all the money you'll soon have for campaigning, you could easily become the prime minister after the war."

"Sounds lovely. Keep walking."

Nate climbed onto the platform and held out his hand to Penny.

Adams held her back. "She can manage on her own. She's a dancer, you know. Very good on her feet. As, I understand, you are."

Nate led the way into the station's lower foyer and thence to the electric panel closet. He drifted to one side, so that Adams would naturally step to the other and place his back to the hallway in which George Perkins hid.

"Your blood money," Nate announced loudly enough that George could hear. "In the middle of bombs raining day and night, could anyone ask for a safer place?"

"Open it."

"Safer than the Bank of England itself, since that's above ground."

"Stop wasting time."

"First, Miss Miles comes over to me."

"I don't think so."

"Put your hands up!" George cried out as he emerged from the blackness with the Browning raised.

Adams pulled Penny against his chest.

"You?" George gasped. The gun wavered in his hand.

The detective swung his revolver up and shot the burglar in the head. The man dropped to the floor like a sack of feed. As quickly as he had shot the burglar, Adams retrained the gun muzzle against Penny's temple.

"He knew you?" Nate managed through his shock.

"Stanley Dudd? Oh, yes indeed. He used to work my side of the river. Pathetic creature. Aptly named." Adams shook his head. "You really are nothing without Mr. O'Shea, aren't you?"

"Now I'm looking at you," Nate said, "And I'd choose Stanley anytime."

"I'm crushed. Open the lock."

Nate smiled. Without moving his eyes from Adams, he squatted and yanked aside the grate at his feet.

"I thought you said the money was inside here." Adams nodded toward the panel closet door.

Nate stood "Time is against you, Adams. You set me up. You were planning to kill me and Danny all along. I don't like you. I cut a deal with Scotland Yard for clemency if I convinced you to come for the money," Nate lied, counting on years of practice to convince the wily criminal. "Unfortunately, I told them to be at the fence at eight. You wrecked my plans by grabbing Miss Miles. I didn't have time to make another call. The money is somewhere down here, and there are bags to carry it. You could make three trips safely. About a hundred thousand pounds. Enough for a lifetime."

Adams studied Nate's face intently. "What's your proposition?"

"Leopards don't changes their spots. You never had any intention of letting either of us go down here." He tapped the drain grate with his foot. "I'll open the panel and show you the money. We both have revolvers. We can put on the safeties at the same time, crack the cylinders and empty all our bullets down here. Penny and I will try our luck running down the track. If you're lucky, we'll both be killed by a train. You carry up as much money as you dare."

"You don't want any of the money?"

"Not a pound."

"Spoken like a man who might have contacted Scotland Yard." Adams pulled Penny wide of the closet panel door. "As time is running out, I must agree. Open the door."

"Penny has to be free to open the lock while I keep an eye on you. Undo the cuffs and step back!"

Adams did as Nate commanded. Nate dictated the combination to Penny, who worked the tumbler with careful precision. She removed and lock and pulled the door back.

Adams's eyes darted to the space beyond the door. He exhaled a sigh of relief at the sight of the solid stacks of pounds.

"First we dispose of Stanley's gun," Nate said. "Or should I say the one you gave me for my protection?"

"You didn't actually trust that dimwit with bullets, did you?" Adams asked.

"No," Nate lied. "But I'm sure you don't want it left here. Down the grate."

"I agree." The detective kicked the gun out of the dead man's hand.

"Let Miss Miles put it in."

Angling directly behind her for protection, Adams encouraged, "Hurry, Miss Miles."

Nate kept his weapon trained. When he heard the grate slide back into place, he said, "Take your finger out of the trigger guard! Point your weapon to the floor. Grab the muzzle in your other hand. First the safeties. On three." Nate counted, and both men locked their weapons at the same time. "Crack the cylinder." Again, they opened the revolvers together. "Now dump the bullets!" The shells rattled to the concrete and rolled. Adams took a step backward and allowed Nate to kick all the shells into the dark hole beneath the grate. Nate closed on Adams, ready to engage in hand-to-hand combat if necessary.

"You have the girl; I have the money. Business concluded." Adams indicated with a flick of his fingers that they should go.

"Come on!" Nate urged Penny, holding out his hand.

Penny ran to him and hugged him. Then they turned together toward the train platform and started into a run.

"Stop!" Adams yelled. "Turn around!"

When they turned, Adams held another gun in his right hand. It was an exact duplicate of the small Webley Danny had taken off Jack Eastwood at the Cockspur Street parking garage.

"What copper only carries one gun?" Giles Adams asked, sneering with disdain. "You're gonna help me transport some of this money. Then you two can leave. Get back here, or I'll shoot you dead right now!"

Penny gasped. Nate gave her hand a reassuring squeeze. "We're still all right," he told her in a soft, steady voice. "Trust me."

Adams stepped away from the electric closet and gestured inside. "Indeed. Trust him. Fill those bags."

Nate and Penny filled the two satchels Danny had purchased for the transfer. When they were finished, they walked down the foyer ahead of Adams, who stuffed two packets into his jacket pockets.

"Hurry it up!" Adams ordered.

The trio moved with haste to the bottom of the ladders. "Set them down!" Adams commanded. "That was a good idea about you two going up the tunnel. Why don't you start off now?"

"Saving bullets?" Nate asked."

"No. Curiousity." I've never seen anyone get hit by a train. They say there's a new one along every few minutes." Adams's smile was demonic.

Penny gasped.

"Still all right," Nate soothed.

"Yes, still all right," Adams mocked. "Walk!"

"My partner was an authority on railroads," Nate said as he began moving.

"Do tell."

"Sleepers and spikes and rails."

The air raid sirens began another chorus of their dirge for London. Nate and Penny stopped and looked up.

Adams exclaimed with exasperation. "Nothing you haven't heard before. Keep moving."

"I hope one of your master race bombs falls on you tonight, Detective," wished Penny.

"You might get your wish. The fortunes of war," he responded in a breezy tone.

The lighting in the main tunnel was not nearly as bright or as concentrated as that on the station platform. Nate counted on that and worried about it. He walked hand in hand with Penny for a dozen paces, then spoke over his shoulder.

"Daniel was especially fascinated by the gap where train wheels cross over tracks so they can switch lines."

"I really don't give a shit about your dead friend's fascination," Adams revealed.

"Neither did I, until he showed me. One should always be learning. Here we are." Nate let go of Penny and swept his left hand wide. "The rail turnout. A marvel of engineering." His eyes strained to pick out the individual crossties. One, two, three, four. "See how they place guard rails to ensure the train wheels don't ride off?" Ten, eleven twelve. He knelt and pointed. "Right here."

"Oh, do shut up!"

A blistering barrage of Victoria Park ack-ack fire reverberated through the tunnel.

"The sirens went off late," Nate noted as his fingers burrowed into the stones, encouraging Adams to look back down the side tunnel for enough time to allow him to release the second Webley from under the two layers.

"What are you doing?" Adams demanded. "Leave those stones!"

A beam of light swept down the tracks from the dark of the main tunnel. Nate, Penny and Adams all looked in that direction.

Under one of the tunnel lights, holding a flashlight, stood a man with red hair. He was dressed in a railway worker's outfit. In his left hand he held a manual switch tool.

"You three!" the man called out. "Nobody's allowed down here!"

Nate ignored the figure the moment he recognized it. He instead concentrated on reaching the gun.

"This is police business. Be off!" Adams ordered.

More aerial noise echoed from the excavation. From the length of the main tunnel came a deep rumble.

"Well, this is my business. Show me identification!" the railway man shouted.

In answer, the detective pointed his gun and fired.

Nate's eyes blinked involuntarily with the report of the revolver. When he opened them again, the redheaded man had vanished.

The detective's head first reared back in surprise, then craned forward to try to find a retreating figure in the tunnel darkness. Failing, he turned to face Nate.

Nate released the safety on the Webley and thumbed back the hammer.

Adams fired at Nate from a distance of eight paces.

Nate collapsed onto his bottom with the impact of the bullet. He thrust his weapon forward, fired once and missed. The blast mingled with the swelling sound from down the tracks.

Penny threw herself at Adams. He caught sight of her out of the corner of his vision and flailed a backhanded fist into her face. She fell hard against the tunnel wall and lay unmoving.

In the three seconds Penny had distracted Giles Adams, Nate grabbed his left wrist with his right hand, and aimed the Webley. He fired twice more.

The first bullet caught Adams in the stomach. He doubled over from the impact and the pain. He roared with anger and fought to straighten up. As his eyes lifted toward Nate, the second bullet caught him in the divot just below his nose. His lips reared back, exposing his crooked teeth. Then he collapsed cross-legged into what looked like motionless Zen concentration.

Nate sought Penny out of the gloom. He saw that she was unconscious, but breathing normally. She would be fine now, no matter what happened to him. Only then did he look down to search for where the bullet had hit him. He thought it might be high on his chest, but he could see or feel nothing. A beam of light down the length of the tunnel grew steadily in size. As Nate vainly commanded his legs to move under him, he wondered if the light belonged to an oncoming train or perhaps the approaching warp of a space-time continuum released by the redheaded man. It grew brighter and brighter, filling the tunnel. Or perhaps, he thought, the portals of heaven opening. His ears were filled with deafening sounds – of engines, war and, above all the rest, the first notes of "We'll Meet Again."

## EPILOGUE

The building at the bottom of the Battery was not very different from
the others around it. It was the standard steel curtain finished with
reflective glass walls. What surprised Nathaniel Allen was its size.
Squinting from the intense light of a sunny day, he counted the stories
twice and satisfied himself that the number was eighteen. Its height
also was not unusual. The structures on either side were twenty and
fifteen stories high. What amazed Nathaniel was the fact that the
building was owned by a charitable organization. He walked into the
lobby and to the glass-enclosed directory. World Population Watch
occupied floors sixteen and seventeen. The well-heeled organization
was precisely what he was seeking. He crossed to the security desk and
offered the guard a smile.

"My name is Nathaniel Allen. I have an appointment with Ms.
Gabrielle Antonelli."

The guard nodded toward the sign-in log. He picked up the house
phone and punched in three numbers. "Mr. Allen to see Ms. Antonelli.
Yes." He lowered the handset to its cradle.

Nathaniel had declined the plastic ballpoint pen lying on the log.
He instead used his own Cross model. As he tucked it into his inside
blazer pocket, the guard gestured to the bank of brass-door elevators.
"Floor Seventeen."

The elevator rose smoothly, signaling each floor for the visually
handicapped by sounding a soft chime. 'Where or When' played softly
from the elevator speaker, and Nathaniel hummed along. At Seventeen
it opened. Nathaniel stepped out onto a small foyer. Directly across
from him stood a wall of glass with one large glass door. Etched in acid
on the door were the large figures of a meridian-hatched globe and,
hovering above it, a dove of peace. Below the figures were etched the
letters WPW. Nathaniel pulled the door open and walked inside.

The foyer of the organization was well appointed. Its floor was a
high-polished golden oak that reflected the diffuse light of six Deco
wall sconces. In between each lighting fixture hung large color photos

of happy children of the world in their native costumes. Six tufted
leather chairs were arranged, three facing three, in front of two narrow
oak coffee tables. The space was large enough to also contain a wide
aisle that led up to a Deco desk. Behind it sat a young, attractive
woman with red hair. She wore a stylish outfit common to fashion-
conscious Financial District office workers. She stood as Nathaniel
passed through the door.

"Mr. Allen?"

"Yes."

"I'm Annette Nolan." She extended her hand.

Nathaniel accepted the greeting. He noted that she wore a claddagh
ring on her right pinkie. Her grip was firm. Then he registered that she
was also studying his hand. The hand she studied, however, was his
left. He smiled inwardly and glanced at her left. She wore no
engagement or wedding ring. She had evidently liked what she saw on
first impression and was checking him out on the most superficial level.
What made Nathaniel smile even more was the likelihood that she was
interested in him because she had a strong suspicion he would be
working for the organization. The thought gave him increased
confidence for the interview.

"I'm pleased to meet you, Ms. Nolan."

"You're early."

"I make it a practice to arrive with five minutes to spare," he
explained. "Nobody can predict New York City traffic."

"Boy, isn't that the truth. Would you care for coffee or tea?"

"No, thank you."

Finally, the receptionist let go of his hand, after allowing her eyes to
roam him from top to bottom. He knew he looked good in his pale
linen suit, red-and-black regimental striped silk tie, crisp, oxford cloth
white shirt and oxblood Gucci tassel loafers. "Then have a seat. The
booklet and bulletins on the tables are about the WPW."

Nathaniel lowered himself to one of the comfortable chairs and set
his shoulder briefcase down on the table just beyond his knees. He
selected the handsome, varnished booklet and opened it. He soon
realized that it contained virtually the same information that the World
Population Watch posted on its web site. He opened his bag and pulled
out the ten pages that he had printed out and stapled together. He
confirmed that they and the booklet pages were almost identical. He
reached for the latest bulletin.

The desk phone rang. Ms. Nolan picked it up. "Ms. Antonelli can see you now." She stood and opened one of the pair of doors just behind her.

Nathaniel grabbed his briefcase with his free hand and entered the office with long strides.

Gabrielle Antonelli stood in front of her desk with her hands clasped below the line of her belt. Nathaniel was immediately impressed and attracted. She was tall. He guessed five-foot-ten in her two-inch heels. She wore a pleated skirt under a tweed jacket. The skirt signaled that she was confident of her figure. Below the conservative hemline, her legs were extremely shapely. Further, there was enough cut in her jacket to allow for ample breasts. She wore a golden pin on the jacket that looked like children skipping in a circle while holding hands. Her skin was like porcelain, with just a bit of rosy color in her high cheeks. She smiled with perfect white teeth. He could not tell if she wore earrings, because her brown, slightly wavy hair flowed down to her shoulders. But the most arresting feature of her face was her emerald eyes. He noted that, in spite of the aura of intelligence she radiated, she indeed appeared no older than he had expected her to. The head of one of the richest charitable organizations in the world looked like she had just graduated from college.

"Nathaniel Allen," she said, not moving. Her words seemed more like a challenge than a greeting.

"The one and only," he replied.

"Did you have a pleasant Labor Day?"

Nathaniel thought the question strange. "I did. Did you?"

"Lovely. To many, September signals the end of the summer. My grandmother taught me that it often begins things." Several strands of hair slipped from her forehead and came to rest covering her left eye. It was a natural occurrence that Nathaniel nonetheless found charged with sexuality.

"Like the theater season," he supplied.

Gabrielle pushed the hair back and secured it behind her ear. "Good example. Did Annette offer you something to drink?"

"Yes."

The chairwoman pivoted smartly and moved behind her desk, leaving Nathaniel to decide whether to sit on his own volition or to wait for an invitation. He pulled one of the two chairs along the bowling-alley-polished oak floor toward the large desk. The piece of furniture was fashioned entirely of wood and high-backed, elegant to look at but not made for comfort. He guessed that either the woman wanted those who sat before her to feel like children in front of their principal or else she never granted interviews long enough to bother with comfort. He put himself down, tugged up his right pant slightly and crossed his leg in what he hoped looked like a relaxed manner.

"I've reviewed your resume. Impressive college grades and class standing. Extensive experience in global charitable work. You seem a perfect fit for us."

"I hope so."

"How old are you, Mr. Allen?"

Nathaniel hesitated to respond. First of all, the woman surely could guess from the dates on his resume. Secondly, it was against the law to ask the question when hiring. Thirdly, it was rude. He found the reply he wanted.

"Twenty eight. How old are you?"

"Twenty two," Gabrielle replied with no hesitation. She glanced over her shoulder, down the mouth of the Hudson River into the sun-brilliant bay where the Statue of Liberty still greeted those yearning to be free. Her face was in profile, so that Nathaniel could see one eye narrow, as if focusing to find the shores of Europe.

When Gabrielle moved, Nathaniel expected her to sit. Instead, she plucked a black and white photograph in an oak frame from the counter that ran the length of the window wall. She circled the desk and placed the picture in Nathaniel's hands.

"Who is this?" she said, more demand than question.

Nathaniel gave the photo a quick glance and looked up. "It's you."

"No, it isn't. Look closely."

Nathaniel analyzed each feature, looking back and forth between photograph and live woman. They were very close but, in fact, not identical.

"I would say your twin then." He handed the photograph back.

"You would say, except you know I have no twin." When Nathaniel declined to contradict her, she revealed, "It's my grandmother. Penelope Miles March. She would say that we were cut from the same cloth."

"Ah," Nathaniel exhaled, even as he wondered just how weak the genes of Gabrielle Antonelli's grandfather and father must have been to allow virtually no change in the facial physiognomy from the grandmother to the woman standing in front of him. "I've never seen a picture of her. I do know she was the genius behind the fortune that allowed this charity."

"I like to hear other people's versions of the story," Gabrielle invited. "Tell me what you think it is."

"She visited America from England soon after World War II was over. Then she returned and became a citizen. She began making a series of wise investments. As I understand it, she was smart enough to hide behind front companies so that those in finance and the stock market couldn't slavishly copy her strategies and lower her profit margins. She never seemed to err in picking winners. That's right, isn't it?"

"Absolutely right."

"She married rather late in life, to a senior vice president of J. P. Morgan. Lewis March."

"I respect thorough researchers," Gabrielle praised. "Go on."

Nathaniel shrugged. "They were a daunting pair. They traveled widely but did not live lavishly, given that they earned millions."

"Do you know how many children they had?"

"One daughter. She has to be your mother."

"Correct. Jennifer March, later Jennifer Antonelli. And what do you know of her?"

Nathaniel's internal radar had long since sounded an alarm. Something was very wrong about this interviewer's line of questioning, but he could not challenge her because he badly wanted the advertised position. He knew he had to be particularly careful with the last question. In her youth, Jenny March had a reputation as a spoiled little rich girl. On one of her several trips to Italy, she had eloped with Antonio Antonelli, a son of one of the Ferrari automotive works vice presidents. Neither she nor he had ever spent a day in gainful employment. Their only goal in life was to enjoy it. According to articles Nathaniel had read in *Forbes* and *The New York Times*, they had been placed on allowances just big enough so they could jet around the world constantly but not enough to ever own anything themselves. Jenny Antonelli had had one child, Gabrielle to her and Gabriella to her father, and that had been too much work and inconvenience to ever consider duplicating the labor. Shortly thereafter, she had divorced Antonio when she caught him having an affair with the same man she slept with. He had been the first of three husbands, with at least twenty known lovers shoehorned in between.

Gabrielle had lived with her maternal grandmother and grandfather since she was two. The philanthropic Lewis March died at age of 85. Her estate, which Dun & Bradstreet evaluated at 1.4 billion dollars and

*The Wall Street Journal* at 1.7, was divided among her daughter, Jennifer, her granddaughter, Gabrielle and the already-established World Population Watch Fund. Gabrielle received eighteen per cent. The charitable organization got eighty per cent. Jennifer, who was forty-eight at the time of her mother's death, received two per cent, or about thirty million. The provision of her bequest was that she sign a document agreeing not to sue for any more of the estate. Lacking ambition to the end, she had agreed.

"I know that Jennifer Antonelli is beautiful," Nate answered the question diplomatically. "And that she lives well."

Gabrielle Antonelli folded her arms across her chest. "Come now, Mr. Allen. Surely a researcher with your skills must know some of the dirt."

Although her face was placid, Nathaniel felt the palpable anger in her voice. "It would be frankly stupid for me to comment on your family, Ms. Antonelli. Why don't you ask me about my work to this point or what I–"

"I'm my grandmother's child," Gabrielle interrupted. "I am twenty-two in years only. Fortunately for me, a number of the financial wizards on Wall Street watched me grow up and know better than to underestimate me. But those in off the street..." The head of World Population Watch took her time drawing a calming breath. "There are men who seek out such charitable organizations as this one for unscrupulous purposes. Some just want a free ride around the world on other people's money. Others have darker motives. For example, they use their seemingly noble work in poor countries as fronts while they arrange deals to export illegal drugs or gems."

"I've heard of such dealings," Nate admitted. "I'll tell you what I think of people who prey on the goodness of others: There should be a special place in hell for them. And I suspect that they carry a personal degree of hell in this life already."

Gabrielle parked her posterior on the edge of her desk. Her arms remained crossed. "So it's not you I've described."

"I'm exactly who I say I am and how I act."

"You haven't ever tried to capitalize on your name?"

"My name means very little to me," Nate affirmed, even as he wondered where this abrupt turn led.

"Why?"

"Because I don't like my father."

"Is he not as good a father as he is a pharmaceutical industry lawyer?"

Nate's eyes widened. It seemed that Gabrielle Antonelli had done research on him and his family.

"In his line of work, being good means being rotten. He's consistent as a father. I'd take my real father's name, but my mother never confided it to me."

Gabrielle seemed mildly amused by the reply. "But Simon Allen did give you the name Nathaniel Allen."

"My mother named me Nathaniel."

"Any particular reason?"

"She named me after a grandfather. She believed in family tradition."

"You said 'The one and only' when you first walked in. Have you found it an uncommon name?"

Nathaniel shrugged. "I've never come across it in this country. I suppose it could be common in England."

"I saw on your resume some education in England."

"Junior Year Abroad. I liked it very much."

"You did research while you were there."

"For college studies. Where is this going, Ms. Antonelli?"

"Was it while you were in England that you learned of the Nathaniel Allen who was there during the London Blitz?"

Nathaniel knew much about the Blitz from his love of history and the strategies of warfare. But he was sure that, in all his readings, from all the war movies and the documentaries on The History Channel and elsewhere, he had never heard his own name mentioned. He was certain he would have remembered such a coincidence.

"I've never met nor heard of any other Nathaniel Allen except myself and my grandfather. Who was this other guy?"

Gabrielle picked up the framed photo of her grandmother. "He was her great love. He appeared mysteriously, with a partner named Daniel O'Shea. They claimed to be Americans. When was your grandfather born?"

"I believe it was 1915."

Gabrielle stared at the photograph. "Might that man possibly have been your grandfather?"

"No. That grandfather was born in the States and never left it. Was this other Nathaniel Allen an American or not?"

"He said he was. There was never any proof."

Nathaniel lost his defensive edge, engrossed by the proffered mystery. "How long was he in England?"

"Only a matter of weeks. But in that short time, he gave my grandmother hope to survive the war. He also created her future."

"I don't understand."

Gabrielle stared hard at the man sitting in the chair in front of her. She sighed. "I must admit that the moment I read the name on your resume, I was on guard. I figured you had learned the soft spot in my grandmother's heart. Of course she's dead, but she lives on in me. Your resume is outstanding, but the name put me off. I instantly thought that you were working on an angle, to use it to get inside WFW and close to me. For all I know, you've got one of those faces that can put on innocence like women apply make-up." She lowered her arms, walked around the desk and sat. Her brilliant green eyes searched his. "But…it's probably just a coincidence."

"I assure you it is," Nathaniel told her. "What happened to this other Nathaniel Allen?"

"As well as guiding her future, he saved my grandmother's life. He died in the process."

"Sad story."

"You have no idea. But that's water long under Waterloo Bridge. I'd like to consider you for the advertised position, but it's beyond what you've done so far. You'd be proving yourself to me on two levels at the same time."

"I don't mind that at all, Ms. Antonelli," Nathaniel said, grabbing his soft briefcase from the floor. "I'm very dedicated to controlling population growth while seeing that every human being already on the planet is cared for."

"You sound just like our promotional materials."

Nathaniel leaned forward with energy. "I've read them all. The advertisements in the newspapers and magazines. The position papers. Your website. I think it's exactly right that WPW lays out only one dollar for every dollar that's contributed by individuals, other organizations and governments. Even the massive finances behind your fund can't last forever without outside assistance. I see your educating the general population to the need to do charitable work as important as your ministering to the poor of the world."

"I'm glad you're not thinking of trying to change that tenet," said Gabrielle.

"Not at all. Charity cannot be allowed to become the cause of a few; every person must understand that work for others is the essence of humanity." Nathaniel pulled out the ten, stapled pages he had copied from the web site. "I envision my first job for WPW as making your philosophy more compelling. Like Jefferson said about the Declaration of Independence: 'To state the cause in such clear, compelling language as to command assent.' Or something close to that. It's been awhile since my high school history." He set the pages on top of the desk and slid them toward the organization's president. "I've jotted in the margins what I believe are subtle but important changes. See what you think."

Gabrielle began reading. Her eyes swept only a few of his lines. Then they grew enormous. She blinked several times. Her head swiveled quickly upward on her neck. She stared hard at him.

"What's wrong?" Nathaniel asked.

"Do you have a nickname?"

"Sure. Nathaniel's way too long. I'm Nate to my friends."

"Not Nathan or Natty."

"No. Nate. Why do you ask that?"

"I'm sorry. Bear with me. Do you have a favorite saying that sums up your philosophy of life?"

"I do. 'I shall pass this way but once. Therefore any kindness I can show or any help I can give, let me give it now for I shall not pass this way again.' That quotation I'm sure of. It was created by Etienne De Grellet."

Although she had sipped nothing, Gabrielle swallowed hard. "Would you pull back your sleeve and show me your watch?"

"Sure. Why not?" Nate was no less confused, but since he felt his potential new employer softening toward him, he indulged her.

"You're left-handed."

"Which means I'm in my right mind," Nate quipped, trying to lighten a confusingly tense moment.

"You like the kind of watch that performs lots of functions."

"As long as they're not gimmicks. This one has a compass and indicates temperature, air pressure and altitude. I find them all useful."

"Are you a slave to technology?"

"Not at all," Nate asserted. "This is one of my few high-tech possessions. I like things simple. I always thought I was born fifty years too late."

Tears welled from Gabrielle's eyes. She stood and crossed to a wall on her left. She swung back a photograph of children singing. Behind the frame was the face of a wall safe. She spun the dial back and forth and opened the secure space. When she closed it again, she held a glassine sleeve with a piece of yellowed paper inside it.

Nate stood. "What's that?"

"It's the gift Nathaniel Allen left my grandmother. It told her all the companies to invest in between 1940 and 2006. It correctly predicted the inflationary patterns and several booms and busts of the stock market. These two pages, front and back, are most of the secret behind her genius."

"Wow," Nate managed. "How could he have predicted the future so perfectly?"

"I don't know. My grandmother had her theories, but she refused to share them."

Nate lifted his left hand. "May I see it?"

Gabrielle stood her ground, ten feet distant from her interviewee. "Do you believe in reincarnation, Mr. Allen?"

"No," he said simply. Then the implication of the question registered fully in his brain. A shiver shook his body. "Me? No!" he repeated firmly. "I have no memory of any past lives."

"Then I don't know how else to explain this," Gabrielle said, finally moving to the desk and laying the protected paper down next to Nate's jottings. The old page had a bit of the bottom corner torn off. She spun both items toward the front of the desk. "Compare them!"

Nate slowly moved close and looked down. His handwriting was identical to that under the clear plastic sleeve. He exhaled in amazement.

"Do you dance, Mr. Allen?" Gabrielle asked.

"Dance? Yes."

"Ballroom dance?"

"That's what I prefer. The waltz, the foxtrot. An occasional time step. My mother taught me."

"I know," Gabrielle said, wiping the tears from her cheeks. "I dance, too."